REVEALED:
THE MISSING YEARS

THE CONCLUSION TO THE CONSEQUENCES SERIES
BOOK #4

D1263042

New York Times bestselling author
Aleatha Romig

REVEALED:
THE MISSING YEARS

Published by Aleatha Romig

2014 Edition

Copyright ©2014 Aleatha Romig

ISBN 13: 978-09914011-5-4
ISBN 10: 0991401158

Editing: Lisa Aurello

Formatting: Angela McLaurin – Fictional Formats
www.facebook.com/FictionalFormats

Cover artist: Melissa Ringuette

All rights reserved. No part of this book may be reproduced or transmitted in any form or by any means, electronic or mechanical, including photocopying, recording, or by any information storage and retrieval system, without permission in writing from the copyright owner.

This is a work of fiction. Names, characters, places, and incidents either are the product of the author's imagination or are used fictitiously, and any resemblance to any actual persons, living or dead, events, or locales is entirely coincidental.

REVEALED:
THE MISSING YEARS

THE CONCLUSION TO THE CONSEQUENCES SERIES

*The tragic or the humorous
is a matter of perspective.
—Arnold Beisser*

Aleatha Romig

Acknowledgements

—◆—

THANK YOU TO all of you who've made this incredible journey with me. Thank you for loving Tony, or hating Tony, for loving Claire, or hating Claire. It has been your emotion that has propelled me to continue this story. You will never know how much your messages have meant and continue to mean to me.

Thank you also to my wonderful team. I began the *Consequences* journey one night alone at my computer. Today I'm not only surrounded by a wonderfully supportive family, I also have some of the best betas, a fantastic editor, a wonderful formatter, and creative cover designer. Without these supportive people my final product would not be the same.

Thank you to all of my author friends, those I see and those I know in great online groups. I have learned so much from each and every one of you!

Thank you to the fantastic bloggers who have not only read, but loved my stories and felt passionate enough about them to tell others! I'm always so glad to meet and hug you in person. I truly believe that without you, only my mother and her friends would have read *Consequences*.

My sincerest thank you goes to my readers. This book is for you. I almost didn't finish it. I admit in many ways it was the most difficult and I believe, my most beloved. I hope you all enjoy the missing years and the future.

As I have done since my second book, I must thank Claire Nichols and Anthony Rawlings. You two characters have taken permanent residence in my heart and soul. I never imagined the amazing roller coaster we would ride together, and though it has turned my life upside down, I wouldn't trade a moment. Though this series is COMPLETELY done, Tony and Claire, you will live forever in my heart and the hearts of thousands and thousands of the best readers that an author could hope to find.

Disclaimer

—————◆·◆·◆·——————

THE CONSEQUENCES SERIES contains dark adult content. Although there is not excessive use of description and detail, the content contains innuendos of kidnapping, rape, and abuse—both physical and mental. If you're unable to read this material, please do not purchase. If you are ready, welcome aboard and enjoy the ride!

~Aleatha Romig

Note From Aleatha

Dear Readers,

When I began writing this last book of the CONSEQUENCES SERIES, I planned to write a companion; however, my characters informed me otherwise. Behind His Eyes Convicted: The Missing Years grew into a full-length novel renamed REVEALED: THE MISSING YEARS. This fourth novel gives you the complete story of what was only mentioned in CONVICTED. It begins at the fateful gunshot and goes into the future. Since most of this book occurs while Claire is unable to tell the story, REVEALED: THE MISSING YEARS is told from the point of view of many of the male characters in her life.

REVEALED: THE MISSING YEARS has become book 4 of the CONSEQUENCES SERIES. Therefore, once you have completed CONSEQUENCES, TRUTH, AND CONVICTED, please join me for *REVEALED.*

Share the struggle as the dominoes begin to fall and the crashing consequences of the past threaten everyones future. Watch as Anthony Rawlings fights for what is his. Join Harrison Baldwin as he discovers the truth that threatens his beliefs, and John Vandersol as he come to terms with his revelations. Witness as Phillip Roach decides with whom his loyalties lie, and Brent

Simmons demonstrates the meaning of friendship—no matter the cost.

Following the epilogue, I have included a complete glossary of characters and a timeline of significant events for the entire CONSEQUENCES Series.

The reading companions, BEHIND HIS EYES CONSEQUENCES and BEHIND HIS EYES TRUTH are full-length books, but were written as an adjunct to CONSEQUENCES and TRUTH. Once you have completed this journey, if you seek more, books 1.5 and 2.5 are already available through most online channels. They answer the burning question: "What was he thinking?"

Once again, thank you for this incredible journey. Please note that I would never have completed this story had it not been for you!

Thank you again for your support!

~Aleatha Romig

Prologue

———⟡———

*For the first time in his life he'd dared
to believe in happily-ever-after. He learned at
a young age it was unattainable. Therefore,
he'd never even tried... until Claire.*
—Aleatha Romig, Truth

TONY'S HEART MELTED as Nichol's soft mews filled their suite, a contrast to the whish-whish of waves lapping the shore. Together the sounds created the perfect melody for the middle of the night. He kissed Claire's forehead and watched the tired emerald disappear behind her closed eyes while their daughter's little body wiggled in his large hands. Stretching contently, she relaxed as he pulled her against his broad chest. Settling into the rocking chair in the nursery, Tony watched Nichol's long lashes flutter as she fought the sleepy lids that threatened to cover her dark chocolate eyes. After a few moments of monotonous rocking, her tiny nose nestled into his soft cotton t-shirt, and sleep won, as she lost her fight with one final sigh.

He could return her to her crib and climb back into bed with Claire, but, instead, Tony continued to rock. The silver rays of moonlight through the open doors to the lanai illuminated their bed, allowing him to watch his sleeping wife. Nichol's feeding schedule had yet to work itself out, and Claire was beyond exhausted. It seemed that their daughter had a ravenous hunger, one that perhaps surpassed her mother's before Nichol was born.

A grin materialized as Tony remembered Claire eating for two. With Nichol present, and demanding to eat every two to three hours, he understood why Claire had been so hungry. Loosening the pink blanket, Tony reached for Nichol's hand. Her little fingers grasped one of his and he gently caressed her soft skin. As the scent of baby lotion filled his senses, Tony realized that in a little over two weeks, Nichol had infiltrated every part of their lives.

There were chairs that rocked and swayed. They called them swings, but to Tony they were more like mechanical seats that played lullabies or made white noise, depending upon the button pushed. He didn't care how many swings or cradles Nichol had: he'd rather hold her safely in his arms. Although Claire claimed he was spoiling their daughter, he'd caught her doing the same thing more than once.

Everyone on the island was smitten and held captive by the beautiful brunette in Tony's arms. Francis and Madeline were more like doting grandparents than employees. Though they never had children themselves, they were well-versed and experienced in anything baby. It was comforting to have the benefit of their knowledge when questions arose. Madeline had been the one to give Tony his first lesson in diapering. It was even before Claire met their daughter. Her encouraging words gave him the confidence to wrap the fabric around her tiny body. She seemed so small that Tony wasn't sure he could do it.

"Oui, Monsieur, that is right. She will not break. Oui, lift her legs..."

Never had Tony envisioned taking instructions from a member of his staff, yet with each word, Tony willingly accepted the role of student.

One evening, when nothing seemed to settle Nichol's cries, it was again Madeline who came to the rescue. At that moment, both Tony and Claire would have willingly allowed Madeline to do her magic, but that wasn't what she did. Or perhaps it was. Yet the magic wasn't performed on Nichol but instead on her parents—the magic to empower.

Although Francis and Madeline had retired to their home for the night, Tony wasn't surprised that Madeline had heard Nichol's protests through the still of the night. After all, Tony had spent hours walking her up and down the lanai, bouncing her gently as he'd been taught. Their daughter wasn't having any of it—nothing would satisfy. Even nursing didn't help. Nichol would begin to eat and then stop, crying and moving her face from side to side. With Claire's sleep deprivation, she too was on the verge of tears—past the verge. Though she'd tried to hide it, Tony saw the evidence on her cheeks.

With Claire in the living room and Tony walking the length of the lanai, he was startled at the touch to his shoulder. Quickly turning around, he found Madeline.

"Monsieur, she is hungry? No?"

"No, I mean, I don't know. Claire's tried to feed her, but after a few suckles, she started crying again."

"Madame el? Or Nichol?"

Tony grinned. "Both."

"Bring her inside. The breeze is too strong."

Willingly, he followed Madeline to the living room.

"Madame el, let me get you something to eat."

Claire shook her head as her red, puffy eyes looked up from her lap. "No, Madeline, I'm not hungry. I just don't know what to do."

"Oui, you do. What does she want?"

"I don't know," Claire confessed. "Her diaper is clean. I've tried to feed her. She doesn't want that. I don't know if I can do this."

"You can," Madeline replied matter-of-factly. "When did she last eat?"

"It was before dinner." Claire looked down. "I feel like I'm about to explode."

Tony stood helplessly as his daughter continued to cry and his wife declared her insecurities. Truth be told, he felt the same way. "Maybe you should—" Tony began as he started to hand Nichol to Madeline.

"Oh, no," Madeline said, waving him off. "She doesn't need me. She needs you—both of you." With that, Madeline disappeared into the kitchen, and Tony sat down next to Claire.

Although Nichol was still crying, it was Claire whom Tony wanted to help. He pulled her closer.

"I'm sorry," she said. "I don't know what to do. I can't..."

"Shhh," he whispered as he kissed the top of her head. He wanted to lift her chin and see her beautiful eyes. It didn't matter to him that they were red. All that mattered was that they were before him. "Look at me. I don't have enough hands to lift your chin."

Claire shook her head against his chest. "No, I look awful, and I'm a terrible mother."

Tony released his embrace and tenderly pulled Claire's chin upward. "You are and always will be the most beautiful woman in the world. Well..." He grinned. "...you do have a little competition now, but in my eyes you'll always win." Gently using his thumb, he wiped the tears from her cheeks. "You're an amazing mother. Remember we said we were going to learn this parenting thing together? Don't you dare give up. My wife is not a quitter. You may remember that I have a rule about failure. We, my dear, won't fail. We're tired and our daughter has a stubborn streak."

Claire's weary eyes sparkled. "I wonder where she gets that."

"Well, we could debate that all night, but I'd put my money on you."

"Oh really, Mr. Rawlings. If you did, I believe I'd have even more of your fortune."

"You can have whatever you want. It's already yours."

"Sleep..." Claire yawned. "...I want sleep."

"All right, you can't have that yet." Tony glanced down to Nichol. Her cries were mere whimpers as she rooted against his chest.

Madeline entered the quieter living room with a sandwich and a glass of juice. "Madame el, this is for you. Eat and drink and then you will be ready to give Nichol what she needs."

Claire nodded and took the glass as Madeline set the plate on the table beside her. After a long drink, she said, "Thank you, Madeline. I didn't even realize I was thirsty."

Tony slowly rocked Nichol while Claire ate. When she was done, Claire leaned back and unbuttoned her blouse. Handing their daughter to his wife, Tony's gaze went from Claire's eyes to her breast and back again.

Exhaling, Claire positioned Nichol and smiled a sly grin.

"You're incorrigible. Do you know that?"

"What?" Tony tried for his most innocent look. "What did I do?"

Before she could answer, they all stopped and stared at their contented baby girl. Nichol's eyes closed as she eagerly nursed. The whole room held their breath, waiting for the next eruption of crying, but it didn't occur, even whilst Claire burped Nichol and switched sides. Nichol didn't complain. By the time she was satisfied, Madeline was gone. When Tony realized that they were alone, he moved closer and once again wrapped Claire's shoulders in his embrace. "Do you think Madeline sprinkled some kind of fairy dust to calm Nichol down?"

"No, I think she calmed us down, which in turn calmed Nichol."

"See, what did I say? You're a great mother."

Claire kissed his cheek. "And you're a great father. I guess we can do this."

"Together and one day at a time."

Neither one mentioned Tony's impending deal with the FBI. They didn't want anything to upset them or Nichol as she finally rested contently in her mother's arms.

Helping with the feedings, especially those in the middle of the night, was Tony's part of *together*. Through trial and error, they learned that allowing Claire to rest when she could, eased some of her stress, which made Nichol more relaxed. Tony had never been one who needed a lot of sleep, and without a doubt, he grew to love his alone time with their daughter. The fact that it helped both of his ladies to flourish was a mere bonus.

The doctor had been to the island the day before and acted very pleased with both Claire's recovery and Nichol's progress. Sometimes they forgot that she was born earlier than expected.

Nichol's little face scrunched and her lips formed a silent O before her contented expression returned. Did babies dream? What could they possibly dream about? Her entire life consisted of eating, sleeping, and soiling her diaper. None of that seemed like the material of dreams, in Tony's opinion. Closing his eyes and maintaining the chair's movement, he contemplated his dream.

He was living it, and it was grander than any dream he'd ever imagined.

His envelope was full.

Chapter 1

March 2014

(Convicted—Chapters 47, 48, & 49)

Tony

———◆———

It is during our darkest moments
that we must focus to see the light.
—Aristotle Onassis

IT HAS BEEN said that everyone gets to experience a moment: an instant when clouds part, fog clears, and the world makes sense. Whether that moment reveals the meaning of *all* life or merely the meaning to personal existence, during that second in time when heavenly beams of light reach down and illuminate the world, the one true matter of importance in one's life is revealed.

Perhaps it was God's way of opening one's eyes, or perhaps it was fate's way of twisting a knife. No matter the cause, for Anthony Rawlings that moment of clarity occurred in the midst of chaos. As icy water fell from the ceiling of his home office, as smoke billowed through the vents and down the corridors, and as voices of unseen faces clamored for attention, Tony's world became crystal clear. The only true meaning in his life was his family: Claire and Nichol.

He'd told his wife to stay away from the estate. It hadn't been debatable. He and Claire had discussed their shared need to keep Nichol safe—at any cost. However, admittedly during those discussions, Tony had yet to truly comprehend the depth of Catherine's depravity. It wasn't until he pushed his onetime confidant into a dissertation of confessions that Tony recognized her limitless boundaries and capacity for evil.

With that newfound knowledge of murders where Tony had thought fate intervened, and years of manipulation where he'd seen friendship, Tony knew that he never wanted his family near the woman he'd trusted for most of his life. For the first time since Nathaniel had uttered the words, *they will pay, their children will pay, and their children's children,* everything was crystal clear. Tony finally understood his unwanted definition: he and Claire were both children of children. Nichol was doubly so. Later, he would reflect on how Claire had tried to explain it to him. Perhaps he hadn't been ready to understand. Now he was.

It wasn't until he saw the utter hatred in Catherine's gray eyes that he felt Nathaniel's words deep in his soul. How could he have trusted Catherine for so long? How could he have willingly placed Claire in her clutches? How didn't he see what Catherine had seen all along?

One thing was obvious. Tony needed to keep his family safe and away from Catherine Marie London.

Unfortunately, the clarity that revealed itself on that March afternoon didn't show Tony a safe and secure family. No, when his eyes were finally opened and he saw his lifelong friend as the monster she truly was—as a monster not only capable of killing his parents, but capable of killing his best friend—fate also showed him the two women in the entire world for whom he'd unquestionably, unequivocally, and unthinkingly lay down his life to save, and they needed him. Only moments earlier, he'd been searching the smoky hallways for Sophia Burke, until he heard Claire's voice. For an instant he prayed that it was his imagination, but then he heard her again. Tony didn't know why his wife was yelling; however, as he raced down the slippery marble floors toward his office, the why of her words wasn't as important as the why of her presence. *Why was she there?* She was supposed to be safe with Courtney. They'd agreed upon that.

Opening the door to his office, Tony's world clarified and collapsed. Terror like he'd never known filled his being when he realized that it wasn't only his wife in the presence of Catherine—no, Claire had Nichol in her arms. Tony would have done anything to reverse time, put them back in paradise, and keep his family from this horror. His deep threatening voice stilled whatever Catherine had been saying. "My God, Claire! Why are you here? Get out, the house is on fire!"

Her taut expression morphed to relief as their eyes met. "Oh, you're safe. I was so afraid."

The rush of the sprinkler system muted the sound of panicked voices in the distance, while intensifying Nichol's cries. From the safe harbor of her mother's arms, their daughter's pleas for attention grew above the commotion. Within seconds, Claire's relief changed once again. It was fear. Tony had witnessed fear in her emerald eyes before and without warning he saw it again. Following her line of vision, Tony saw the small handgun Catherine now wielded in her steady grasp. The open drawer indicated that it had come from his desk. In a moment of utter confusion, Tony wondered why or how there could be a gun in his desk. He didn't like guns, never had. That was why he hired security. There was no reason to own a gun unless you were willing to use it. However, at that moment, Tony knew he was more than willing to use it. He'd rather kill Catherine with his bare hands, but for speed's sake, he'd gladly use the gun. He also knew that there was no way he'd allow Catherine to be the one to pull the trigger. He needed to get Claire and Nichol out of the house. "Get out; get Nichol out!" he screamed.

As Claire moved to obey, Catherine turned toward Tony with a malicious grin and asked, "*Nichol? Nichol?* You named a Rawls *Nichol?*"

Instead of answering, he used her distraction to knock the gun from her hand, sending it flying toward Claire and Nichol. When it landed near Claire's feet, Tony commanded, "Claire, get the gun!"

Did his words refocus Catherine's attention? He didn't know; however, in a microsecond Catherine was scurrying toward Claire and the gun. Without thinking, Tony dove forward. As he neared the women, he realized that Catherine wasn't going after the gun: she'd pulled a crying Nichol from Claire's arms. The earlier clarity glowed with new radiance. His daughter's safety was paramount to everything else. Momentarily forgetting the gun, Tony's strong hands steadied as he secured Nichol's small, wet, blanket-covered body and pulled her toward his chest. Though Catherine grappled for control, she was no match for Tony's strength and determination.

With their daughter once again safe in his arms, Tony looked to Claire with reassurance as Phil came into view. Tony hadn't seen him enter the office, yet Phil's intention was clear as he neared Claire, whose gaze was fixed on Catherine, completely unaware of Phil's presence. The gun in her grasp shook violently as she lifted the barrel toward Catherine who stood in front of Tony and Nichol. Phil's soothing tone was barely audible over the mayhem. Reaching for the gun, he said, "Claire, it's all right. Give me the gun."

Placing a hand on Claire's shoulder, Phil reached for the gun at the exact moment their world exploded with a flash and a bang. Tony instinctively twisted away in an effort to protect Nichol, as Catherine fell backward, toppling the three of them onto the wet carpet. The room filled with people, and footsteps rushed toward them.

"Claire! Claire!" Tony screamed as he assessed Nichol, made it to his knees, and fought to get to his wife. Easing himself and Nichol away from Catherine's body as she twisted and moaned, Tony's dark eyes searched through the smoke and artificial rain. He called out again, "Claire!"

Tony needed to get to Claire and let her know that he and Nichol were all right. He wanted to touch her and hold her, to hold both of his ladies and have them safe in his embrace. He saw her across the room, lying limp where only seconds earlier she'd been standing. Tony and Phil both rushed to her side. With Nichol still in his arms, Tony picked up the gun. Suddenly, the room filled with people.

"Help me! They tried to kill me!" Catherine's voice begged for attention.

Tony ran his hand over Claire's cheek.

"I'm not sure what happened," Phil replied to Tony's unasked question. "She just collapsed. I don't know if she hit her head. I wasn't fast enough to catch her."

Unexpectedly, someone turned up the volume. What only seconds earlier had been a dull roar of activity grew to an explosion of voices. The sound of his name came into range. "Mr. Rawlings. Mr. Rawlings."

It was a member of the Iowa City Police Department. Tony

recognized him, though he didn't know his name. *Was he one of the officers who'd searched the house after Claire disappeared?* Tony couldn't remember. He turned toward the officer and spoke, "Yes, my wife needs help."

The officer spoke calmly, "Mr. Rawlings, give me the gun."

It wasn't that he didn't know he'd been holding it: he did. It was that he didn't care. The only thing that mattered was Claire and Nichol. They were safe and the police were there. They'd take Catherine away and his family would be safe. Holding out the gun, Tony implored, "Here, take it. Someone help my wife."

Another officer took the gun away, while the man with the name Hastings stitched on a patch above his badge stepped between Tony and Claire and said, "Your wife? Who's your wife, Mr. Rawlings? Ms. Nichols is your ex-wife."

Thankfully, the sprinklers had stopped and the smoke had begun to dissipate. Tony stood. Hastings' words were ridiculous. Shaking his head, Tony freed droplets of water from his saturated hair, causing them to descend down his forehead and blur his vision. Continuing to hold Nichol tight, Tony said, "Get out of my way. I don't know what you're saying. Claire Rawlings is my wife." His voice rose in volume. "Get out of my way!"

Two individuals began to assess Claire as a female police officer came forward. "Mr. Rawlings, is that Ms. Nichols' daughter?"

"This is *our* daughter." He spoke as his attention went to a gurney being lowered on a scissor-like contraption with wheels next to Claire. Simultaneously another similar contraption was wheeled next to Catherine, as more people with dark blue coats surrounded her.

The female's voice empathized, "Please, Mr. Rawlings, let me take your daughter out of this chaos. Let me get her in the fresh air."

"No." Tony stood resolute. "No, I'll take her. But first she needs to see her mother. Claire needs to know we're all right."

"Ms. Nichols will be taken away to some place where we can assess her needs, and then she'll be held while we determine what happened here."

"Mrs. *Rawlings*! Her name is Claire Rawlings. Stop calling her Nichols!" As Tony's voice grew louder, Nichol's tiny face contorted, and her cries resumed. "What do you mean *held*? Claire didn't do anything wrong. We were acting in self-defense." Tony stopped. "I'm not saying anymore until I have my attorneys." He stood helplessly as an unconscious Claire was moved to the gurney. "Where are you taking her? Is she hurt? If she is, she needs medical attention." Turning his attention away from the two police officers, Tony searched for Phil. "Roach? Roach?! Where are you?"

Officer Hastings spoke, "Mr. Rawlings, why would Ms. Nichols be hurt? Did you hurt her?"

Tony stared incredulously. "Of course I didn't hurt her. Stop. Calling. Her. Nichols. Her. Name. Is. Rawlings."

"Mr. Rawlings, I must insist that you hand the child over to Officer O'Brien."

Ignoring Hastings' command, Tony saw Phil heading out of the office with Claire's gurney. "Roach! Roach?"

Hearing Tony's call, Phil stopped and looked his way. Obviously torn between staying with Claire or returning to Tony, Phil hesitated for only a second before he walked back to Tony. Not waiting for a question, he explained, "They said they're going to take her to the hospital first and assess her for injuries."

Tony tried to make sense of it all, yet nothing made sense.

"Mr. Rawling—" Hastings began. Tony pulled his arm away from Hastings' reach. "Mr. Rawlings, you are under arrest for the

14

attempted murder of Ms. London."

"Mr. Rawlings," Officer O'Brien pleaded, "please, allow me to take your daughter."

"No! No, you're not touching my daughter. She needs to see her mother." Tony looked toward Phil. "You take Nichol to Claire. Keep her with Claire until Claire can care for her. I'll get this settled in no time. I didn't attempt to murder Ms. London. If I had, I would've succeeded."

Before handing Nichol to Phil, Tony gently placed a kiss on her forehead and tugged her closer to his chest. Three months of memories swarmed his mind, from the first time Madeline laid his daughter in his arms to their nightly private rock and chat sessions. He imagined the sweet smell of her after a bath, the way her little legs kicked in the warm water, and the way her eyelids became heavy after she'd eaten. The thought of being separated from his daughter for even a minute hurt like no physical pain ever could.

Inhaling her sweet baby scent, Tony calmed his voice and whispered, "It will be all right, my princess. Momma will be with you soon, and Daddy will be back to you just as soon as he can." Gazing into her big brown eyes, he continued, "Take care of your momma and don't forget me."

One more kiss to her forehead and Tony handed Nichol to Phil. Once Tony's arms were free of Nichol, Officer O'Brien placed handcuffs on Tony's wrist.

"Mr. Rawlings," the first officer said, "you have the right to remain silent. Anything you say—"

"Roach," Tony interrupted. "Have Eric contact Rawlings Industries. I want my legal team to meet me at the police station."

Phil nodded as they led Anthony Rawlings away, continuing his Miranda rights.

———◆———

THE NEXT FEW minutes were a blur. Once they got Tony to the police station, his litany of crimes would come to light. It was Claire's nightmare, the reason she hadn't wanted him to travel to the United States. Their one-year reprieve would be null and void. The FBI would never swoop in and save them. They wouldn't allow their family to return to paradise for the remaining nine months. Tony knew in the pit of his stomach that his time was up—at least for a while. He silently prayed that it wouldn't take too long. He had money. He'd spend every last dime to get back to Claire and Nichol as soon as possible.

Tony's normally quiet estate bustled with people and vehicles. Fire trucks ran long hoses through the corridors, creating an obstacle course as Officer Hastings led Tony toward the outside. His house staff stood huddled together on the bricked driveway, silently watching their runaway boss. He'd been missing for months and now he was being forced into the back of a police car—arrested. It didn't matter that he hadn't tried to kill Catherine: if it weren't for the damn videotapes, he'd confess to being the one who shot her, anything to save Claire. He couldn't bear the thought of his wife spending one day or even one hour in a prison cell. He'd done that to her once; he would move heaven and hell to stop it from happening again.

Just before settling into the back of the police car, Tony saw Emily rush toward Roach. Hatred seeped with reddening intensity as Tony took in his sister-in-law. This was all her fault. He and his family would be safe in paradise if she hadn't been so damned determined to learn Claire's secrets from Catherine. And now she was reaching for Nichol. Tony closed his eyes and prayed—silently demanded—for Claire to wake. She needed to be there for their daughter.

Tony stiffened his shoulders as he searched for answers. How could everything go so terribly wrong in such a short period of time? Despite the cool March Iowa air, perspiration beaded upon Tony's brow and a wave of nausea sucked the breath from his lungs.

Brent.

Brent Simmons. Was. Dead.

Claire would wake. Tony would undoubtedly have a price to pay, but Brent was dead. Tony couldn't buy back his friend's life. He couldn't alleviate the pain that Courtney must be enduring. It was all Catherine's doing!

What about Derek Burke? What about Sophia? Red grew. Questions multiplied and lurched forward in his mind. It was all happening too fast to register. Did they find Sophia asleep upstairs? Did anyone even go look? How was she dealing with the loss of her husband? It was too much! More questions than answers raced at untold speed. The vendetta continued to snowball out of control.

Crimson covered his world!

Claire. Nichol. Brent. Courtney. Sophia.

The mental toll needed an outlet: physical release took hold. He lunged forward and purged the red as vomit splattered the floor-mat to the right of Tony's feet.

Chapter 2

March 2014

Phil

———◆———

The mystery of human existence lies not in just staying alive, but in finding something to live for.
—Fyodor Dostoyevsky

DESPITE THE WAY his training screamed at Phil to disappear into the chaos, he couldn't do it, especially not after Rawlings so trustingly placed Nichol in his arms. Phil didn't know anything about babies, but common sense told him that the little girl with her daddy's eyes and lungs was not happy. The saturated blanket wrapped around her tiny body had been her only protection from the icy water that had rained moments earlier from the sprinkler system as mayhem erupted all around her. Removing the wet blanket, Phil unzipped his jacket and pulled Nichol to his warm chest. Covering her again with the warm dry material, he pulled the zipper over her, all the while being cautious to avoid her fine dark hair. Almost instantly, her loud cries mellowed, her little fist found its way to her mouth, and her eyes contently closed.

Fleetingly, Phil wondered how he'd thought to hold her against his body. He was warm: she was cold. It made sense. Only a few times in his life had he been this close to a child, and every time was with Nichol. He wasn't the type of man to show affection. It wasn't in his DNA. Without a doubt, his comfort level was higher in setting his sights on a marked man than cradling a baby under his jacket. The other times that Phil had held Nichol were at Claire's insistence. Shielding Nichol from the stiff breeze, he made his way out of the estate as memories surfaced of the first time Claire had placed her daughter in his arms. Nichol was only a day old and Phil had done his best to avoid Claire, Rawlings, and Nichol; however, there were only so many places to hide on an island.

Overwhelmingly, Phil had been relieved by Claire's condition. When he risked his life to get the damn doctor to the island—if he'd been forced to admit the truth, it wasn't to save Nichol. Phil was worried out of his mind about Claire. Getting in that boat and braving the rough seas wasn't selfless. No, it was selfish. He couldn't stand to stay near Claire with no ability to ease her distress. After all, he'd agreed to protect her and her child, and while on the run, he'd succeeded. The idea that his efforts had been for naught, thwarted by a tragic medical accident outside of his control, was agonizing.

On the day after Nichol's birth, Claire was in the shade on the lanai when Phil came around the corner. He hadn't expected her to be up and out of her room. Though tired, she looked amazing. He stood and watched as she held Nichol, seemingly in a world by herself. Contentment resonated all around her. Perhaps it was curiosity: Phil had never seen such a young baby, or just maybe it was a desire to share in a miracle of this magnitude. The reason wasn't clear, but instead of going on to the kitchen for a bite to eat,

Phil walked toward Claire and Nichol and made his presence known. He remembered her happy expression as he sat on the chaise longue near her outstretched legs.

"Thank you for getting the doctor yesterday," she said with her green eyes open wide.

"I wish you'd stop thanking me for doing my job."

"Risking your life is not your job."

"My job is to keep you safe. And now look at you."

Pink returned to Claire's cheeks. "Yes, thank you for that. Let me introduce our daughter..." she shifted the bundle in her arms. The tiny face and scrunched eyes were like nothing Phil had ever seen. In a way, she reminded him of a pale raisin. "...Nichol Courtney Rawlings."

He leaned closer. "You made quite an entrance, little lady. You should really take it easy on your mom. She had a rough night."

"She's been as good as gold since she last ate." Claire's eyes widened. "Would you like to hold her?"

Phil sat upward. "No."

Claire giggled. "You answered that pretty fast."

"Remember, I said that I don't do diapers."

Claire reached for some hand sanitizer and pushed it toward Phil. "No one's asking you to change diapers. Here, rub this on your hands and you can hold her." Maybe it was his blank stare, perhaps it was the flushing of his face as blood drained, but Claire continued, "You're supposed to protect me? Well, I need to get up for a minute and take care of something. Nichol is part of me, so I need you to protect her until I return."

Phil rubbed the alcohol-scented sanitizer on his hands as he asked, "A minute? What if she cries?"

Ignoring his concern, Claire shifted her legs from the longue *and gently placed Nichol in his arms. "Just support her head. You won't break her. Hold her closer... yes, like that." Once she was satisfied, Claire kissed her daughter's head and added, "Now, if you'll excuse me for a minute, just a minute, I'll be right back. Oh, stay in the shade."*

Claire wasn't gone long, but in those few minutes—yes, more than one—Phil fell in love. Of all of the things he'd done in his life, never had he held such a precious, innocent being in his hands. He knew Claire was right: his assignment had just doubled. The little girl in his hands had her daddy's eyes, but he saw Claire, too. No longer did he see a raisin. He saw Claire's nose and lips...

Phil wondered how some poor kid would feel when Phil drove Nichol and him on their first date, because there was no way he was letting her go with that kid alone. Hell, he'd been a teenage boy once. No way!

When Phil was younger and on assignment with the military, his objective had been defined by others and incredibly simple: life or death. While observing Claire for Rawlings in California, Phil's world changed. For the first time in his life, his target had been achieved, yet his mission wasn't complete. Each day he found himself more and more enthralled with his assignment. Truth be told, it probably began in San Antonio when she outsmarted him; however, that was only the beginning. What impressed him beyond belief was her ability to manipulate the master manipulator. Phil saw how others responded to Anthony Rawlings. Claire's actions truly earned Phil's respect. Then, Claire was attacked while on his watch, and Phil was relieved of his duties.

Never without a connection, Phil moved on to other jobs: most were short and finite. He followed a husband and verified his involvement with another woman. He tracked down a runaway teenager and alerted her parents to her location. Not ready to give up his newfound obsession with Claire Nichols, he welcomed the directive from Ms. London. In his mind he was helping to create the perfect ruse for Claire to leave Rawlings. Phil firmly believed Ms. London's story that in a moment of weakness following Chester's attack, Claire agreed to go to Iowa. It was a decision she immediately regretted, but one that she was unable to reverse without assistance. Rawlings had already proven that he would track her down with relentless fortitude. As the seeds of *Rawls-Nichols* threats were being planted, Phil was planning her ultimate escape. To that end, he willingly mailed the notes, cards, and packages.

It wasn't until he helped her escape the United States and they spoke again in Geneva that Phil learned he'd only been a pawn in Ms. London's strategically planned game of chess.

Back at the estate, the unusually cool spring air nipped Phil's face as he stepped from the warmth of the house onto the lawn. Police cars and fire trucks littered the drive. For all practical purposes, he should disappear. But how could he disappear with Nichol in tow? He'd surely be accused of kidnapping. Smirking, Phil knew that kidnapping charges would be the least of his worries. Feeding, changing, and bathing a three-month-old baby ranked much higher on his list of concerns.

The crowd of people became quiet as a policeman led Rawlings from the house with his hands secured in handcuffs. Just seconds ago, two ambulances left: one contained Claire, the other Ms. London. As Phil watched the scene unfold, Claire's sister approached.

"Who are you?" she asked.

"Excuse me?"

"Who are you? Do you work for *him*?"

Phil's stance straightened. The way Emily stressed the word *him* left no doubt as to her meaning. "I work for *her*—your sister." Maybe it was his change in demeanor, but as he spoke Nichol made her presence known.

Emily covered her mouth failing to stop the gasp. "Oh, my God, do you have her child?"

Phil nodded as he lowered the zipper on his coat. "Her blanket was wet. I'm trying to keep her warm."

"Her?" Emily repeated with wonder.

John Vandersol, Claire's brother-in-law, joined the conversation and immediately removed his jacket as Emily reached for Nichol. Phil wanted to protest and pull the little girl back to his chest, but he knew this was the right thing to do. Emily was her aunt. She would know better how to care for a baby until Claire was well and released. Besides, Phil wanted to go check on Claire at the hospital and tell her what had transpired with Nichol and Tony.

"There, there..." Emily cooed, as she wrapped her niece in John's coat. Looking up to Phil, she asked, "Do you know the last time she ate?"

Phil shook his head. "Claire just brought her here minutes before this all got out of hand. She's, umm..." his cheeks uncustomarily reddened, "...not fed with a bottle."

"Oh," Emily responded. "Then I guess we need to get her to Claire at the hospital." Again to Phil, "Do you know what happened inside?"

"I wasn't there for all of it. But I have a good idea—"

John interrupted. "It was Anthony, wasn't it? That's who Claire was trying to shoot?"

Emily nodded as her husband spoke.

"No." Phil answered definitively. "No, she wasn't trying to shoot anyone. She was trying to save Nichol from Ms. London."

Emily's head shook. "I don't believe you. Claire never said anything but good things about Catherine."

"You're defending the woman who had you locked in a suite, instead of the man who saved you?" Phil retorted.

John's brows cocked. "How do you know that? How do you know where we were? Maybe you're working for Anthony and he was the one—"

Phil glared. "I'll give my official statement to the police. I assure you, though, that you're mistaken." Despite being muffled by John's coat, Nichol's cries called out. "But before we argue this point, you need to get Nichol to Claire."

Emily's eyes widened. "Nichol? My niece is named Nichol Nichols?"

"Nichol Courtney Rawlings." Phil stated matter-of-factly.

Emily's green eyes glared. "What do you mean Rawlings? Did Claire agree to that?"

Phil's tone deepened. "Mrs. Vandersol, you'll need to speak with your sister. But I'll tell you that she and Mr. Rawlings remarried. They were married when Nichol was born. Just let your sister explain it to you."

John spoke as they made their way toward the cars. "You know he's a wanted man. Did you know where he was? How can we trust you?"

"You can't. However, things are different when it comes to Mrs. Rawlings. I wouldn't do anything to harm her or allow her to be harmed. She really is the one you should be talking to."

"So," Emily pushed, "she wanted you with her because she was afraid of him harming her again?"

"Mrs. Vandersol, you are misinterpreting—" Phil's explanation was cut short as an Iowa City policeman reached for his arm.

"Sir, we need to ask you a few questions. You were in the office at the time of the shooting..."

Phil replied to the officer as John and Emily carried Nichol away. Unexpectedly, John turned around and walked back. "Is there an infant car seat?"

The officer nodded as Phil took John to the car Claire had driven, the one belonging to Courtney Simmons. Phil wished with all his might that he could keep Claire's friend out of the turmoil that would come from helping Tony and Claire. He might have been able to, had Claire not driven Courtney's car. His mind spun. As soon as John walked away, the policeman asked, "Whose car is this?"

"It belongs to another of my employers. He allowed me to use it."

"You? You drove Miss Nichols here?"

"Her name is Rawlings. She and Mr. Rawlings were remarried, and I believe I should have an attorney present before I divulge any more information."

That became Phil's answer to each question. He'd already said more to the Vandersols than he should have. He wanted them to know, however, that despite Claire and Tony's past they were raising Nichol together. Undoubtedly, all of the hiding from the FBI would come back to haunt Rawlings, but Phil hoped Claire's family would understand. Both Rawlings and Claire would need their support.

Finally, the officer became bored with Phil's response, or lack of one. "Mr. Roach, what do you do and who do you work for?"

"I'm an independent contractor. I do many things and work for many people."

"Maybe we should take a drive downtown and check your résumé a little closer."

"Although that sounds like a fun afternoon, I'm rather busy. Do you believe that you have a reason to charge me with something? If you do, let's drive. If you don't, I have more work I need to do. The first thing is checking on Mrs. Rawlings."

"Mr. Roach, how do you know that she and Anthony Rawlings are remarried?"

"Officer, when I speak with my attorney, we'll let you know." Phil hesitated. When the officer didn't respond, he continued, "I will assume we're done for now?"

"For now. Do not leave the state—for *business* or personal reasons without contacting the ICPD first."

Phil shrugged. "Independent contractors are in constant demand all over the world. If you need me, you have my number." With that, he turned and walked toward Courtney's car. When he'd retrieved the car seat, Phil saw a purse on the floorboard. He hoped, for appearance sake, that the key was there. As soon as he sat in the car, his phone buzzed with a text from Eric.

"I'M STILL IN THE SECURITY CENTER. I'VE MADE BACKUPS OF EVERYTHING. WHERE DID THEY TAKE EVERYONE?"

Phil responded. *"LONDON AND CLAIRE TO THE HOSPITAL AND RAWLINGS TO THE POLICE STATION. HE SAID FOR YOU TO CALL RAWLINGS INDUSTRIES AND GET HIS LEGAL TEAM THERE ASAP. I WOULD HAVE COMMUNICATED EARLIER BUT THINGS ARE CRAZY."*

"NICHOL?"

"EMILY VANDERSOL. I'M OFF TO CHECK ON CLAIRE. YOU'LL GET RAWLINGS HELP?"

"YES." Eric replied.

Phil riffled through the purse and found a key fob. Within seconds he was headed away from the Rawlings estate toward Iowa City.

IT HADN'T OCCURRED to him that there were multiple hospitals in Iowa City, and it would have been an issue, except when Phil handed John Vandersol the car seat, he placed an inconspicuous GPS tracker under the soft fabric. Rawlings had put Phil in charge of Nichol's care, and he had no intentions of losing track of her location. After a few swipes on his phone, the blinking light led him exactly to where he needed to be. Phil didn't consider contacting Courtney as he parked and locked her car. She was too busy with the news of her husband to be concerned about Claire, Nichol, or her car. Phil tried not to think about Brent. There were many people in Phil's life who'd come and gone; nevertheless, the lingering sadness at the thought of Brent Simmons' untimely death was another example of how Phil's life had radically changed since Brent contacted him a year ago. He was getting soft.

Slipping into the overcrowded emergency room, Phil nodded at the nurse sitting behind the desk and crossed the threshold to the draped examination rooms. In no time at all, Nichol announced their location. Before he could decide if he wanted to be seen, Emily emerged from a sliding glass door of a concealed room and their eyes met.

"I didn't get your name," she said matter-of-factly.

"Roach, Phillip Roach. How is Claire?"

Emily bristled. "My sister's information is private."

"I can assure you, Mrs. Vandersol, I'm privy to your sister's private information. It's my job; I need to know. Keeping her safe is what I'm supposed to do. I can't do that if I'm unable to be near her."

Nichol's cries grew in strength.

"As you can see, she has a police guard. I don't believe your services are needed."

"Why is she still crying?" Phil asked, moving his gaze toward Nichol.

"I'd assume she's hungry. I'm on my way to get formula from the pediatric unit."

"But... Claire won't be happy—"

"Thank you, Mr. Roach. Obviously, if your job was to assure my sister's safety, you've failed. She has her family now. We'll take care of her and Nichol. If you're owed any money, see *him*. I mean according to you, he's her husband. Please don't bother my sister again."

"Thank you, Mrs. Vandersol, I will gladly resign my position when my employer, your sister, relieves me of my duties, and not a minute before."

"My sister is in shock from whatever occurred. When she recovers, the police will question her. If you have any information you'd like to share, please contact me. They've already done some kind of test and know for a fact that she fired a gun. Luckily, I don't believe Ms. London is gravely injured. I just wish my sister had had better aim and it was him who was shot."

"You don't have the necessary facts to make the assumptions—"

"I need to get Nichol fed. I have instructed the police guards as to who may or may not enter her room. Goodbye, Mr. Roach."

Clenching his teeth, Phil nodded. Tony had said more than once that he disliked Claire's sister. Phil concurred.

If he couldn't see Claire in person, he'd hack into the hospital's records and learn about her that way. Turning around, he walked toward Courtney's car.

Chapter 3

March 2014

Brent

———◆———

Why should we look to the past in order to prepare for the future? Because there is nowhere else to look.
—James Burke

BRENT SIMMONS SIGHED as he settled against the leather airplane seat and enjoyed a minute of relaxation. It seemed that more recently his life was a whirlwind: as soon as he extinguished one fire, another went from smoldering to blazing. Was it his profession? That could be expected with law. Or was it the company he kept? During his tenure with Rawlings Industries, he either spent his time ascertaining whether protocol was followed or steering the offending policy back on an even keel. Brent was a rule follower. He didn't make waves. No, he was the one who calmed the passengers as the storms of life blew them about. That was probably why his and Tony's relationship had worked from the beginning. Tony created rules, and Brent followed them. That was until now.

Closing his eyes, he contemplated his current *illegal* status. He and Courtney were willingly harboring a fugitive. For the first time in his memory, Brent Simmons was knowingly breaking the law, the same law that he had taken an oath to uphold. He hadn't stumbled into his new world of law-breaking: he'd volunteered. When Roach informed him that Tony and Claire wanted to return, temporarily, to the United States, Brent suggested without hesitation, that they come to his home. Brent knew without a doubt that Courtney would agree. After all, it wasn't the first time he and Courtney had risked consequences to help Claire. What made this unique was that now they both also wanted to help Tony.

Although Brent and Tony had been friends for years, their relationship wouldn't have been considered equal—perhaps it never will be. But the last time Brent saw Tony, before last night, they'd had words, words that evened their friendship in a way as never before. Actually, that night in Boston, Brent said things he never thought he'd ever say to his friend, and it felt good. Anthony Rawlings had a way about him, an arrogance. It worked for business, but not for his personal life. Being both a friend and an employee, Brent spent most of his life walking a damn tightrope. It had gone on for too long. He'd known about Tony and Claire's history since before their divorce. When presented with the FBI account of their past, Brent couldn't—no, he wouldn't—maintain his silence any longer. He had to lay it on the line.

Then Tony disappeared.

In the weeks and months that followed, Brent relived their argument a hundred times. His satisfaction at clearing the air wavered with the reality of never seeing Tony or Claire again. Brent and Courtney talked their way through a million scenarios. They hoped and prayed that both of their friends were safe. The part they weren't sure about, what neither one knew what to pray for, was if Tony and Claire should be together. Brent knew in his heart that

Tony wasn't injured in an emergency plane landing. He knew that the man he'd worked beside and gotten to know as an esteemed businessman and his best friend was out searching for the woman he loved. Through endless hours of deliberation, he and Courtney debated about the missing piece of the puzzle. Why had Claire left?

Neither Brent nor Courtney wanted to believe the story Claire's sister and brother-in-law spun. They didn't want to believe that Claire was once again motivated by fear of Tony, yet, with the publication of Meredith Banks' book, that lingering concern loomed ever-present in both of their minds.

On a whim, Brent contacted Phil Roach. After all, Brent had been the one to hire him in the first place. Being a consummate professional, since Brent was not his client, Roach didn't divulge anything. And then the call came. Roach had discussed it with Tony, and the lines of communication were opened. Roach explained to Brent, and thus to Courtney, the intricacies of the Rawlingses' temporary departure. The Simmonses became privy to the real story of their disappearance and Catherine's role in it all.

Over the years, as situations deemed necessary, Brent mastered the skill of being less than forthcoming. Depending upon the circumstance, the level of difficulty varied. One of the hardest scenarios was Claire's pardon. To work every day beside Tony and know the answers to all of Tony's questions, yet remain detached, warranted Brent an Academy Award. There were even a few times when Courtney deserved, at the very least, a nomination for Best Supporting Actress in a drama series. Although the role was sometimes tedious, what fueled Brent's motivation were the words of Claire's testimony. He'd remember the frightened young woman who accompanied Tony on a business trip to New York, or the beautiful bride who lived a hidden life of domination. It made Brent physically ill to think of the things that she'd endured at the hands of his *friend,* the things that occurred right before their eyes, while they'd done nothing to help.

Maybe it was Claire who deserved an Academy Award? After all, neither he nor Courtney knew what was happening behind the iron gates of the Rawlings estate.

Even more difficult than facing Tony day to day while he ranted and raved about Claire's pardon, had been the past few months of facing Catherine London. Knowing what Brent knew, each inquiry that Ms. London made into Rawlings' personal financial matters or Rawlings Industries, each time she used her position as executor of Tony's estate to influence something or the other, Brent's blood boiled. He had to force himself to return her calls. Sometimes he wouldn't do it for days, claiming an overwhelming workload or forgetfulness. Each interaction was loathsome. Normally a gentle man, Brent couldn't interact with her without wishing her physical pain. Her smug countenance grated on him as he contemplated her role in the upheaval of his friends' lives. After so much time, Brent had come to the conclusion that Tony and Claire were both people he'd grown to love.

The flight attendant refocused Brent's attention. If there hadn't been a glitch in the finalization of the proposal, he'd have been home already with Courtney and Claire. He would know what was happening with Roach and Tony at the estate. He might not be in need of more antacid!

The glitch wasn't big; nonetheless, by spending a few more minutes—that turned into an hour—with the appropriate people, Brent preempted the need to return to Chicago to rectify the potential contractual misinterpretation. He didn't mind. Taking a commercial flight gave Brent the opportunity to regroup and think about all that was happening. No doubt, if he'd flown back with Sharon Michaels and Derek Burke, they'd have spent the entire flight rehashing the proposal, crunching numbers, and verifying statutes. This alternative gave Brent a moment of uncustomary peace and anonymity.

Even though he wasn't initially scheduled to be involved with the negotiations, Brent believed the meeting in Chicago had gone exceptionally well. It was his first opportunity to personally witness Derek in action. In hindsight, Brent wondered about the promotion that brought the young man to corporate. It seemed strange that Ms. London had found the necessary requests on Tony's home computer, but regardless of the mode of hire, Derek Burke appeared to be an asset to Rawlings Industries. Brent wasn't sure when, or if, Tony would once again be personally involved in the day-to-day workings of Rawlings Industries, but he made a mental note to tell Tony about Burke. He was a natural: professional, eloquent, and a wonder to watch. The young man's negotiating skills were stellar. With his potential, Brent believed that he had a bright future with Rawlings Industries.

With time to allow his mind to wander, one thought led to another. Thinking about his own day's duties and telling Tony about Derek reminded Brent of Tony's plans for the day. More than once, fleeting thoughts manifested themselves as Brent wondered what was transpiring at the estate. He was concerned: could things—for once—go the way they were meant to go for Tony and Claire? It seemed that the deck had been stacked against them since before they knew one another. Truth be told, it was. Tony had confirmed it months ago, as had Claire to Courtney. As much as they both loathed their friends' history, seeing them last night with their beautiful daughter helped to confirm Brent and Courtney's wishes for their future. After all Tony and Claire had endured, they both deserved better. Brent hoped that their coming back to the United States and helping John and Emily wouldn't dampen their future. With Nichol in the game, the stakes were much higher.

After the captain announced their altitude and the little bell dinged, Brent leaned his chair back and opened the eBook app on his phone. He'd placed it on airplane mode much earlier than necessary. It helped with the relaxation. Despite the fact that Brent had been actively involved in the attempts to stop the publication of Meredith Banks' book *My Life as It Didn't Appear*, he still purchased the book out of morbid curiosity the day it came out. He wondered how Ms. Banks would sensationalize what Brent had read in a more clinical legal brief.

Brent wasn't blind or deaf. He heard whispers and murmurs. He knew that he wasn't the only member of the Rawlings Industries legal team to buy the book. Everyone was intrigued. However, as a close friend of both Tony and Claire, when asked, Brent maintained his stance, continually professing that he had no desire to add to Ms. Banks' rankings or bank account. Perhaps it was a misleading statement, but it was not an outright lie.

When Brent first downloaded the book, he was only able to read as far as the author's introduction that explained Meredith and Claire's relationship, setting the stage for the details to come. Brent had tried to read Claire's words, but couldn't. Knowing without doubt that what he was about to read was completely accurate made it too painful. Nevertheless, curiosity is a strange beast. Despite best intentions or convictions, it doesn't fall asleep and quietly fade away. No. If left unfed, curiosity becomes a hunger that grows in strength and voracity until it monopolizes unconscious thoughts and dreams.

Seeing his friends last night gave Brent the sustenance he needed to move past Meredith's introduction. Seeing firsthand that Tony and Claire's relationship had matured, and watching them with Nichol, gave him the necessary strength to continue reading. He was ready to read the words, knowing that through Meredith, Claire spoke of the past—a dark past, but nonetheless, a time that was gone, never to be repeated.

Brent also justified his reading as company research. If the world had a perception of Anthony Rawlings, as his personal attorney, Brent needed to understand it. Sitting in a commercial airplane at thirty thousand feet gave Brent that opportunity. It was undoubtedly a better place to read Meredith's story than on a Rawlings Industries plane.

My Life as It Didn't Appear: Chapter 1...

Imagine, if you will, that you are suddenly keeping company with one of the country's most eligible bachelors. What would you expect? Perhaps flowers and romance? Maybe candlelight and soft music?

I'm Claire Nichols, formally Rawlings, and I wish I could say that was what I experienced. I wish I could tell you how Anthony Rawlings wooed me, seduced me, and romantically worked his way into my heart. Unfortunately, my reality was starkly different.

Although it now seems inconceivable, when I first met my ex-husband—before my life changed forever—I didn't know Anthony Rawlings nor did I know of him. I've read numerous accounts that paint me as nothing more than a calculating gold digger. I may never be able to convince the world otherwise, but the truth is that

I never wanted wealth, or fame, or any of the things that entered my life on that fateful evening when I saw his dark eyes for the very first time. Before that night, my life was amazingly simple and yet complex. As an out-of-work meteorologist, I tried to make ends meet by tending bar at a local restaurant. I had friends, a family, and my life was content. I didn't realize how truly happy I was until my life was taken away.

Never has nor ever will money be my barometer of happiness. I can tell you with all certainty that money does not buy happiness.

There were many other truisms that I learned after March 15, 2010. The most important was about appearance: never doubt its power or importance. It was a lesson that I mastered to perfection. My outstanding dedication to that lesson helped to perpetuate the misconceptions regarding my relationship with Anthony Rawlings.

Am I writing this book for money? No. Am I writing it to exact revenge? No.

I'm telling my story for one reason and one reason only because I need to have a voice in my reputation. I'll no longer sit quietly and allow the world to be misinformed—or more accurately, disinformed—at my expense. You will soon learn that I was complacent for far too long. Some of the details from my story will be difficult for me to share as well as difficult for you to read. I can't make you believe me. All I can do is tell my story to anyone willing to listen.

My reality began on March 15, 2010, in an establishment where I worked as a bartender. Anthony Rawlings appeared out of nowhere and sat down at my bar. Throughout the evening he was witty, charming, and debonair: all the qualities you'd expect. He asked to meet me for drinks after my shift. Although I had a firm rule against dating customers, Anthony Rawlings had a way of making you forget your rules and play by only his instead.

Brent swallowed back a bitter laugh. Damn—she was spot on. He continued reading.

Although I agreed to his invitation, as a safety net I refused to leave my place of employment. He willingly acquiesced and waited for me. When my shift was over, we sat, drank wine, and chatted effortlessly about nothing in particular. Sometime during our conversation, he asked about my aspirations and dreams. With a deep baritone voice that has graced both my nightmares and my dreams, he began, "Claire, surely you don't want to spend forever serving drinks to stooges like us."

Clearly, he was a successful man, and I was flattered by his genuine interest. I explained my wrinkle in employment, and he offered to help: he proposed that my dreams could be as simple as a signature away. With a rush of enthusiasm, he presented me with a napkin from the bar, and asked, "Would you be willing to give this all up for something bigger? What if this napkin were truly a contract and what if it said WEATHER CHANNEL at the top? Would you be willing to sign on the line for something like that?"

Perhaps it was the wine, but I'd say it was his magnetism. His words and tone enveloped the booth where we sat and filled me with a false sense of hope for a future and a career I'd lain awake nights dreaming of experiencing. For a brief moment in time, he made it seem obtainable. I bit—hook, line, and sinker—and, willingly accepting the pen he offered, signed my name.

What I thought was an imaginary agreement to my life's

dream, was in actuality a literal agreement to a nightmare.

Though I didn't see Anthony at all the next day, he called the restaurant and asked me to dinner. I was so surprised that he remembered my name, much less asked me out on a date, that I didn't realize that he knew my schedule. Not only did he know when I was working so that he could call, but he also knew the time I would finish work the following day.

Another rule I faithfully practiced during my dating years was to never ride with a man in his car on the first date. I always drove separately. It was my escape. That practice had proved useful on more than one occasion. However, once again, Anthony had his own plan, his own rule. Before I knew it, I'd agreed to a dinner date and to having him pick me up at my place of business. That date was March 17—the date I ceased to exist.

Perhaps if there were to be any hearts and flowers in our courtship, it was that night. He took me to a beautiful Italian restaurant, and once again, I missed warning signs. He ordered my meal, my drinks, everything. I'd never met a man like him before. He threw my world off-kilter. No matter what I thought or said, he seemed to be one step ahead of me and for some unknown reason, I liked it. After living independently with no one else to rely upon, an evening with a man in total control was a nice break in routine. I had no illusions about a long-term relationship with Anthony Rawlings. Our worlds were too different. But for a night I was treated like a princess and this dark-haired, dark-eyed gentleman was my prince.

When he offered to take me back to his hotel suite and I accepted, little did I realize that it was one of the last decisions I would make for nearly three years. Little did I realize that my fate was sealed and my prince was truly the beast of every fairytale I'd ever read. I now understand that my future was predetermined, and my pseudo-decisions—like agreeing to dinner and his hotel suite—were just that: a ruse for a bigger, darker plan.

Though my nightmare began later that night, I can't recall any of it until the next day when I woke in my prison—my cell for the next three years of my life. Of course, that wasn't what he called it. He called it my suite at his estate.

The captain announced their approach into Cedar Rapids as Brent turned off his app and closed his eyes. He'd heard rumors and whispers around the office. Hell, the Internet and television buzzed with the stories, but part of Brent wanted to believe that Claire hadn't truly disclosed their darkest secrets to the world. A cold chill brought goose bumps to his arms as he imagined Tony reading this account for the first time.

As the plane touched down in Cedar Rapids, Brent fumbled with his phone, turning off the airplane mode. An onslaught of buzzes and vibrations told him that his momentary reprieve from reality was done. He obviously had messages galore awaiting his reply. Then, just as quickly, the screen went black.

"Damn," he whispered to himself. "That battery is shit."

As the plane taxied to the gate, Brent realized that he'd forgotten to text the office to have a car pick him up, and his car was at the Rawlings Industries private airport. With his phone dead, he couldn't even call Courtney, not that he wanted to disturb her. She and Claire were probably catching up. Fine, he'd take a cab. Although there was plenty of work at Rawlings, Brent wanted to go straight home. He hoped that when he arrived, he'd find Tony and Claire safe under his roof, with harrowing stories of outsmarting

Catherine and saving Emily and John.

Rotating his head from side to side in an effort to relieve the tension, Brent wondered when he'd become an optimist. The tight muscles in his neck and shoulders warned him of the alternate possibilities of what he'd find at home. Perhaps even a police officer. If Tony were taken into custody, would Brent and Courtney's roles be discovered? Would they too be taken in for questioning?

Those questions and more rattled through his consciousness as Brent exited the causeway to the airport. He wasn't looking at the televisions sprinkled throughout the waiting area of the gate, but the headline caught his attention: **RAWLINGS INDUSTRIES PLANE DOWN: 5 BELIEVED DEAD.**

Perspiration dotted his brow as he fought to comprehend. Rawlings had more than one plane. Surely they didn't mean the plane he was supposed to be on? He stared at the silent screen. The closed caption finally registered. Brent Simmons. Derek Burke. Sharon Michaels. Andrew McCain. Tory Garrett.

Brent rushed to a pay phone and fumbled for change. He called his home—no answer. He called Courtney's cell phone—voicemail. "Courtney, I wasn't on that plane!" he yelled into the receiver. "I'm on my way home. Oh, my God! I'm coming home!"

The ride from Cedar Rapids to his home was nothing more than a blur. He wanted to call the office, to try other phones. He hadn't left a message on their home phone, but he couldn't do any of that. His phone was totally dead. Brent couldn't think straight.

As the cab turned in to his driveway and approached his house, the number of cars on the brick drive brought the tension in his neck fully to Brent's temples. Easing his way in the front door of his home, Brent listened to the din of hushed voices coming from his kitchen. Stopping dead in his tracks, he heard his son's voice.

"Mom, we'll be there as soon as we can." Caleb was obviously on speakerphone. "Julia found a flight leaving in a couple of hours. We'll stay here as long as you need. Don't even try to argue. Nothing's more important right now than taking care of you."

"I-I need to do something. Anything." The sadness in Courtney's voice pulled at Brent's heart.

He turned the corner, met his wife's puffy-eyed stare, and rushed to her side.

The entire room gasped in unison as Courtney flew from her seat and wrapped her arms tightly around Brent's neck, surrounding her husband in a frantic embrace. "Oh, my God. Oh, my God..." Her words became unrecognizable as she shuddered with sobs.

"How? How? It's a miracle," Courtney managed between sniffles.

"I didn't know anything about the accident until I landed. I tried to call..."

Courtney's unwavering embrace stilled his words. Finally, she asked, "Why weren't you on the Rawlings plane?"

Caleb's voice came through the speaker. "What's happening?"

Bev and Sue smiled as Bev picked up Courtney's phone, turned off the speaker, and said, "Caleb..." She couldn't keep the tears from falling. "...there's someone here to talk to you."

Prying his arm free from his wife, Brent took the phone. "Hi, son. Apparently, the reports of my death are a bit exaggerated."

Caleb and Julia could both be heard gasping. Brent smiled. "Let me put you back on speaker. I had a few papers that needed to be tweaked and at the last minute decided to grab a commercial flight. I didn't know anything about it until I landed. My battery was dead so I tried to call from a pay phone. I left your mom a message." His eyes twinkled toward his wife. "But you know how she is: she never checks her messages."

"We're still coming home, and I just got a text from Maryn. Her plane lands about the same time as ours. We'll all be home this evening."

It had been Christmas since he'd had both of his children and daughter-in-law together. "Thanks for taking care of your mom. I love you all and can't wait to see you," Brent said before he disconnected the line.

The joyous mood turned somber as Sue came forward and hugged Brent. "I wish the others had waited too."

Brent's eyes misted. "I've been thinking about them since I heard. I can't believe it. Do they have any idea what happened?"

Courtney's head moved slowly from side to side. "I'm so sorry. I feel guilty being happy. I know what Sophia is going through."

Brent made no attempt to conceal the tears as he scanned the room. Looking to Sue, with her arms wrapped around her growing midsection and her cheeks dampened by emotion, he asked, "Poor Tim. As if he doesn't have enough happening. I need to help him."

Sue nodded. "I just texted him. He should call in a few minutes. He'll be so happy to learn you weren't on that flight, but Brent, there's so much more."

Brent sat silently as Courtney and Sue tag-teamed the significant details of the past few hours. When Courtney received the news about the flight, Claire panicked. She was upset, but also concerned about Tony's reaction if he learned about it while with Catherine. Claire was certain that Catherine was responsible. Once Sue was on her way to stay with Courtney, Claire took Nichol and headed over to the estate. No one really knows what happened there. They only know that Tony is currently in police custody, and

Claire is at the hospital with pending charges of attempted murder as well as aiding and abetting a fugitive.

"Thank God, Emily's here. She has Nichol," Courtney added.

Brent tried to process as he fought the onset of emotion. His brow glistened with perspiration at the realization: he was supposed to be dead. Derek Burke, Sharon Michaels, the pilot, and copilot were all dead. That wasn't all: Tony had been arrested and Claire had charges pending. That wasn't how it was supposed to happen. The FBI promised that no charges would be filed against Claire.

"I need to get to them," Brent said.

"You two need some time alone, before the kids arrive," Bev suggested.

Brent thought about Claire's words in Meredith's book. She'd already lived through hell, and he'd done nothing to help. He wasn't dead—he was alive. Brent wouldn't sit back again and do nothing. He couldn't. "I'm fine. I'm not doing this because it's my job. I want to help them. I have knowledge and proof. I need to get the FBI involved. The Iowa police don't realize all that has been done and the deals that have been made. With Meredith's book out there, I'm guessing they won't be willing to listen to Tony. I have to go."

Courtney wiped her eyes and nodded. "Then I'm going with you. I'm not letting you out of my sight, and I need to be sure they're both all right—and that Nichol Courtney's safe and sound."

Chapter 4

March 2014

Tony

Friendship multiplies the good of life and divides the evil.
—Baltasar Gracian

THE CINDER-BLOCK walls matched those from his memory. Only now, it wasn't his grandfather who was led to and fro by a guard; it was Tony. This was different than when he'd been questioned by the FBI: at that time Tony had hope. He'd had hope of finding Claire, hope that the FBI would reveal something to him, and hope of being free. Sometime in the past year, his hope bloomed and blossomed. In paradise it was alive and well. During the last few hours, it wilted before his eyes and lay at his feet gasping for its final breath. Tony gathered the fortitude to fight the overwhelming cloud of doom that threatened everything he held dear.

He suddenly realized how simplistic his existence had been. Decision-making had been much easier without emotional attachment. Now, every thought process pointed in one direction—his family.

While in paradise, the arrogance Tony had possessed for most of his life transformed into something different, something deeper. Tony couldn't explain it because he didn't completely understand it. However, a year ago, Anthony Rawlings would've used every resource at his disposal to free himself from the Iowa City Police and clear his name. For what? The answer was simple and ingrained. He would have done it to maintain appearances. Never would he want to admit to the world or anyone else that he was capable of the heinous acts described in Meredith Banks' book, much less the litany of crimes yet to be revealed.

Now, waiting alone for Tom and others from Rawlings Industries' legal department to arrive, Tony wasn't thinking about his own freedom, or even his own reputation. His thoughts were a blur with concerns about his wife and daughter as well as the mind-numbing blow of Catherine's confessions.

His grandfather.

Tony could barely stomach the reality: Catherine Marie London, the woman he'd trusted like a sister, confessed to willfully poisoning and ultimately killing Nathaniel. He tried to grasp that new reality. His grandfather's imprisonment and resulting death had been the catalyst for everything—every plan, every name on their list, and every consequence. Sherman Nichols and Jonathon Burke had collected evidence that led to Nathaniel's conviction, but they weren't responsible for his death, as Tony had believed for most of his life. It had all been a farce.

Tony recalled his dream...the envelope.

In his dream a year ago, Nathaniel had told Tony he'd failed. For the first time, Tony saw through the veil of crimson that had clouded his vision for so many years. Nathaniel never wished Anton a life of vengeance. Family, no matter how dysfunctional, had always been of utmost importance to him. He wished a full envelope for all of his loved ones. Never would he have wished harm to Anton, his wife, or his child, no matter who they were or to whom they were related. Even with Samuel's testimony, Nathaniel never condemned Samuel to pay. Family was exempt.

In the still of the interrogation room, Tony's memories screamed for attention as thoughts of his grandfather's medical records clamored for recognition. When Tony closed his eyes, he saw Nathaniel in a room similar to the one where Tony sat. He remembered his grandfather's voice, still strong and demanding, rambling about debts and children of children. Now, in the clarity provided by the new information, Tony wondered if any or all of those ramblings could have been brought on by the dementia-like side effects of the medication.

The person who ultimately deserved to pay for the crimes against so many was undoubtedly Catherine Marie. She took Nathaniel's wishes, vindicated them, and orchestrated a life-consuming scenario. A red hue seeped from the corners of the small room within the Iowa City jail as Tony assessed the damage. Everything began with hate and lack of forgiveness. That said, Catherine wasn't the only perpetrator. Samuel, Tony's father, was also responsible. His hatred of Catherine influenced his decision-making regarding Nathaniel's medication. That vengeance created the symptoms in Nathaniel that Catherine misconstrued as dementia.

Tony wanted to believe that Catherine's poisoning of Nathaniel was the selfless act of a concerned wife, not the homicidal act of a psychopath, but he was done seeing her through his grandfather's lens. Nathaniel had only been months away from release. Catherine Marie Rawls had had the proverbial world at her fingertips. She had a man who loved her, respected her, and promised her a future.

Maybe Nathaniel's wealth had dwindled, but at the very least, Nathaniel had the money overseas. If only she'd waited, taken him home, and allowed his medications to be re-evaluated.

Tony shook his head. *If only...*

Wasn't that the phrase of the day?

If only Nathaniel had lived. If only Brent hadn't gotten on that plane. If only Derek Burke hadn't found his way into Sophia's life. If only Tony and Catherine had never complied their list of names. If only his life had crossed paths with Claire's in another way...

Tony could go on for hours thinking about that list: Sherman Nichols. Tony remembered the first time he saw that name. It was during his investigation of Cole Mathews, Sherman's alias. He remembered the pride he felt as he supplied Nathaniel with that information. He'd done what he'd been asked to do, what Anton knew Nathaniel was incapable of doing. Tony's report didn't only contain Sherman's name, but the names of his family. It was more than his grandfather had requested, but that's what Anton did—more, above and beyond. That report contained the names of Sherman Nichols' wife, Elizabeth; son, Jordon; daughter-in-law, Shirley; and granddaughters, Emily and Claire.

Tony's empty stomach twisted. Every time he pointed his finger at Catherine, four pointed back toward him. He couldn't blame her for everything. Without his initial research, the entire Nichols family would've been spared. His face flushed. When Tony disclosed that list of names to his grandfather, Claire was six years old. A sickening feeling brought a bad taste to his mouth as he imagined what Nichol would be like at that age. What did Tony want for his daughter at that age? The answer was simple: security and innocence. Wasn't that the same thing Jordon and Shirley had wanted for Claire?

Catherine not only murdered Nathaniel, but Sherman, Jordon, and Shirley Nichols. During her confessions, she'd admitted to singlehandedly eliminating an entire branch of Claire's and ultimately Nichol's family tree. Remorse and guilt took a backseat to red-hot rage as Tony remembered the scene at the estate and envisioned the determination and hatred in Catherine's cold, gray eyes. She'd had the gun and had wanted to hurt *his* family. If she'd succeeded this afternoon, the entire Nichols line would be gone. The way she looked at Claire and Nichol. Hell, not only them: she had John and Emily locked in a suite with poisoned water. The bounds to her depravity knew no limits.

How had he been so wrong for so long? Had Samuel seen something in Catherine all those years ago that she'd somehow hidden from Nathaniel and Tony?

The door opened and Officer Hastings entered, bringing Tony's thoughts back to the present. "Mr. Rawlings, we have a couple more questions for you."

"Where are my attorneys?"

"They called and are on their way."

Tony sat taller. "I believe I'll wait. It's in my best interest to postpone your questions until their arrival."

"Mr. Rawlings, you aren't calling the shots here. We want to know where you've been for the last six months?"

Tony's jaw clenched in defiance as he silently stared at Officer Hastings.

"Perhaps you'd like to know about Ms. Nichols?" the officer baited.

"Mrs. Rawlings." Tony glared. "Where is she?"

"Do you have proof of your marriage to Ms. Nichols?" Hastings clarified, "Your second marriage."

Tony looked down at his left hand. Shit, he didn't even have a wedding band, but Claire did. Their marriage was legal. After the ceremony on the beach, they'd gone to the city with Francis and completed the necessary legal documents. In an effort to remain hidden, they'd decided to not forward that information on to the United States government. That may make verifying their marriage more difficult; however, it didn't nullify the legality of it. People married in different countries all the time.

Hastings taunted, "Without proof of your marriage, you have no claims or rights to information regarding Ms. Nichols."

The thin veneer of control Tony had held on his decorum, splintered as his fist hit the metal table. The otherwise still room exploded with the echoing vibrations as his determined voice rose above the clatter. "Rawlings! Mrs. Claire Rawlings," Tony said through gritted teeth. "Do not make me correct you again. And, no, I don't have our marriage license in my damn pocket, but I can get proof. We remarried on October 27, 2013. Ask Claire."

The doors once again opened and Tom Miller, the co-lead attorney at Rawlings Industries and Tony's personal friend entered. Without a word, he stopped Tony's rebuttal, silently warning him to say no more. Laying his briefcase on the table he turned to Hastings and politely asked, "Officer, I'm sure you're not questioning my client after he's asked for legal counsel, are you?"

"I'm not questioning him about the case. We need preliminary information."

Tom leaned forward and slowed his speech. "His name is Anthony Rawlings. He is the CEO of Rawlings Industries. Unless you charge him with a crime, I will be taking him out of here today." He lifted his brows. "What other preliminary information do you require, Officer?"

"Mr. Miller, at the very least, we need answers. Your client has been missing for the last six months. He needs to explain—"

"My client is a wealthy man," Tom interrupted. "As such, he took an opportunity to travel and relax. I'm sure many people would like that ability. However, my client also oversees a billion-dollar company and therefore was never completely inaccessible."

Tony spoke over the terse exchange, "Now that my counsel is here, I want to speak with him privately." Tony suddenly worried that Tom's speculations could further compromise his agreement with the FBI since he'd promised the feds he'd be completely inaccessible. After all, it was a very tangled web, one that would take days of explanations to unravel.

Biting back his rebuttal, Hastings glared toward Tony and replied, "This isn't done. I'll be back." With that, he stood, knocked on the door, and left.

Once they were alone, Tony's eyes widened. "Tom? Do you know about Brent?"

Tom nodded. "Yeah, this has been the day from hell. Bev went over to Courtney's. She's the one who told me that you and Claire were back, and then I got the call saying to come here. Where the hell have you been?"

Tony pinched the bridge of his nose and exhaled. "It's a long story. Let me just start out by saying that Claire and I remarried. We have a daughter, Nichol. I'm going crazy here. I need to know that Claire and Nichol are all right."

"I don't know anything about your daughter. I've sent Stephens to the hospital to serve as Claire's counsel. The last message I received before I turned over my phone was that she's still unconscious." Before Tony could reply, Tom asked, "What the hell happened?"

"I need to get to her, Tom. I don't want anyone to make assumptions and hold anyone else responsible for my actions. I've been in contact with the FBI. There's an agent—his name is Jackson—in Boston. If you contact him, he'll corroborate my story and hopefully talk to the Iowa City police." Unable to stay seated any longer, Tony stood and paced the length of the room and back. "Today was a train wreck. I came back, *we* came back," he corrected, "because we were worried about John and Emily. We learned that they'd be at the estate, and we didn't trust Catherine."

Tom shook his head. "What? Wait. John and Emily? As in your ex-brother and sister-in-law, the same people who've told anyone and everyone that you were on the run after possibly killing Claire?"

"Yes, only no longer ex. I know what they've been saying. I also knew that if we contacted them they would stop. It doesn't make sense, but I hoped that if they continued their allegations, it would keep them safe."

"Safe? From...?"

"From Catherine!" Tony's volume rose. "Tom, you need to pay attention. I said that before. Catherine London, she's crazy. The woman is a psychopath. She's responsible for so much." He spun in a circle, as if his pacing was no longer sufficient. "Brent!" His movements stilled. "She's responsible for Brent's death."

"Tony, calm down. You're not making sense. You're talking about the executor of your estate, the woman who's worked for you for as long as I can remember, and one of the gentlest women I've ever known."

The small room shrunk as the walls closed in, threatening to suffocate, to steal the very air from his lungs. Appearance—the lesson Tony had learned and the one he'd taught—was mocking his every move. He was perceived as the tyrannical businessman, and

Catherine was the kindly housekeeper. Tony took a deep breath, sat back down, and steadied his voice. "Tom, I can't explain everything right now. Just find out if they plan to charge me, and what those charges are. Then get me the hell out of here. I need to find out what's happening with Claire and Nichol. I need to help Courtney, and I don't want to spend another minute in this damn room, much less a jail cell." His voice deepened with determination. "I don't fuck'n care how much it costs. You're my attorney. Get me the hell out of here."

"You were gone for six months. I can't promise that we can get a judge to agree to bail. They'll consider you a flight risk.'"

"I'll surrender my passport."

Tom lifted a brow. "Did you use *your* passport the last time you left the country?"

Tony squared his shoulders. "We're in Iowa for Christ's sake. Any damn judge better grant me bail, or that judge will never achieve a higher bench in his or her whole damn career. I don't care if they want to make the bail excessive for appearances. I'll pay it. Just make it happen."

Tom nodded. "What about the FBI? Are you sure they'll corroborate this story?"

"Agent Jackson, with the Boston field office," Tony bristled, "or Agent Baldwin, with the San Francisco field office. They've been our contacts. Get a hold of one of them. They knew where, or approximately where Claire and I were residing. They know more than I'm willing to—or have time to—say right now. Just make it happen. I need to get to my wife and daughter."

"Tony, I'll do what I can. Wherever you were, did you hear that Meredith Banks' book..." Tom didn't need to finish the sentence. Tony understood what he was implying.

Exhaling, he closed his eyes and sighed. "Get me out of here. Then we'll talk."

"I can't promise it will happen today. I need to make some calls..." Tom's voice trailed away as they both turned toward the opening door.

Tony glared, expecting another interruption from Hastings or another of Iowa City's finest.

"I heard you were here," Brent said with a sad gleam in his eyes.

Both Tom and Tony stared: their conversation momentarily muted by the appearance of their friend. The hope that had been wilting at Tony's feet found new life as Tony and Tom simultaneously stood in amazement.

After a moment, Brent clipped, "Are either of you going to say anything?"

The three men collided as Tony and Tom slapped Brent's back and fought the battle of their raw emotions. "But...how?" Tom managed.

Suddenly, the dull, pale room filled with the brilliance of optimism. "The plane didn't go down?" Tony asked. "Everyone is all right? Derek Burke?"

Darkness overtook their reunion. "No," Brent replied. "I wasn't on the plane. It did go down." Raising his brows, he asked, "So, you really know Burke? You wanted him brought to corporate?"

Tony shook his head. "I did know him and his wife. It's a long story, one that seems to keep getting longer by the minute. However, I didn't want him at corporate."

"He deserved to be here, Tony. He was good." Tom interjected.

Brent concurred. "Yes, just today in Chicago..." His voice trailed away.

Tom refocused the conversation. "I'm sorry about Burke and

Michaels, but," he slapped Brent's back again, "I'm thrilled you're here. We have a lot of work ahead of us. Tony was just telling me a little about his time away and a connection with the FBI."

Brent turned to Tony. "I just got off the phone with Agent Jackson." Tom shot Brent a look of disbelief as Brent continued, "Part of your agreement was to not return to the US. He said you nullified your agreement."

"What does that mean?" Tony demanded. "They're going to throw our whole agreement out the window? What about Claire? They promised that she wouldn't—"

Brent interrupted. "One step at a time. Let me see what I can do."

"Get me out of here. Get any and all charges removed from Claire and anyone else. I'll take responsibility for what I've done, but my list of crimes is miniscule in comparison to what I learned today at the estate. It's all recorded. The cameras in the office should have gotten it all. Make sure you get that evidence."

"This is so farfetched, yet obviously you both know more than I do," Tom said.

"Tom," Tony's dark eyes turned toward his friend. "It was a need-to-know basis. The FBI wouldn't allow—"

"No. Don't worry about that. I'm happy to know you're not losing it. I was beginning to wonder," Tom replied with a grin. "We'll get you out of here as soon as we can."

"Today. And get me information on my family."

Brent and Tom nodded.

"Tom," Tony said, "I want you to go to the hospital. Stephens is a good man, but when Claire wakes, she needs someone she recognizes. I have a bad feeling about Emily and John."

"The people you risked everything to save?" Tom interjected.

Nodding, Tony continued. "They don't even know what you know, and that is so little of this story. Everyone keeps questioning our marriage." Tony's eyes widened as he turned toward Brent. "I will not implicate anyone else, but as my counsel, please contact the person who can help get the necessary documents to prove we're married. He's good, Brent. I'd bet he could obtain what you need in a matter of hours. It would take the State Department days or weeks."

Tom listened and shrugged. "Need to know?"

"Yes, some things are better left unknown for right now. Just go to Claire. Let Brent get me out of here."

Tom nodded. "I will."

"So will I," Brent replied, and added, "Don't answer any questions. Don't let them bait you into anything. Tony, this is not as simple as before. You need to listen to me."

A slight grin came to Tony's lips as he once again slapped Brent's shoulder. "Who am I to refuse the man who just overcame death?"

"What about Courtney?" Tom asked.

"She's waiting for me here." Brent's eyes held the first spark of hope that Tony hadn't seen in hours. "She wants to go to Claire, but right now she seems to have an issue letting me out of her sight."

"Thanks Brent. I mean that." Tony said, with the most heartfelt gratitude he'd ever known. "You too, Tom. I have total faith in both of you. Now get me the hell out of here."

Chapter 5

March 2014

Tony

———◆———

**When everything seems to be going
against you, remember that the airplane
takes off against the wind, not with it.**
—Henry Ford

DESPITE BRENT AND Tom's best efforts, the booking of Mr. Anthony
Rawlings did occur, as did the booking of Claire Nichols Rawlings.
Her name was no longer in question: documentation had been
produced verifying their marriage. It didn't matter who they were or
what their last name was. The accusations were too blatant to not be
addressed. The Iowa City Police Department had recorded the call
from Ms. Catherine London. The transcripts were leaked to the
press. She claimed that she feared for her life, said that Anthony
Rawlings had returned from hiding and was talking irrationally
about killing her and her guests. She wasn't only scared for herself
but for the Vandersols. Why else would he have returned, but to
stop their constant public accusations? When the police arrived, the
evidence substantiated her claim. Ms. London had been shot.

Simple ballistic tests found gun residue, proving that Claire Rawlings was the shooter. According to the Iowa City chief prosecutor, the case was sad, simple, and straightforward.

Due to the severity of the crime, the defendants were not granted stationhouse bail and were kept in custody until the complaint was filed and the first appearance before the judge was scheduled. Claire Rawlings was still in the hospital, and the debate had started about her future. In a bold move, the prosecutor had booked Claire in absentia.

The small Iowa City jail cell wasn't like anything Tony had ever experienced. Each minute inside of it lasted an eternity. He paced the confines for hours. Thankfully, Brent visited frequently. Of course, it was all in the name of generating Tony's defense, but it was more than that: it was Tony's only reprieve, his saving grace. Each time Brent arrived at the jail, a guard would escort Tony from the claustrophobic cell.

"Tell me what's happening with Claire." Tony demanded, once they were again alone in the visitor's room.

"We don't know much. Roach is our main source of information, and Emily has banned him and anyone else from contact with Claire."

"I'm her husband. Roach got the documentation from Francis. How can she refuse me? I want to know what's happening with my wife and daughter. Besides, when Claire gets out of that hospital, she's not going to jail. I won't let that happen, not again. I don't know how she survived in here the first time. She has the full legal staff at Rawlings ready for her defense. Emily can't possibly want to deny her own sister legal representation."

Brent shook his head. "She isn't denying her representation. John is representing her. He has his license back."

"In Iowa? He was never licensed for Iowa."

"No, he's acting as co-counsel with Jane."

Tony pinched the bridge of his nose, closed his dark eyes, and released a long breath. "I'll pay them whatever they want. I don't like it, and I'd rather you were involved in her defense, but I think that John and Jane will have her best interests at heart."

Brent leaned forward and lowered his voice. "Roach is laying low. I told him to leave town, but he won't. I'm worried that he'll be charged with aiding and abetting or possibly accessory to commit a crime. He has a rather colorful history. It definitely could be used against him."

"He doesn't know a thing. No one does."

Brent's brows rose in question.

"That's my story—I'm sticking to it."

"You know," Brent continued, "all of your, Claire's, and Nichol's things were found in a hotel in Cedar Rapids. Apparently that was where you were staying once you came back to Iowa?"

"Roach is good. Don't expect him to take you up on that offer to leave town. I know he isn't sticking around for me, but damn, I'm glad he's sticking around. He probably has the hospital's network totally accessed and knows more about Claire than Emily does." Tony stood and walked toward the wall. "I've never liked her. She's never liked me." He spun around. "But I fuck'n saved them from that house and this is how the bitch thanks me? Keeping me totally out of the loop. She can't deny that we're married."

"Claire, according to Roach, is awake but unresponsive."

"What does that mean—unresponsive?"

"She isn't speaking to anyone, not even Emily or John."

"What about Nichol? Surely she'll respond to Nichol."

"We're going totally by doctor's notes only, but I don't think she has."

"Get me the hell out of here and let me see her. She'll respond to me."

"I'm working on it. Your first appearance before the judge is scheduled for early tomorrow morning." Before Tony could blow at the prospect of spending another night in the jail, Brent continued, "Judge Jefferies will accommodate your proposal. It took a little longer to get on his docket, but the end result will be guaranteed bail. It was a trade-off: I thought it was the right move. If your bail request were denied at first appearance, it would be more difficult to have that decision reversed. You're getting a lot of press on this as it is. I don't want to add fuel to the fire."

"Fine, one more night in this hell-hole and then I can sleep in my own bed. What about Claire? When is her first appearance?"

"I'm trying to learn. I've got a clerk at Evergreen's office who will let me know as soon as the complaint is officially filed and the date is set. I'd assume today or tomorrow. They can use her medical condition as an excuse, but rarely does the first appearance go longer than seventy-two hours from the time the complaint is filed."

"Whatever the amount is for her bail or mine, have it ready. Neither one of us will be in jail long. And what about Catherine? She needs to rot in this jail."

"Tony, Eric showed me the footage from the office at the estate. Right now, you're being charged with intimidation, accessory to commit murder, and eluding the FBI. If we show anyone that footage, I'm sure that your list of charges will increase. Are you sure you want all of that to get out there?"

Tony stared incredulously. "Are you kidding me? Hell yes! I'm willing to admit to anything to show the judge what that bitch is capable of doing."

"Let's get you out first. Then you can take the tapes to Evergreen."

Tony's head ached as he massaged his temples. "She sure as shit better not be anywhere near my house."

"She's still in the hospital. That's why I believe we have time. She's playing the victim card, and I don't expect her to change her tune anytime soon."

"Get me out of here."

"Tomorrow morning, you'll be out."

"If Jefferies screws me, he'll regret it."

"He won't," Brent assured.

THE RAWLINGS ATTORNEYS made a little headway. Instead of being part of the normal parade of defendants, Anthony Rawlings was granted a private first appearance in Judge Jefferies' courtroom. All members of the press and spectators were removed, leaving only Tony and Brent, as well as the prosecutor, stenographer, and judge.

The judge's tone resounded through the cavernous courtroom, speaking with the authority expected of one in such a position. He never faltered in his reiteration of the charges levied against the great Anthony Rawlings. Tony too, never wavered, as he stood before the judge dressed in his customary Armani tailored suit.

"Mr. Rawlings, you have been charged with intimidation, eluding federal agents, assault with the intent to commit bodily harm, two counts of false imprisonment, and accessory to attempted murder. While most of these charges are misdemeanors, accessory to commit murder and false imprisonment are felonies. Accessory to attempted murder can be punishable by up to five years in a federal penitentiary, while each charge of false imprisonment can reach a maximum penalty of twenty years. Do you understand these charges?"

Standing confidently, Tony's dark eyes shot toward Brent. He hadn't mentioned the false imprisonment charge. Turning back toward the judge, Tony replied, "I do, Your Honor."

"Do you also understand that you may not leave the country before or during these proceedings?"

"I do."

"Very well, it is the opinion of this court that bail will be set at—"

"Judge Jefferies," Marcus Evergreen interrupted. "While I want to believe Mr. Rawlings that he will not flee, he definitely has the means, and due to recent events, the ability to disappear. We recommend that Mr. Rawlings' request for bail be denied."

"Thank you for your recommendation, Counselor. This is my courtroom, and it is my opinion that Mr. Rawlings has ties to this community, as well as a family. I have decided to grant bail in the amount of $10,000,000."

Tony's shoulders relaxed as he flashed a grin at Brent. It was one thing to have a promise of bail: it was quite another to have it said aloud in court.

Mr. Evergreen pleaded, "Judge, then we ask that Mr. Rawlings surrender his passport into the custody of the court until such time when all the proceedings have completed."

"Mr. Rawlings, will that be necessary?"

"No, judge, I will not leave the country. I intend to be near my family."

"I believe you have your answer, Mr. Evergreen. Now, Mr. Rawlings, you are aware that you have a right to counsel, and if you cannot afford an attorney, one will be provided for you."

Brent replied, "Mr. Rawlings has counsel, Your Honor."

"Very well, we're done here. Next…" Judge Jefferies proclaimed with a strike of his gavel, allowing Tony to walk as a free man out the doors of the courtroom. Suddenly, the stillness of the nearly empty room was replaced with a gallery of reporters shouting questions.

"Mr. Rawlings, tell us your side of this story."

"Was your wife trying to kill you—again?"

"Where have you been?"

"Why did you remarry?"

Tony and Brent remained silent as they pushed through the crowd, exited the Johnson County District Courthouse, and slipped into a waiting car. Eric smiled into the rearview mirror as he sat behind the steering wheel. "It's good to have you back, Mr. Rawlings."

"Thank you, Eric, it's good to be back. Take me to the hospital. I want to see my wife." Tony turned to Brent. "What the hell was that false imprisonment charge?"

Brent looked up from his phone. "I just heard about it minutes before we went into the courtroom."

"Who the hell did I restrain?"

"We can get that charge dropped once we produce the tapes. Don't worry about it."

Tony tried to concentrate, but concerns about Claire kept interrupting his thoughts. "Wait—what are you saying? Who am I charged with imprisoning? I didn't imprison Catherine."

"Tony, concentrate on Claire and Nichol. Let me worry about this."

"Two counts at twenty years a piece seem worthy of my concern." Tony sighed. "Fine. I still can't believe it about Sophia. Did you do what I asked?"

"Yes, Derek's parents were contacted and Rawlings Industries has offered to help in any way with the arrangements."

"Good." Tony's mind went back to his wife. Roach's reports had gone to Brent and ultimately to Tony throughout Tony's seventy-two hours of incarceration. Roach had accessed the hospital's network, as well as Emily and John's phones. He was getting an array of medical notations from the hospital and personal comments from their text messages. The latest information was that Claire was awake, speaking, and exhibiting amnesia type symptoms: incoherent speech, lack of recognition of loved ones, and the inability to answer simple questions. Though Emily authorized tests and scans to try to learn the cause of her sudden psychosis, the results were inconclusive. Tony wondered if Claire could be faking it, trying to save herself from prison. He knew she didn't mean to pull that trigger. It was an accident. Tony claimed it was self-defense. When he spoke with her, he planned to reassure her and explain that with her lawyers and all the resources that Rawlings' legal could provide, she'd be cleared in no time.

The consequences of Tony's decisions continued to harm his family. He swore that Claire would never again be subjected to the inhumanity of a jail cell. Then he'd think about Nichol. It broke his heart to think of their daughter without her mother or father. It wasn't right.

From Roach's monitoring of the Vandersols' cell phones, Tony knew that Emily was caring for his daughter. That wouldn't last. Tony intended to bring her home with him immediately. He'd hire a nanny to help until Claire was better. First and foremost, Tony wanted to get to Claire.

As Eric weaved through traffic, Tony barked orders into his cell phone, telling Patricia to get recommendations for reputable nannies. He also touched base with Roach, happy to be able to contact him directly. Tony, too, told Roach that he should leave town. Of course he refused.

"I'm not done with my job. I don't leave unfinished work."

Tony grinned. "I know I'm not the appreciative type, but Claire is. So, for right now, I guess it's my job. Thanks for everything. She was definitely right about you."

ERIC PULLED THE car up to the front of the hospital.

"You don't need to babysit me," Tony said to Brent.

"Yes, I do. I know how you feel about the Vandersols and how they feel about you. You don't need any more charges filed against you."

Tony shrugged. Brent was probably right. They made their way up to Claire's room. As the elevator doors opened, a woman with short dark hair stepped forward. "Mr. Anthony Rawlings?"

"Yes."

She reached in her bag and pulled out a large envelope. Handing it to Tony, she said, "You have been served."

"What the hell?" Tony asked in disbelief as the woman entered the elevator, the doors closed, and Brent and Tony were left staring at the envelope.

"Let me see that," Brent said as he reached for the envelope and opened the flap.

Tony moved to Brent's shoulder so they could both read the words. It didn't take long for the meaning to be clear. Tony staggered. "A restraining order, for both Claire and Nichol? They can't be serious! I'm going to see my wife."

"No, Tony. You can't afford to break this order. It'll land you back in jail."

"I don't give a damn about some piece of paper. I haven't seen Claire since the shooting. No one is keeping me away from her or Nichol," he added.

Brent reached for Tony's arm.

"Don't do it, Brent. Don't try to stop me." Tony's dark eyes glared.

"I'm doing what needs to be done. I'm going to bet when we turn that corner, there are policemen outside of her room. Husband or not, Anthony Rawlings or not, you can't walk through a restraining order. The day is young. Let me find out the allegations and why this was granted. We'll get it overturned, hopefully today."

Through clenched teeth, Tony seethed. "Get me out of here before I add murder to my list of charges. So help me God, if I see my in-laws..."

Chapter 6

March 2014

Brent

———————◆———————

**Power tends to corrupt, and absolute
power corrupts absolutely.
—Lord Acton**

THE NIGHT BEFORE, Brent had ventured further into Meredith's
book. It wasn't that he wanted to know the details, but with
everything that was happening, he believed that he needed to know.
The recent memories of the three of them, Claire, Nichol, and Tony
in his kitchen and living room, gave Brent the strength to read with
an open mind. It was a luxury not held by many. Other than Roach,
Courtney, and himself, Brent wasn't sure of anyone else who knew
how far the Rawlingses' relationship had progressed.

My Life as It Didn't Appear: Chapter 2...

*I couldn't remember what happened, but I knew it had. I knew
that somehow and for some reason, my life had changed. My body
ached, each movement evidence of the atrocities I suffered,*

atrocities cloaked in veiled memories that my mind kept locked behind my conscious recollection. When I finally awoke, I didn't move or make a sound, fearful of what or whom my actions may alert. I lay still for the longest time, utilizing my other senses. I heard silence. It's true that it's audible: a buzzing that drones on and on. While the blankets against my exposed skin were soft and comforting, I fought to deny the aroma of the bed where I lay. Instead, I drifted in and out of sleep. With time, my mind cleared and the calmness of the room gave me the strength to move.

Though the suite where I was kept was beautiful and lavish, I was too focused on survival and escape to notice the opulence. Despite my circumstances, I held onto false hopes that I could make both goals a reality. With each step on my tender legs or the sight of my marred reflection, the hope dimmed. The reality was suffocating: I'd been used, physically abused, and undeniably raped.

I remember thinking that things like this didn't happen to real people. This was the storyline for TV shows, movies, and books— not for real life. Yet, for some reason...it was now my life.

I had vague memories of fighting, none which ended well. As the recollections began to surface, I understood with painful clarity that I was no match physically for the man I'd recently met. Not only had he overpowered me, but my reception of his advances in Georgia had also opened the door to his mental domination. With an overwhelming sense of defeat, I recalled surrendering, not having the strength to continue the fight. As I cried under the hot spray of a much-needed shower, I found it difficult to blame anyone but myself. I'd lived my life independently and safely by following my rules. In a matter of days, Anthony Rawlings had broken my rules and shattered my world. No longer was I safe and independent. At twenty-six years of age, I was huddled in the corner of the cavernous shower, petrified of what the next hour would bring, and terrified of the suite door opening.

The ambiguity of my future was numbing. All I knew with some certainty was that I was trapped in a large suite with windows that looked out for miles and miles onto a dormant forest of gray, leafless trees. No longer was I in Atlanta... but where was I? How did I get here? And... could I handle the answers?

The fear of learning my location was equally as upsetting as the prospect of seeing the dark eyes that I knew in the pit of my stomach would return to that opulent cell. I was a prisoner at the mercy of my captor. At some moment in those first few hours of wakefulness, I convinced myself that there'd been a mistake—a terrible mistake. Perhaps it was a misunderstanding or maybe a mistaken identity. No matter the reason, survival instincts told me that it wasn't enough for me to believe there'd been a mistake: I needed to convince the man with the key to my freedom. Naively, I believed that was possible.

In what I later realized was a game of wits, I was informed of Mr. Rawlings' impending return. I was told that he would come to my suite at 7:00 PM, and that I was to be dressed and ready to dine. It was as if each minute were more absurd than the one before. My brain truly had difficulty keeping up.

Instead of being left alone to my own devices, which in hindsight would have more than likely resulted in another painful lesson, I was assisted with dressing, fixing my hair, and makeup. The entire scenario was unreal and vulgar. I was being helped to make myself presentable for the man who'd kidnapped and abused me. As much as I planned to state—or even plead—my case of mistaken identity, in the pit of my stomach, I feared that with the *help of the kind housekeeper, I was doing nothing more than preparing myself for more abuse.*

The man who entered my suite that night was somewhere between the charismatic man at the bar and the monster I'd seen glimpses of during my abduction. Though intimidating, he was also debonair. It's an odd combination, one that left me reeling with uncertainties. To say I was scared to face him would have been an understatement; however, after an afternoon of attempting to escape, I knew my only mode of freedom was through him. Though I tried to hide my trepidation, the physical cues were obvious: my entire body trembled merely at the sight of his black eyes.

Anthony Rawlings had the darkest eyes I'd ever seen. With time I learned to read the emotions that swirled in their abyss. But on that night, all I witnessed behind his eyes was an impenetrable hunger that I didn't understand. How could I? I was figuratively walking the tightrope of my life.

We did dine—or should I say that he ate. My nerves were too stretched to even consider consuming food. I wanted to appear strong; however, I doubt that I did. He spoke casually about the meal, dining, and trivial things. Had my body not throbbed with the abuses from the night before and my muscles not been as taut as metal stretched to its brink, I could have pretended I was on a date with an eloquent gentleman. That mirage—or should I say charade—faded into the reality of my situation once he'd finished his meal.

He told me to stand and I did. It wasn't until he told me to remove my dress that I found my voice.

"I think we need to discuss this..." was what I remember saying. He didn't want to discuss it. Anthony Rawlings had other

plans. A second later my dress lay shredded on the floor, torn from my body. Unfortunately, that night will live forever, burned into my memory.

Does one fight when one knows she can't win? Does one protest when she knows it falls on deaf ears? Does one pray for escape, even if death is the most viable alternative? I only know how I can personally answer those questions. I pray that those of you reading this will never need to learn your answers.

The chapter wasn't over, but Brent couldn't read anymore.

❖

THOSE WORDS FROM Claire's memoirs rushed to the forefront of Brent's mind as he stared at his best friend in the hospital corridor. The look in Tony's eyes was darker than Brent had ever seen. Was that what Claire had been forced to face years ago?

Truly, Brent's bravado spoke volumes about the evolution of their friendship. The reality of Brent successfully removing Tony from that hospital hallway was something that years ago would probably not have even been attempted. Somehow, Claire's plight gave Brent strength. She moved mountains when it came to Tony— it was doable. The last thing Anthony Rawlings needed to do was to walk through a restraining order, and just because they both knew that, it didn't ease the tension as they rode back to Rawlings Industries in impenetrable silence.

The lack of conversation didn't bother Brent. He had a lot to do. Once he had Tony back to the office and safely tucked away, Brent planned to visit the judge who'd signed the restraining order. Maybe it was against protocol, but he'd learned to work the system. As they rode, he sent a message to his assistant telling her to set up the meeting.

From what little Brent had read, he believed that Meredith's book was the cause or at least the bias for the order. He didn't doubt the accuracy. Beginning with Claire's testimony from what seemed like a lifetime ago, to the book now sitting comfortably on the New York Times bestseller list, Claire's story had stayed consistent. There was no reason to doubt what the entire world now knew. However, as he'd counsel Tony, there was no reason for Anthony Rawlings to publicly confirm it, either.

While reviewing emails, Brent came to the one he received just prior to Tony's first court appearance—the one stating that two charges of false imprisonment had been added to his list of infractions. Brent was confident that the same two people who alleged they had been falsely imprisoned were the same ones who'd filed for the restraining order. He was immediately thankful he hadn't told Tony anything more about the charges. He was even happier that the Vandersols hadn't made their presence known at the hospital. Entering Claire's room could have been the match to ignite the explosion that none of them could survive.

They weren't far from the office when Brent asked, "Are you sure you want to go into Rawlings? You haven't been there in months."

Tony turned as if pulled from a trance. "Where the hell else would I go? Well, other than to my wife and daughter, but I can't. I have an order restricting me to stay at least one hundred yards away and to make no attempt to contact. My home is still being investigated as a crime scene, not to mention the fire, water, and smoke damage. Hell, I can't even go there."

"I've got a call into Judge Temple about the restraining order. Give me some time. And Courtney wants you to come and stay with us."

"I think a hotel would be better right now."

"It's your decision, but our home is less likely to draw reporters."

Tony nodded. "Good point."

They'd been through Tony's rendition of the events a hundred times, but Brent wanted to hear it again. "Before we get to the office, tell me what happened from the moment you got to the estate with Eric and Phil."

"I've told you, and you've watched the office tapes. What more do you want to know?"

"Specifically, I need to know about John and Emily. They weren't on the office tapes."

Tony's brow furrowed. "No, they were locked in Claire's suite. There are cameras in there," he added somewhat sheepishly, "as you know." His normal tone returned. "Those tapes should also be available. Have Eric or Roach find them. Roach and Eric should also be able to compile the entire chain of events leading to the Vandersols' entrance to the suite. There's even a way to electronically verify that the lock is set on the suite door. Hell, most of the damn house is under surveillance. That's how I knew where to go to find them. Roach texted me their location..." He lifted his phone. "...check my phone records; it should be on there." Tony's voice trailed away as he added, "I didn't know where Sophia was. I didn't get her location..."

"No one's blaming you for Sophia."

Darkness once again prevailed. "What the hell are you saying? Is someone blaming me for John and Emi—are you telling me they're the cause of the false imprisonment charges?" Tony's thoughts and sentences overlapped each other as they came forward at untold speed. "I risked everything to help them, and they're saying it was *me* who put them in there and locked the damn door? It wasn't *me:* it was her!"

"I think you're right about sharing the surveillance tapes. I wanted to wait and hopefully keep them suppressed, but I don't think we can. I think we need them. I'll call Evergreen's office and set up a meeting."

"Get this damn restraining order lifted first. I need to see Claire, and I want to see Nichol."

— ◆ —

IN ORDER TO get the restraining order dismissed, Brent needed to contest the order on Tony's behalf and ask for a hearing before Judge Temple. Before he followed protocol, Brent wanted to hear the grounds that the good judge heard to get a better understanding of why the order had been granted. His request may be slightly out of order: in most cases forms were filed and time went unaccounted for; however, this was different—this was Anthony Rawlings.

By the time they arrived at Rawlings Industries, Brent's assistant had his response. Esquire Simmons had been granted a 3:00 PM meeting with Judge Temple in his chambers. Once he arrived, the judge wasted little time.

"Good afternoon, Counselor. Make this quick. My docket's full." Judge Temple said, looking up from his desk. He was a stocky man with a thick neck. No doubt he was more comfortable as he currently appeared with his robe hanging around his shoulders, unbuttoned at the collar, revealing a loosened gray tie and wrinkled white shirt.

"Thank you," Brent began, "for granting me this meeting. I'm here about the restraining order—"

"Ah yes. You see, I thought perhaps you were here to apologize for shutting me out of Mr. Rawlings' first appearance. As a judge in district court who hears a wide array of cases on a regular basis, I've always been a supporter of your client. You can imagine how surprised I was to see his first appearance taken from my docket and put onto Jefferies'. Well, that's no matter. You got what you wanted. I heard Mr. Anthony Rawlings made bail."

Brent stood dumbfounded.

"Come, Counselor, time is money."

"Yes," Brent said, "my client was granted bail. I'm here today about the restraining order that you granted for Jane Allyson, representative of Emily Vandersol, who assumes that she is speaking for..." he emphasized, "...*Mr. Rawlings' wife.*"

"The medical records submitted as evidence state that Mrs. Rawlings is currently incapable of making her own decisions or even voicing her opinion."

"*Mrs.* Rawlings is married, and as her husband, Anthony Rawlings is legally—"

"At the time of the complaint, Mr. Rawlings was being held in the Iowa City jail. As a prisoner, he was relieved of his rights."

"He's out."

"On bail."

"Yes," Brent conceded, "on bail. Innocent until proven guilty. He is her husband."

"Mr. Simmons, I assume you've heard of the book *My Life as It*—"

Brent felt his blood pressure rising. "Surely this court is not making decisions based on works of fiction?"

Judge Temple's neck and cheeks reddened as his voice lowered. "If you're suggesting that I look at anything other than the facts, Counselor, I will find you in contempt."

"Judge, Mrs. Rawlings remarried Mr. Rawlings. We have legal documentation of their union—or reunion. They have a daughter who needs her parents. Since Mrs. Rawlings is incapacitated at this time, their daughter needs her father. There's no evidence to suggest that Mr. Rawlings is a threat to his wife or his dau—"

"Are you confident?" Judge Temple interrupted.

"I'm confident that he is no longer a threat. His family means the world to him, and he'd do—"

"Save it for court, Counselor, or maybe the *Lifetime* movie. In the meantime, there's protocol for this, and you're not following it. I don't care who your client is. I will *not* in good conscience allow a man who has obviously physically and mentally abused a woman and stolen her from her life—twice, I may add—access to do it again when that woman is suffering a mental break at his hands. The evidence appears to support the premise that Mrs. Rawlings was reaching out in desperation, as she did once before, in an attempt to free herself from your client's clutches. How many times does Ms. Nichols need to *attempt to murder* your client before she succeeds? Mr. Simmons, this restraining order can be seen as a benefit to both your client and Ms. Allyson's. Regardless of the validity of Ms. Banks' book, these two people do not belong together. As an officer of the court, I must look at what is best, not what is popular.

"Besides what is best for Ms. Allyson's client, I must also consider the best interests of the minor. Her safety is a top priority. At this time, both her mother and father have felony charges pending against them. I'm in full support of Ms. Allyson's contention that for the child's safety, she needs to be removed from this volatile environment. Currently, the Vandersols have been granted temporary custody. Child protective services have been involved. I suggest that you do your research before we meet in court."

Before Brent could respond, Judge Temple concluded their meeting. "Consider that advice my support of your client, since I was deemed unable or untrustworthy enough to be the one to grant him bail." Temple sat taller and squared his shoulders. "I guess we'll never know how that would have gone." He shrugged. "That is all. I look forward to seeing Mr. Anthony Rawlings on my docket."

Brent left the judge's chambers in a daze. Damn political hard-balling—that was all this was. Allyson found the judge who'd been denied the ability to decide bail and played to his ego—not like it was difficult to play to Temple's or any other judge's ego. As soon as he got back to Rawlings, Brent intended to subpoena Claire's medical records. Until they officially arrived, he knew how they could get a head start: Roach's information. It might not exactly hold up in court, but it would kick-start the medical legal team at Rawlings to get going on their research.

Brent called Roach. "This is Brent Simmons. Can you get me everything you can find on Claire's medical treatment, diagnosis, and prognosis? We'll subpoena the official records soon enough, but this will help our research get started."

"I'll have everything I can find to you as soon as possible."

"Thanks, we appreciate your help. You know, usually I wouldn't ask—"

"Unusual circumstances warrant unusual procedures," Phil replied.

"Yeah," Brent said. "This definitely qualifies as unusual. Thanks again." He hung up.

While Brent put those wheels into motion, the next stop would be Evergreen's office. He sure as hell hoped that would go better than his chat with Judge Temple. His goal was to get the false-imprisonment counts dropped before the additional accessories to murder and attempted murder charges went on.

The raise that Brent gave himself about six months ago wasn't going to cut it. If Rawlings Industries didn't fail entirely under this burden, Brent's 2013 taxes would show a significant increase in income. Friend or not, with Brent's head pounding, this shit deserved more money!

Chapter 7

March 2014

John

———◆———

*There are times when the mind is dealt such
a blow it hides itself in insanity. While this may
not seem beneficial, it is. There are times when
reality is nothing but pain, and to escape tha
pain the mind must leave reality behind.*
—Patrick Rothfuss

SITTING IN THE quiet hospital room, John assessed his sister-in-law. Claire was married. She'd actually married that bastard again! Once the foreign documentation was delivered to Jane Allyson, John had stared at it until he'd nearly bored holes in the pages. The attorney in him wanted to prove the documentation was false or unlawful but he knew it wasn't. Perhaps it wasn't the lawyer in him; maybe it was the brother-in-law. There'd been a time when Emily, Claire, and he'd been close. John truly did consider, or used to consider Claire a sister. She still was like a sister, John reminded himself. After all, it wasn't unusual for families to have disagreements. Glancing toward the woman lying asleep on the bed, John wondered if the disagreements in this family could possibly be overcome.

Emily was at the hotel with Nichol, trying to rest. John was worried what the stress of this whole situation was doing to his wife and unborn child. Weren't pregnant women supposed to take it easy? Instead, Emily was dealing with not only her sister but also her niece and so much more. Memories of the fire at Rawlings' estate and being trapped in that room continued to haunt them both. Would the horrors of Anthony Rawlings ever end?

As John watched Claire sleep, his thoughts went back in time, to a time of innocence—when grades, sports, and girlfriends were the only concerns, when life was black and white. How do people not appreciate that age when it occurs? Instead, everyone wishes for maturity. John sat in the vinyl chair with a sigh. Growing up wasn't all that it was cracked up to be. Their growth had started out well enough. Somehow, from early on, John knew that Emily was the girl for him. Truthfully, throughout everything they'd endured, he'd never doubted that. After all the recent darkness, it seemed as though life was finally looking up. He and Emily had a baby coming, John had a new job, and they were living the life in California. When he first started dating Emily, Claire was barely a teenager.

As John remembered her at that age, the tips of his lips rose slightly recalling the lanky adolescent with frizzy dark hair and an undeniable stubborn streak of independence. Though John found it endearing, it was something that often infuriated her older sister. He recalled many occasions when Claire chose her own path, despite her sister's advice. He blinked the moisture from his eyes as he mourned the woman Claire was never allowed to become. He also mourned the woman she had become. Either scenario was undeniably better than the one lying before him. Despite it all, or perhaps *because* of it all, his sister-in-law was a survivor. Whether it was the death of her parents, the loss of her job, or surviving her first marriage, Claire survived. Not only did she survive, each time she came back stronger. For that, John believed Jordon and Shirley would be proud. For that, he believed she would triumph once again. His sister-in-law was a phoenix. Whatever had occurred in her brain to make her the way she currently was would smolder and die. Claire would once again rise from the ashes.

John wanted to believe that. No, he *needed* to believe that, not just for him, but for Emily and Nichol.

Thinking about Nichol and the mess at hand, John remembered Claire's visit to California last summer. It had been the last time he or Emily had seen Claire—until now. During that visit, John had seen that same stubborn streak he'd known since she was a teenager. The only difference was that this time she directed it at them. Claire came to announce her engagement, claiming she was in love.

Really? In love with Anthony Rawlings?

Emily did her best to dissuade Claire and convince her to stay in California, reminding her of the things Anthony had done in the past. Truly, with their history, John and Emily were amazed that Rawlings had permitted Claire to travel to their home. It seemed like the perfect opportunity to persuade her to escape.

Claire assured them that it wasn't like it had been before—that this time was different. John remembered a conversation:

"Claire, look at you. You're starting to show," Emily said as she feigned excitement for her sister.

Claire's hand fluttered over her midsection. "I know. It's amazing. I'm starting to feel our baby move." With each word, she glowed—not only her green eyes, which reminded John of his wife's, but also her entire expression.

That glow faded as Emily retorted, "Really? Must you use the word *our*? You know this is 2013. There's nothing wrong with raising this baby on your own. You made a mistake. It's all right. Get away while you can. I mean, fine, if you want to take his money or child support or whatever, do it. But why, oh why, would you want to subject yourself and your child to a man like him?"

"I'm not having this conversation with you," Claire replied matter-of-factly.

"Why?" Emily asked, "Because he'll find out? That Clay-guy will tell him, won't he?"

John didn't try to hide his feelings regarding Anthony Rawlings. In his eyes, the man had ruined his career and sent him to prison. If it weren't for Amber McCoy and SiJo, the life he and Emily lived wouldn't be possible. Thankfully, the New York Bar Association had found new evidence and revisited the case. His license was in the process of reinstatement. Despite all of that, John was a litigator and as such tried to see both sides of the story, no matter how difficult. Therefore, when Claire stood and walked to the window of their Palo Alto home, John touched his wife's hand, shook his head, and whispered, "Do you want to push her away?"

Knowing how much Claire meant to his wife and how much she had looked forward to her visit, Emily's teary stare burned a hole in his heart. "Claire," John said, "you know we love you. We always have. You have to understand where we're coming from. He ruined your life. He ruined our lives. We're just now making a recovery."

Expecting to see sadness, Claire turned with a vengeance. "I'm not going to subject our child to this negativity regarding his or her father. Honestly John...and Emily," she added, "I'm looking out on a pristine tree-lined street in one of the most affluent areas of the country. Emily, you say you're taking a break from teaching. Why? I'll tell you why. It's because you can afford to do it. For the first time, you can afford it. You say Tony ruined your lives. I'm not saying he didn't do things that are regrettable. I'm not downplaying the hell you or I went through. I'm saying we came out the other side and you know what? You don't look too worse for wear. And I'm tired of hearing about Clay's presence. Do you know why he's here? Because both Tony and I knew that Tony wouldn't be welcome. Clay isn't spying on me: he's protecting me. Did you all forget about Patrick Chester? My laptop still hasn't been found. And, yes, Tony has money. That makes me a target for crazy people. I'd rather have Clay nearby than live in fear."

"But if you weren't with him, you wouldn't be a target," Emily tried.

"Our child would be. No matter what you say, or what you want me to do, this is my life, and I choose to live it with Anthony Rawlings. We've taken a long and unconventional road to get to where we are. But let me tell you: where we are is a good place. I want to have the two of you in our lives and the life of our child. That choice is yours. My child will not pay the price for the sins of his father, from you or from anyone else."

Emily stood shell-shocked. "I'd h-hoped..." her words trailed away.

"What, Emily? You'd hoped I would come to California and decide to stay?"

Emily shook her head and then shrugged her shoulders. "I'd hoped that when John decided to take the job at SiJo we'd be together again, the three of us. Like it used to be."

Though Emily's cheeks were damp, Claire had yet to shed a tear as she spoke each word with conviction, "I'm not the little sister who needs you to tell me what to do. I'll admit that I've lived through hell, but so has Tony. You don't know the half of it, and frankly, it's none of your business. But we've come out stronger. I'm stronger, and I want our child to have both parents. It's more than that: even without our child, I want to marry Tony again."

"It seemed like you and Harr—"

"Stop," John interrupted. "Claire's made her point. She didn't come here to escape. She came to tell us about her engagement. We don't have to like it, but I don't believe Claire came to Palo Alto for our permission."

Emily exhaled. "How can you take her side? We've discussed this. Think of everythin—"

John cupped his wife's cheeks. "I'm not taking her side. I've always been on your side and I always will be. Don't you see? So will Claire. She'll always choose Anthony, just like I'll always choose you. Isn't that how it's supposed to be? We can also be on Claire's side and the side of our niece or nephew." He turned to Claire. "That's the best I can offer you right now. I admit that I have a lot of resentment. I'm not as ready to forgive as you. Maybe that makes you a better person. I've always thought you were pretty special."

Tears teetered on Claire's lids. "Thank you, John...Emily?"

Emily took a ragged breath and leaned into John with her head shaking from side to side.

"Emily, we're all the family we've got. I want our child to know and love his aunt and uncle. I hope someday Tony and I can be the same for your children. Maybe someday you will want the same thing."

Emily left John's embrace and walked to her sister. "Baby steps. I'll support you and your baby. I want to be Aunt Em," she added with a sad grin.

The irony helped to coat John's cheeks in fresh tears. Emily was being Aunt Em, and he was Uncle John. Nichol was absolutely beautiful. After a few days of fussing at the formula, she was eating and sleeping like a champ. The first time Claire had awakened, John called Emily and told her to bring Nichol to the hospital.

Claire acted confused, but John felt confident that her daughter would snap her back to reality. She didn't. The first time they tried, Claire held Nichol and cried. The next time that Emily brought her in the room, Claire just turned away and stared out the window. It was the saddest thing he'd ever seen.

The doctors explained it as a psychotic break—like a reprieve for the mind. Being a healthy, young woman, the prognosis was good. Yet no promises for the length of the episode could be made. The doctors said to take it one day at a time.

What made that increasingly difficult were the criminal charges facing Claire.

The police had tried to question her. She wouldn't answer anyone's questions about anything. Even Jane Allyson had been in and out trying to work on Claire's defense. Increasingly, it seemed that self-defense and temporary insanity would be the best route.

Once again, focusing on his sister-in-law, John prayed that her condition was *temporary*. As hard as this was for Emily and him, he couldn't imagine what Claire was enduring. Trying to pass time, John paced the hospital room. He'd done it for more hours than he could count. He knew the number of tiles in the floor as well as the number of tiles in the ceiling. At some point he had a random thought about why that number wasn't the same. The answer was obvious: the size of the tiles. The ones on the floor were square, while the ones on the ceiling were rectangle. His interior monologues were a simple means of diversion: one he'd used successfully while incarcerated. Life seemed to have a repeat button.

Whenever his thoughts returned to incarceration, John's blood pressure rose and his hands clenched unconsciously into fists. The next logical step in his stream of consciousness was Anthony Rawlings. Maybe Claire did love him, and maybe he was the father of that beautiful baby girl back at the hotel; nevertheless, he still deserved to be the one rotting in a prison cell—not John and not Claire. The idea that his sister-in-law could be convicted for a crime and once again Rawlings would go free was absurd.

That was why he and Jane went to Catherine London's hospital room. They were in search of the truth—of answers. They asked her what exactly had happened at the estate. After that conversation, accusing Rawlings with false imprisonment seemed a foregone conclusion. There was no way they could let Claire face felony charges and Rawlings some misdemeanor charge. Knowing his depth of influence, especially in Iowa, he'd probably get off with a light sentence or pay a fine, get a slap on the wrist, and walk away scot-free.

John remembered the pain in Catherine's eyes, her expression one of devastation as she spoke of the fateful events. The only reason John and Jane were granted access to Catherine's guarded room was because they were Claire's attorneys. Even still, Catherine's attorney was also present.

"Catherine, how are you feeling?" John asked with true concern in his voice.

"Mr. Vandersol, I-I..."

John stepped closer. "Catherine, we've been through this before. I'm nothing like that man. Please call me John." Motioning to his side, he said, "This is Jane Allyson. She's Claire's defense attorney. We're hoping you could tell us something, anything, that would help with Claire's defense and help nail Rawlings to the proverbial wall."

The gray behind her pained eyes showed a spark of interest. "That's why you're here?"

Jane tenderly replied, "Ms. London, I understand this is difficult for you. You've worked for him for so long. It's understandable how devastating it would be to have someone you've trusted most of your life turn on you."

A single tear descended Catherine's cheek. "There's so much. Did you know Sophia Burke died?" More tears cascaded as she closed her eyes and shook her head. "And you, Mr.—I mean—John, the police said that you were trapped in the suite during the fire? I don't know how that could have happened. How did Mr. Rawlings even know where you were? I hadn't seen him in months. I thought he and Claire were dead..." Her voice trailed away.

Jane touched Catherine's hand. "Can you please tell us why you called the police?"

Catherine adjusted the buttons on the hospital bed. As she sat straighter, her expression turned into a grimace.

"How are you doing?" John asked.

"I'll be all right. The bullet didn't do any lasting damage. Thankfully, they were able to remove it, and it missed my vital organs." She winced as she settled into a more comfortable position. "I'm pretty sore. I don't think I'll be running any marathons for a while."

"Ms. London, why did you call the police?" Jane asked again.

Her gray eyes clouded as she replayed the memory of the crucial afternoon. "I had just had lunch with..." she looked toward John. "...you, your wife, and Sophia. Then I went into the home office to check my emails. When I opened the door, imagine my shock. Mr. Rawlings was seated at the desk. It didn't take long for him to start accusing me of vile things. I had no idea what he was even saying. It didn't make any sense. He spoke about his grandfather and his parents. The way he was ranting and raving..." She closed her eyes and another tear found its escape. When she opened them, her voice was meeker, "It was like how he used to be to her. I was frightened."

John's license to practice law didn't give him that ability in the state of Iowa; nevertheless, he couldn't stop the question that had burned in him since he'd first learned the truth about Claire and Anthony's beginning. "Catherine, why didn't you help Claire back then?"

"I did all I could do. I tried to make it better."

John nodded. He'd heard the stories of how Catherine had been Claire's saving grace, especially during the first months. "But surely you knew what he was doing. Why didn't you report him?"

"I wanted to." She looked down to her lap and her voice trailed away. "I should have. I'm sorry, I was so scared..." After a deep breath she straightened her shoulders and continued, "That's why I called the police. After being away from him for so long, I felt stronger than I had in years. I refused to go back to the way things were. I didn't want that for Claire or for me. Then when she arrived, she was so scared. I could tell she felt trapped."

Jane pushed forward. "Why would Claire, the person you'd helped, try to shoot you?"

Catherine's head tilted from side to side. "I don't know. Was she? I mean, I was trying to protect the baby—Nichol, right?—from Mr. Rawlings. Claire was yelling. I don't know if she was trying to shoot me. That wouldn't make sense. Perhaps she was trying to finally be free. I can certainly relate." She turned again to John. "Is it true what the press is saying? Is it true that Claire isn't communicating with anyone?"

This time, John was the one to nod. "Damn press. Yes, it's true."

"How long do the doctors think it'll be...I mean, before she can remember?"

"They don't know. We'd hoped that she'd snap out of it before now. She rarely wakes, but when she does, she doesn't speak and only stares. It's like we're not even there. I've never seen anything like it."

Catherine's brows peaked. "She's not saying anything?"

"She only speaks in her sleep. She calls out for him."

"John, please tell Emily that I'm sorry I didn't do more for her sister. I truly tried to help, the only way I knew how."

"I will. Perhaps she'll be by to visit?"

For the first time since their arrival, Catherine smiled. "That would be nice. I'd like that."

Catherine's attorney spoke, "My client has been through a lot. If you'd like to return, contact me first. If you have no further questions..."

After their visit, John and Jane spoke for hours contemplating Claire's defense. It appeared clear: Claire didn't try to shoot Catherine. She was trying to get away from Anthony Rawlings, again. Unfortunately, the Iowa City police weren't as easily satisfied.

Although her previous record had been expunged, everyone knew that the current charge of attempted murder levied against Claire Nichols Rawlings, was not her first. The question for her new legal team was how would Claire respond? The longer she remained incoherent, the more likely it seemed that Jane would be forced to file a *not guilty by reason of insanity* plea. While often an attempt at a lesser sentence, or more accurately hospitalization versus incarceration, this plea would be Claire's true stance. If things stayed status quo, medical authentication wouldn't be a problem.

John's visit to Catherine, seeing the fear in her eyes as she talked about Anthony's temper, helped him decide to pursue the protective order. This woman had worked for Rawlings for the better part of her life, and yet she seemed terrified. There was no way that John could sit back and let Claire and Nichol go back to him. Many years ago, when Emily and Claire's parents died, he took on the role as man of the house. It wasn't an old-fashioned *do as I say* role. No, it was one of protector and provider. Never had he considered it cumbersome. On the contrary, after knowing Jordon and Shirley Nichols, John felt it an honor to watch over both of their precious daughters. The way he saw it, he'd failed Claire too many times. Later that night as he rocked his niece to sleep, John Vandersol swore he wouldn't allow it to happen again, not to Claire and not to Nichol.

The morning of Anthony Rawlings' first court appearance, Jane Allyson insisted that neither John nor Emily be present in Claire's hospital room. She had a sheriff's deputy strategically positioned, ready to serve Rawlings with the protective order. The Iowa City policemen outside of Claire's door didn't hurt. Of course, they were present because Claire was officially in police custody. Jane promised that she'd stay with Claire, and if need be, she'd speak with Mr. Rawlings.

Had it not been for the gleam in her eye as she discussed a possible confrontation, John may have refused. However, that sparkle was present. Jane assured them that she'd had more than one run-in with the infamous Anthony Rawlings, and she wasn't intimidated. Though Emily didn't want to leave, John agreed. It would be better to have Rawlings walk through a restraining order and be greeted by Iowa City's finest and Jane Allyson than by Emily and John. The volatile scene had the potential of becoming a full-out war. John was done being Mr. Nice Guy.

❦

IT'D BEEN A long few days. As the memories of everything began to quiet and much-needed rest crept upon John's tired body, he did his best to find a comfortable position in the hospital recliner by Claire's bed. So far, Anthony hadn't attempted to break the restraining order, and the police were still present. After all, she'd recently been officially booked and charged with attempted murder. John's only disagreement with the charge was the victim. Claire would never try to kill Catherine.

Just as sleep was about to win, the hospital door opened and Emily entered carrying the car seat Roach had given them only a few days ago. John rushed forward, kissed Emily's cheek, and reached for the small seat. "You shouldn't be carrying this all over."

Emily scoffed. "I'm fine. I'm tired, but carrying Nichol isn't going to hurt our baby. She barely weighs a thing."

His brow scrunched as he lifted the pink blanket. "Hi, little girl, why don't you weigh more? Aren't you eating for your Aunt Em?"

Stifling a giggle, Emily answered. "Oh, no. She's finally eating—and, boy, is she eating. I think maybe we're finding a routine."

John lifted Nichol, removing her from the confines of the straps and blankets as her little legs kicked. "I think she likes getting free of that seat." He glanced toward the bed. Though the monitors hadn't changed their monotonous beeps, Claire's eyes were open. John walked toward the bed. "Claire, look who came to see you. Can you please sit up?" Instead of moving, her eyes shut as if not hearing or recognizing the commotion around her.

"Claire, why don't you sit up? I'll get you some water," Emily prompted. More out of obedience, as Emily pushed the buttons on the bed, Claire moved herself to a sitting position. Once she was upright, Emily handed her a Styrofoam cup with a straw. When Claire didn't reach for it, Emily placed it closer. Claire leaned forward, and sucked from the straw. Lowering the side rail, Emily scooted next to her sister. "Hi, sweetie, I know you're hearing me. I think Nichol needs her mommy. What do you think?"

Again, she didn't respond.

John came forward and placed Nichol across Claire's lap. Emily encouraged Claire's movements while her daughter kicked with glee, rooting toward her mother. Unfazed, Claire sat stoically, gazing not at her beautiful child, but toward the blind-covered window. When Nichol's cries broke the trance, hers weren't the only cheeks that were damp.

Chapter 8

March 2014

Harry

———◆◆◆———

I do solemnly swear that I will support and defend the Constitution of the United States against all enemies, foreign and domestic; that I will bear true faith and allegiance to the same; that I take this obligation freely, without any mental reservation or purpose of evasion; and that I will well and faithfully discharge the duties of the office on which I am about to enter. So help me God.
—**FBI oath of office**

ASSOCIATED PRESS:
Iowa City, Iowa, USA

The Iowa City Police Department has finally confirmed that Anthony Rawlings, missing CEO of Rawlings Industries, has been located and arrested in regard to an alleged incident occurring at his estate outside of Iowa City, Iowa, USA. This alleged incident also included Claire Nichols Rawlings, who was reported missing on September 4, 2013, by Mr. Rawlings himself.

According to Iowa City police records, unbeknownst to family and friends, Anthony and Claire Rawlings remarried at an undisclosed location in October of 2013. It has not been confirmed, but it has been mentioned that the two wed outside of the United States. Mrs. Rawlings's family confirmed that while missing, the couple gave birth to a daughter. No more information regarding the child has been released.

In regard to the alleged incident, Mr. Anthony Rawlings has been charged with intimidation, eluding federal agents, assault with the intent to commit bodily harm, two counts of false imprisonment, and accessory to commit murder. Mrs. Claire Rawlings has been charged with attempted murder. The alleged victim was identified as Ms. Catherine London, a longtime employee of Anthony Rawlings. She is still hospitalized with non-life-threatening injuries, said to be the result of a single gunshot.

The motive for the return of this high-profile couple, as well as the motive for the alleged crime, has not been disclosed.

The door bounced off the wall as Agent Baldwin determinedly entered SAC William's office in the San Francisco FBI field office. Indignantly, Agent Williams looked up, disgust evident in his expression. "Baldwin, I assume your entry is in relation to your resignation."

"Sir," Harry managed through gritted teeth. "The Associated Press? I devote over a year of my life and career to a case, and I learn that Rawlings and Claire have been arrested in Iowa from the *Associated Press*?"

"It's no longer your concern."

"That's bullshit," Harry replied as he threw the printed press release on Agent Williams' desk. "I know I was no longer their contact, but you know I have a personal interest in this case."

Agent Williams pressed his lips together, deliberating his response. After a prolonged, uncomfortable silence he said, "Yes, Agent, I'm well aware of your *personal connection,* as are many others. That does not give you the right to barge into my office or to demand information. Do I need to remind you of your position within the FBI?"

"Sir, my reviews have been outstanding since leaving the Rawlings case. I just want to know what the FBI has done for the Rawlings."

"*You just...* really, Agent? Would you like me to perhaps log you into their private files?"

Harry shifted his footing. That *was* what he wanted. The last few times he'd tried to access anything, even from within the bureau, his access had been denied. There were ways to access cases through backdoors, but there was always the possibility that such digging could set off alarms and alert others to his activities. Harry cleared his throat and said, "I know I screwed it up—I screwed it *all* up—but that doesn't negate the fact that I know this case backward and forward. I know that Claire said she was running from Catherine London. She believed that the woman was a threat to her, her child, and even to Rawlings. Ms. London scared Claire enough to force her to disappear. Now Claire's been charged with attempting to murder the woman. Sir, surely you see that somehow this all came to a head. Right now, everything I've read makes Ms. London out to be a saintly, kind woman who's been victimized by Claire and Rawlings. Before I left the case, I heard audio of Rawlings' confessions. Everything he confessed to doing was in conjunction with London. We can't sit back and let those local-yokels prosecute either of them without coming forward with our information."

SAC Williams shook his head. "Son, this case has moved past you and even me. What the FBI reveals is not up to either one of us." He leaned forward. "However, I will say, it's refreshing to have you speak about testifying for both of them. If nothing else, you've made personal growth. That may temper my response to the insubordinate way you entered my office." He motioned to a chair. "Have a seat. I have the feeling you know more than you've let on."

Harry exhaled and sat facing the SAC. He stretched his long jean-covered legs out before him. Being between assignments, Agent Baldwin was currently working daily at the San Francisco field office and living in Palo Alto. "I may have done some more research in my spare time."

"Perhaps the bureau isn't monopolizing enough of your time. We can always use more desk jockeys if research is your new forte."

Ignoring his comment, Harry continued, "It didn't and it still doesn't make sense. I'm not talking about Claire. I may still believe that her decision to go back to that ass—I mean man—was a bad and possibly dangerous move, but that isn't what's been eating at me and keeping me awake at night."

"Go on."

"I've listened to Rawlings' confessions over and over. The evidence doesn't match his statements."

"I'm listening."

"Sir, will this go any further? You said the case is beyond both of us. Will what I tell you make a difference?"

"Let me be the one to decide that. You obviously believe you know something. What is it?"

Harry looked down momentarily before bringing his bright blue eyes back to the SAC. "*If* you decide to take this beyond this office, and *if* it's possible, I'd like to be officially back on the case."

SAC Williams didn't verbally reply; instead, he nodded. It wasn't a promise but it wasn't a refusal. It was a spark that gave Harry the fuel to share his research and intuition. Harry began, describing in extensive detail Tony's confession: his claim to have paid someone to sabotage Simon's plane.

"Rawlings couldn't say how the transaction worked, other than that he initiated contact with someone who took his money and promised results. A few weeks later, Simon's plane crashed. To Rawlings the transaction was complete. It's rather narcissistic of Rawlings to believe he had that power, but I guess not surprising. What bothers me was the NTSB's final analysis of Simon's plane."

Williams lifted his brows, wanting Baldwin to continue.

"The NTSB didn't find any evidence of tampering."

"Why was this not discussed earlier?"

"I didn't bring it up..." Harry confessed "...because I wanted to see his ass rot in prison for what he did. I didn't care if it made sense or not. The man paid to have my best friend's plane sabotaged. Simon Johnson wasn't only my friend: he was my sister's fiancé. He was a good man who didn't deserve to have a hit put out on him simply because he wanted to close part of his life before he moved on to the next. I also hated what Rawlings did to Claire. So, even though I knew the evidence didn't fit, I was happy with Rawlings' confession."

"What changed?"

"I've done some messed-up things in my life. My priorities have been skewed, but every time that happened, it was in favor of the bureau. I gave up the rights to my daughter. I told Ilona, and myself, that I did it to keep them safe. I've backed away from commitment with Liz and anyone else because I never know where my next assignment will lead or if I'll come home. Again, I've told her it's for her. I don't want to leave her hanging for months or years on end. While all of that is true, it isn't the full truth. Can I assume that you know what I mean?"

SAC Williams nodded. "Yes, son, the day we take that oath we're all married, and the FBI is a bitch of a wife. She demands all of your attention."

Harry's lips formed a straight line. His characteristic grin and blue-eyed smirk disappeared behind his solemn expression. "I agree. The FBI is my other half, and I can't ignore that the bureau stands for something other than revenge. I chose to give up my life to uphold the laws of this land. It's more than that. I believe in that oath that I took years ago. That doesn't mean I didn't screw it—figuratively and literally," he added with a slight upward turn of his lips, "but I can't sit back and watch a man take the blame for a crime he didn't commit. Don't get me wrong: Rawlings is guilty. He hired someone with the intent of ending Simon Johnson's life, which is conspiracy to commit murder. But in this case, it was just that—conspiracy. Simon's death did not result from a sabotaged plane. In my opinion, his crash was related to an overdose or perhaps a poisoning. I'm not sure."

SAC William's brows furrowed. "You're not sure. You construct this entire story and end with *I'm not sure?*"

"I don't know if it was accidental or if it was intentional. I don't believe Simon would've intentionally taken a medication to which he had a sensitivity. Perhaps it was an ingredient of another medication? I don't know."

"What are you saying?"

"Although Simon's body was badly burned, I was able to order an analysis of his tissue remains." When the SAC's expression changed, Harry added, "I ordered the tests while I was on the case. It took a while for the results. Honestly, I was expecting to find actaea pachypoda. More than expecting—I *wanted* to find it. If I had, it would've confirmed Rawlings' connection."

"I should've been notified if actaea pachypoda was found."

"You weren't notified, because it wasn't found," Harry admitted.

"What did you find?"

"The only unusual marker was a normal-high level of diphenhydramine."

"Normal-high? What does that mean?"

"Simon had 17.5 micrograms/liter of diphenhydramine in his tissues. A lethal dose isn't obtained until over 19.5 mg/L. Simon's dose was high, but not out of the normal range."

"Why is this worth my time or the bureau's?"

"Because, sir, according to Simon's mother, he had an unusually high sensitivity to diphenhydramine."

"Benadryl," Williams said.

"Yes, Benadryl, which is available at every drugstore and convenience mart throughout the country. Mrs. Johnson said that it was nothing new. It's something Simon dealt with since a small child. He knew how to avoid it. Just a little Benadryl would make him incredibly sleepy. Mrs. Johnson vehemently swore that Simon would never knowingly consume Benadryl or any medication containing Benadryl, like Tylenol PM, prior to flying. I'd have to agree. Simon was very conscientious. He had his whole life ahead of him. Unfortunately, I was away on assignment when he died, but I was around when he proposed. Amber was ecstatic and so was Simon. It just doesn't make sense."

"Let me get this straight: you want to reopen this closed case because Mr. Johnson's plane was *not* tampered with and he had an unusually high sensitivity to the only foreign substance found in his body. Do you believe that he was poisoned?"

Harry contemplated his answer. "Do I believe? I don't have enough information to believe or disbelieve. I've been taught to look at information objectively. Objectively, I have more questions than answers. Another piece of the puzzle that doesn't fit, in my opinion, was my attack and the threat against Jillian. I mean, Rawlings was with Claire. It wasn't very much later that he confessed to conspiracy. Why would he have me attacked and threaten my daughter? How would he even know about her? That was the point of what I did when I chose the bureau over parenthood. I wanted to separate that part of my life and assure her safety. I know Rawlings has money, and initially that's what I told myself. I said he paid to get all the information he could on me. I believed he saw me as a threat. Even I don't believe that anymore. I was no more a threat to him and his relationship with Claire than her bodyguard was, especially in his eyes. He's too egotistical to see anyone as a threat. People like him believe they own the other person. No one belonged with Claire but him—he didn't care enough about me to threaten my family. I believe someone wanted to stop my research. I just don't know who that someone could be."

"Are you insinuating a mole? Here in the bureau?"

Harry chewed his cheek for a second while his blue eyes looked down and then back up again. "How many people here at the bureau know about my daughter?"

Williams leaned back and contemplated the question. "Prior to your attack, only myself and the deputy director."

"I suppose it's your call, if you feel an internal investigation is needed—"

"Son, who outside of the bureau knows about your ex-wife and daughter?"

"No one knows. They're no longer part of who I am. I have no past."

"Everyone has a past."

Harry mulled the SAC's last comment over in his thoughts. "Sir, that's what I know. I also know that we had a deal with Rawlings. I knew about it, you knew about it, and the Boston field office was in on it. The FBI may be a demanding wife, but she doesn't go back on her word."

"That's very upstanding of you. Again, it isn't your call."

"May I travel to Iowa?"

"As an agent or a private citizen?"

All moisture disappeared from Harry's mouth; his tongue suddenly became thick. "Are you saying that if I go to Iowa, I'm no longer a part of the FBI?"

"No, unless you entered this office with the intention of resigning?"

"I didn't, sir."

"If you choose, as a friend of the Vandersols, to take a few days of leave and visit Iowa, I won't try to stop you. However, if you use your position in the FBI with the local authorities or anyone else while there, you will be subject to disciplinary action. The call is yours. This case almost cost you your badge. Consider your options and tread lightly."

"Hypothetically, if I go to Iowa, as a friend of the Vandersols, and I learn anything particularly useful, may I share it with you?"

"I don't see any violation in that."

"Thank you, sir."

"Agent, never enter my office with that attitude again. I don't care what bone you have to pick with me."

"Yes, sir, I apologize. Will you take my concerns to the deputy director?"

"Put in for your leave, son. We'll talk when you return."

"Yes, sir."

<hr>

THE SCRUMPTIOUS AROMA of garlic and the light rhythm of jazz overpowered Harry's senses and loosened the tension as he entered his condominium in Palo Alto. Walking quietly toward the kitchen, he stopped and gazed toward the stove, more specifically toward the woman unaware of his presence. Her hot black skirt, long tanned legs, and bare feet could make him forget everything else that he'd endured throughout his day. Still unaware of his voyeurism, Liz stood near the stove swaying rhythmically to the music coming from her phone, her attention monopolized by the amazing Italian sauce in the pan. He watched as she'd stir, taste, and hum. Quietly, he stepped behind her, wrapped his arms gently around her waist, and planted a kiss at the base of her neck.

Jumping, she shrieked, "Hey!" Immediately, the stovetop was dotted in a rain of tomato sauce. Turning into his embrace, she chided, "Look what you made me do."

"Hey, yourself," Harry chuckled. "I know what I'd like you to do." His finger swept across the stainless stovetop swiping sauce in its wake. Placing his red-coated finger between his lips, he tasted her delicious concoction. "Hmm, this is good."

"Good?" Her lower lip pushed forward in a feigned pout.

"Hmm..." He nuzzled her neck. "...yes, good."

"I've been cooking for hours and all I get is *good*?"

"Well," Harry teased, "all things are relative. The sauce is good. This..." His lips once again found the soft skin above her collarbone, each kiss dipping lower and lower along the scooped neckline of her blouse. "...is delectable."

"Oh?"

"Do you doubt me?" He asked as his bright, innocent eyes met hers and his thumb found the roundness of her breast. "I'm fairly confident that as delicious as your neck is, under this blouse..." He ran his hand over the firmness of her behind searching for a zipper on her skirt "...and under this skirt, it's even better."

The spoon which had commanded Liz's attention now lay on the tomato-splattered stovetop as her head fell back, giving Harry better access to her exposed skin. As his hands wandered, she said breathily, "I think I may see where you're going with this."

Turning off the stove, Harry tugged on Liz's hand and pulled her toward their bedroom. "I think I'm suddenly famished."

Caressing the hardness in his jeans, Liz giggled. "Maybe I'm the one who's hungry?"

"I like the way that sounds."

"B-but," she stuttered, putting on the breaks. "Amber and Keaton are coming to dinner tonight."

Lowering her to their soft bed, Harry watched her golden hair fan behind her blushed cheeks. "Let's cancel. I like the idea of our own private dinner."

Liz looked over at the clock, her blouse now untucked and her bra exposed. "They'll be here in a half an hour."

"I'd rather take longer," Harry said. "But I'm never against fast food."

Liz playfully hit his shoulder. "You're crude. I need to finish dinner." Standing and adjusting her clothing, she added, "Besides, if I'm the dinner, I'd rather be a three-course meal. I'm not fast food."

Harry lay alone on their bed, staring up at the ceiling. "Then let's change places. I'm all right with being the meal, and I'm pretty sure I can do fast, if necessary."

Liz laughed as she threw a pillow his direction. "Sorry, buddy. Besides, I love your being between assignments. We have plenty of time for all the dining you want." Looking at his exaggerated pout, she said, "Just wait until after they leave."

"Fine, I can wait, I suppose."

"You don't have a choice. I still need to set the table and make the salad."

Propping himself up on his elbows, Harry said, "If I help with dinner, can I make reservations for later?"

Shaking her head, she walked back toward the kitchen.

The conversation flowed light and easy as Amber and Liz talked about SiJo, and Harry and Keaton discussed their predictions for the upcoming basketball tournament. It wasn't until Amber kicked Harry under the table that he even listened to his sister's question. "Why didn't you tell her? I've been dying to say something all day. Liz, I can't believe you haven't seen the news,"

Harry searched from Amber to Liz. "Well, you see, sis, I just got home and, well, we had better things to do than talk about the latest news." He took a bite of garlic bread and smiled a toothy grin. "We were kind of busy."

Amber kicked him again.

"Ouch!"

"You're gross. TMI!" Amber retorted.

"What are you talking about?" Liz asked.

"Fine, I'm spilling the beans. Keaton and I've been talking about it all day." Amber's eyes sparkled with untold secrets. "Both Anthony Rawlings and Claire have been arrested!"

"Arrested?!" Liz said. "For Simon's death? Claire had something to do with Simon?"

"No," Amber replied. "Not for Simon. The article said that Claire shot someone."

"Oh, my God, she is nuts. And you had her living with you."

Harry's shoulders straightened. "I think there's more to it than that. And no one said she's nuts." His modest attempt at defending Claire earned him cold looks from the two women at the table. "The woman she's accused of shooting is the same one who was at the estate when Rawlings first took her."

"Didn't you go and talk to that lady?" Liz asked.

"I did."

"And Claire killed her?" Liz questioned.

"No," Harry replied.

When he offered no more information, Amber responded. "I called John. He said it's a mess. The lady's name is Catherine, and she was shot, but her wound isn't life-threatening. Of course, I was all concerned about Claire. He said that she's not doing well. She hasn't spoken to anyone since it happened."

"She isn't as dumb as she acts. I bet she's faking it to avoid jail time," Liz said.

Harry thought about her transition from prison the first time, the way she reacted to simple things like sky and sunlight. He didn't want her going through that again. It wasn't right. The FBI made her a deal. She had immunity.

Amber's laugh refocused him. He wasn't sure what he'd missed in the conversation, but Liz and Amber were clinking their glasses of red wine and grinning.

"I scored us four great tickets to the Lakers game this coming Saturday. They're in the Google suite: drinks and food on me," Keaton offered.

"On you or on Google?" Amber teased.

"I work for Google, so without me you wouldn't be there," he answered smugly. "I'd say it's on me."

Amber kissed his cheek. "Sounds great."

"Yeah, sounds fun," Liz replied. "What time?"

"I'm sorry," Harry said, interrupting their plans. "I need to be out of town for a few days. You have fun without me."

Liz's expression dropped. "What else didn't you have time to tell me? Do you have a new assignment?"

"Yeah, but it won't last long—just a couple of days."

"When are you leaving?" Amber asked.

"Tomorrow."

Pressing her lips together, Liz slumped in her chair and sighed.

"Well, this party just took a downturn," Keaton observed.

After a long drink of her wine, Liz refilled her glass and faked a smile. "Don't be silly. I'm not that insecure. It isn't like Harry's running off to Iowa or something."

Amber's gaze cut to Harry.

"Would anyone else like some more wine?" he asked with a purposeful tone of innocence as he refilled his glass.

Chapter 9

Late March 2014

John

One of the secrets of life is that all that is really worth doing is what we do for others.
—Lewis Carroll

MY LIFE AS It Didn't Appear: Chapter 3...

It's difficult to look back at a time of despair and isolate the most difficult moment. They all worked together to accomplish the same goal. In my education as a meteorologist, I learned how essential elements combined in just the right way to create the perfect storm. Finding the one element, the one piece of the puzzle that completed the devastation would be like choosing the single raindrop responsible for a ruinous flood or the upward draft that completed the destructive funnel cloud. Each drop of water or gust of wind played a role in the destruction. In my education as Mrs. Rawlings, I learned how each storm, no matter how small, played a role in creating the perfect companion.

As a town is never the same after a destructive storm, neither was I.

The isolation in my suite was my first storm. It should have been the kidnapping and the physical abuse: surely they contributed. They were rumblings of impending desperation, like the threatening winds before a hurricane. During those times that seemed unsurvivable, I erroneously believed I could make a difference. I held on to the hope that I could say or do something to change my destiny. While left alone—literally alone—for almost two weeks, the dams broke and I changed forever. I found myself almost wishing for the threatening precursors.

After Anthony's proclamation of ownership, he left my suite. Though my cheek stung from the slap of his hand, it was the impenetrable silence that hung about me like a cloud. I'd already tried and failed to escape my cell: I was alone with no way out.

The windows wouldn't break with the pounding of the chair against the glass. First, I tried the tall French doors that led to a balcony. Of course, the doors were locked, but I hoped that I could break the glass to get outside and climb to freedom. That seemed safer than the windows. The small panes repelled the blows. After numerous failed attempts, and despite the distance from the other windows to the ground, I tried breaking the windows. Unfortunately, no number of strikes shattered the glass, only my hope.

The Weather Station had told me I was in Iowa. When I escaped, I didn't know where I would go or how long it would take me to get there. I just knew that freedom was beyond the sea of trees. From my view, they seemed to go on forever. I also feared that if the windows broke, an alarm of some kind would sound; however, with each passing day my desperation grew. Running through the trees was my recurring dream—and nightmare.

Often, I'd wake panting from the realness of my illusions with my heart pounding too quickly in my chest. During the day I imagined freedom, but with night, reality intruded: I couldn't get free. I'd be chased and caught. Though I wasn't sure what would happen after my recapture, I knew instinctively that it wouldn't be good.

Day after day, I saw only one person. The choice was extremely calculating, as the young man of Latin descent spoke little English. Three times a day, he'd enter my room and bring me my meals. Each time he'd avoid my eyes and say, "I bring Miss Claire her food." That was all. No other words were uttered.

Each day while I showered, my room was cleaned and clothes were taken, laundered, and returned. As the dreams of escape faded, they were replaced by desires of companionship. I had never truly been alone in all of my life. There had always been people. Even in Atlanta when I lived alone, I had friends, neighbors, coworkers, and even strangers. I never realized how much it meant to pass a stranger on the street with a nod and a smile. As the days turned to a week, I longed for a smile, a nod, anything.

Since my waiter didn't speak beyond his one sentence, I hoped to speak with one of the invisible people who cleaned my suite. Repeatedly, I tried to catch someone in the act—anyone—but I never did. They were too quick. One day, I was so distraught that I devised a plan. It was quite simple. Instead of showering, I would lie in wait and spring from the bathroom when someone entered the suite. The anticipation was overwhelming. I was so excited at the prospect of hearing my own voice and another responding. Such a simple desire, yet it monopolized my thoughts and took away my appetite. Finally, I left the tray of food, went into the bathroom leaving the door slightly ajar, and waited.

No one came.

Lunchtime arrived and my breakfast tray remained.

The reality struck with a blow more painful than Anthony's hand. I was a grown woman hiding behind a door, praying for the companionship of anyone. Salty, pathetic tears fell from my eyes as sobs resonated from my chest. As the day progressed, my hope dimmed. At one point I even prayed for the young man—oh, to hear him say "Miss Claire." I knew it would give me strength. Hearing my name would validate my existence.

He didn't come.

Anthony had never left me without food, and though I wasn't hungry, I naively believed that my next meal would soon arrive. The silence and despair combined to create a time and space continuum. Did I sleep? Was this real? Every now and then I'd open the door a little wider to be sure that I hadn't fallen asleep and missed the invisible people. The sight of my room taunted me: my bed remained disheveled and my cold eggs had turned to rubber on the plate. I believed the people were coming and was so obsessed with seeing them that I refused to shower and even waited until I could wait no more to enter the lavatory.

Still no one.

I continued to wait as the storm raged in my shattered mind.

The Iowa sky became dark and the hard tile floor of the too-white bathroom became my chair and my bed. The plush purple towels served as my pillow as sleep intermittently took over. I dreamed of conversation—not food, shelter, or even freedom. I lay curled up on the bathroom floor fantasizing about speech. I remembered hours spent with friends. I recalled the sleepovers I'd had as a child and a smile would briefly grace my lips. There were nights when I'd talk with my friends, as little girls do, until we were too tired to finish a sentence. On that white marble tile I cried for the times I'd fallen asleep. Oh, to have that opportunity again. I swore I'd never again take it for granted.

During that night the winds changed direction. My consciousness was no longer blaming Anthony but myself. Of course, no one would enter my suite. I was pathetic—a grown woman behaving like a child. Who would want to come and talk with me? I'd hit bottom—or so I'd thought.

I'd later learn that bottom was much deeper than I ever suspected.

The next morning when I awoke on the hard, cold floor with my body aching, I knew the storm had passed. I hadn't hit bottom but a shelf on the floor of the ocean. It was lower than I'd ever been, but I refused to allow myself to sink further. Instead, I evaluated my elevation and concluded that I would survive, and I would never be alone again.

That didn't mean that I wouldn't be without others: it meant I wouldn't let it destroy me. He may have believed he owned my body, but as long as I was in control of my mind, Anthony Rawlings, or anyone else, would not have the ability to isolate me. With my new resolve, I showered, dressed, and walked into my clean suite. The invisible people had returned. My cold eggs were gone, and I had a warm meal waiting on the table.

That storm taught me another lesson. If I followed the rules, I could expect favorable consequences. I'd already learned about unfavorable ones, and I had more to learn. Instead of feeling defeated, that day gave me strength. My actions had consequences: whether those were positive or negative was up to me. I was in control.

It never crossed my mind to wonder how Anthony knew I was hiding and lying in wait in that bathroom. I just knew that somehow he did. He knew I wasn't following my daily routine. My only hope at manipulating the circumstances of my incarceration was to appear compliant. I had another new goal.

My theory was soon to be tested. After thirteen days, I heard a knock on my door. The young man who brought my meals always knocked once before entering, but this knock was different. No one entered. I waited. It happened again. When I called out, I was miraculously answered.

"Miss Claire, may I enter?"

Her question was quite comical. I couldn't have bid her entrance if I'd wanted nor could I deny it. I was on the wrong side of the locked door. Nonetheless, I said, "Yes, Kate (name changed to protect the innocent), please come in."

The familiar beep preceded the opening of my door. I stood motionless as her gray eyes filled with compassion, silently confirming that I was no longer alone. "Miss Claire, I have a message for you." Kate's accent was unique and formal and her words were music to my heart. I didn't care what they said, only that they were spoken to me. I longed to hug or touch her in some way, craving contact, but that would have been too much—too much for my attention-starved psyche. Unable to verbally respond, I nodded, savoring the interaction and trying to make it last.

"Mr. Rawlings will be coming to see you tonight..."

I listened with a mixture of fear and anticipation. The storm had broken my defenses and revealed my greatest vulnerability: I *would do anything to avoid being alone, even if it meant facing him.*

The bile rose in John's throat as he closed the book and laid it on the bedside stand. Little bits were all he could tolerate—it was too much. As he tried to settle for sleep, a line in Meredith's book came back to him: *as long as I was in control of my mind, Anthony Rawlings, or anyone else, would not have the ability to isolate me.*

He turned to Emily. "I didn't think it was possible to hate him more than I did, but I do."

With her head on the pillow, she opened her tired eyes. "I hate that book. I told you not to read it."

"I couldn't when she was missing, but now—"

Emily sat up and kissed her husband. "Now, I think, may even be worse. She's still missing."

John shook his head. "I just read something about her thinking she was in control—how she would never allow anyone to isolate her. I get it."

"What do you mean?"

"When I was in prison..."

Emily nodded.

"The loneliness was the most difficult part for me. I remember reliving so many conversations. It's like you have this continual movie playing in your head. Sometimes I'd remember something you said that was funny, and I'd hear myself laugh. It felt wrong, yet right. It helped me."

"John, I'm so sorry..."

"No, that isn't my point. My point is that in this book she talks about *remembering*. Em, why isn't she remembering now? How can we, or the doctors help her remember? I mean, she has a daughter!"

"Shh," Emily chided. "Let's not wake that daughter up."

John exhaled. "Do you ever think about what we were doing while she was going through that shit—before?"

Emily nodded and leaned against John's chest. "I do. I especially did while reading that damn book. I wish I could say I think Meredith sensationalized it, but it's a lot like what Claire told me. There are more details in the book..."

"Yeah, I could do without those."

"Me too, but as long as the rest of the world knows them, I felt like I should too. John?" Her green eyes looked up.

"Yeah?"

"I don't think I can go back to California."

He closed his eyes and nodded.

Emily continued, "I can't leave her here in that state facility alone. I'm afraid if I go before his trial, somehow he'll get out of it, and I need to keep her safe, keep him away from her and Nichol."

"I understand, but I have an obligation to SiJo and Amber."

"I know you feel indebted to them. Can we just take it a day or a week at a time?"

John nodded. "Did I tell you that they called? I spoke with Amber and Harry. They're both concerned. Amber told me to take as much time as I need."

Emily yawned. "She's been great. What did Harry say?"

"He asked if he could visit."

Her attention was once again focused on her husband. "He wants to visit? Us or Claire?"

John shrugged. "Both, I think."

A smile fluttered across Emily's lips. "Well, all right."

John's eyes narrowed. "Why do you have that smirk?"

"Because I like the idea of keeping that bastard away and

allowing Harry to visit. If I could, I'd take pictures!"

John hugged his wife's shoulders and pulled her down to his pillow. "I'm glad we're on the same team. You definitely have a wicked side."

"Don't you think he deserves it?"

It was John's turn to yawn. "After what I just read, he deserves more."

———◆———

"IT WAS SO nice of you to visit," Emily said to Harry as she rocked Nichol.

"Yes, I'm sorry we're hidden away in this hotel suite," John said, "but I'm sure you understand. We're doing our best to keep Nichol out of the spotlight."

"I get it," Harry replied.

John sat back against the soft chair and watched as Emily lulled their niece to sleep. Although Harry wasn't making it uncomfortable, it seemed odd to have him here with Claire's baby. After all, there was a time when they'd all assumed he was the father. Looking at the tufts of dark hair making their way out of the soft blanket and back to the blue-eyed man with wavy blonde hair, there was no question: Harry was not Nichol's father. Her resemblance to Anthony Rawlings was as unnerving as it was undeniable. The first time John looked into his niece's big brown eyes, he shivered at the recognition. That was only the first time. From that point on, her eyes were *hers* and hers alone. The long lashes and round cheeks that turned crimson at the first sign of fussing were all Nichol—Claire's daughter and their niece.

Never could John bring himself to blame her for her father's sins.

"Amber couldn't get away," Harry said. "But she sends her love and support. She said to let you know that she understands allegiance to family. Take as long as you need John. Your job is waiting for you in California."

John nodded. "I spoke with her the other day. I can't thank her enough for all that she's done for us."

"Yes, after Claire left..." Emily began and stopped. "Oh, I'm sorry, Harry. I'm so sleep-deprived that I'm talking without thinking. I'm sure you don't want to talk about that."

"It's all right. There's nothing I haven't already heard or thought about. It was a little uncomfortable for a while, but John wasn't hired because he was Claire's brother-in-law. He was hired at SiJo because of his ability."

"But you left SiJo right after that. I hope I wasn't the cause. We miss you," John said.

"That wasn't it at all. I missed police work. I couldn't pass up the opportunity to go back with the California Bureau of Investigation."

"It's nice that you can still consult with SiJo. You obviously care a lot about your sister's company," John replied.

The three of them chatted as Nichol slept contently in her aunt's arms. It wasn't until the subject of Claire's current condition came up that the tension seemed to seep in from the corners of the room. It was one of the first times they'd discussed Claire outside of their legal team.

"After what I've heard, I'm a little nervous to see her. My visit won't upset her, will it?" Harry asked.

Emily shook her head. "I doubt it. She probably won't even

realize you're there." Her voice turned stern. "Harry, we can trust you, can't we?"

"Of course you can."

"Very few people have been allowed to see my sister. It's been solely for her protection. She's not doing well. I know she wouldn't want the media learning the truth about her state of mind."

Harry sat straight. "I would never talk to the media."

John smiled. "We know that. It's just that we need to be sure. Please be careful about what you tell others too."

"Liz?" Harry asked.

Emily nodded. "She's nice enough around us—really she is. And I'm thrilled to see you happy, but I get the feeling she didn't like or maybe even still doesn't like Claire. I don't blame her either. Amber told me that you dated Liz and broke up with her right before Claire moved to Palo Alto. But my point is that I would hate for you to say something to her that she might repeat to someone else. You know how it goes."

"I won't. She doesn't know I'm here."

John glanced at Emily's wide eyes and back to Harry. "Why?"

"You're right. She isn't a fan of Claire's and I was worried. I hoped that you'd let me see her and tell me more about what happened, but Liz wouldn't understand my concern. She'd think I was somehow trying to rekindle..." Harry's voice faded.

"Oh, how I wish you were," Emily mused. "But Claire isn't ready for anything like that. You'll see when you visit."

"So, when you return, please don't say anything about my visit," Harry said.

"No worries. I won't," John said. "And Emily doesn't know when she'll be back."

Emily smiled. "I can't leave Claire in the place where she is. I go there every day and so does John. In her condition, I worry about how she'd be treated if we weren't on them, twenty-four-seven. And then there's Nichol..."

Harry's blue eyes dulled. "A little girl..." His words trailed away not finishing his sentence.

"Would you like to hold her?" Emily asked as she stood.

"I'm not good with babies," Harry admitted. "I'd better not. I have the feeling her parents wouldn't approve."

Walking toward him, Emily lowered Nichol toward Harry's lap. "They're not here. We are and we approve. You're a good friend and it's sweet of you to travel all this way after what Claire did to you."

Hesitantly, Harry cradled his arms and accepted a sleeping Nichol. After a long gaze into the blankets, he looked up with his toothy grin. "She has her mommy's nose and lips."

"She does," Emily agreed, gleefully.

"Her eyes?" Harry asked.

John's lips pressed together before he replied, "Are dark brown."

Acceptingly, Harry nodded. "I assumed. I just wondered."

Walking from the room, Emily's voice was barely audible as she said, "I wish they were blue."

John tried to avoid Harry's gaze as Harry shrugged with a sad smile.

SINCE CLAIRE WAS technically under arrest and not fit to be in a jail cell, the court moved her to a state-funded institution for further tests and treatment. The state institution required an array of clearances prior to visiting a patient. John and Emily had already filed the necessary authorization for Harrison Baldwin. All that was needed on his part was to show his identification and sign the visitor's log.

Each step down the corridor filled John with dread. As much as he hated the old hospital room where Claire had been, he hated this new place more. There were noises and murmurings coming from the closed doors along the hall. Because Claire still had her pending charges, her room was beyond more locked doors. However, her room was empty. Hurriedly, John searched, finding her in a common area. She was sitting in a wheelchair, still dressed in her hospital gown with her hair a tangled mess.

John's face burned as anger built behind his deceptively calm facade. He turned to the attendant. "Why the hell is she out here?"

"All patients get time out of their rooms."

Harry stood helpless as John took the lead and knelt before Claire. "Good morning, Claire."

She didn't look his way. Her eyes were fixed on the bar-covered window.

John continued, "I think it's a good thing your sister isn't here right now. I'm taking you back to your room." He looked back up at the attendant. "Has she eaten? How about a shower?"

"I just get them from their rooms. Don't ask me."

Before John could respond, Harry said, "Don't ask you? Then who the hell is he supposed to ask? Can't you see she needs help?"

The young man put up his hands. "Back off, dude, or I'll call security. You think they'd let me shower female patients?" He chuckled. "It'd sure make this job better." Then he shook his head and slowed his words, as if that made for better comprehension. "I just get them and bring them here. That's my job."

"Well, I'm taking her back to her room," John announced.

Harry followed as John pushed the wheelchair. Once they were with Claire behind her closed door, John fought the emotion. "Harry, I'm sorry. You shouldn't have to see her like this."

"What are you going to do?"

John reached for the brush. "Emily will be here later. In the meantime, I'll brush her hair."

Harry ran his hands through his blonde mop and looked out the small, rectangular window, five feet above the floor. "She can't even see out these windows." It was more an observation than the start of a conversation. "She loves sunshine."

John listened as he gently tugged against the tangles, smoothing his sister-in-law's sun-lightened hair. "I don't know exactly where they were, but when everything first happened, Claire was suntanned. It's starting to fade."

Harry nodded.

"Thanks for coming. This is really hard."

"Do you need help?"

John looked up and smiled. "Not with brushing her hair... all of it is hard. I hate leaving Emily here to deal with it alone."

"She won't be coming back to California, will she?"

John shrugged. "She said she wants to take it a day or week at a time, but I don't think she will. I don't think she'll leave Claire, not like this."

"Claire was the one who left you guys—twice," Harry reminded.

"She's family. No one knows you like your family. The past is..." He looked back down at Claire. Her closed eyes appeared as though she were sleeping, but the slight twist of her neck that gave the right amount of resistance to work out the tangles told him she was awake. "...the past. We know it, but we can't let that stop the future. It's the right thing to do."

Chapter 10

Early April 2014

Tony

———◆———

You never find yourself until you face the truth.
—Pearl Bailey

"WE'RE MEETING WITH Judge Temple in his chambers, but there's something you should know." Brent said, as he and Tony rode to the courthouse. "He agreed to this meeting with a few stipulations."

"What kind of stipulations?" Tony asked.

"He demanded equal representation. He refused to meet with us without the claimants being present or at least their representation."

Tony's brows furrowed. "So?"

"Jane will be there."

"And John?"

"I don't know for certain. When I spoke with the judge, I tried to emphasize that John's presence wouldn't be beneficial to this situation."

"I don't give a damn who's there, as long as the end result is that I get to see my wife and daughter. It's not like John and I will get in a brawl."

"I'd hoped that wasn't an option but, nevertheless, I'd rather that this meeting not morph into a hostile environment. I don't want you saying anything that can be misconstrued. Recently, the momentum has shifted in your favor. Since showing the video from your home office to Evergreen and the ICPD, your defense has taken an upward swing. Even though your pending charges aren't relevant regarding this restraining order, I don't want anything that may potentially negate the progress we've accomplished."

Tony huffed under his breath. "I want to see my wife. Despite what Roach is saying about her medical prognosis, I think that I can reach her—snap her out of whatever has happened. I'll fuck'n do whatever I need to do to get me to her." He turned toward the window, not watching the scenes of the city pass before him. His back straightened. "The damn state has her, Mrs. Anthony Rawlings, in a state-run mental hospital." He turned back, the brown of his irises almost completely overwhelmed by black. "That's absurd! I want her home where she can be cared for properly. She deserves the best doctors money can buy, not some state institution—"

"Home probably isn't an option, yet." Brent interrupted. "She's been officially charged with attempted murder, but I agree: getting her moved to a private facility would be better. I think Emily may even agree with you on that."

"Imagine that," Tony replied sarcastically. "I think it may be the first time in the history of mankind that we've ever agreed—monumental day."

Brent narrowed his eyes. "That type of remark is why I don't want you and the Vandersols together in Judge Temple's chambers."

"Vandersols?" Tony emphasized the last letter. "As in Emily, too?"

"Remember..." Brent reminded him, "...they didn't balk when the state dropped the false imprisonment charges against you and charged Catherine."

Changing the subject, Tony said, "After this meeting, I plan to get Nichol. I've hired a nanny and have a nursery at my temporary apartment ready, as well as a room for the nanny."

"Yes, I think that should show the court that you're capable and willing."

"Hell, yes, I'm willing and I'm more than capable. I can take care of her myself, but I thought with everything pending, the nanny would be a good idea."

"Well, if things go the way we hope, she'll come home with you today." Looking away from his notes, Brent asked, "When will the repairs be done on your home? I haven't seen it since they started."

"A couple more weeks. The fire damage was mostly limited to the first floor of the southwest corridor. However, the water and smoke damage was more widespread. Everything has to be cleaned. That smell of smoke is difficult to remove."

"I read the fire investigator's report. The fire originated in Catherine's suite. She's not talking. Do you have any idea what she was trying to accomplish?"

"The woman's crazy. According to the fire chief, there were remnants of melted electronics and plastic in her fireplace. Claire told me that the reason she left last fall and started running was because Catherine produced her laptop, the one taken before her attack by Chester. It pisses me off that I had everyone searching for that damn laptop and it was in my house the whole time. Catherine told Claire that it was my way of tricking her into returning to Iowa."

Brent listened as the car moved in slow bursts, indicating they were nearing their destination.

"I hate that she believed her," Tony admitted, "but I also understand. Claire was frightened for Nichol. Truthfully, I had no idea what had happened to it." Tony sighed. "I think she successfully used that laptop against both of us. Showing it to Claire scared her. Not knowing its whereabouts had me on edge."

"Do you think she was burning evidence? Do you think she knew everything was caving in around her?"

"I think she burnt the laptop. I have no idea what she was thinking. I'd say she knew I was no longer falling for her bullshit."

"Why start the house on fire?"

Tony shrugged. "The investigators weren't certain if it was intentional or if she forgot to open the flue. They said that electronics aren't the most combustible material: she probably threw other things in the fireplace to get the fire going quickly. Based on some evidence, they're presuming bed linens. It would make a lot of smoke. The fact that the fire spread may have been accidental—or not."

"They're waiting on more definitive evidence before they charge Catherine with Sophia's death. It'll most likely be manslaughter."

Tony's head slowly moved from side to side. "As much as I want to see her spend the rest of her life in prison, I can't believe Catherine intended to kill her own daughter."

"This whole thing gets more twisted every day," Brent replied. Refocusing on the tablet in his hand, he returned them to their task at hand. "Judge Temple will ask you some questions. The purpose of this meeting is to talk with you, and assess the need for the order. The Vandersols claimed that due to your past history, you're a threat to Claire and to Nichol."

Tony's lips made a straight line as he fought to remain silent. There's no way he'd ever hurt Nichol: it wasn't even plausible. He'd never hurt Claire again. But with that damn book out, he couldn't deny the past.

Brent continued, "No matter what he says or what he asks, don't get upset. Jane will also ask you questions. I guarantee she wants you to lose it."

Tony turned his dark gaze on his friend. Anthony Rawlings didn't need lessons on public appearances. He was the master. Before he could comment, Brent continued, "I'm saying that because if I were her, that's what I'd want. I'd want to provoke you. I know that you know not to do it, but I also know that you have triggers. Expect those to be exploited."

"I'll watch it," he conceded as he reflected on the past few weeks. With every passing second, he missed paradise—not the location but the bond. Lamenting the loss of what he, Claire, and Nichol shared on that tiny island wouldn't bring it back. Besides, Anthony Rawlings wasn't a watcher: he was a doer. He'd do whatever was necessary and swore that he'd never give up. If playing nice with the Vandersols, Judge Temple, or even the devil himself was what Tony needed to do to get even a sliver of paradise back, he'd do it.

Returning to Iowa City had been both pure hell and a resemblance of normal. The hell part was obvious. The return to his previous *normal* came after the meeting with Evergreen. Everyone had rehearsed his part, even Eric. Tony didn't want anyone other than himself to be held responsible for the actions at the estate. He also didn't want anyone else charged with aiding and abetting; however, they all agreed that Eric's involvement wouldn't trigger red flags. At the time of the incident, he was employed by the *estate*. By virtue of Tony's will, Catherine assumed the role of executor of the estate so, in essence, she'd become Eric's employer.

Working with the estate's security had always been a component of Eric's job. As Tony's driver and pilot, his presence was for more than transportation. He was Tony's first line of protection. Once Tony became missing, Eric assumed that role for Ms. London. Reviewing the surveillance video was an acceptable component of his job. Who would be more likely to find the evidence that could potentially implicate Catherine as well as exonerate Tony?

Though the estate had turned everything over to the police, their forensic teams had a lot of footage to dissect. Eric claimed that it was his personal concern for everyone involved that prompted him to scan the videos. Despite the incriminating evidence against his new employer, he had an overwhelming sense of conscience to set the record straight.

With Evergreen and Chief Newburgh, the Iowa City police chief, present, Brent showed them the video. Once it was confirmed that the video hadn't been doctored, that it was the same as what had been confiscated by the police, it was logged into evidence. Of course, it was only a small step along the legal process. Catherine's attorneys had motioned to have the video evidence dismissed. Although no definitive decision had yet been made, Brent believed that it would stand. After all, Catherine ran the estate at that time. She'd lived there for many years and was well aware of the surveillance cameras. Eric even had video evidence of her accessing the feeds from multiple locations. Even though it was true, there was little to no chance that she'd be able to claim that she'd been video-recorded without her knowledge. Why would a judge or jury believe that she assumed the office was not recorded when she knew that the rest of the estate was under surveillance?

The footage that Eric presented also showed Catherine engaging the electronic lock on the suite where the Vandersols were held. The crime lab's analysis of the water bottles within the suite found that the water contained the deadly toxin actaea pachypoda. Once that particular poison was identified, the FBI joined the case and confirmed their previous knowledge. After a few turf wars and posturing, the two agencies seemed to have found a common ground.

They all knew more charges would come against Tony; they just hadn't happened yet. The video had made it clear that Tony had knowledge of other crimes but it also overwhelmingly showed Catherine's involvement. After she was charged, her bail was set at the same amount as Tony's—$ 10,000,000. When she professed her right to the estate's assets, Tony vehemently denied the request, as well as forbidding the use of Rawlings Industries' resources. In order to secure counsel, she laid claim to overseas accounts. Imagine her surprise when the accounts no longer existed. It was a mystery. According to the bank's records, it was C. Marie Rawls who had made the final transaction. They promised to investigate. Currently, Catherine Marie London was resting comfortably—or uncomfortably, Tony didn't care—in the Iowa City jail awaiting her next court appearance with her new legal representation, a court-appointed attorney. The charges levied against her included two counts of false imprisonment with the threat of harm, thus felonies, as well as multiple counts of conspiracy to commit murder, murder by hire, and falsifying sworn statements. With the FBI and ICPD cooperation, there was the potential for more charges.

Even though it showed incriminating evidence against him, Tony didn't regret sharing the video footage to the authorities. Not only had it incriminated Catherine, it also helped to vindicate Claire. For that reason, Jane and John were not fighting the admittance of the footage into evidence. It showed Claire acting in self-defense. John even admitted that, in the video, it appeared as though Tony and Claire were working together.

***

JUDGE TEMPLE'S CHAMBERS couldn't comfortably hold the number of people in attendance; therefore, their meeting was relocated to a conference room down the hall. Brent and Tony followed a young woman to the new location. Brent audibly sighed as they entered, and Tony felt his chest tighten as he took in Jane Allyson, and John and Emily Vandersol. "Ladies and gentlemen," the young lady said, "now that everyone is present, Judge Temple will be with you shortly."

A murmur of courteous replies filled the tight air.

"John, Emily," Brent said, as he extended his hand.

John shook Brent's hand. "Mr. Simmons."

Turning to Jane, Brent said, "Ms. Allyson, the last we spoke you were planning on attending this meeting alone."

"Mr. Vandersol is my co-counsel, and as you know, Judge Temple wanted equal representation. Mrs. Vandersol is the plaintiff."

"Well," Brent said, using his most affable voice. "I'm pleased that we can all be together. Hopefully, we can reach an amicable conclusion to this unfortunate situation."

"That is our plan," Ms. Allyson replied, stopping as the door once again opened and Judge Temple entered.

"Good afternoon," he offered, as he pulled out the chair at the head of the shiny table and sat.

Again, murmurs of acknowledgements filled the room.

"I see we were all able to make this meeting. I'm all about disclosure. Nothing will be done in my courtroom behind closed doors." He eyed Brent. "Is that clear, Mr. Simmons?"

Tony bristled at Temple's tone. Could this guy be that out of sorts over losing his first appearance?

"Yes, Judge. It's clear."

"Very well, Mr. and Mrs. Vandersol are present, representing Mrs. Rawlings who, according to these documents..." he held a manila folder, "...is mentally incapable of making this complaint on her own." He looked up at the Vandersols. "Is that correct?"

"Yes, Your Honor, it is. We also have been granted guardianship and temporary power of attorney over Ms. Nic—Mrs. Rawlings," John replied.

"As Mrs. Rawlings' husband," Brent countered, "my client has issued an injunction of that power of attorney. It is common practice for the husband—"

"We are getting ahead of ourselves," Judge Temple interrupted. "I assume that we've all read the affidavit?" When his question was met with resounding affirmative responses, he continued, "The affidavit was filed on behalf of Mrs. Rawlings immediately following the incident at the Rawlings estate; however, that particular matter is not being heard by me. It's my place to decide if the petition has warrant."

"Yes, Your Honor," Tony said, believing he sounded controlled.

"Mr. Rawlings, do you believe the affidavit has warrant? Do you believe your brother- and sister-in-law have reason to question your wife and daughter's safety in your presence?"

Tony inhaled. That wasn't the question he'd anticipated. "I love my wife and daughter unconditionally. There is no way I'd do anything to harm them. I believe Claire needs me during this difficult time."

"That wasn't the question," Judge Temple replied. "I asked you if you believe Mr. and Mrs. Vandersol have grounds for questioning your volatile temper."

"I object," Brent replied.

"Mr. Simmons, we're not in court. You do not need to object."

"Judge, I believe that Mr. and Mrs. Vandersol are making assumptions."

Jane replied, "Then I'd like to ask a few questions, if I may, Judge Temple?"

"Go ahead, Counselor."

"Mr. Rawlings, have you ever lost control of your temper in the presence of your wife and daughter?"

"My wife *and* daughter? No."

Brent interceded, "May I also ask a few questions, Judge?"

Judge Temple leaned back against the vinyl chair. "Please, I'm interested in the way this will play out."

"Mr. or Mrs. Vandersol, have you personally witnessed any behavior by Mr. Rawlings that you deem violent?"

Emily's chin rose indignantly. "Violent, no. Controlling and manipulative, yes."

"Mr. Vandersol?" Brent continued.

"I've always had a gut feeling that something wasn't right."

Brent turned back to Judge Temple. "I don't believe there's a legal precedent for issuing orders on gut feelings, is there?"

"No, Counselor, but there is more at play here than a gut feeling. Mr. and Mrs. Vandersol claim that the incident at the Rawlings estate was evidence that Mrs. Rawlings was trying, once again, to free herself from Mr. Rawlings. Ms. Allyson, has that changed?"

"Yes, there has been new evidence regarding the incident. At the time of the filing, neither Mr. nor Mrs. Vandersol knew for sure that Claire and Mr. Rawlings were remarried. They also believed that Mrs. Rawlings was trying to free herself from him, as she'd done in the past."

"Speculation," Brent interjected. "As you so eloquently stated on a previous occasion, Ms. Allyson, Mrs. Rawlings did not plead guilty to attempted murder in 2012. She pled no contest. That wasn't an admission of guilt. Mr. Rawlings filed for divorce from their first marriage. She did not *free herself* in the past, as you state. And the previous charges, as well as her plea, were expunged. They are not relevant."

"Thank you, Mr. Simmons, for that clarification," Jane replied. "As I was about to say, there has been new evidence. First, we now have reason to believe that Mr. Rawlings and Claire Nichols were legally married on October 27, 2013. We also have reason to believe that Mrs. Rawlings was not trying to harm Mr. Rawlings. That however, does not render this petition null and void. As court-appointed representatives of Mrs. Rawlings, necessitated by your client's incarceration and based on their status as next-of-kin, the Vandersols still believe that Mr. Rawlings has been and continues to be a threat to their sister."

"What evidence do you have? Other than sensationalized fiction?" Brent asked.

"Mr. Simmons, I warned you about insinuating that this court is taking anything other than the facts into consideration," Judge Temple reprimanded.

"I apologize, Judge, but I've yet to hear anything except hearsay—"

Jane produced documents. "I have evidence."

Tony took the papers that were passed. The first was a bound folder. He'd seen one very similar in the past. Of course, he hadn't read it then, and he didn't want to read it now. It was Claire's non-sworn testimony from 2012. It was her account of their first marriage.

"This testimony was not given under oath..." Brent began. As he spoke, Tony watched Emily's agitation rise. Her unusually quiet demeanor was no doubt at the prompting of her husband. She appeared as ready to spring as Tony felt.

Finally, she interrupted, obviously unable to contain her words any longer. "You almost killed her! Do you deny that?"

Brent's hand quickly went to Tony's arm, warning him to remain silent. Tony bit the inside of his cheek and pressed his lips together forming a slight grin as his unwavering stare remained fixed on his sister-in-law.

"Mrs. Vandersol, your attorneys will ask the questions," the judge reminded Emily.

"To that point, Judge, we also have recently obtained medical data," Jane said as she passed more documentation Around the table. "This is a preliminary report regarding Mrs. Rawlings' mental state. It has been noted through various tests that Mrs. Rawlings suffered a concussion approximately three years ago."

Tony and Brent scanned the papers. Thanks to Phil Roach,

they'd seen the report. It didn't take long before Brent replied, "This is not conclusive."

"No, Mrs. Rawlings has only been recently evaluated. These tests take time. However," Jane continued, "her current state is theorized to be a psychotic break—a break with reality." She turned toward the judge. "It was theorized to me, by the doctors, that such a break is brought on, in most cases, by one of two reasons. The first is traumatic brain injury. While we just received this report this morning, we haven't been able to thoroughly research, but the idea is that Mrs. Rawlings was so violently injured in 2010, that her brain formed scar tissue. This is a very painful process as the gray matter around the brain shrinks. It can sometimes cause debilitating headaches." Her eyes went to Tony.

He remembered Claire's headaches. She'd been suffering with them for as long as he could remember, but he couldn't recall if they'd occurred prior to her accident. Though she often tried to pretend that the headaches weren't happening, Tony also knew that there were times when nothing but sleep would relieve the pain he had witnessed in her emerald eyes.

Jane continued, "Mrs. Rawlings was also attacked by a perpetrator in 2013, once again sustaining trauma to her head, though, according to medical documentation, not as severely as in 2010. There is ongoing research that verifies that, with time, the lingering results of the TBI (traumatic brain injury) can result in a psychotic break. Therefore, it's the belief of my clients that Mr. Rawlings is the cause of Mrs. Rawlings' current condition and is obviously a threat to her future wellbeing."

"Ms. Allyson, let's stick to the facts and dispense with the beliefs," Judge Temple said.

Brent looked at his notes, things he'd scribbled as Jane spoke, as well as information from the medical experts on Rawlings' legal team. "Ms. Allyson, you said there were *two* possible causes for a psychotic break. What is the second?"

"The evidence points to the TBI."

"Psychotic breaks can also be brought on by a traumatic life event." Brent handed documentation to Jane as well as Judge Temple. "I too have research. It cites many well-documented examples."

"Judge," Jane retorted, "I have seen some of this research. These people didn't have brain injuries."

Brent sat straighter. "Do you deny that the incident that occurred at the Rawlings estate could be defined as a *traumatic life event*?"

"I do not. However—"

"Sometimes the brain just cannot handle the stress. Mrs. Rawlings was undoubtedly undergoing excessive anxiety. According to witness testimony and the video surveillance, she'd just learned about the downed Rawlings Industries plane, she'd gone to the estate to assure her husband and family's safety from Ms. London. The home was on fire, and she'd just had a gun pointed at her. Can you honestly say that it wasn't this traumatic event that caused her psychotic break? Can you even say with one-hundred-percent certainty she has suffered a psychotic break? Come now, Ms. Allyson, do you have proof that a TBI caused her current condition?"

"It is too early to say definitively," John admitted, as his wife shot silent daggers in his direction.

Judge Temple interjected, "Let me get this straight: it's believed that Mrs. Rawlings' current mental state was caused by previous injury or possibly a very stressful situation?"

"Yes," Jane replied.

"Are both options viable?"

"Yes," she said again.

Turning toward Tony, the judge asked, "Mr. Rawlings, in the best interest of your family, though you are not under oath, I'm expecting a truthful answer. Do you know how Mrs. Rawlings received the initial and most severe injury to her brain that is evident on the medical scans?"

"Judge, my client does not need to answer that question," Brent interjected.

"Counselor, I need the facts to make my decision. Mr. Rawlings, I'm waiting."

The rush of blood to his face made Tony feel faint. Maintaining the eye contact he'd demanded of Claire in the past, Tony gazed only at the judge. "Yes, I do."

"There is a sensationalized bestselling book on the market right now that claims to have been narrated by your wife. Are you aware of this book?"

"Yes, I am."

"Have you read the book?"

Tony stoically replied, "No, I have not."

"Were you aware that you're mentioned in this book?"

"Judge, where is this going?" Brent asked.

"Counselor, I want to hear your client's answer. Mr. Rawlings, were you the cause of that brain injury? Did you harm your wife?"

Tony turned toward John and Emily. "I'm not proud of the things I've done in the past, and I would never do them again. I would do anything to have never behaved as I did. You need to know that this time things were different."

"Mr. Rawlings..." Judge Temple's voice deepened, "...while

we're not in a courtroom, I will still hold you in contempt if you avoid another of my direct questions. Did you cause your wife grievous bodily harm in 2010?"

"Tony, don't answer this," Brent urged.

"Grievous?" Tony asked.

"Did you wound her with intent?"

"I didn't intend to harm her. It just..."

Tony's words faded, tears descended Emily's cheeks, as the small room buzzed with silence.

"Mr. Rawlings," Judge Temple continued, "are the things in Ms. Banks' book based on fact?"

"I haven't read her book."

"How did Mrs. Rawlings first come to live at your house, in 2010?"

Tony looked toward Brent and then remembering the judge's statement about contempt, he replied, "I'd rather not answer that question."

"Oh my God," Emily breathed under her breath, "you're a monster."

"I'd never hurt Nichol. I haven't hurt Claire since before our divorce. We've worked things—"

Judge Temple inhaled and sat taller. "Based on the best interest of this family and of the minor child, I believe I have enough information regarding the protective order. We will reconvene in court, and I'll announce my decision."

Tony's heart ached.

Chapter 11

Late May 2014

Tony

—————◆—————

I'd rather be hated for who I am,
than loved for who I am not.
—Kurt Cobain (paraphrased from André Gide)

THE OFFICES AT Rawlings Industries corporate were quiet. Being after hours, most of the people had gone home to their families. Tony didn't have that luxury. He didn't want to go to his house— ever. The repairs were complete but the entire structure made him ill. The contractors said that the smell of smoke was gone, but when he entered the grand doors and walked the corridors, a putrid smell infiltrated his senses. No one else could smell it—but Tony could. It was the manifestation of years of hate and vengeance. It was the sickening loss of happiness that would never be his. It was the death of innocent people, and the death of innocence.

Was it only the structure in Iowa, or would he smell the same thing if he were to ever enter the house in New Jersey, the one where he was raised? After all, didn't it all begin there? Tony wasn't blaming anyone: he'd done enough of that. But the fact remained that he was raised in an opulent pit of evil. Like the red of his rage, it lurked in every corner and slithered through the halls. His grandfather's greed, grandmother's illness, father's passive-aggressive hatred, and his mother's submissive acceptance all mingled together to create the environment that spawned both Tony and Catherine. In no way was he forgiving her for any of her actions: nonetheless, she'd come to live under that roof at a mere twenty years of age. Would she have turned out differently had her parents accepted her and Sophia? Would he have turned out differently raised by someone else?

Tony pondered Sophia. She was a London, yet she was so different from her mother. Didn't the woman Sophia became speak volumes about nature versus nurture? Every day he thought of the life lost too young.

Tony also mourned Derek. The man deserved better. He'd met every test and challenge with flying colors. Mr. Cunningham from Shedis-tics gave him glowing recommendations, as did Brent, from the short time they'd worked together. His death was another piece of the tragic puzzle.

The home Tony constructed was built as a testament to a man that Tony never really knew, a man who influenced events long after his death. Nathaniel fought hard, lived large, loved secretly, and fell from grace. He allowed his ambitions to overpower his better judgment.

As Tony swirled the amber liquid around his glass, he admitted, if only to himself, he was no better. If anything, he was worse. Nathanial made mistakes out of greed and ambition. Tony's sins were based on misguided need. It was pitiful, he concluded, as he swallowed the contents of the glass and poured another two fingers of Johnny Walker. Relishing the slow burn as the whiskey dulled his senses, Tony mourned the loss of everything he knew to be true. His entire life was built on lies, retribution, and the need for validation. The money, the power, the prestige were all for one thing—to finally hear Nathaniel say, "well done, son."

He couldn't even dream that. In his dream, Nathaniel told him he'd failed.

Tony laid his jacket across a chair and stretched out on the long leather sofa in the far corner of his office. Hell, he'd sleep the night there; he'd been doing it quite frequently. It was better than going back to that house. He'd sell the damn thing if it weren't for Claire. His eyes closed as he fought the memories. Even the recollections weren't as bright as they'd been. Even they'd been dulled by the loss of color. There was some hot selling book that talked about shades of gray. Tony concluded that it was now his life. The color was gone. The vibrant greens of the island couldn't transcend the veil of despair in Tony's whiskey-numbed mind. There was a time when color was all around...

He'd invited Claire to Caleb Simmons' wedding. He didn't know if she'd come, but she did. The first evening, after they returned from Tim and Sue's house, Tony remembered standing on the brick drive beneath a blanket of Iowa stars. With a gentle June breeze blowing Claire's hair, she looked up at him and said, "I'm surprised how much I like being here. I was afraid the bad memories would overpower the good." The next day she guided him through his woods to her lake. Her beautiful emerald eyes sparkled as they tossed pebbles into the clear water and watched the sun reflect in prisms of light dancing on the waves.

That was why he couldn't sell the estate. It belonged to her. She was the only one to ever bring life and color to 6,000 acres. Before her, it was only a monument. After her, it was as dead as the man who it had been built to impress. It was only with her that the stone and brick structure was a home, even when she didn't want to be there. Her presence infused life and spirit into the brick and mortar.

Roach's reports were discouraging. The damn doctors at the state facility where Claire was still being held were uncaring and inept. Their records were inconclusive. Most of the information he was able to glean was from the taps on the Vandersols' phones. Tony shrugged. Hell, they might as well add that to his list of charges—just pile it on!

Perhaps another drink was in order.

Tony refused to give up on Claire. Even if he couldn't see her, he would never stop watching her. He couldn't. She was part of him. The separation obviously added to his funk. Despite it all, he believed with all of his heart that she would get better. She just needed better doctors—the best money could buy. There was a reason for his success, other than Nathaniel. With Tony's money he could provide Claire and Nichol with the best the world had to offer, even if he were going to be spending the next three to fifteen years behind bars. The plea agreement was in place, the final decision for sentencing was up to the judge. Claire and Nichol deserved that and more.

Tomorrow, Tony had a meeting with the Rawlings Industries board of directors and then a web conference with the presidents of the subsidiaries. He prayed that his admission of guilt and quiet plea agreement would help to take the focus away from his company. It wasn't just for him, but for the thousands of people employed by him. Even that reminded him of Claire. That damn little company in Pennsylvania. She'd saved their jobs and now his past could take them all away.

No. He'd walk away from the company before he let that happen.

Tony looked at his watch; it was a little after 8:00 PM. Sitting back up, he knew it was too early to fall asleep. But it wasn't too early for Nichol to fall asleep. His arms ached with the desire to hold and rock their daughter. He turned on his phone to a picture taken only a few days ago. Her cheeks looked rounder than he remembered, and she was smiling. While it broke his heart, it also encouraged him. Tony hated Emily with everything in him, but he was thankful she was caring for Nichol. The picture came from Courtney. She'd finally convinced Emily to allow her to visit. A faint grin came to Tony's lips. Courtney had a way with everyone. Hopefully, she'd soon be allowed to visit Claire, too.

Thankfully, John and Jane had successfully worked out a plea agreement for Claire. The FBI came forward and agreed to drop the charge of aiding and abetting: that left only attempted murder. The video made it clear that Claire acted in self-defense. The prosecutor discussed aggravated assault; however, it was her mental condition that sealed the deal. Declared unfit to stand trial, Claire was exonerated of all charges.

Tony and Evergreen had come to a conclusion. It was Tony's conclusion, but Evergreen agreed. Dropping the charges against Claire didn't make the prosecutor look bad. He'd caught a much bigger fish in Anthony Rawlings.

Before Tony could celebrate Claire's freedom with another drink, he heard the knock on his office door. Curiously, he asked, "Who is it?"

"It's me, Mr. Rawlings. May I come in?" Patricia's muffled voice came from behind the closed door.

Tony rose and opened the door. "Patricia, why are you still here? You should be home."

She lifted a plastic bag with what appeared to be Styrofoam containers and grinned. "You need to eat."

Shaking his head, Tony ran his hand through his unkempt hair and allowed her entry. "Thank you, but you didn't need to do that. I could have called—"

Patricia opened the bag and set the containers at the conference table. As she smiled, she said, "You could have, but you wouldn't have."

She was right. Tony had no intention of eating. He honestly hadn't even given it much thought. Noticing the way she was setting two places he asked, "Did you get something for yourself, too?"

"I did." She tilted her head toward the liquor cabinet. "I didn't think you should be drinking alone, either."

Since his return from paradise, Patricia had been instrumental in catching him up on all things Rawlings. He'd never be able to thank her for the long hours she'd spent running reports, filling him in on the numbers, and all around helping him re-acclimate to the world of CEO. It wasn't that Tim, Tom, and Brent hadn't been helpful—they were. But Tom and Brent were overwhelmed with legal issues, and Tim was still making the day-to-day decisions regarding operations. Tony didn't see the need for resuming the role just to lose it when his prison sentence began.

He lifted the bottle of Johnny Walker. "I'd offer you something else, but this seems to be all I have."

Patricia raised her eyebrows. "I'm not much of a drinker. Oh, but..." She hurried from the room. Seconds later she was back with a bottle of red wine and an opener. "...I've had this in my file cabinet for months. It was a Christmas present that I forgot to take home."

Tony grinned and reached for the bottle. He closed one eye, helping his focus, as he lined the little curly Q opener over the cork. When the cork popped, he said, "Well then, here's to your forgetfulness."

Patricia produced two new crystal tumblers from the cabinet. "Oh, my memory isn't that bad."

"No, no, it's not," Tony said as he pulled out her chair and sat. "Thank you for this kindness. I seem to be taking self-pity to a whole new level."

"Well," her voice came out an octave higher. "Mr. Rawlings, none of that tonight. I'd say you've had enough for one day." As she lifted her tumbler, her brows knitted together. "Should you drink wine after liquor? What's that saying?"

Tony chuckled, lifting his glass and clinking hers. "I believe it has to do with beer, not wine. Beer before liquor, never been sicker. Liquor before beer, all in the clear."

Taking a sip, she laughed. "Then I guess you're safe."

Opening the container, the delectable aroma of garlic whiffed around the table, reminding Tony that he truly was hungry. After a few bites he remarked, "This is delicious, thank you again."

"Mr. Rawlings, you don't need to keep thanking me—"

"Patricia, how long have you worked for me?"

She feigned a pout. "You don't remember?"

"I do. You've been my assistant for eight years. As I recall, you were the one candidate I never expected to choose for the position."

Her eyes opened wide. "And why was that?"

"My assistant before you was extremely capable—"

"And you didn't think I would be?"

"No." He shook his head. "No, let me finish. She was capable, but she couldn't keep up with the growth and technology. I wanted someone who would do both."

"And, it wasn't me because..."

Tony shrugged. "You were energetic enough, and your résumé..." He thought reflectively. "Graduated top of your class from MIT, with your MBA from Stanford." He raised his glass again. "Impressive."

Patricia smiled and lifted her glass too. "Thank you, Mr. Rawlings."

"That's why I asked you how long you've worked for me. Please, after all you've done, you may call me Anthony, outside of work hours."

Crimson glowed from her cheeks. "Thank you, Anthony. I'm glad you took a chance on me, despite that dismal education."

"Your education was superb, as you know. I was concerned about your age."

"You do know that age isn't a legal reason for not hiring someone? I believe they call that discrimination."

He grunted. "Damn. Glad I hired you then. The last thing I need is another legal charge against me."

Patricia reached out and covered his hand. "Shh, stop. Remember, you're taking a break from that right now."

Tony nodded, removing his hand from hers. "Fine..." he lifted the bottle of wine. "...as long as I can refill your glass. I'm glad I hired you, too. You've proven your weight in gold around here. I just imagined you getting settled and then—damn, this *will* sound sexist—leaving to have a husband and babies."

Her eyes diverted to her food. "It did sound sexist. If I wanted that, I could do both."

"If?" His alcohol-infused mind had no idea of the dangerous

road he was maneuvering. Her shoulders squared, reminding Tony of Claire when she was about to tell him a piece of her mind. However, instead of stern, Patricia sounded sad.

"I mean, I'm not too old... but... you know what they say?"

Tony looked at her questioningly.

"All the good ones are taken."

The food and wine helped lift a layer of grayness. He chuckled, "I thought you were going to say the good ones were gay."

"No, I'm extremely confident that isn't the case," she murmured as she ate another bite of pasta.

As the last morsel of noodle was consumed, Tony's phone buzzed. "Excuse me. With all that's going down, I hate to miss any messages."

Patricia nodded.

It was a text, from Brent.

"I JUST HEARD FROM EVERGREEN AND WANT TO REVIEW THIS PLEA AGREEMENT WITH YOU. WHERE ARE YOU? CAN ERIC DRIVE YOU?"

Tony wanted to take issue with his last comment, but truth be told, he shouldn't drive. The pasta had helped to lower his blood-alcohol level, but not enough. He replied.

"I'M AT THE OFFICE. I SENT ERIC HOME FOR THE NIGHT. I CAN DRIVE, BUT PROBABLY SHOULDN'T. A DUI WOULDN'T BE GOOD FOR MY REPUTATION."

See, he thought, I still have a sense of humor.

"I'LL BE THERE IN FIFTEEN MINUTES. DO YOU NEED FOOD?"

"NO. I JUST ATE—REALLY. JUST COME HERE."

"SEE YOU IN FIFTEEN."

Tony looked up to Patricia's doe eyes.

"It's none of my business," she began, "but you were grinning. Was that good news?"

"Probably not. I'll find out soon enough. Brent's on his way here to discuss the plea agreement."

"Oh," she sounded sad. "I should go."

Tony nodded. "Thanks again for the food and wine... can *you* drive?"

"I'll be fine. Two glasses of wine with a meal, no big deal."

He smiled again. "I don't think that's a real saying."

Shrugging, Patricia gathered the containers and the wine. "I'll leave this in my office, just in case you run out of whiskey."

"I'll see you tomorrow, big meeting first thing."

"I'll be there Mr.—I mean, Anthony. You can count on me."

FIFTEEN MINUTES LATER, Brent walked through the open door. "So," he motioned toward the couch. "Is this your new bed? I told you to come to my house. You would have saved me a drive, and Courtney's one hell of a cook. She wouldn't let you drink your dinner."

"You're getting damn pushy, and I didn't drink my dinner. That was my hors d'oeuvres. Patricia brought me some pasta."

"Good. I'd like you thinking straight while we discuss this. Once you agree, there's no turning back." Brent threw the envelope on the table. "Afterward, I'll join you for a drink."

"Is it that bad?"

Brent shrugged. "I'm not a fan of any of it. I still would rather that you plead not guilty. There's enough circumstantial—"

"No. I'm not doing that. Then I'd be taking a chance on a jury and who knows how long it would all take. I want to do this and pay my debt. I want to come clean. For the first fuck'n time in my life, I want to do the right thing."

"Tony, that's not true. Don't get me wrong: you've done some messed-up shit, but you've done good things too. Don't be a martyr."

"I'm hardly a martyr. I'm not doing this to save anyone but myself. I already confessed this shit to the FBI. I can't live with the idea that one day, when I have my family back, there'll be a knock on the door and my world will crash in around me. I'm laying my cards on the table and cashing in my chips. Tell me what kind of deal you and Evergreen came up with so that I can get out of prison sooner rather than later."

As Brent sat and opened the envelope, his tired eyes swirled with emotion. "I sat in on Catherine's arraignment this afternoon. She's been charged with seven counts of murder. There isn't enough evidence yet with the Rawlings' plane to incriminate her."

"She fuck'n admitted it to me in my office—it's on tape."

"She implied it. There wasn't an explicit confession. Now she's claiming total innocence."

Tony pinched the bridge of his nose. "Are you sure we should wait on that drink?"

Brent shrugged. "Do you have anything less strong than the Johnny Walker? I'd rather save that for later."

Tony's dark eyes widened. "As a matter of fact I do. Wine?"

"All these years and I never knew you were running a damn liquor store in here."

Tony left the office and returned with Patricia's bottle of wine.

"Might as well finish this off." As he poured, Tony asked, "Seven? Did they list names?"

"Yes, Nathaniel Rawls, Samuel and Amanda Rawls, Sherman Nichols, Jordon and Shirley Nichols, and Allison Burke Bradley."

Tony lowered his head to the table and wearily lifted it back up. "That's the better part of Nichol's family tree."

Brent nodded.

"Those names go way back."

"There's no statute of limitation on murder."

"She didn't personally... I mean other than Nathaniel and my parents... right?"

"Murder for hire resulting in death carries the same penalty as murder."

"Will they be able to prove it? That she was involved?"

"I'm not privy to all the information. From what I've gleaned, the FBI has extensive research connecting the cases with the poison that she used." Brent took a drink. "There's more."

"More charges? Are we still talking about Catherine?"

"Yes, we'll get to you later. They're also charging her with attempted murder—four counts."

Tony's brows rose. "Maybe I've drunk too much. There's John and Emily. Who else did she try to murder, but fail?"

"From the video, there's evidence of her pointing the gun at Claire."

"All right, that makes three..."

Brent leaned forward. "You, Tony. She poisoned *you*. She's claiming you knew all about it, but Evergreen is fighting her on it. He didn't like being played, with your accusations against Claire and then your public change of heart and recantation. It made him look bad. Charging her puts an end to that case forever. You had that same unique poison in your system. He's running with it."

Tony collapsed against the chair. "Will I need to testify?"

"Would you perjure yourself?"

"I don't want to. But then again, I want her to rot."

Brent swallowed the deep red liquid from his crystal tumbler. "I recommend that you stick to your original testimony. You didn't know anything other than drinking the coffee and waking up."

Tony nodded.

"The press is calling her a serial killer."

"Who else was at the arraignment?"

"They barred the press, but people with a connection were given special dispensation."

Tony peered over the rim of the tumbler before he drank, and said, "The Vandersols were there, weren't they?"

"Yes."

"What about Cindy? I haven't spoken to her since she's learned the truth."

"She's pretty broken up. We're trying to work something out with her to avoid a civil case. I mean you've taken care of her for years."

Tony looked down. "I thought we were, but she did work. It's not like we just let her live at the estate."

"She was paid, had a roof over her head, and her education was being paid for. So she served food and cleaned. It was a hell of a lot better than what would have happened to her had you not stepped in after the death of her parents."

Tony shook his head. "Yes, which sounds great, with one exception: her parents died because of us."

"Let's talk about that."

Chapter 12

June 2014

Phil

———✦———

**Each player must accept the cards life deals him or her:
but once they are in hand, he or she alone must decide
how to play the cards in order to win the game.**
—Voltaire

MY LIFE AS It Didn't Appear: Chapter 4...

Like an obedient child, I listened to the rules and there were
many. The most important one was to do as I was told. Truly, that
was all encompassing. There were rules regarding attire—no
underwear. My boundaries were defined. I could roam the house
as long as I didn't enter the corridor of Anthony's office or suite
without his permission or summons. Those rooms held the means
to contact the outside world, and I was forbidden to communicate
with anyone but him and his staff. Most days I had to myself,
unless otherwise informed by Anthony or Kate. I could wake when
I wanted, work out in the gym and swim in the indoor pool, watch
movies in the theater room, or read in the library. Each evening at

5:00 PM I was required to be in my suite and await the evening's instructions.

During the day my options were many and few. My cell had grown larger, but it was still a cell. Each glance outside my windows reminded me that I was trapped inside the walls of the mansion. Spring had arrived to Iowa, bringing longer days and life where only gray and dormancy had resided. The dead trees showed faint shades of color as buds formed and turned to lush green leaves. I longed for the freedom of walking outside, the ability to go to a store or a restaurant. I had designer clothes and luxurious surroundings, yet I desired what others took for granted. I craved the mundane life I'd lost.

My job duties were defined broadly. For lack of a better word, I was forced to become Anthony Rawlings' whore. My existence and presence was for one purpose: to please him. If he didn't want or have time for me, I was left in my suite, like a doll left on the shelf. If he wanted me, I was required to accommodate. The word no had been removed from my vocabulary.

During the days I'd assure myself that I had choices. The evenings and nights convinced me otherwise. Failure was not an option. That was not only something that Anthony liked to say: it was the truth. Failure had consequences—some very painful and demeaning consequences.

My first punishment was when I was late returning to his office. I quickly learned that displeasing him was not something that I wanted to do. I believe that fear of seeing the darkness arise behind his eyes was the true key to my captivity. I'd thought I'd seen the depth of his rage—I hadn't yet—and I knew I didn't want to see it again. If I disobeyed, ran through the grand doors and made it into the trees, yet failed to find freedom, I knew that my punishment would be severe. That didn't need to be spelled out for me.

I'd been at his estate for nearly a month when I was awakened by a member of the staff and told that Mr. Rawlings was working from home, and I was to be in his office by 10:00 AM. It wasn't that I didn't usually wake by that time, but I'd developed a routine, and I wasn't always showered and dressed. Of course, I did as I was told, yet as I prepared for my day, each decision was monumental. Usually during the day I dressed casually. If I were to see Anthony at night, Kate informed me what he wanted me to wear.

My first, mid-week summons to his office was a new, daunting assignment. I debated everything. Finally, deciding upon a pair of slacks, silk blouse, and high heels—because other than workout shoes, that was my only option—I arrived at his office door with minutes to spare. I'd been in his office on the occasional Sunday afternoon for lunch, but other than my first time in the regal room, I'd never been called there and required to fulfill my new duties. With each step down the grand stairs and along the marble corridor, I knew this would be different. He had plans. I just didn't know what they were.

With my hand shaking, I knocked on the door to his office. I didn't know if it was locked, but he had a way to open it from his desk. The door opened and I entered. He was talking on the telephone and motioned for me to be quiet. Silently, I walked to his desk as the door closed by the pushing of a button. Though the temperature of the room was the same as the rest of the mansion, I felt a chill that sent shivers to my core. He was upset with the person on the other end of the line. I didn't know or care what he was discussing, but I had learned to read him well enough to know he wasn't happy.

For minutes upon minutes, I stood, unsure of what to do. Each second hung in the air as his eyes grew darker and he wove some trinket around the fingers and knuckles of his other hand. It was the first time I saw this habit—one of his only nervous habits. I'd later consider it the rumble of thunder, warning of an impending storm.

My heartbeat quickened as he leaned back in his chair and told the person on the other end of the line that he had a personal matter, and he would put him or her on hold, momentarily. After hitting the button, his dark eyes found mine. "Claire, you have a job. Do it."

I was lost. I had no idea what I was supposed to do, and yet I feared not complying. Timidly, I asked, "What do you want me to do?"

The pent-up frustration from his business dealing burst forth as he sprang from his chair and rounded the desk toward me. Defensively, I stepped back. He grasped my arm pulling me toward him. His warm breath smelled of coffee as he growled, "Do not pull away from me. Do you understand?"

I understood. I understood that if Anthony Rawlings was having a bad day that I was having a bad day, probably worse. "Yes. I didn't mean to pull away."

My cheek burned with the slap of his hand. "Don't think that you can pacify me with lies. I want the truth from you. You meant to step back—it wasn't done on accident. Admit your mistakes and I won't need to punish you for them."

Tears threatened to stream as I faced his rage. Though every muscle in my body wanted to turn away and run, I knew that wasn't an option. I stood resolute as his anger spilled forth. My

choice of clothing was inconsequential in the equation of the day.
As I stood before him, with his business associate still on hold, he
told me to undress.

I did.

Phil hated the damn book. He'd done enough research to know
that Rawlings and Claire had an unusual relationship, especially in
the beginning. However, he'd also spent a lot of time with the two of
them and knew that what he was reading was not what he'd
witnessed. Yet he also knew the book was based on truth. He'd been
around each time Claire and Meredith met.

The topic also came up during a recent meeting with Mr.
Rawlings and Brent Simmons at Rawlings' office. Once they were all
seated, Rawlings was the first to speak.

"I've reached a plea agreement with the prosecutor."

Phil nodded.

Tony continued, "I know you probably have the opportunity for
more exciting jobs than watching the Vandersols with Nichol and
trying to learn about Claire, but I called you here to ask you to keep
working for me."

Phil considered reminding him that he actually worked for
Claire, but there was a tiredness about Rawlings' demeanor that
stilled his words. For the first time since he'd met him, Phil felt a
pang of sadness at Tony's weary expression. He wasn't the
domineering man who'd hired him to find and trail his ex-wife. No
longer was he the man who had all the answers or made all of the
decisions. He seemed older. Phil was glad he'd decided not to share
the information about Harrison Baldwin's visit. He wasn't sure
Rawlings could've taken it.

Trying to lighten the somber mood, Phil responded with a

slight grin, "I wasn't planning on stopping, even if you told me you wanted me to."

Though his eyes didn't join the party, Tony smiled back. "Thank you. It'll be easier being away knowing that you're watching over both of them."

"Do you know how long you'll be *away*?"

Brent answered, "The length of incarceration can change depending on circumstances in prison, but the current agreement is for four years, minus time served."

Four years. Phil had enough criminal knowledge to know that something had changed. Even after Rawlings was cleared of helping Catherine with her poisoning deaths, there was still Simon Johnson's murder. It was murder for hire, but he'd admitted to it. Phil doubted that even Anthony Rawlings could get a life sentence reduced to four years.

"I'll be honest: I thought it would be longer," Phil replied. "What happened?"

Brent responded, "The FBI dropped the murder charge for Simon Johnson. They said that the NTSB found no signs of tampering with Simon's plane. Since Tony confessed to making the contact with the intent to murder, the murder charge was reduced to conspiracy, a second-degree felony. Tony also admitted to supplying Catherine with the money for one known hit—that was the second conspiracy charge. Due to his cooperation with prosecuting Catherine and turning state's evidence, those two charges were negotiated to time served and a hefty fine."

Phil looked puzzled. "Then what's with the four years?"

"Kidnapping and sexual assault," Tony said matter-of-factly.

Brent corrected, "Kidnapping is the only charge that's standing."

Phil sat straighter. "I know Claire isn't pressing charges. It's the book, isn't it?"

"Yes," Tony replied. "The state of Iowa can't stand the persecution it's getting over the case. Besides the Vandersols, there are victims' rights groups going nuts."

Brent added, "Tony hasn't read the book. His admission is not to all of the contents, publicly, only that he took Claire from Georgia and brought her to Iowa without her consent. Crossing state lines makes it a federal offense."

"The sexual assault charges?" Phil asked.

"There's a statute that states the exception to the third degree class C felony is if the act is between persons who are at the time cohabitating as husband and wife. The book doesn't claim anything nonconsensual happening until Claire was living in Tony's house. I argued that they did become husband and wife—twice. Without physical evidence or Claire's testimony, they let that charge drop, as long as he admitted to the kidnapping. The law has varying options for sentencing with kidnapping. Since Claire was an adult, not sold into human trafficking, and there's record of Tony compensating her for her time with the paying of her debts, the court agreed to a lesser sentence. Tony's lack of criminal record also helped in reducing the penalty. However, there's also a hefty fine."

Phil nodded. Looking at Tony, he said, "If I didn't know you and witness the two of you in the South Pacific, I'd want to kill you right now. I still kind of do. I sure as hell hope that book has been sensationalized and it's not an accurate account of what happened."

Tony shrugged, his confident demeanor temporarily gone. "I haven't read it, but apparently I'm the only one in the room who can say that." His dark eyes glanced toward Brent.

"I have a job to do," Brent said.

The hairs on the back of Phil's neck stood to attention. The words from Claire's book came rushing back. *You have a job to do. Do it!*

Brent went on, "I can't defend you if I don't know what I'm up against. And as much as I'm your friend..." he turned to Phil, "...I think I'd help you hide the body."

Tony shook his head. "I told her not to talk to Meredith." He looked toward Phil. "Remember?" His domineering voice returned with conviction. "This whole damn thing started in San Diego. I should have put an end to it then. I should have had you stop the meeting before I ever got there."

Phil casually leaned back against the chair and crossed his arms over his chest. Tony was obviously on some unbalanced emotional roller coaster. "I believe this *whole damn thing* began in a bar in Georgia, or before, if I understood her laptop."

Tony glared. "The information on the laptop about the Rawls family doesn't need to be public. I've got enough shit out there."

"You do have enough shit to spread far and wide," Brent said. "But as far as keeping it private, I think you'd better focus on damage control. Catherine hasn't been keeping her mouth shut. Tom's been working his ass off on gag orders regarding her case. The whole world is going to know your family's name."

Tony shook his head and pinched the bridge of his nose. "My family's name is *Rawlings*. Claire and Nichol Rawlings—they're my family. I'm doing all of this so that I can get them back, so there won't be any damn skeletons waiting around to shock their world. Do you really think I'd put myself through all of this if it weren't for them?"

Nodding, Phil replied, "That's why you're not dead." Turning to Brent, he asked, "Will Rawlings' plea be done in a closed court?"

"Yes, however, the judge is allowing special dispensation."

"I want to be there."

Tony's dark gaze returned Phil's way. "What the hell for?"

With his arms on the table, Phil squared his shoulders. "Because I have a job to do and I'm going to do it. My job is to protect Claire. I'm the one who took you to her. I won't stop doing my job. I want to see this for myself. Don't get me wrong, I can hack the courthouse records and read it, but I want to hear it. I want to know I did the right thing getting you two back together. If I didn't, I might have to reconsider my next assignment."

Brent's eyes opened wide and he looked at Tony. When Tony nodded, Brent replied, "Well, all right. I'll see what I can do."

Tony leaned across the table. "I know you have her best interest at heart. I've seen that. But don't fuck'n threaten me again."

Undeterred, Phil closed the gap. "I do have her best interest at heart, as well as Nichol's. *No one* is going to hurt them: you don't need to worry about that. And..." he paused, "...it wasn't a threat."

Tony inhaled and sat taller. "Brent will be your contact until you can talk with me. The prison is minimum-security. Once I'm settled, you can again report directly to me. Brent will be the one paying you and your expenses."

"We have a deal."

FOR A CLOSED hearing, the courtroom had more than a few people watching from the galley. As Phil made his way to a seat, he heard Emily whisper to John, "What's *he* doing here?"

"I don't know, but as long as he's on the list, he can be here,"

John replied, sitting next to his wife in the galley. The current charges were being filed on behalf of the United States. Grinning smugly, Phil nodded and sat a few rows behind them. Obviously, nearing the end of her pregnancy, Emily was much larger than the last time Phil had seen her. It amazed him how fast pregnant women changed. The last few times he'd watched Nichol from afar, she was with a nanny. Although, that made it easier for Phil to go unnoticed, he worried about her safety. Most of his observation of the Vandersols was electronic. Smirking, Phil thought about their private text messages. He'd learned many things: he knew they were having a boy and that Claire was being moved to a private facility in Cedar Rapids called Everwood.

He watched them from his vantage point. Although Emily's hair was shorter, seeing her, with her hand resting on her enlarged midsection, reminded Phil of Claire. The private facility where they'd gotten her admitted had outstanding ratings, a great reputation, and phenomenal security. Phil wholeheartedly approved. Of course, he'd also already infiltrated their data. They'd started some preliminary tests on Claire. Despite the inconclusive results, Phil planned on knowing what they did, when they did it.

Emily and Nichol had moved out of the hotel suite and rented a home outside of Cedar Rapids. John was commuting from California as often as he could. Since the charges had been dropped, John's legal acumen was no longer needed. He mostly visited on weekends, but Phil wasn't surprised when he learned that he'd be traveling to Iowa for this hearing. Jane Allyson was also present. She was sitting to John's right. Being as he and Jane weren't involved in the current legal proceedings, Phil was curious to see their reaction to Rawlings' negotiated sentence. There hadn't been any correspondence between the two of them indicating that they were in the know.

Ahead and on Phil's right was Courtney Simmons. Before he'd made his presence known, he saw Courtney speaking with Emily and assessed that it must be a difficult position for her. She obviously wanted to support her friend and her husband's boss, but if she were to maintain a relationship with Nichol, she also needed to stay in Emily's good graces. Since that was more than Phil had been able to do, he was glad she'd made some headway. There were others from Rawlings Industries with Courtney. Phil knew their names, but other than their job titles, he wasn't familiar with them. There was Tom Miller, legal, Tim Benson, acting CEO, and Patricia, Tony's personal assistant.

One of the last people to enter caught Phil by surprise. It was Harrison Baldwin, accompanied by an older gentleman. Harrison nodded in Phil's direction as they found two empty seats behind the Vandersols. Emily appeared pleased to see Harry. Well, wasn't this a fun group.

The small courtroom filled to capacity as the prosecution, Marcus Evergreen, and the US Attorney came from a closed door and made their way to one table, and the defense, Brent and Tony, followed behind and made their way to the other. Tony's gaze assessed the crowd, stopped momentarily on Baldwin, and then shifted to the front of the courtroom. In his customary thousand-dollar suit, Rawlings didn't look like a man about to head to prison. He looked more like the CEO he was known to be. The courtroom fell silent as the judge entered, followed by the clerk.

Shattering the palpable stillness, the clerk announced, "The honorable Judge Jefferies presiding…"

Judge Jefferies didn't waste any time. After some directions to the attorneys, he said, "Mr. Rawlings, in the matter of the United States versus Anthony Rawlings, how do you plead?"

Standing, Tony glanced at Brent, turned toward the bench, and proclaimed, "Guilty, Your Honor."

Judge Jefferies asked, "Counsel, have you reached a settlement?"

The US Attorney replied, "Yes, Your Honor. The people have agreed to four years in a minimum-security federal prison camp, minus time served, $75,000 in fines, and probation."

Emily gasped and turned to John and Jane. In a stage whisper she asked, "Tell me that isn't all that he's getting. Tell me there's more."

John reached for her hand and silently tried to soothe her.

Judge Jefferies continued, "Mr. Rawlings, do you know that by pleading guilty you lose the right to a jury trial?"

"Yes, Your Honor."

"Do you give up that right?"

Tony never wavered, "Yes, Your Honor."

"Do you understand what giving up that right means?"

"Yes."

"Do you know that you are waiving the right to cross-examine your accusers?"

Tony replied, "Yes."

Judge Jefferies continued his questions, "Do you know that you are waiving your privilege against self-incrimination?"

"Yes."

"Did anyone force you into accepting this settlement?"

"No. No one forced me."

"You are being charged with two counts of conspiracy to commit murder and one count of kidnapping. Are you pleading guilty because you in fact conspired to kill Allyson Burke Bradley and Simon Johnson?"

"Yes."

"Are you also pleading guilty because you in fact transported Claire Nichols across state lines without her knowledge or consent?"

"Yes."

"From where to where did you transport Ms. Nichols?"

"From Georgia to Iowa, Your Honor."

Emily's shoulders shuddered as the proceedings continued.

"Did you know that what you were doing was illegal?"

Tony's shoulders lifted and fell, but his chin remained high. "Yes, Your Honor."

Judge Jefferies concluded, "Mr. Rawlings, you are hereby sentenced to four years in a minimum-security federal prison camp. I am also making the recommendation that while incarcerated you attend counseling with a state-appointed therapist. While not at the suggestion of the counsel, I believe it would be an excellent use of your time and helpful for your future. Upon completion of your sentence, you will serve two years' probation. Is that clear?"

"Yes, Your Honor."

"Do you have any questions before we adjourn?"

"No, Your Honor."

Judge Jefferies addressed the attorneys, "Any further questions or comments, Counselors?"

"No, Your Honor," came from both tables.

"Mr. Rawlings, as agreed upon, your sentence will begin immediately." Addressing the courtroom, "Ladies and gentlemen, you were permitted to attend this closed hearing. Be aware that it was closed for a reason. Any information regarding this hearing that is released to the press without the written approval of this court will be evidence to hold you in contempt." Hitting his gavel, Judge Jefferies proclaimed, "We are adjourned."

Phil watched as Tony shook Brent's hand, leaned across the bar and hugged Courtney, and was then led away by the waiting bailiff.

Once the judge and Tony were gone from the courtroom, the people from Rawlings murmured amongst themselves as Patricia dabbed her eyes.

Emily's voice rose above the whispers. "How could you?" she asked Marcus Evergreen. "With all of the charges against him, how could you agree to four years? What happened to sexual assault? What happened to murder? Allyson Bradley is dead! Simon Johnson is dead!"

Chapter 13

June 2014

John

***Take the first step in faith. You don't have to see the
whole staircase, just take the first step.***
—Martin Luther King, Jr.

"AND YOU!" EMILY growled toward Brent. "You claim to be Claire's
friend. How could you in good conscience defend him?" She pulled
her arm from John's grasp. "I'm not stopping. I want answers!"

"Not. Here," John implored.

Jane whispered, "Emily, this is a conversation to be conducted
in private." Turning to Marcus, she asked, "Mr. Evergreen, could we
possibly enter a private room and discuss what occurred?"

"I'll see what I can find," Marcus said as he closed his briefcase
and stepped away.

Emily's moist green eyes peered up at her husband, but it
wasn't sadness that he saw: it was full-out rage. Though they'd
discussed Anthony's pending charges *ad nauseam,* they'd never
come to a conclusion like the one they just witnessed. "It will be all
right. At least he isn't free. Four years is a long time."

"Not long enough, not after what he's done to my family. I don't understand. How could this happen?"

"I found a room," Marcus announced.

"Brent and Courtney?" John asked. When they both looked his way, he said, "For Nichol's sake, would you join us? It won't change the outcome, but it may help us better understand."

Courtney looked to her husband and nodded. Brent replied, "Yes."

Courtney was the one who added, "Thank you for asking. Please know, we'd do anything for Nichol and for Claire."

Courtney squeezed Patricia's hand as she and the others filed from the room. Before leaving, Tim came up to John. "I know this isn't a good time, but I'd like to discuss something with you, when you can."

John looked questionably at Tim. "If it's about the things we've said about Anthony—"

Tim shook his head and interrupted, "Not directly, but I'd like to talk to you. I guess I could say it's indirectly about Claire."

At the mention of her sister's name, Emily looked their direction. She'd been shaking her head and twisting from side to side as she spoke quietly with Harry.

"This way," Jane announced. "We don't have the room for long."

Tim handed John his card. "Please call and hear me out..." His eyes widened. "...for Claire."

John took the card. "For Claire," he repeated as he placed the card in his jacket pocket. Taking Emily's hand, he gave it a squeeze and walked with her to the small conference room. As they neared, he whispered in her ear, "Please, hear them out."

Inhaling deeply, she pressed her lips together and nodded.

The table only had six chairs as Marcus, Brent, Courtney, Jane, John, and Emily made their way to seats. John began. "Thank you for discussing this with us. I hope you can understand my wife's outrage as well as our disbelief in what just happened. Mr. Evergreen, could you please explain to us the charges and how the plea agreement was reached."

"Many things were taken into consideration. This is part of the closed negotiations. I'm sure you're aware of the gag order."

"We are," John answered. "However, our special dispensation allows us—"

Brent interjected, "I believe everyone present is aware of the importance of confidentiality."

"Yes," Emily murmured. "We'd hate for the great Anthony Rawlings to have more bad press."

John silenced her with his stare. "Thank you, Brent. We want to understand what happened and how it happened."

Evergreen began, "Many of these crimes have been under investigation by the FBI for a long time. Although the use of actaea pachypoda is highly unusual, it's been documented in the death and poisoning of individuals who were initially thought to be related in some way to Anthony Rawlings. With his help, it was discovered that although he was connected, he wasn't the culprit. As you know, it was—"

"Catherine London," John answered.

"Yes, I can't go into specifics, but Mr. Rawlings was instrumental in helping them put the pieces of the case together. Prior to their return from the South Pacific, Mr. and Mrs. Rawlings had worked out a deal with the FBI."

Emily covered her mouth, stifling the sound of her gasp.

"There was no money trail for the FBI or the Iowa City police to follow that specifically connected Mr. Rawlings with Allyson Bradley's death. The only information they had was his confession. The same can be said about Simon Johnson. And although they had his confession, it couldn't be substantiated by physical evidence. Mr. Rawlings admitted to paying for a crime. He paid to have Simon Johnson's plane sabotaged. The NTSB verified that the plane was in perfect flying condition. Mr. Rawlings' hit man didn't do his job."

"Then why did Simon crash?" Emily asked.

"I don't know. If the FBI knows, they aren't saying."

"Okay, so that's why the murder charges were reduced to conspiracy. What about the sexual assault?" John asked.

Brent answered, "Again, there was lack of evidence. The court can't use a book as evidence without physical evidence or Claire's testimony."

Jane replied, "There was testimony, during her 2012 defense. She told us all about it. I took it to *you*." She nodded toward Marcus Evergreen.

"That testimony was not made in a court of law or under oath. It can't hold up in court."

"This is ridiculous," Emily sighed.

"That isn't all," Brent added. "In Iowa, there's a statute that nullifies the charge if the two individuals are living together as husband and wife. The book claims that the assault occurred while Claire was living with Tony, in his house. And they later became husb—"

Emily interjected, "*In his house*, where he'd kidnapped her and taken her against her will. Where he'd trapped her!"

Marcus spoke calmly, "Mrs. Vandersol, that leads us to the most serious charge that Mr. Rawlings faced: kidnapping and transporting across state lines. As you know it's a federal offense..."

He went on to explain how he fought to keep that charge above everything.

"But *four* years?" John asked. "As a federal offense it can be punishable by up to twenty years, in some cases, life."

Marcus replied, "There are many different stipulations that go along with kidnapping. Ms. Nichols was not a minor. There's a stiffer penalty with minors. She was not sold into human trafficking. That too has a stiffer penalty. By her own admission, she had opportunities to flee and didn't."

"Because she was scared." Tears coated Emily's cheeks in a visible display of her frustration. She turned to Courtney. "You were her friend during that time. You know she was scared, don't you?"

Courtney sat forward. "Emily, I had a feeling—a gut feeling— that something wasn't right. Please know that I did, and still do love your sister. I asked her over and over if there was a problem. She never once told me there was." She paused. "Well, not until later, after she was out of jail."

"Jail!" John said. "What about filing a false report? Claire didn't try to kill Anthony, yet she served fourteen months."

Marcus cleared his throat. "The state of Iowa is responsible for that. I won't admit to that publicly so don't ask me to. But honestly, Mr. Rawlings woke in the hospital not knowing who poisoned him. The evidence, including video evidence, all supported that it was Mrs. Rawlings."

Emily shook her head. "So that's it. He pays $75,000, which to him is like pocket change, and he gets a slap on the wrist."

"He confessed. He pled guilty," Brent reminded her. "If he hadn't, he would be free right now and exercising his rights as a free man."

Emily's green eyes opened wide. "He's not getting to my sister or my niece. Not now, and not in four years. I didn't protect her in 2010. I will now."

"Thank you. Thank you for explaining this all to us. We're not happy, but at least we understand." John's words were the dismissal for the meeting. Slowly, everyone rose from their seats, murmured their goodbyes and silently made their way out of the courthouse into the hot, sunny Iowa afternoon and through the throng of reporters.

"Mrs. Vandersol, could you give us a statement?"

"Mr. Vandersol, how do you feel about Mr. Rawlings' sentence?"

"Did he really plead guilty?"

"Mr. Simmons, tell us how your client feels..."

No one replied as they made their way to their cars.

NICHOL ROCKED BACK and forth on her knees as she giggled and inched forward toward the brightly colored toy in front of her. A little progress and she was back to her tummy, arms and legs flailing in glee. With single-minded determination, she made the distance and reached for the soft black and red rattle. Once it was hers, she took it straight to her lips, her little jaw moving up and down.

"I think she's teething," Emily said.

"I thought babies were fussy when they teethed," replied John.

"Becca said she had trouble going down for her nap, but since she woke, she's been great."

John scooped her from the floor and brought her to his lap.

Contently, she chewed on her prized possession, until it fell from her grasp. Kicking her legs she arched her body in protest. As her cheeks reddened, John asked, "Whom do you think she gets that strong will from?"

Sighing, Emily leaned back and massaged her enlarged midsection. "I'd say both of them. Did you know that they'd worked together on a deal with the FBI?"

"No. I knew they didn't pursue the aiding and abetting charge, but I didn't realize there was an FBI connection."

"Do you think they were really happy..." Her voice trailed away and then regained strength. "...wherever they were in the South Pacific?"

John shrugged. "I don't see how. I mean, the more I read—"

"I told you not to."

"I know. I'm not rushing through it, although I should, to get it over with. But I read it while flying. I just read about the first time she was *allowed* to call us. It was your birthday. Do you remember that?"

Tears descended as she managed to say, "I do. I was so happy to hear from her. If only I'd known..."

John moved to pull Emily into his arms. "I know... I'm so sorry we didn't know... Courtney was right. Claire never told anyone."

Emily nodded. "I hate that he got off so easy."

"I was incarcerated. Trust me: he isn't getting off easy."

"Unless someone beats him into unconsciousness, I think it's too easy."

John shrugged. "Well, if he pisses off the wrong people—"

Emily grinned. "You're just trying to make me feel better!"

After dinner, John settled at his desk in the study and looked at Tim's business card, the one he'd been given earlier today. It was lying innocently on the desk... pleading for attention. Truly, John was curious as to what Tim wanted to say. Though the card had only his business numbers, in pen, Tim had added his personal cell number. John punched the number into his phone.

Contemplating the conversation he'd just had, John made his way through the house and found Emily lying on their bed, hands over her enlarged midsection, with her eyes closed. She looked so peaceful that John hated to disturb her. As he was about to walk away, her eyes fluttered open. "I thought you were sleeping," he said softly.

"No, I was just enjoying our little man's tap dance."

John's smile broadened as he made his way to the bed and placed his hand next to Emily's. "I felt him! Man, he's really moving."

Emily nodded. "He is."

"Is Nichol asleep?"

"I think so. I just put her down a few minutes ago. She was pretty tired." Emily glanced toward the baby monitor on the bedside stand. "I haven't heard a peep out of her."

"Are you ready for *two* babies?"

Emily shrugged with a tired grin. "I'm ready for Michael to make his appearance, and after the last three months, I couldn't imagine not having Nichol. So I think the answer is yes."

"I love her too, but you know, she does have parents."

Emily brushed a tear from her eye. "These stupid hormones have me all emotional."

"You don't think maybe it was the day. I mean it's been pretty stressful. I think you need to get some sleep."

"With everything going on with Anthony's hearing, I forgot to tell you about my visit with Claire yesterday."

John scooted up to the headboard and pulled his wife closer.

With her head on his shoulder and both of their hands on her midsection, Emily continued, "I like her doctor: she's not only compassionate but incredibly intelligent. They're trying some different things."

"Like what?"

"Well, they asked me a lot of questions: like what does she like to do in her spare time? It occurred to me that I didn't know. I could tell them things she *used* to like to do, but I discovered the sad truth: I don't know my sister anymore." More tears blurred the room. "When we decided to move to California, before we knew about Nichol, I had such high hopes. I thought Claire and Harry seemed happy. I imagined all of us being a family one day." She took a ragged breath. "It's all *his* fault. Everything is his fault. Now, we're not together as a family—even us. I miss having you around. But I can't leave her..."

John held her shuddering shoulders as Emily's tears dampened his shirt.

Smoothing his wife's hair, John said, "Tim Bronson gave me his card today, just before he left the courtroom. He asked me to call him."

"Why?"

"I was curious, too."

Emily looked up. "You *were*? Does that mean you called him?"

"I did. I just got off the phone. That's why I came to find you. I wanted to talk to you about his offer."

"His offer? Does he want to bribe you to stop saying things about Anthony? I've been watching Rawlings Industries stock numbers. The company's taken a hit."

"Is that really what we want?"

Emily shook her head. "I don't know. I want *him* to suffer."

"You do realize that it's not just *him*: there are the thousands and thousands of employees, and more importantly, there's Claire and Nichol."

"What are you saying?"

John continued, "Tim offered me a job."

Emily's eyes opened wide as she studied her husband. "You're serious, aren't you? You said you'd never work for Anthony. You said you wouldn't even work for one of his subsidiaries, no matter how far down the food chain."

Shrugging, he continued, "I didn't say yes, but I didn't say no. The thing is that he approached it from the standpoint of helping Claire and Nichol. Rawlings Industries is Nichol's legacy. There's no doubt that I hate Anthony Rawlings, but you have to admit that when it comes to financial support of Claire, her medical bills, treatment, anything, he's offered unlimited funds. The same can be said about Nichol's care. I know the money for her is in a trust, but helping to rebuild Rawlings Industries would assure their financial future. Hell, I can't even get Claire to make eye contact with me. This is something I could do, and as a bonus, I'd live in Iowa with you, Michael, and Nichol. This traveling back and forth to Palo Alto is getting old."

"What about SiJo?"

"I feel bad about leaving Amber, but I suspect she'd understand. I started a new position at SiJo and got it up and running. She could definitely get someone else with more experience in gaming. Really, since everything went down here, my heart hasn't been in it."

Emily laid her head back and grinned. "Oh, did you feel that kick?"

John chuckled. "I'm thinking soccer or football player."

"I'm thinking *no*," she giggled. "What about Nichol?"

"What about Nichol? Are you kidding? She's got the world on a string."

"You know what I want for both of the children?" Emily asked.

"What?"

"I want them to be happy and normal. None of this vendetta crap. None of the hatred that's consumed too many lives. I just want them to be kids."

John sighed. "Maybe working for Rawlings is the first step."

"It sounds like you've already made up your mind."

"I really haven't. I'm going to meet with Tim and discuss it further."

"When?"

"We're going to meet for lunch tomorrow. I fly back to Palo Alto on Sunday," John added wearily.

"I'm taking Nichol to Everwood tomorrow," Emily said. "Doctor Brown believes that if we have Claire in a more home-like environment with Nichol, it could help to trigger some memories."

John nodded. "That makes sense."

"Yes, they're trying other things. Mostly, I like how they're getting her up, out of bed, and out of a chair. I hated that other place. They just put her in a wheelchair and moved her around. She's capable of walking. I remembered her stories about hiking and gardening here at his estate."

"It's hers, too." He reminded her.

"I told them she liked the outside," Emily continued. "So they've added that to her schedule."

John yawned. "I'll get over there before I head back to California. I already like the way they take care of her better at Everwood."

Emily cuddled against his side. "I think you should be open-minded about the job offer. Make sure it's sincere and not just a ploy to keep us from telling the world the truth."

"The court's limited us on what we can say about the legal proceedings, but I get what you're saying."

"I think it could be good too. I liked all of those people when we first met them."

"At Claire's first wedding," John said.

"I know I shouldn't blame them for not knowing what was happening any more than I can blame us."

John hugged Emily again as she closed her eyes and her breathing became steady. They weren't dressed for bed, but he couldn't bring himself to nudge her awake. He wanted this. He wanted to be able to cuddle and talk—not on the phone and from across the country. Could he look past the name on the letterhead? Could he work for Rawlings Industries—at corporate? Obviously, the company was successful and substantial, but was it legitimate? All the things Anthony has done personally: what if John got into the legalities of Rawlings Industries and found skeletons? Then again, what if he didn't?

What if he could come home every night to Emily and the kids? What if he could help assure Claire and Nichol's financial future? So many questions swirled as his eyes closed.

Chapter 14

Summer 2014

Tony

———❖———

It is not the strongest of the species that survives, nor the most intelligent that survives. It is the one that is most adaptable to change.
—Charles Darwin

NOTHING COULD HAVE prepared Tony for incarceration in the federal prison camp in Yankton, South Dakota. Perhaps, to the experienced prisoner, or even from the outside, it was lovely, better than most. After all, it had only been a federal prison since 1988. From the outside, it still looked like the small, private, liberal arts college that it had once been. Most buildings were on the historical register and bore the names of alumni and benefactors. The grounds were beautiful with flowers, trees, and well-manicured grass. There wasn't even a fence around the perimeter. Nevertheless, it was a prison.

Tony's legal department had done their research: not only was Yankton relatively close to Iowa City, it was said to be one of the best all-male, minimum-security prisons in the United States. As most of the prisoners there were convicted of nonviolent crimes, it took some negotiation from the Rawlings' legal team to secure Tony a spot in the highly sought-after facility. A large subsection of inmates were middle-aged men who'd been convicted of *white-collar* crimes. Anthony Rawlings wasn't the only successful entrepreneur on the grounds. Brent and Tom had hoped that would help Tony's transition. It didn't.

Undergraduate school at NYU was the last time Tony had shared a room with another man apart from his travels through Europe while on the run from the FBI. During that time, he'd stayed in a few hostels with large shared-sleeping areas, but this was different. At Yankton, the inmates didn't have private or even semi-private rooms. Prisoners slept in dormitories that in some ways reminded him of Blair Academy, only a million times worse. These rooms had beds, lockers, and desks. All the beds were bunked with an unspoken understanding that the eldest bunkmate received the prized lower bunk. Some of the dormitories held sixty men. Thankfully, Tony's only held twenty, which was still nineteen more than he wanted.

Over the years he'd heard how these minimum-security prisons were just country clubs for the wealthy criminals. Anyone who said that had never been behind the walls. Though he'd researched the prison camp before he arrived, he wasn't prepared. He remembered that most testimonials stated that the first few days were the most difficult. He hoped that was true. His first day was filled with interviews and screenings, but as Tony received his khaki shirt, khaki pants, cumbersome shoes, underwear, and bedding, the reality was overwhelming. There was no doubt that the next four years of his life would be drastically different from any of the first forty-nine. Not only did he yearn for the life he'd left behind, but his heart also ached for the time Claire had lost behind similar walls.

During the mental-health screening, Tony agreed to anger-management counseling. Before he was transported to Yankton, Brent told him that Judge Jefferies' recommendation had truly been a gift. Since it wasn't court-mandated, Tony's willingness to undergo therapy would look good on his record and help when his case came up for review. Though parole wasn't offered in federal penitentiaries, there was always hope of early release. After only hours as a number, not a full name, Tony knew he'd do whatever it took to make an early release a reality.

As if sleeping in a room with nineteen other men wasn't difficult enough, he soon learned about *counts*. Counts happened every day at 12:01 AM, 3:00 AM, 5:00 AM, 10:00 AM, 4:00 PM, and 10:00 PM. The last two were *standing counts*. During a standing count each man was required to stand unmoving by his bunk while the correctional officer counted inmates. With wake-up being every day at 5:50 AM, Tony wondered why they couldn't wait until then to do the count. Heaven knows that lights coming on and a correctional officer walking bunk to bunk three times in the middle of the night was not conducive to a good night's sleep.

The other men in his unit didn't care who he was outside any more than he cared who they were. Each man was cordial and respectful, yet not overly communicative. That was until evenings: most of the men thrived on television time. From 4:30 PM until midnight, the television was on. Never being much of a television watcher, the incessant noise—*every* night—wore on him as much as the stupid counts.

Sleeping wasn't the only activity that was communal. Showering, too, was done by unit. As the first week progressed, it seemed that each hour was worse than the one before. As his old life slipped further and further away, the therapy seemed like a good idea.

Besides his thrice a week counseling sessions, Tony, like every other inmate, was required to hold a job. Not only was he responsible for cleaning his part of the dormitory, he had an actual *job*. Every day after breakfast, Anthony Rawlings, Number 01657-3452, reported to the warehouse, where he unpacked supplies from delivery trucks. That bit of manual labor earned him $0.17 an hour. Hadn't this place heard of minimum wage?

The money he earned, plus money he had sent to him, allowed him to purchase non-issued supplies. That was everything from headphones and an MP3 player to drown out the incessant television, to shampoo and additional clothing. Though Tony could have unlimited money sent to his account, there was a $320.00 per month spending limit. He almost choked when he read that. Hell, he'd spent more than that on a haircut.

In an effort to avoid the dormitory, Tony signed up for educational services. He'd always appreciated education, but as a man with an MBA, he wasn't interested in a GED. The subject he chose to study was horticulture. It reminded him of Claire. As he learned to care for the plants on Yankton's grounds, he'd remember her chatter about the flowers and plants on the estate. Just being outdoors, with his hands in the soil, made him feel closer to her. While learning about or tending to some plant, Tony would think about Claire and hope that she was doing well enough to be doing the same. He knew how much she loved the outdoors and believed that if she were outside, it would give her strength.

The schedule included time to exercise, and, during the allotted time, a quarter-mile track was frequented by the inmates. While many used the track as a time to talk with a little more privacy,

Tony's playlist kept him occupied. Purchasing music was one of his bigger expenses. To occupy his mind, he had the Wall Street Journal, as well as other business publications delivered, and he was allowed a minimum amount of Internet time. The Internet as well as phone calls were monitored, but they were a connection to the outside world. As days turned to weeks and weeks to months, the routine became easier to handle.

Tony recalled Claire's description of prison, saying that it was very *routine*. He could add lonely, boring, and other adjectives, but routine was accurate. In the first few months of incarceration, Tony learned that not only could he make rules, he could follow them. He didn't like it, but each message from Courtney about Nichol, from Roach about Claire, from Patricia about Rawlings Industries, or Brent about his sentence gave him the substance and stamina to continue.

The best and worst days of the week were weekends and holidays. Those were the days when visitors could visit Yankton. Upon his arrival to the prison camp, Tony was required to compile a list of friends and family who could visit. The list was then verified and approved by the prison. Tony knew that there were people on his list who would probably never visit, but he added them anyway. His list included Brent (although as his attorney he had additional license to visit), Courtney, Tim, Patricia, Roach, Claire, Nichol, John, and Emily.

He doubted that John and Emily would ever bring Nichol to see him, but he wanted the option available to them if they decided to come. Tony wasn't sure about Claire, but believed that she would get better. When she did, he prayed she'd come to see him. He even fantasized about her visiting, especially on days he had no visitors. When the weather was warm, there was outside seating for visits.

Seeing the other inmates with their spouses and children was probably the worse punishment Tony endured.

Utilizing the Rawlings' jets, people could get to Tony in less than an hour. There was a small municipal airport not far from the prison. Driving would have been over five hours, and flying commercially meant another hour's drive from Sioux City, the closest international airport.

By law, inmates were allowed four hours a month of visitation. However, it was the belief of the prison that visitors were good for the inmates' morale. Therefore, contingent upon available space— every visitor and inmate were required to have a chair—visits were granted. They had to be planned ahead and approved. Brent and Courtney visited every three weeks, like clockwork. Roach came at least once a month, and Tim or Patricia alternated their visits. It was without a doubt the highlight to Tony's week.

Besides visiting, Courtney was the best about sending letters. They were usually just little notes about nothing. When one would arrive it was impossible to keep the smile from Tony's face.

Occasionally, something would occur that the visits didn't happen. Those were dark, colorless days.

Autumn came a little earlier in South Dakota than it did in Iowa. By early September the days as well as the nights had begun to chill. In Tony's horticulture class he learned about hardy, weather-resistant flowers. After Labor Day, they removed the summer's flowers and planted mums. He'd seen them before but never paid them any attention. Throughout the prison's campus yellow, orange, and deep red mums added color.

Tony's counseling had progressed beyond insignificant discussions about Tony's adaptation to Yankton. His therapist wasn't a doctor but a counselor named Jim. At first, Tony wasn't sure what to think about Jim other than he wasn't very talkative for a therapist. Tony had always imagined that therapy was where the therapist told the patient what his or her problems were and what to do about them. He knew his problems: he was stuck in a prison while his wife was in a mental facility and their daughter was living with his brother- and sister-in-law whom he hated. Of course, it took Tony weeks to divulge even that much. He had a personal rule about sharing private information. Speaking to Jim about Tony's private life, outside of Yankton, seemed like a violation of his own rule.

Speaking about prison life, however, was acceptable. That was how they started each session. But they'd been at this now for months and the mundane was getting to be that and more.

"Anthony, how are things going?" Jim asked. Tony liked that Jim referred to him solely by his name. The correctional officers as well as any announcements or call outs always included the inmate's name and number. It didn't take long for Tony to tire of hearing *Rawlings, Number 01657-3452.*

He shrugged. "As well as can be expected, I suppose."

Jim waited. When Tony didn't offer any more he went on, "Why? What did you expect?"

"I don't know. I thought I could handle it better."

"What do you mean?"

"I hate it—every minute." He stood and paced to the window and back. It was the only place where he could freely get up and move while with a member of the prison staff. That realization struck him. "Like this! I can't even fuck'n do this."

"What?" Jim asked. "What are you doing that you can't do?"

"Just move, walk, pace, whatever. I've been trying these last few months, but I don't think I can make it another forty-four months.

Damn, that sounds like forever." He collapsed into the chair before Jim's desk.

"Why?"

Color came to Tony's cheeks as red threatened his vision. "You know, that drives me crazy."

"What?"

"That! If you're going to ask me questions for three hours a week, be more specific."

"Give me an example," Jim said.

Did he need to tell the therapist how to do his own job? "Instead of *why* or *what*, ask why I don't think I can make it or what drives me crazy—use complete sentences."

"Is that something you always do?"

Tony thought for a minute. "I think I do. I know I used to. Hell, I don't even know what I do anymore."

"How does that make you feel?"

"I feel like after only three months, I'm losing who I am. Just Saturday, my assistant was here to fill me in on things happening back at my work. I am totally out of the loop."

"Have you always been in the loop?"

"Up until a year ago, yes."

Jim put down his pencil. "What happened a year ago?"

"Surely you have my records, Jim. Surely you know my history. I mean, haven't you done your homework?"

"If I did, what would I know?"

Tony stood again and walked toward the window. "I hate this. I'm not the person I'm forced to be in here. I can't stand it."

"You weren't saying this Friday. What changed?"

Tony remembered Patricia's visit. She wasn't allowed to bring papers or her phone or anything back for the visit, so everything she said, she had to remember. She was telling him about some recent fluctuations in the stocks, and about a few changes on the administrative level of a recently acquired subsidiary, but instead of listening and following what she was saying, as he would have in the past, he was watching the inmate at the table next to them with his wife and two kids.

"Do you think kids should be allowed to visit here?" Tony asked.

Jim leaned back and took a deep breath. "I think that children can be a motivating factor for people to want to better themselves. Therefore, seeing that child is a reminder of why a person is trying to follow the rules and be a better person."

Tony contemplated his answer. "But for the kids," he asked, "won't it mess them up to be visiting their father in a prison?"

"What do you think?"

"I'm asking you."

"Anthony, are you used to getting your questions answered when you ask them?"

"Yes. I accept no less."

"Does the Anthony who lives outside of this prison get what he expects?"

"I-I..." he was about to say *I do*, but the reality of his life since he returned from paradise came crashing down. "I used to."

"How does it make you feel to not get what you expect?"

"It disappoints me. I don't like to be disappointed."

"We always talk about Yankton. You brought up a year ago... were you disappointed a year ago?"

Tony remembered a year ago. It was last September when Claire left, when his world fell apart. "Yes," he replied quieter.

"Was it something or someone who disappointed you?"

"I think I'm going to request a change in job. I mean, there are jobs in the business office. I have a lot to offer in an office."

Jim didn't argue Tony's change of subject. "What would you do? Clerical work?"

"Hell, no. I could do much more than that. I already have seen how poorly the supplies are managed by working in the warehouse. I think I could help them utilize..." Tony went on to describe his plan for supply logistics.

"Don't you think that any of the other inmates could do the same?"

"I'm sure they could, but they haven't."

"Why do you think that is?" Jim asked.

Tony thought about that. "I would assume that most people don't believe the prison truly wants to accentuate our abilities."

"Do you think that?"

"I don't know. I guess I want to find a reason to get up every day. I used to hate to sleep, like I was missing something. Now I would kill to get a good night's sleep."

Jim grinned. "As a rule of thumb, in a prison anger-management session, saying you'd kill isn't a good idea."

The tips of Tony's lips perked upward. "Yes, I didn't give that much thought. Perhaps it's my lack of sleep?"

"Between now and your next session, I have something I want you to do."

Jim had never asked Tony to do anything other than arrive on time. "What do you want?" he asked suspiciously.

"I want you to think about who or what disappointed you a year ago, and I want you to decide if you're going to trust me with that information. If you decide you're not going to trust me, I want to know why. Can you do that?"

He didn't want to do that. Tony didn't want to think about a year ago. He didn't want to remember how great he thought he and Claire had it at the estate, how she'd accepted his ring, how he thought she was safe. He didn't want to remember the crushing sadness at her disappearance or that it was Catherine who turned their world upside down. Not only did Tony not want to share that with Jim, he didn't want to share it with himself.

When he didn't answer, Jim asked again, "Anthony, can you do what I asked?"

Was failure an option? "I'll try."

Early Fall 2014

"MY LIFE AS It Didn't Appear, Chapter 6...

Actions have consequences. It was a phrase I heard over and over. There were negative consequences and positive consequences. Everything I did or said was evaluated: by Anthony, and by me. I found myself walking on egg-shells at every turn. It began the moment I woke, and ended after I finally fell asleep. I didn't want to fail: I couldn't fail. I learned very quickly that failure had consequences.

The physical punishments didn't continue with any kind of regularity after the first few weeks. They weren't necessary. Though I was being treated in many ways, like a small child, I wasn't. I was a college-educated adult who'd been placed in an extreme maze of operant conditioning. Something as simple as a look from Anthony's dark eyes could still my words. The slight grasp of his fingers, lifting my chin would bring me to submission. I didn't need or want to feel the slap of his hand. I learned the rules and strove to obey.

It was the fear of re-igniting his anger that continually weighed on me. There were days and weeks when his gaze remained light. Despite my circumstances, it was almost pleasurable living as I did during those times. I was still a prisoner, but one in a huge home with people to take care of my every need. And then, without the luxury of a warning rumble, the darkness would return."

"Stop there," Jim said.

Truly, Tony wanted to stop before he ever started. Working desperately to rein in the red, Tony placed the book on Jim's desk and walked toward the window. The damn view only reminded him that he was just like the other men he saw walking from place to place. He was wearing the same khaki clothes and living the same hell.

"Tell me what you're thinking," Jim implored.

"I'm thinking that I can't wait to wear another color."

"Really, after what you just read, that's what you're thinking?"

"Really," Tony answered stoically.

"Then think about what you just read."

Tony clenched his jaw, holding back the red that had just started to fade. "Are you trying to get me to explode? Is that your goal? Because I'm pretty sure you picked that fuck'n passage for a reason. Why don't you tell me what that was?"

"What made the *darkness* that Claire describes return?"

"I have no idea. She didn't give me a time frame. It said days or weeks. When the hell was that, exactly?"

"Well, we can assume it was early in her captivity. She said she was still a prisoner. She hasn't mentioned leaving the house. When did she do that?"

"Read the damn book. It will probably tell you."

"Anthony, how does this book make you feel?"

"You want to know? Fine, I'm so pissed I can hardly see straight. I'm pissed that it happened, and I'm pissed that she gave the fuck'n interview. This is private information. No one else needs to know any of this shit. Besides, it was a long time ago. Things change."

"When did they change?"

"Everything was different after she got out of prison. It was all different. The penalty was over. I could finally admit... Fuck!" Tony collapsed in the chair. "I don't know. It doesn't make sense."

"During those times of light, how did you feel about Claire?"

"I didn't. Not in the beginning. I didn't feel anything for her... she just was there. She had a job to do."

"Does that even make sense?"

Tony shrugged.

"Explain it to me," Jim said.

"I can't. It just is."

"We need to work on this. Think about it, until our next meeting."

"Think about what?"

"You watched your wife for years before you ever introduced yourself. You're telling me that when you first risked everything by kidnapping and keeping her held hostage in your home, that she meant nothing to you?"

"No—yes. You're messing up my words. She's always meant something to me. I love her."

"Did you then?"

"Now, I think I did. But then, I didn't think so."

"Would you do to her again what you did to her in 2010?" Jim asked.

Tony replied immediately, "No. I told you that. Everything was different."

"Because?"

"Everything was different because I couldn't do that to someone I love."

"But you did."

"I didn't know that I loved her."

Jim looked at the clock. "Our time is up. Think about this. Think about how you felt. Was that darkness she describes anger or control—or perhaps loss of control? Did you punish Claire when a business deal went south or was it because of something she did or said? Remember, you've told me how much you enjoyed her smart mouth during your second marriage. Yet during your first, you've admitted that you wouldn't have tolerated it. Could the reason that you lashed out be that you didn't want to admit your own feelings? Could it have been your way of keeping her as your possession and not becoming emotionally invested?"

Tony didn't want to think about it.

Chapter 15

October 2014

Harry

———◆———

Facts do not speak for themselves. They speak for or against competing theories.
—**Thomas Sowell**

THE RISING SUN cast a warm glow from behind the blinds as Harry slipped from the condominium. He needed time to think, and lying in bed next to Liz as soft breaths infiltrated the predawn silence wasn't the place. His mind swirled with answers to questions he didn't want to ask. Pieces of the puzzle lay blatantly before him, yet he struggled not to connect them. He couldn't. He needed more evidence, something concrete. Then again, he didn't want it.

The last five years had been some of the best and worst of his life. He'd made decisions, some good and some bad. Unfortunately, as he stuffed his hands into the pockets of his worn jeans and walked toward the cafés in Palo Alto, Harry couldn't decide which ones were good and which were bad.

Warm coffee had a way of clearing his mind. He thought about going to his sister's condominium each morning and sharing a cup.

At first it may not have been *sharing:* it was his way of avoiding grocery shopping. Truly though, it was more than that. It was also a time to reconnect. He and Amber hadn't been overly close as children, yet when he moved to San Francisco after his divorce, they slowly worked their way into one another's lives. Warm memories intermingled with sad as Harry thought about Simon. Their friendship was instantaneous. He was probably the reason Harry and Amber had become close. There was something about Simon that pulled people in and made them feel comfortable. Whether it was sports, work, or recreation, they had hit it off.

Harry and Amber had a shared past, but siblings or not, forging a friendship as adults was not always easy. That's especially true if one or the other harbors childhood feelings and insecurities. Harry needed to be sure that the feelings he had as a young boy—watching Amber receive the love and attention of two parents—weren't playing a role in his current conflict. In all actuality, he thought they'd made it past that. Besides, his vision was much clearer as an adult. He now saw that it wasn't her fault. She was just the lucky one to be born to two parents. The man who'd left Harry's mother was the culprit. Harry couldn't even blame his stepfather. No, those issues weren't even worth considering.

Amber was the lucky one. She always had been. Imagine at her age being the CEO of a growing Fortune 500 company. With the exception of losing Simon, everything has always worked in her favor. Now that she had Keaton in her life, she was no longer lonely. She truly had it all.

Moving into Amber's building after Simon's death was Harry's first unselfish brotherly act. Though he and Liz had to give up the little house they rented in San Mateo not far from the beach, it was worth it. Amber was devastated. She poured her heart and soul into

SiJo. Having Harry and Liz right down the hall gave her a reason to come home. It was in those early weeks after Simon's death that Harry and Amber began their morning routine. It was during that time, as an adult, that Harry got to know—really know—his sister. They talked, listened, laughed, and even cried. They'd both lost someone dear. Though Harry mourned Simon, too, he knew his loss of friend wasn't the same as her loss of a lifemate. Nevertheless, he could relate. Ilona and Jillian weren't dead, but he'd let them go. For all practical purposes, it was the same. Despite the fact that his had been voluntary, Harry understood loss—there was a time in his life that he'd thought that he and Ilona would be together forever. It was during those early mornings, over steaming cups of coffee, that brother and sister created a connection that surpassed blood ties.

Then Claire happened. Their routine changed participants, but didn't go away. Sometimes Amber would join them, but she often claimed work responsibilities. During those mornings in Amber's kitchen, Harry learned more about his assignment—Claire—than he ever could have as the occasionally visiting brother. He wondered sometimes if Amber wouldn't have developed a deeper kinship with Claire if she'd been with her more. Amber always privately blamed her attitude on the connection to Anthony Rawlings. After all, Claire claimed that Anthony could have known about Simon's death. While originally Amber wanted to know more about that, she never fully trusted Claire. Of course, she played the caring-friend role well.

Thoughts of Claire twisted his stomach. Emily took him to see her again when he went to Iowa for Rawlings' plea hearing. The facility where the Vandersols had moved her was a hell of a lot better than the one where Harry had first seen her. However, it was her condition that blew him away. When he'd seen her in Geneva, she was so strong and determined. He remembered her telling him off and telling him to leave her suite. Though he had only heard her message before the case was given to Agent Jackson, even then she sounded strong. Harry couldn't fathom what had occurred to cause her current status. If it was, as Emily claimed, due to past traumatic brain injury, Harry believed he was also responsible. Yes, Rawlings beat her, but Harry had been the one to introduce her to Patrick Chester. Though the Vandersols never mentioned that, Harry felt responsible.

He wished there was anything he could do to relieve her suffering. Perhaps that was his motivation for pushing SAC Williams to step in, to go to the powers that be and persuade the FBI to come forward about both Claire and Anthony's agreement. Apparently, there was reluctance due to the Rawlings coming back to the United States before they were supposed to do so, violating the stipulation of the agreement. Agent Jackson contacted Agent Baldwin who explained that the reason the couple traveled was fear for the Vandersols' safety. Jackson wasn't impressed. In his words, if Rawlings had done as he was ordered and stayed out of contact with people from his past, he wouldn't have known about the threat to the Vandersols. Sometimes, Harry wished he could tell John and Emily the truth about his job and what he truly knows. Do they realize all that Claire and Anthony risked to save them?

The cafe began to fill, yet Harry's thoughts were still scattered when his phone buzzed.

"WHERE ARE YOU? I WOKE UP AND YOU WERE GONE. (sad face)"

"I'M AT THE OVEN ON WAVERLY. I DIDN'T WANT TO WAKE YOU."

"ARE YOU COMING HOME OR DO YOU WANT ME TO JOIN YOU?"

Harry shrugged, thinking that he was leaning more toward option number three.

"I THOUGHT YOU HAD PLANS TODAY WITH AMBER?"

"SHIT! I FORGOT. WE CAN CATCH UP FOR A LATE LUNCH?"

"SOUNDS GOOD."

He sighed as he laid the phone back on the table. Even though it was a Saturday, Harry knew he needed to work this out in his head. After Liz's comment last night, he couldn't ignore the facts any longer. They were discussing John's decision to move to Iowa and work at Rawlings Industries.

"I can't understand how he can work for that company after all the things he's said about Anthony Rawlings. I mean, it's like working for the enemy," Liz said.

"According to John, he had every reason to hate his brother-in-law, but things change. I think he's doing it more for Claire."

Liz huffed. "What is it with her? I mean people uproot their lives for her. I don't get it."

"Liz, she's ill. She has a daughter and needs help."

"Ill? Like what kind of ill?"

Harry inhaled, "I really don't know. I just know John said that Emily wouldn't leave her, and he didn't want to be away from Emily and Michael. Apparently, Rawlings Industries offered him a tremendous deal to move to Iowa City and work with their legal division."

"Yeah?" Her nose wrinkled. "I never thought of John as someone who'd sell out for money."

"I think the money was an incentive, but he did it for... family."

Harry was about to say for Claire but he didn't want to keep that conversation going.

"Well, Emily surprises me too. Did you see them while you were in Iowa?"

Harry tried to process: he hadn't told her he was in Iowa to visit Claire.

Liz glanced at his expression. "I know you went there for the plea agreement. You didn't have to hide it. Amber explained that it's part of your job. SAC Williams went, too, didn't he?"

Breathing easier, Harry replied, "I wish my sister would learn to keep her mouth shut. She wasn't even supposed to know. And yes, I saw Emily and John. They were surprised to see me at the hearing. They still don't know my true job."

"Well, since the whole thing is over, why can't you tell them?"

"Because that's the job. Being undercover means... being undercover. I can't go back to all the places and people I've met and be like, oh, I wasn't really who you thought I was..."

Liz scoffed. "I get that, but how often are you you?"

Harry's light blue eyes clouded. "What do you mean?"

"I mean, for most of your assignments don't you have some kind of alias? I hope you do. I don't want to go through something like we did—ever again."

He remembered her terror after his attack. She handled it well at first, but there were nightmares and panic attacks that she tried to hide. Harry wrapped her in his strong arms. "Yes, you're right. I'm not me on other assignments. All of my information is changed. There's no way to get back to you, Jillian, Ilona, or Amber. You don't need to worry."

Liz laid her head against his chest and the scent of strawberries rose from her hair. "I don't think about it that much."

Veiling her big blue eyes with lashes, she looked up at him. "I don't. Forget that I mentioned it. My point was that John and Emily know you. They know us, and Amber. Don't you think they deserve to know—"

"What? Don't they deserve to know that my relationship with their sister was a job? I don't see the reason to hurt them like that. They're good people."

"Maybe you're right. Besides, they've moved away. It's not like you have to see them as regularly as you did when they lived here."

"Harry?" she asked shyly. "Can I ask you something?"

He could tell by her voice that it was something he didn't want to be asked. "Go ahead, but if it's about the job, I can't promise that I can answer."

"I don't know if it's the job or not. It's about us." *When Harry didn't respond, she went on.* "Is there something you're not telling me about Claire? You said she's ill. I thought she was probably in jail. I figured with all of Anthony's money, they're keeping it covered up. I know Amber was pissed that she couldn't find where he was charged with Simon's death. I thought you were working on that—" *Harry started to speak, but Liz went on.* "—wait, I want to say this. I don't even care anymore about you proving anything about Simon. I miss him, but I think Amber just needs to move on. I want to know if you really have. That's my question."

His brows knitted together. "What's your question?"

"Have you really moved on? Do you not want the Vandersols to know that Claire was your assignment, because in reality she was more? Remember, I saw that picture of you two holding hands in Venice. Did you visit her in Iowa?"

"I went to Iowa with SAC Williams. I saw the Vandersols and spoke with them as friends, but I was there on behalf of the FBI.

There's another case related to Rawlings coming up soon. I will probably go back there again. Claire's been gone from here for over a year. I'm getting sick of having her constantly thrown in my face. You and Amber are the ones who keep bringing her up, not me." Harry's words flowed, but he'd said them before, or some version of them. His mind zeroed in on the picture. Liz had mentioned it a long time ago, but it had never registered like it did now.

"Methinks he doth protest too much!"

She stood to walk away when Harry grabbed her arm. "Tell me again who showed you that picture."

Pulling her arm away, Liz replied, "Hey, I'm not some criminal under interrogation! I told you before—Amber showed it to me. She knows what it's like to have your boyfriend obsessed with someone else. After what happened, she didn't want me setting myself up for another disappointment." Her blue eyes pierced. "Is that what I've done, Harry? Are you just playing me? Rawlings is in prison. Maybe now is the time to make your move!"

He saw her anger, the way her cheeks flushed, and the tone of her voice, but his reaction was off. He wasn't Harry Baldwin, boyfriend. He was Harrison Baldwin, FBI agent. "You're overreacting. I have no intentions of making a move on Claire. She told me off the last time I spoke to her—and for the record that was in Venice. I told her I was FBI. She was pissed off."

Tears coated Liz's cheeks. "Y-you told her?"

"Yes, I told her the truth and she hates me."

"W-why didn't you ever tell me?"

Harry reached for her hand. After a moment of hesitation, she surrendered it to his tender grasp. "Because it is my job. I wasn't in Venice to pursue a relationship with her. You and I were back together. I don't want to fuck this up, again. I was there to protect her. I can't tell you any more, other than that she told me to get lost."

"So this is real. I don't have to be afraid that you'll go back to her? Wait..." She pulled back and looked into his eyes. "...why were you holding her hand?"

"It was a set-up. She didn't know about the FBI, yet. I needed that picture to show Rawlings. I really shouldn't be talking about this. Besides, it all blew up in my face."

Liz wiped her eyes with the back of her hand. "But you spoke with the Vandersols. They've been living here. They really don't know the truth about you?"

Harry shook his head.

Liz continued, "I'm surprised. I mean, if I were going to move across the country to some remote place for my family, I'd expect that family to be honest with me. Why hasn't Claire told them about you? I mean, who knows you like your family?"

Harry had heard that before. He replied, "I think their family has had a lot going on. I'm confident that the Vandersols are still in the dark."

Sitting with his empty cup of coffee, Harry lifted his phone as Liz's question reverberated through his mind. *Who knows you like your family?*

He accessed his contacts and called the one man who may be able to put his mind at ease. SAC Williams answered on the second ring. "Yes, Agent? What can I help you with?"

"Sir, can I speak to you, in person?"

"Can this wait until Monday?"

Harry closed his eyes and shook his head. SAC Williams

couldn't see his anguish, but Harry knew it was evident. "I really need to speak to you today."

"All right, son, I can be at the office in an hour."

"Thank you. I'll see you then." Harry hung up the phone and stared at the empty cup. In the middle of the café filled with people, he prayed: *Please God, let me be wrong.*

———————◆———————

THE FBI DIDN'T stop for weekends, yet depending on the caseload and schedule, many agents had the luxury of the occasional weekend off. Therefore, the San Francisco field office wasn't as busy as it was during the week. Harry made his way to SAC Williams' office. One rap on the door and he heard Williams' voice.

"Come in."

As Agent Baldwin entered, he said, "Thank you, sir, for taking the time to see me."

Williams' forehead stretched. "What is it, son? You sound different."

"May I sit, sir?"

Williams stood and walked around his desk, motioned to one of the chairs, and seated himself in the one beside it. As Harry sat down, Williams said, "You're being way too formal. I'd think you were a new recruit if I didn't know better. What's happening?"

"It's about the Rawlings—"

Williams' expression of concern morphed to agitation. "How many ways do I need to tell you that it's over—"

"No, sir, I don't think it is."

"Agent—"

Harry interrupted again, "It isn't about him, per se. SAC, do you remember when I was attacked? When they took Liz and threatened Jillian?"

Williams relaxed against the chair. "Yes. Did you remember something new?"

Harry shook his head. "What happened to my phone?"

"I believe it was recovered but it was unusable. The perpetrators destroyed it."

"But you got all the pieces?"

"Yes, the lab was able to access all your data."

"This is very important." Harry moved to the edge of his chair. "Was the SD card found?"

"I don't remember, but now that you ask, I remember your being concerned about that. There was a picture, right?"

"Right," Harry agreed. "There was a picture that I took with the intention of showing it to Rawlings. I had a plan that obviously didn't work, but in the picture I was holding Claire Nichol's hand. SAC, did the bureau get that SD card? Does the FBI have that picture?"

Williams shook his head. "Not to my knowledge. After what happened before between you and Mrs. Rawlings, I'm sure that if it would have materialized, the deputy director would have brought it to my attention."

Harry closed his eyes and fell back against the chair. With a shaky voice, he asked, "What do you believe happened to my SD card—based on what I've told you and what the FBI found?"

Williams shrugged. "I could say that the FBI missed it at the scene, but honestly, I doubt that. The area was swept clean more than once. You're one of us. We take the attack on you, as well as the threat to your daughter and ex-wife, very seriously. More than likely, I'd assume that the perpetrators took it. Who knows, maybe it was to be used as blackmail, but if you haven't heard anything yet..."

The rush of blood caused his ears to ring. Harry could no longer hear his supervisor. There was no other explanation. The words kept repeating: *No one knows you like family—everyone has a past.* It all pointed to one person: *his sister.* Could she have been the one to have him and Liz attacked? How else could she have gotten that picture? Who else would have known about Jillian?

Oh God! Harry's chest hurt.

Why? Why would Amber have done that to him?

Harry finally stilled the voices long enough to speak above their din. "Sir, I have a theory, one that I'd like the bureau to disprove."

Chapter 16

November 2014

John

———◆———

***If you don't like something, change it. If you
can't change it, change your attitude.***
—Maya Angelou

JOHN MADE HIS way toward the courthouse for the third day of
Catherine London's grand jury trial. The grand jury was still hearing
testimony and debating the evidence. It wasn't their job to
determine guilt or innocence, only if there was enough evidence for
Catherine to stand trial. Since all grand jury proceedings were done
in private, this was the one phase that the Rawlings Industries' legal
team didn't need to fight to keep away from the press. However,
there were many other probable sources of bad exposure. To that
end, the Rawlings' legal team, with the help of their newest
member, had been successful in limiting the release of information
during the preliminary phase. That didn't stop the crowds of people
from lining the cold steps of the US District Courthouse in Cedar
Rapids. Many of the onlookers were hoping to get a glimpse of
Anthony Rawlings. Though it was only speculation, if he were to be

subpoenaed, the reporters didn't want to miss his arrival.

Since the list of possible witnesses wasn't public, John wasn't sure if Anthony would be asked to testify or not. He did know that it was one thing to indirectly work for his brother-in-law, but John wasn't sure he was ready to see him and look him in the eye. The decision to take the job at Rawlings Industries had not been made lightly. John and Emily spent many hours and days discussing the pros and the cons. Without a doubt, Tim timed the offer perfectly. First, there was Emily's desire to stay close to Claire and the court's decision that kept her in Iowa. Then there was the salary. Tim's offer made Anthony's proposal from four years ago look like minimum wage. And while those reasons were enticing, it was the possibility of helping Claire and Nichol, helping to secure their financial future and the future of Nichol's legacy that truly sold John. Well, that and Tim.

Tim Bronson, the acting CEO of Rawlings Industries, was one of the most upfront and honest CEO's that John had ever met. They'd met socially years ago, but time and responsibility had not only matured, but also added confidence and charisma to Tim's demeanor. Despite all of the problems that Rawlings Industries was having with Anthony's private life, Tim was steadfast and confident in the company and its future. Truly, John was impressed from the first lunch. Tim didn't beat around the bush or try to avoid the giant elephant in the room. No, Tim laid it on the line.

Standing and extending his hand as John approached him at the restaurant where they met, Tim said, "John, thank you for meeting with me. I know this isn't a good time. I also know that you'll be leaving town again soon, and I so wanted to discuss this offer with you in person before you did."

John shook Tim's hand and had a seat. Being one of the nicer restaurants in the area, the waiter was present immediately, assessing the needs of the two men. Once he walked away, John responded, "I'm curious, Mr. Bronson, not to mention very surprised."

"Please, call me Tim. We've known each other for years. I'm not much into titles. I'm into this company. Despite decisions that Tony has made in his private life, his work ethic and business sense has always been spot on and impeccable."

John listened.

"You have been very vocal about your feelings toward your brother-in-law. I respect that. From what I've seen, you're a family man, and you feel that your family has been wronged."

John nodded, "My family as well as me."

It was Tim's turn to nod. "Yes, Brent filled me in on some past history. I assure you, that the business side of Rawlings is and always has been separate from the personal side. I didn't know about..." he hesitated "...well, any of the personal dealings." He corrected. "I of course knew about Claire, that they were married. Sue and I were there. However, we didn't know about any of the other things. I can honestly tell you that I wouldn't have cared if he were my boss or not; I wouldn't have been able to sit idly by if I had any idea—"

John interrupted, "Please, Tim, I've heard all I want to hear about Claire and Anthony's first marriage. I've read the book, and I don't care to see the movie. I've heard the same thing from everyone. They did a good job keeping it hidden. Obviously, neither Emily nor I were aware. We can't hold others accountable if we ourselves weren't to blame. No matter the reason he did it or she didn't tell, was their choice. I don't have to agree, but I think I've come to terms with it. They remarried, and from all accounts, it was a mutual decision based on feelings versus contracts. I can only hope that at some time my sister-in-law was happy."

What John didn't say—what he couldn't say—was the why of how he'd come to terms with it. Ironically, it was the same reason Emily couldn't. It was Claire. For a while the doctors questioned her ability to speak. Most of what she said was difficult to understand and jumbled. However, what she did say with some clarity was the name Tony. Over and over, especially while in a sleep-like state. It seemed like it was at those times, when she was absent in mind, that she was the most at peace. John couldn't explain it, and Emily didn't see it the same way, but there was something about seeing her during those times that touched John's heart.

"That's what I want to discuss—Claire and Nichol."

John leaned forward, his voice lower than usual. "Tim, I respect you and what you're doing for Rawlings Industries, but I will not discuss Claire's condition nor will I allow Nichol to be part of the media circus that seems to surround Anthony."

Tim shook his head. "No, John, that's not what I mean." A slight grin came to his lips. "But I do have to say, if you would include Claire and Nichol's company—their financial future—in that protective umbrella you have over them, I believe you'd be the perfect addition to Rawlings Industries."

Leaning back, John relaxed a little. "I'm listening."

"You and I aren't far apart in age. Brent Simmons has been an asset to Rawlings and to Tony. His allegiance is to his friend and his friend's company. No matter what happens to Rawlings Industries and the tens of thousands of employees, Anthony Rawlings will do fine when he is out of prison. I believe that Brent

has been through some difficult times over the years. Through it all he's stayed steadfast with Tony. I can only imagine that when Tony decides to retire, so will Brent. Tom too has been wonderful. I want someone else heading up the legal department who can both learn from those two men, as well as stick around, hopefully with me, and take Rawlings Industries into the future."

"You mentioned Claire and Nichol," John reminded.

"I don't think that they will ever be destitute. Tony is too smart for that. However, with the publicity regarding Nichol's parents, the best way to make her future easier is to have the good outweigh the bad. I want to see Rawlings Industries not only continue as the powerhouse that it was, but to forge a path for the future. I believe that with the right people we can not only bring back what we once had, but make it better..."

John listened as Tim laid out his goals and objectives. Wealth builds wealth, power builds power. Anthony Rawlings began Rawlings Industries with nothing. He and his friend had an idea and from there it mushroomed. It was an atomic bomb in the world of computers. Right time. Right place. Along the way there have been difficult decisions. Companies have been closed, but more have been opened. The economy is trying to rebound. It will take companies like Rawlings Industries, ones who are willing to reach down to the smallest of subsidiaries and lend the needed guidance, to keep people working.

Tim wasn't afraid to address the difficult subjects, yet he added the personal touch. "When Tony first re-introduced Claire into our fold, I'll admit that Sue and I were skeptical. After all, the last we'd heard, she was incarcerated for attempted murder."

John started to respond, but Tim went on.

"We forgot about the woman we knew and liked. I can say

loved when it comes to Sue. Sue thought and still thinks the world of Claire. Their ages helped to make them fast friends. Then, after Claire returned, it only took being with her for a few hours to remember. We remembered the woman we knew, the one we never believed could have hurt Tony. John, she could have hated us all. She could, and maybe should have hated Tony, but she didn't. I'm not asking you how she's doing now. I'm telling you that she has one of the most forgiving hearts I've ever known. I hope that you can see that by working for Rawlings Industries, by forgiving the injustices that were done to you and to your family, and by concentrating on what Claire would want... building a better future for not only her and Nichol, but for thousands and thousands of employees who need their paychecks, that you will be helping so many."

"I have to ask where Anthony stands on this?"

Tim nodded. "I expected that question." He reached into his breast pocket and retrieved an envelope. "This is for you. If you'll excuse me while I make a call, I'll leave you alone for a moment. By the way, I have not read what's in there. All I know is that I proposed your hiring to Tony a few weeks ago. I was still technically in charge, but he was back. Anyway, he said he wanted to think about it and asked me to wait. Four days ago he gave me that envelope and told me to follow my gut. He already knew his sentence and said that he felt secure with Rawlings Industries in my hands. He said that I should do what I want to do: currently the decisions are mine. However, if I still wanted to pursue offering you a position, he made a few requests. The first was that I discuss it with Brent and Tom. If I found support, he asked that I bring it up to the board of directors. He said if I had the support of the company, I had his. His last request was that I give you that envelope before you make a decision." Tim grinned. "I hope he doesn't screw up everything I've just said, but despite it all, I have faith in him, too."

John tried to swallow the anticipation as he laid the envelope on the table. He wasn't sure why his hand had begun to tremble. Looking up at Tim, John nodded. Smiling, Tim walked away to make his call. Once alone, John lifted the letter, broke the seal, and removed the page. The letter was hand written.

John,

I don't know where to begin. If you've received this letter then you're at least considering working for Rawlings Industries. You should know that I had nothing to do with this job offer. It is not like the last time. I have no excuse for what I did in the past, but I do have an explanation.

I saw you as a threat—which I hope you know is a compliment. I'd followed your career and knew all about you. From your modest roots to your Midwest education, I saw how you took what I honestly believed to be a mediocre beginning and turned it into success. Your record was impeccable. Before meeting you, I knew you were a force with which to be reckoned.

That said, I did what I do. I decided to capitalize on your ability and at the same time create a situation in which you would be indebted to me. At the time, I didn't consider Claire's feelings. When she found out that I'd offered you the job, she was apprehensively pleased. She spoke about us living closer and being a family. All I could think about was having you under my control.

It's no secret that I wasn't happy with you at our wedding rehearsal when you didn't give Claire away. At that moment, when I saw the anguish in Claire's eyes, I was determined to stifle your paternal, protective instincts. Claire was no longer your concern. She was MY wife and your actions caused her anguish.

I said she was apprehensively pleased. The apprehension came because Claire was concerned that you'd refuse the offer. She told me it was a possibility. I didn't give her concern credence, until you refused. After all, I, via Tom, had offered you so much more than you had in Albany. I was certain the money alone would entice you. However, as you know, Claire was right, and once again, you demonstrated that you were indeed a formidable opponent.

As I stated, that wasn't meant as an excuse or even a feeble attempt at an apology. I believe we are beyond that.

You currently have guardianship of two of the most precious and important people in the world. The only reason that I have not fought harder to regain my rights regarding my wife and my daughter was that I knew I had a debt to pay. I've accepted that commitment and will pay what I owe. Once I am done, be forewarned I will fight for what is mine.

In the meantime, I have to believe that those protective instincts that I witnessed years ago, and loathed, have resurfaced. For peace of mind, I have to believe that the decisions you're making in your life and for your family have my family's best interest at heart.

To that end, I want you to know that I welcome you at Rawlings Industries. My company is Claire's company. One day it will be Nichol's. I have the utmost faith in Tim. If he believes in you, I do too. I also want you to know that I will not interfere in his decisions regarding your employment. If you choose to work for him at Rawlings Industries, he will be whom you are working for.

I trust that you will take that arrogant, protective attitude that I hated and use it to better the lives of my wife and daughter, as well as the employees of Rawlings Industries. All of these people need what I will temporarily be unable to provide.

To that end, if you choose to do that in my absence, I thank you.

Anthony

Shaking his head, John placed the letter back into the envelope. He wasn't sure what to think about his brother-in-law's attempt to communicate. However, for the first time that John could remember, it didn't seem manipulative or calculating. It seemed like—in Anthony's own way—he was almost humbled. Before John could give it too much contemplation, Tim returned.

"Are you still considering my offer?" Tim asked with a grin.

Extending his hand, John said, "Yes, Tim, I'm considering it."

John didn't give Tim an answer the day they met or even the next week. He talked to Emily and to Amber. The prospect of practicing law again excited him more than he'd anticipated. Though he could accept the offer, he had his own legal hoops to jump through before he'd be licensed in Iowa. But that could be done, and when it came to SiJo, John believed he'd done all he could do. Since the incident, his heart hadn't been in it. He was truthful when he told Amber that he believed she could find someone new to take the position further.

Did Anthony's letter confess to being the person who set him up and took away his life? Not directly. Nevertheless, John chose not to share the letter with Emily. He knew she'd see manipulation and deceit in every word; however, during their discussions he explained that though Anthony was still part of Rawlings Industries, Tim was the one who wanted to hire him. Tim would be the one to whom John would report. Both he and Emily liked the prospect of being together again as a family, especially with Michael on the way. After much debate, John accepted Tim's offer, resigned his position at SiJo, and moved to Iowa.

In the past five months, he and Emily added Michael to their family, purchased a home, and began a new life—again. It was true that every upheaval in their lives could be associated with Anthony Rawlings. Nevertheless, with time, it even surprised John that he could now say the word *Rawlings* without feeling the deep-seated hatred from before. He supposed that was because along the way, the meaning of the word had changed. *Rawlings* no longer solely represented the man: instead, it stood for the company, a part of Claire and Nichol.

Though it was undeniably Nichol and Claire's last name, Emily had done her best to remove it from anything associated with Claire. John knew his wife meant well. She'd explained her stance many times. In her mind, Anthony was inarguably responsible for everything negative in Claire's life. Not only was he responsible for the concussion she'd sustained while with him, but the injury she had in California. After all, she reasoned, Chester wouldn't have been after Claire, if it weren't for Anthony. Emily interpreted the doctors' findings to say that Claire was suffering a psychotic break brought on by the TBI. She believed that by creating a stress-free, anti-Anthony environment, Claire could heal and recover. She forbade anything that would in any way remind her sister of her life over the past almost five years. Though Emily couldn't legally have *Rawlings* removed from Claire's name, she made it clear to everyone at Everwood that her sister was to only be addressed as Claire Nichols. Since Emily was her court-appointed guardian and was the one who paid the medical expenses—with Anthony's money—her wishes were followed.

Arriving at the federal courthouse, John made his way to the grand jury chambers. John was glad that Catherine wasn't present during this phase. He hadn't spoken to her since the day in the hospital when she'd so brazenly lied to him and Jane. He shook his head at the mangled web of deceit. Could it be that she'd lied to Anthony, too?

Each day at Rawlings Industries tore a little of John's hatred away and built his respect for the businessman in Anthony Rawlings. In the months of his recent employment, with Tim's permission, John had scoured years and decades of records of acquisitions, employment, and dissolution of contracts. It was just as Tim had promised. The lies and sins of Anthony's personal life had not transcended into his company.

John waited outside the grand jury chambers and thought about the lengthiness of the judicial procedure. This was only the grand jury phase. If the sixteen to twenty-three people inside the room decided there was enough evidence for a trial, then Catherine would finally be indicted. It had already been eight months since John and Emily had been locked in that suite. Although they'd only been held for a few hours, as he read about Claire's days of seclusion, he could relate better than most.

He'd been subpoenaed to testify at 9:00 AM. Though the subpoena hadn't specified what questions he would be asked, he suspected it was about the day at the estate. As he thought back to that day and remembered the realization of the locked door, he recalled the terror as the room began to fill with smoke. He'd tried to break the windows. Not even the glass doors to the balcony would open. John was more afraid for Emily and their baby. Then, the door opened. It was Anthony. Before he could process any more memories, the chamber door opened and the woman said, "Mr. Vandersol, please come back."

Chapter 17

December 2014

Tony

———◆———

Face reality as it is, not as it was or as you wish it to be.
—Jack Welch

"MY LIFE AS It Didn't Appear, Chapter 14...

I couldn't believe I was engaged and marrying Anthony Rawlings. When I woke the morning after his proposal, our engagement filled my every thought. At the time, I didn't realize that my single-mindedness was exactly what he wanted. In merely eight months, I'd lost myself, learned my role, and played it without question. Rarely did I have independent notions. It wasn't that I didn't think and process, but every concept was skewed. Every moment of deliberation centered not on my own desire or aspiration but his. Each movement and action had one purpose—to please him and keep the darkness at bay.

The night before, as we discussed the wedding, my thoughts filled with illusions of fairytales. I believed that I'd lived through the worse, and I held tight to his promises for better. It wasn't his *money I desired: it was his name. I longed for validation in my new position. I craved to hold my head high without trepidation. From the very beginning, Tony required that physical poise. Yet, with my chin held high and my eyes glued to his, I felt like an imposter. He'd forced me into duties that I'd been raised to know were wrong. When we'd go into public, or even with his friends, I constantly feared that everyone knew the truth.*

Then, in a magical, unexpected moment, everything changed. On that frost-filled night, with lights twinkling in the trees, we sat in a horse-drawn carriage, and his beautifully worded proposal took away my shame. He offered me the option of saying no. I could have done that and walked away—but to where? Anthony Rawlings was my job, my life, and my world. If I walked away, what would I be? What would that make me? Would I forever have been nothing more than his whore? He'd taken away my past, and I despised my present. That left only my future. It was like the journey necklace he'd given me. The diamond representing the future was the biggest and brightest for a reason—it held hope for better. That night in Central Park, Anthony Rawlings offered me a future without disgrace. The sparkling engagement ring that he presented was more than a symbol, much more. It was my dignity. I wanted it back. Truly, there was very little deliberation: I would be his wife.

No longer would I feel as though I didn't belong. No longer would I feel like the world could see behind the veil of perfection. I would be Mrs. Anthony Rawlings. As husband and wife, our personal business would remain personal. Yet, no matter what it entailed, I could endure it with pride, knowing that now it was socially and morally acceptable.

I'd learned too well the importance of confidentiality. What happened in the past, present, or future, behind the iron gates of our estate, or the closed doors of one of our apartments, wouldn't be shared, yet, as his wife, somehow I could accept it with my head truly held high.

My past and my future worked together to create a new paradigm. I knew I had my new sense of self-worth, but I remember wondering what my new title would mean to him. Did he too understand the significance of being his fiancée?

That morning, after I woke and ate, I went to look for him. From behind the closed door of his home office, I heard his voice. I was now his fiancée, not his mistress, possession, or whatever I had been. I also knew my rules. As his acquisition, I was not allowed to enter without permission or advance summons. Now that I'd willingly accepted my new role, what did it mean? Could I now pass into his sacred domain without fear of punishment? Standing for minutes debating my entrance, an all too familiar fear swept over me. I wanted to believe that I could enter and show him the love and happiness that I was feeling, but at the same time, I was terrified that in doing so, my illusions would be shattered irreparably. Without knocking, I returned to our suite."

Tony leaned back and closed the book. Though his eyes were open and staring toward Jim, he was seeing the past. He saw his fiancée of four years ago. He remembered finding her in their suite. His thoughts had been filled with wedding plans and his conversation with Catherine. He had no idea that Claire had been standing outside of his office door or that she was fighting an internal battle.

"Why did you stop reading?" Jim asked, bringing him back to present. Truly, Tony wasn't sure which place was worse—his memories or his therapy sessions in prison.

"I can't read any more right now."

"Why *can't* you?"

Tony inhaled deeply as he fought the urge to rebuke Jim's question. This was his counselor's way of making Tony weigh each word. Was it that he was incapable of continuing to read? Tony corrected, "I don't *want* to read anymore right now."

Jim nodded. "Very good. Why don't you *want* to read any more? You'd said you wanted to read happier parts of this book. It sounds like she was happy about the wedding. Was she happy?"

Tony could control the red outside of therapy. Hell—he could control the red *in* therapy when they talked about anything, except Claire. But when the topic was his wife, the crimson seeped through his shields and filled his thoughts without warning. "Does it fuck'n sound like she was happy to you?" he asked. "Maybe you're hearing something I'm not."

"Then tell me what you're hearing."

The chair screeched across the linoleum floor as Tony stood to pace toward the window. The view of the prison's campus was much better from Jim's office window than from any of the windows in his dormitory. In the summer, it'd been beautiful, but now with the grayness of winter, it reminded Tony that the green was gone. He tried to remind himself it may be dormant, but it wasn't forgotten. He worked to articulate his thoughts. "She said she wanted to come in my office and show me the *love and happiness* that she was feeling." He turned toward Jim. "That sounded happy—right?"

"What do you think?"

"I think what I've thought before. I fuck'n hate having questions answered with questions."

"Okay, tell me why you aren't convinced she sounded happy."

The soft soles of his shoes muffled his footsteps as he traveled from one side of the office to the other. "I'd just proposed. I was in the office making arrangements, and she was scared to walk in." His dark eyes shot darts toward his therapist. "Didn't you hear that? She was fuck'n petrified to knock on the damn door."

"Would she have needed to knock?"

Tony's eyes opened wide at the question. Well, yes, she would... but later, after their divorce, she wouldn't have. Fuck! He'd never thought of it like that before.

"Anthony, would she have been *required* to knock?"

"Yes."

"What would have happened if she knocked without being asked to your office, say... upon her arrival to your estate?"

Tony dropped back into the chair, his gaze once again transfixed beyond his counselor's eyes as his jaws clenched pulsating the muscles in his neck. Finally, he replied, "We've been through that shit. I don't want to talk about it. I don't want to fuck'n read anymore of the damn book. Let's talk about something else."

"No. I want to talk about this."

Tony's hands clenched in an attempt to rein in the red. Glaring with what Tony was sure was what Claire referred to as his *dark gaze*, he stared at Jim.

"How often do you hear that word?"

"I hear it too often."

"Now you do. What about before? What about during the time of this book? Did anyone tell you no?"

"No," Tony replied.

"How did you feel back then?"

"I don't know. I didn't have someone who stared at me three

times a week asking me about my damn feelings. I just did. I just was. I didn't think about it."

"Did you think about what Claire was feeling?"

"I told you I want to talk about something else. I wrote the letter that you said I should."

Jim's words slowed dramatically. "Anthony, did you think about Claire's feelings?"

"Sometimes."

Jim's brows rose questioningly.

"Like during the proposal. I wondered what she was thinking and feeling."

"So now you have an idea. What do you think?"

"I don't want to think about it. All right?" Tony replied. "I don't want to think about how she felt like a *whore*. I hate even saying that word. She wasn't!"

"Is that you talking now, or how you felt back then?"

"I *never* thought of her as a whore."

"How did you think of her?"

The moisture burnt Tony's eyes. He stood and walked back to the window. Snow had begun to fall. It was almost the fourth anniversary of his first wedding, almost Nichol's first birthday, and almost Christmas, and he was stuck in a freak'n hellhole.

"Anthony?" Jim didn't repeat the question.

"I thought of her as an *acquisition*. She's used that word in the book because I told her that—later."

"What did you tell her in the beginning?"

The red threatened again. Tony had said this before. What was the damn point of repeating it?

Jim cleared his throat, as he stood and began walking around the desk. "I believe you told me that you didn't like to repeat yourself." Stepping next to Tony, looking out the window, he added, "Neither do I."

"I told her that I owned her. She belonged to me. I made her repeat it." Tony turned on his heels. "That didn't mean she was a whore!"

"If you would've known the way she felt, what would you have done?"

He closed his eyes. "Today, I'd take her in my arms and convince her that she was wrong, that she deserved all the love and respect, and to keep her chin held high because she had nothing to ever be ashamed of. She was never a whore. She's always been my queen. In our fuck'n wasted game of chess, the king can survive without the queen, but he doesn't want to—he needs her."

"That's today. What would you have done and said on that morning after you proposed?"

Tony sighed. "How the fuck should I know? I don't remember."

"Anthony, we have few rules in this office. You're allowed more liberties with your speech, demeanor, and even your movement than anywhere else. That's because I want you to be comfortable enough to talk. But do not lie. If I ask you a question, I want the truth."

"Even though I demanded that same thing of her back then, I don't think she would have told me."

"But if she had?"

Tony shook his head. "I'm not lying. I don't know what I would have done. I probably would have told her she was wrong and chastised her for not behaving like a future Rawlings. A Rawlings would never be self-deprecating."

Jim glanced at his watch. "One more thing before our time's up: Claire said something else in that passage that I'd like you to think about between now and our next session."

Tony didn't want to think about any of it. "What?" he asked.

Jim smirked. "Is it just me, or is it Yankton that has taken away your predilection for using complete sentences?"

"What do you want me to think about?" he corrected.

"How long have you been here?"

"Twenty-six weeks and four days," Tony answered matter-of-factly.

"So, about six and a half months. What did Claire say, in what you just read, that had happened to her in only eight months?"

Tony contemplated. "Something about not having her own thoughts and conforming to what I wanted."

"How would it feel to be forced to do that? Forced to conform your previous way of life to someone else's rules and direction?"

It didn't take a genius to know where Jim was going. "I don't need to think about it," Tony replied. "It sucks."

"I'd like you to think about it. Think about the guards and the corrections officers. Think about their roles and yours. Then think about how Claire was feeling. When you come back, tell me exactly why she didn't knock on that door. Then, without the aid of continuing your reading, I want you to tell me what happened when you went to the suite."

"It sounds like you've read ahead. It sounds like you know."

Jim shrugged. "We've found a few things in this book that you've contested as accurate. Let's see how true the next scene is."

"We talked about the wedding plans and made love. Then I surprised her with her sister and brother-in-law."

"Next time." Jim stepped back behind the desk and looked up, meeting Tony's gaze. "Also, think about our definitions. Having sex and making love aren't the same thing. Think about it."

As Tony made his way back to his dormitory, he wondered what the fuck there was to think about, besides the fact that it was almost 4:00 PM, and he had to be back and present for the standing count. As he hurried from one building to the other, Jim's words came back. What was Claire thinking?

Tony wanted to go back and ask him to clarify. He wanted to go get that damn book and throw it in the incinerator. He wanted to do many things, none of which included standing by his bunk and being counted. Was that how Claire felt?

April 2015

SPRING HAD FINALLY sprung and the South Dakota air was warm enough for outside visitation. Tony liked sitting outside with his visitors much better than being cramped inside. For one thing, with the openness and fresh breeze, it seemed more private. That was an illusion: nothing at Yankton was private. Nonetheless, as Patricia sat across the small table from him and recited numbers and proposals, the illusion felt real. For a brief moment in time, he was living his old life.

The winter had been hard. Not only had the weather been exceptionally cold, the dormant landscape, as well as Roach's reports about Claire, all worked to add to his funk. Jim even recommended medication. He said that it wasn't unusual for prisoners to become depressed. Though he made it seem acceptable, Tony's thoughts went back to his grandfather. The antidepressants in conjunction with his other medication created symptoms of dementia. Tony didn't want that. He was having enough trouble remembering Claire and Nichol.

No. That wasn't true. He remembered everything about them, except now and then he'd think about the scent of baby powder and forget the fragrance. Or another wife would bring in a young child and Tony would wonder about Nichol. How big was she? What was she doing? Courtney sent pictures whenever she could. No one was allowed to bring cell phones near the prisoners. Visitors weren't even allowed to bring papers or pencils; however, she could mail them. As much as he appreciated it, each time he looked at the images of his sixteen-month-old daughter walking or laughing, another piece of his heart broke. If he was having trouble remembering how she felt in his arms, he had little doubt that she'd completely forgotten him. His stomach twisted at the thought. In her young mind, John was her father. No one had to say that to Tony—he knew.

As if that wasn't enough, Roach's reports were the same. He'd found a source inside of Everwood who was willing to divulge information—at least some. It seemed as though Claire was a mystery to most of the residents and staff. They saw her from afar. Yet, she never joined the other patients in group activities or even in the dining hall. According to Roach's source, Claire was treated with kid gloves and well cared for. Her needs were met in every way. The source said that Nichol hadn't been to visit in the last few months. Since Emily never entered Nichol's name on the registry, it was difficult for Roach to confirm or deny. Now that the weather was improving, he could report that the nanny had both children outside and to the park while Emily was at Everwood.

Tony's request to work in the business office had been granted. He'd endured it for most of the winter months, but it hadn't been what he'd expected. It was clerical. He was a damn secretary—not an assistant, like Patricia, not someone who had a thought or an opinion. No. For $0.17 an hour he filed papers and filled out invoices. As soon as they began planting the flower seeds in the greenhouse in Tony's horticulture class, he put in for a transfer. Now, his job was landscaping. It was a great way to combine his new knowledge of plants with his job. Perhaps because he had acquired the knowledge through Yankton, the supervising staff actually asked for and accepted his suggestions. It was a joke that he could recommend a geranium versus an impatiens based on the amount of sun exposure and they'd listen, yet in the business office where he'd made a fortune outside of these walls, they weren't interested in what he had to say.

Patricia continued her information dump. "Mr. Bronson said to tell you that Bakers in Chicago accepted the first proposal. He'd been prepared to increase the bid, but they bit at the first offer."

Tony shook his head. "Maybe it was too high?"

"Oh, he didn't think so." She leaned forward. "It was all about timing. They had a balloon payment coming due..."

He listened as she gave more details.

"I almost forgot," Patricia said with a grin. "A remarkable offer came in the other week to purchase a small company... in Pennsylvania, I think. Darn, it's hard without notes. But it was almost too good to believe. The company's been doing all right but there's no reason to hold on to it."

She had his attention. "What's the name of the company?" Tony asked.

Pressing her lips together, she pondered. "Mar-tins? No Mar—"

"Marque?"

"Yes! In Pennsylvania." Her eyes lit up. "That's it. It only employs about a hundred people."

"A hundred and twenty-six, the last time I looked," Tony corrected. "No. The company can't be sold."

"But—"

"No." His baritone voice deepened. "Tell Tim I said absolutely not. I don't care if someone offers ten times its worth. I will *not* sell."

She reached across the table and gently touched his hand. "Anthony, Mr. Bronson's made some great decisions that have kept Rawlings Industries strong. He doesn't believe—"

Tony pulled his hand away. "Don't treat me like a child. I'm well aware of the chaos I've created. The answer regarding Marque is still no."

"Yes, Mr. Rawlings, I'll let him know."

When her brown eyes looked down into her lap, Tony realized the tone of voice he'd used. In many ways he liked it—it felt good. He hadn't used that tone in almost a year. However, the expression on his assistant's face washed away his momentary relish. Tony lightly touched her arm, and she glanced his way. "Patricia, I appreciate your traveling all this way to keep me up to date. I'm sorry I barked. Marque has special meaning to me, and I don't want it sold."

Her eyes softened as she smiled. "I really don't mind traveling. I'm glad to help. I hope you know, Anthony, that I'd do anything you need me to do. I'm happy to help you to not be so lonely."

The way her dark hair blew around her face in the gentle breeze reminded Tony of Claire. He pressed his lips together and grinned. "You've been great. Thank you. Just tell Tim I said no about Marque. If he wants to discuss it further, he can when he visits again."

"I will, and I can come here more often if you'd like. I mean, I don't need to always fly. It's only a five-hour drive. I could come up and stay overnight. I read that in the warmer months visitors can come on Saturday and Sunday."

Tony shook his head in refusal. "I would never ask that. You have a job, a demanding boss, and a life. You don't need to waste an entire weekend in nowhere South Dakota."

She reached out again. They'd both read the visiting rules. Touch was limited to the beginning and end of each visit. Rules were to be followed or the visitor would be banned and the prisoner punished. "Right now I'm still helping Mr. Vandersol get better acquainted with Rawlings Industries."

"Brent said he's doing well."

"You really don't mind having him work there?"

"I don't." His voice deepened. "Don't let his past with me influence your opinion. You know a lot about the company, and he could use your help."

Patricia shrugged. "If that's what you want. What about the stuff last year?"

Tony's brows rose.

"The packages you told me to watch out for, the ones addressed to Rawls-Nichols?"

"What about them?"

"Is that something Mr. Vandersol should know?"

"No," Tony replied. "Why would you even ask?"

"Well, he asks a lot of questions. I wondered if it would help him understand what happened."

Tony wasn't sure where this was all going. "What do you mean?"

"You were worried about the packages and said that you didn't want them scaring Mrs. Rawlings, then she left. I just figured—"

"Well, don't."

Again her eyes fluttered to her lap.

"That's all over. John doesn't need to know about it, and you don't need to worry about it."

Patricia closed her eyes and inhaled deeply. "I love the smell of springtime."

Tony agreed.

When their time was up, Patricia touched his hand again. "I meant what I said. And I don't think my boss is too demanding. It's not demanding when I want to do it."

"Thank you. I'm not demanding or asking. Don't worry about me."

"But I do, Anthony. I do."

Chapter 18

July 2015

Brent

———————◆———————

It's no wonder that truth is stranger than fiction.
Fiction has to make sense.
—Mark Twain

AFTER WHAT SEEMED like a lifetime, it was finally time for the opening statements of Catherine London's trial. Tony had already served over a year of his sentence for his crimes, and hers were finally making it to the light of court. It wasn't that there hadn't been pretrial motions—there had. Catherine's attorney had filed almost every one possible. They'd requested a change in venue, to no avail. They'd filed challenge after challenge to the evidence and the witnesses. There was a plethora of expert witnesses who were expected to testify for the prosecution. Catherine's attorneys had challenged every one of them. At one point they'd even attempted to have the charges dismissed. Since the grand jury had convened and found probable cause, the likelihood of a dismissal was low; nevertheless, they gave it a shot. It seemed like her attorneys were following a handbook on how to delay trial proceedings and checking each box as they went.

It wasn't only the defense that filed a pretrial motion. The prosecution filed a request for a gag order. It seemed as though Catherine had no issue with telling the world about her sordid history: however, her story wasn't hers alone. The gag order on her trial was part of Tony's plea agreement. He argued that by releasing the information of her trial, it would negatively affect thousands and thousands of workers. Though technically libel and slander were considered civil charges, being part of his plea in conjunction with his sworn testimony against Catherine the order was granted. As Brent, Courtney, Emily, and John all sat and prepared to listen to the government present their opening statement, Brent feared what they'd all learn. It was, after all, the government's job to prove burden of guilt. From what little Brent knew of the case, they'd done their homework.

Originally, he assumed that Emily and John would be sequestered from the courtroom. However, during the negotiations, the US government decided to concentrate on the murder charges and dropped the attempted murder of John, Emily, and Claire. Their reasoning was that although John and Emily were locked in the room, the intent to harm was difficult to prove. There was no evidence verifying that Catherine had been the one who placed the poison-laced water bottles in the suite. While Catherine admitted to starting the fire in her own fireplace, the spread of the fire was deemed accidental. There was no longer a reason why either of the Vandersols would be called to testify. Therefore, sequestering was no longer a concern. John applied for special dispensation: after all, Catherine was accused of killing Emily's parents as well as her grandfather. It was granted and they were now able to attend each and every day of the trial.

Their conversation came to a halt as Catherine was led into the courtroom. Quickly assessing her, Brent saw that she'd lost weight in prison and allowed her hair to go gray. The end result was that she appeared older and frailer. She definitely appeared older than her true fifty-three years. Brent wondered about Tony's rule and how well Catherine had learned it. Appearances were of the utmost importance. From his eye, Catherine appeared to be more a frail grandmother, than a serial murderer. He hoped it wouldn't work.

When it came to evidence, Claire's computer had been destroyed in Catherine's fireplace. Nevertheless, she'd saved all the paper documents. All of her research connecting Tony to his past had been confiscated by the Iowa City police in 2013 after her disappearance, and labeled as evidence. As the Simmonses and Vandersols listened, the US Attorney used that information to spin a well-fabricated web for the jury. If Brent hadn't known it to be true, he would have questioned its veracity. For small-town America, it was a thriller! The story began with a young girl who'd been abandoned by her family. By the time the prosecution was done, he'd set the stage for the most fantastic game of vengeance and revenge that Brent had ever heard. Unfortunately, the story wasn't a novel, and it wasn't fiction. Innocent lives had been lost and others destroyed in the name of this twisted vendetta.

His statement had gone on for over two and a half hours. Throughout, Brent watched the jury. Not once did they seem bored or disinterested. As a rule of thumb, the opening statement should be short and concise. Brent glanced at John and raised his brows. It was an unspoken question, attorney to attorney. What did you think? John shrugged. Brent prayed that it was a hit out of the park. After everyone who'd suffered, he wanted the frail woman at the front table to die a lonely death in a lonely cell. It wasn't a nice wish, but it was the one he harbored.

Not far from the courthouse was a popular diner. As long as the judicial system stayed in business, the restaurant was assured a good lunch crowd. It was frequented by judges, lawyers, staff, and the public. In essence, the entire room was filled with ears. Truthfully, it wasn't only the law and lay people who were listening. As the two couples made their way to lunch between the morning and afternoon sessions, they were witness to reporters. Even though it was only the first day in front of a jury, the reporters were hungry for news. It seemed as though the granting of a gag order did nothing more than whet their appetite.

Over the last year, especially with John's employment at Rawlings, the two couples had become closer. If Brent had to pinpoint one reason, he'd say it was because Courtney was determined that she was going to be part of Nichol's life. Thus far, access to Claire had been adamantly denied, but Courtney had been given the ground rules. "If you ever are to see her, you may not mention him—at all." Without a blink of her eye, Courtney agreed.

As much as the Vandersols and Simmonses wanted to discuss the morning's opening statement, they tried to keep the conversation away from the proceedings. There were ears at every turn. If any one of them was deemed responsible for leaking information, they'd be banned from the remaining trial. None of them wanted that: the morning had only been the beginning.

As they finished their lunch, John asked, "Would you two like to come over for dinner? I think Emily and I would both like to discuss some of this background information."

Emily nodded, adding under her breath, "Claire had mentioned some of this years ago, but it seems pretty farfetched. I hope they can make it believable."

Brent watched Courtney's eyes glow at the invitation.

"The prosecutor had me totally enthralled. I had no idea he'd been talking for so long," Courtney said.

Knowing that his wife was always willing to do whatever it took to get close to Nichol, Brent said, "That sounds good. Give us a little time to stop by home after they wrap up for the day, then we'll be over. Let us know what we can bring."

"Ridiculous! Farfetched! Fiction!" Catherine's attorney began, capitalizing on the US Attorney's earlier flair for the dramatic. "I hope you're all ready for a show, because that is exactly what the government wants to give you. Just look at my client. She's worked her entire life as a servant. Oh, the wealthy have other names... housekeeper, maid, whatever. How many of you have someone who picks up after you, manages your household, and assures that your dinner is on the table? Catherine London has done that for three generations of the same family. She has worked and worked." He lowered his voice. "She has witnessed things that no one should witness. But yet, she didn't betray her employer. No—not until he did it first..."

Late August 2015

BRENT AND COURTNEY knew the routine at Yankton. Instead of surrendering their belongings, it was easier to carry only the authorized items into the visiting room. With just their keys and identifications, they arrived at the prison. Being too early for the prisoners, they migrated with the other visitors into the visiting room. As they found their way to seats, and sat quietly, they watched the other people. Some appeared confident, while others looked side to side, wondering what would happen next. Brent found it strange that only a year ago this had been a difficult and uncomfortable process. It wasn't that they now enjoyed it, but the entire routine had become normal. The metal detector seemed less invasive. The guards and questions seemed less subjective. Brent equated it to the airport security system. Though it was a pain in the ass, it was no longer troublesome to step into the glass cubical, lift your arms, and allow the machine to scan your entire body. It just was. That was the process at Yankton—it just was.

Not long after 10:00 AM, he and Courtney watched as the inmates entered through the north door of the building, the opposite end from where they themselves had entered. They were all dressed in their khaki shirts and pants. Their black shoes with soft soles created a muffled thunder as the visitors stilled, waiting for their loved ones.

On the way, they'd discussed how nice it was to visit outside. Although it was summer and the morning temperature was conducive, it was evident that wasn't happening. The threatening South Dakota sky and forecast of severe storms had them trapped indoors.

The inmates scanned the crowd from veiled lids, searching. Near the middle of the pack, Brent saw Tony, his height giving him away, and noticed how once Tony spotted his friends, his gait changed. No longer did he blend into the masses with his head slightly bowed and steps shuffled. In an instant, he was walking confidently with his familiar stride. Though the latter made Brent smile, his heart ached at seeing his friend as the former.

Tony extended his hand, but before Brent could shake it, Courtney was up out of her seat, and wrapping Tony in a quick, friendly hug. "How are you doing?" she asked in her cheeriest voice.

"I'm all right. How are you?"

Brent shook Tony's hand just before he took his required seat. "We have some news," Brent offered.

Tony nodded. "I saw it already. There was an article in this morning's Wall Street Journal." He rolled his eyes. "It's so nice of them to spell out the whole Wall Street connection between me and Nathaniel."

Brent inhaled. "I'd hoped you hadn't seen it yet. Keep in mind that it wasn't negative against you. As a matter of fact, they made a big point out of how Rawlings Industries has been carefully scrutinized and come out clean as a whistle."

"I'd rather avoid any publicity, especially any connected to Catherine."

"They're adding *Rawls* to her name, now. The reporters are, I mean," Courtney added.

"Isn't that great?" Tony asked. "She's going to spend, what was it? Five life sentences in prison, but she finally gets my grandfather's name back. Ha!" Tony forced the laugh. "Think of all the lives that could have been spared if only they'd given her that honor years ago."

Courtney reached out and touched Tony's hand. "It's over. It's all over."

His dark eyes clouded. "Not for thirty-four more months."

"I know I'm here today as a friend, not your lawyer," Brent said, "but let me remind you, you'll go up for review in less than a year and then every six months after. There's always a chance that it could be less."

"And I could go batshit crazy, and it could be more."

"Don't say that, Tony," Courtney said. When Tony smiled in her direction, she cocked her head to the side and asked, "What?"

"It's dumb I suppose, but no one here calls me that. I think I miss it."

"Well, *Tony*," she said, emphasizing his name, "what else do you miss? What can we do to make this better?"

Though his expression didn't change, Brent saw a spark of something in Tony's eyes: a recognition or connection like he hadn't seen in some time. "What is it? What did you just think of?"

Tony shook his head. "Damn, am I that easy to read? I didn't used to be." He paused and looked at Courtney. "I can't tell you how much your letters have meant to me, especially the pictures. Thank you."

"Of course, I'm glad to do it. Nichol is beautiful. You should be proud."

"Of her, I am."

"You have a lot to be proud of," Brent offered.

"Thank you." His gaze fixed on Courtney. "I can't imagine not having the visits or your letters. That's just who you are and always will be. Thank you for taking the time. I was wondering if I should continue to write to you at your home or if I should send your letters to your P.O. box in Chicago?"

Brent turned to his wife and watched as the color drained from Courtney's cheeks. "What P.O. box?" he asked. Turning back to Tony, he continued his questioning, "What are you talking about?"

Tony's tone was gentle, almost sad. "Thank you, Courtney. Thank you for being J. Findes."

Tears fell from her eyes as Courtney tried to remain composed.

"Someone tell me what's happening," Brent demanded in a hushed tone.

"Y-you're not mad?" Courtney asked.

Tony shook his head. "I probably would have been, but not now. Not only am I not mad, I'm happy. I failed her then. I didn't realize how awful this was... and this place is better than where she was. I'm so glad you helped her."

Courtney inhaled, trying to stifle her cries. "I never wanted to lie to you..." she turned to Brent "...either one of you. But I couldn't... I just couldn't..." her voice trailed away as she lowered her face.

The temperature of the room rose exponentially; Brent and Tony had come so far. It truly felt as though the two of them were friends, connected as never before. Was it right to leave deception between friends? Or would the truth separate what had finally been solidified?

"I'm not going to lie to you, Tony," Brent confessed. "I knew about that. I didn't know the name she used or where the address was, but I knew and I supported Courtney... and Claire.

Tony leaned back.

While Brent reached for Courtney's hand, he saw the question in his wife's moist blue eyes. Inhaling, Brent continued, "You've come clean with us. I guess it's time to come clean with you. Just promise me that you won't be upset with Claire."

Tony's brows knit together. "What are you talking about? Why would I be upset with Claire that you wrote to her in prison?" It was as if they watched the light bulb illuminate. The spark of understanding ignited a flame behind his eyes and Tony's voice brimmed with emotion. "It was *you*... Oh, my God. You're the ones who freed her." This time he was the one to look away.

"Tony?" Courtney implored. "It wasn't against *you*. It was for *her*."

At first Tony only shook his head; however, when he turned back, his eyes were red. "Thank you, for saving her. I understand. Two years ago, I might have been irate." He scoffed. "I would have been—hell, I was, but things are different. What you did, the petition, the money... by freeing Claire, you gave me back my life.

"I've spoken to Roach, and I just don't understand what's happened to her. But if you can... if it is ever a possibility to save her again... I don't care who you have to deceive... just please, for both of us, for Nichol... do it."

Courtney wasn't even trying to hide her tears. "I want to hug you so badly."

Tony swallowed. "I wish you could."

"Tony, she didn't know—at first. Once she did, the only reason she kept it from you was for us."

Tony reached out and covered Courtney's hand with his own. His soft brown eyes were bordered in red. With his famous grin, he said, "We're good. I'm not upset at all. I'm indebted to you." He widened his grin. "About $100,000, I guess."

Courtney shook her head. "No—"

"No you're not," Brent said. "And you're not paying us back. You already have."

Tony's eyes widened, questioning.

"I've had a few raises over the last couple years. I figured I deserved them."

Tony's grin morphed into a full smile. "You do, my man, you do."

Brent leaned forward and spoke quieter. "I may have some news you don't yet know."

"What?"

"Amber McCoy has been charged in connection with the death of Simon Johnson."

The clouds over Tony's dark eyes showed his processing. "I don't understand. I thought the NTSB found no signs of tampering."

Brent shrugged. "They haven't released any more information, only that there was sufficient evidence to press charges."

"What's happening to SiJo?" Tony asked.

"I really don't know."

"Tell Tim to look into it immediately. As you know, this kind of shit makes it vulnerable."

"What? Do you want to buy it? It could go under the Shedis-tics umbrella—"

"No," Tony interrupted. "I want to help it. No matter how Amber and Harry lied to Claire, Claire cared about Simon and that company. Find out what they need."

Courtney smiled.

"I'll call Tim as soon as we leave," Brent assured him.

Chapter 19

A few weeks earlier—Mid-August 2015

Harry

———◆———

My family is my strength and my weakness.
—Aishwarya Rai Bachchan

HARRY WATCHED FROM behind the glass, unseen by his sister or the officer from the California Bureau of Investigation. It was the same division where Harry had gotten his start in law enforcement—the same bureau that fueled his desire for justice. It was the same bureau that was now questioning his very own sister in regard to the senseless death of Simon Johnson.

SAC Williams patted Harry on the back. "I'm sorry, son. I'm sorry it all came to this."

Harry nodded. Words weren't forming without emotion. He was a damn FBI agent; crying wasn't part of the job.

"You did the right thing. I know it may not seem like it at this moment, but the truth, the law, is always right."

Inhaling deeply, Harry managed to say, "You're right. It sure doesn't feel like it at this moment."

"Have you talked to her?"

"No. I have about a thousand texts and voicemails from Liz. She's out in the waiting room going crazy. She doesn't know I'm here." He turned his sad blue eyes to his supervisor. "SAC? I don't know how to do this. Do I come clean and tell her that I'm the one who..." He couldn't finish the sentence.

Williams reached for his arm. In the midst of turmoil, the point of contact was comforting. The older man had been as much of a father to Harry as his stepfather, and more of a father than the man who helped to create him. "That's your call. I know that you'll know what to say, if you do let her know you're in on it. But remember, you weren't the one who followed the phone trail. You didn't dig up the text records or question the witnesses. You can't take all the blame."

Harry sighed. "I'm the one who put her on your radar. Without me, she would never have been discovered."

"Think about your friend. Think about Mr. Johnson. Would that have been right for him? For his family?"

Harry had lain awake at night thinking about exactly that. "I can't imagine the Johnsons. I mean, they still think of Amber like a daughter. They're going to be devastated."

"One fire at a time, son."

Harry turned toward the window and wiped his eyes. He couldn't hear what they were saying because he'd turned off the sound but he could tell by his sister's expression that she was pleading her innocence. "She needs to shut up. I know we have the evidence, but she just needs to shut up!"

"Then go be a brother: a brother who's also an agent. Tell her what she can do to make it better."

Harry turned on his heels. "Nothing! She can't do a damn thing to make it better. She killed Simon Johnson..." He shook his head.

"...and it goes back to Claire. How does every damn thing go back to Claire? Simon's obsession was what pissed Amber off so much. How could I be right here in San Francisco and hang out with them and not know?"

"Simon never mentioned Mrs. Rawlings?"

"He did, but not a lot. It was one of those things you say in passing. I'd get pissed at Liz about something and mention Ilona. He'd be pissed at Amber and mention Claire. She was his girlfriend in college—freshman year! That was forever ago. I remember thinking that it was weird that he'd gone so long without someone serious in his life. He chalked it up to devoting his energy to his work. That's why he and Amber were so perfect. They met at Shedistics and she followed him to help with SiJo. They were friends before they became an item. I'm not sure Simon even saw her as girlfriend potential... for a while." Harry shrugged. "I can't testify to any of that. It's what he said and she said. That was all before I moved back to California. Once I got here, they were definitely together. Other than a mention here and there of Claire to me, he seemed totally devoted to Amber."

"So you didn't know that he'd gone around the country to see her?"

Harry shook his head.

"Ms. Matherly knew."

"We never talked about it." Harry's eyes widened. "What else does Liz know?"

"If you're asking if we think she knew that your sister allegedly poisoned Mr. Johnson, we don't. There's no evidence—at this time—to suggest that. In an interview with the CBI, she mentioned that Mr. Johnson had an obsession with a person from his past and that upset Ms. McCoy. She claimed that his preoccupation was the only source of contention she'd ever witnessed between the two of them."

Harry's head shook slightly from side to side, allowing his too-long blonde hair to fall across his eyes. Pushing the unruly curls away, he said, "They *all* need to shut up." He turned back to the window, just in time to see the officer exit the room, leaving Amber alone at the metal table.

Harry handed SAC Williams his phone. "Here, the damn thing's going to explode if I get another message from Liz. Can you hold it for me while I go in there?"

Williams' lips twitched into a slight smile. "You want me to hold your *exploding* phone?"

Harry grinned. "Yeah, thanks."

When Harry opened the door, Amber's head popped upward, and her tear-filled eyes looked directly at him. Instantaneously, her expression morphed to need. "Oh, thank God, Harry. You need to help me. They're saying things that don't make sense. They're saying that I was involved in Simon's death and that attack on you. Please... please..." she reached out to him "...tell me that you know I wouldn't do that."

Walking toward his sister, she stood. Harry wrapped his arms around her, hugging her shuddering shoulders. He fought his own emotions as her tears dampened the cotton of his shirt. After a moment, he helped her to sit again and sat across from her. "Amber, they read you your Miranda rights, didn't they?"

"Yes, but why? Why would they even think that I would—"

Harry interrupted, "You need to get a lawyer. Stop talking to them or even to me... I'm an agent—"

"I know what you are! You can help me. Find out who's saying these vile things. Make this all stop. I loved Simon. I love you! I would never do anything to hurt..." her words faded into tears. Suddenly, her eyes opened wide. "I bet it's that bitch. Claire Nichols! She's the one saying these things about me! It's not enough for her to have her billionaire jailbird and *you*, but she wouldn't let Simon go either. She tried to kill Rawlings. I bet she found out that Simon and I were engaged and she tried to..." Her anger turned to sadness. "...no, she didn't *try*. She succeeded in killing him."

"She isn't telling anyone anything. You sound delusional."

"No!" She stood. "You don't know. You don't know what it's like to have someone who you love willing to travel all over the damn country to get one last chance with a woman he hadn't even talked to in years! Years!"

"Stop," Harry said calmly.

"No! I'm not stopping. You need to know what she's capable of doing. Hell, you know, don't you? She has some kind of power over men. I don't understand it. I mean it's not her looks and definitely not her brains." Her eyes widened. "Emily said she's having issues. Well, she's crazy if she thinks she can tell the world lies about me!"

"Amber, stop talking. Everything you say can be used against you—"

Her eyes narrowed. "Why, Harry? Are you going to tell them what I say?" She looked around, turning until she faced the window. "Or are they watching?" She walked to the darkened glass and turned back. "Are you in here as my *brother* or an *agent*?"

"I'm both, but I'm in here right now as your brother. I'm telling you to stop talking and get a lawyer."

"I have lawyers," she said smugly. "I have lawyers, assistants, accountants. I have a whole damn company at my disposal. The stupid bureau will never get any of this to stick. I'm innocent. Sure, I was pissed when I found out that Simon was going all over the damn country trying to get his wimpy nerve up to talk to that bitch. Wouldn't you be upset? I mean, who goes to multiple events and then doesn't even talk to her? Ha! I loved reading that stupid book. I hope that after Simon talked to her, Rawlings beat the sh—"

Harry stood. "Stop it! Now! Shut the fuck up and listen to yourself. Are you really that stupid? You're in a damn interrogation room. Shut up! I'm getting Liz and getting one of your many attorneys over here. And I'll call Mom and Mrs. Johnson. You don't want either one of them hearing about this from some news report. In the meantime, *shut up!*"

Amber crossed her arms over her chest, pressed her lips together, and continued to glare as Harry walked from the room. Instead of heading out to Liz, Harry knocked on the door to the observation room. Williams opened it, and Harry entered, falling into one of the empty chairs. Williams sat next to him where they stayed—silent—for minutes upon minutes. Finally, Harry turned and said, "I need to get her that attorney."

Williams nodded. "You gave her good advice, son. You can't make her take it." Williams handed Harry his vibrating phone.

Taking a deep breath he walked through the crowded hallways toward the waiting area, avoiding eye contact with everyone he passed. Once there, he stood and watched as Liz paced a small area near the corner of the room. She was holding her phone with one hand, willing it to ring, and had the other arm wrapped around her stomach. "Liz?" he asked.

Her anguish imploded as she ran towards Harry. Flinging herself against his hard chest, she sobbed. Finally, she asked, "What's happening? I'm so glad you're finally here."

He wrapped her in his arms and whispered into her hair, "I've been here. I didn't have my phone on me. I'm sorry I didn't let you know."

She looked up. "You've been here? Why? How long? What's happening?"

"Amber needs an attorney—"

"No! That's ridiculous." Her indignation came forth with each word. "They can't charge her with anything. She would never—"

"They already did," Harry said, as Liz's head shook back and forth. Taking her face in his hands, he closed the gap. "Liz, Amber needs you to be strong. Please, call SiJo. Get someone from legal over here right away. Call public relations and get them to run some kind of defensive maneuver. This won't be good for SiJo."

Liz lifted her phone, but looked back up. "SiJo? You're worried about SiJo? What about Amber? You're an FBI agent—do something to help her."

"I am, and so are you. She needs legal representation before she says something that she can't retract."

Liz lifted one finger as she spoke into her phone. When she was done, she looked back at Harry. "They're on their way. Can I see her? Have you seen her?"

"I've seen her, but you can't."

"You don't want me to see her or I can't?"

"Both. We can't do any more here. Let's go home."

She planted her feet. "Home? I can't leave her. She's my best friend, and she's my boss. I won't just leave her."

Harry forced a grin and placed a kiss on her forehead. "I love your stubborn streak, but now isn't the time. Fine, we can wait until legal arrives, but then we're leaving."

"Harry, you know that Amber wouldn't do what they're saying..."

He placed his finger over her lips. "Stop talking about it. We're in a police station. Both you and Amber need to just stop talking."

As they sat in the plastic chairs and waited, exhaustion as Harry had never felt before filled his being. His temples throbbed at the thoughts going through his head. He needed to call his mother. He needed to call Simon's mother. He needed to file a report about his non-interrogation. None of that, though, was what he wanted to do. Harry wanted to climb into his bed and not come out for days. He wanted to pretend that everything was all right. He wanted to go back in time to when Simon was alive... no, farther back than that, back to when Ilona told him she was pregnant.

Harry closed his eyes and squeezed Liz's shoulder. She had her head resting against him. It would be so easy to lay his head on hers... and try to forget.

Chapter 20

December 2015

Tony

———◆———

Love is not a feeling of happiness. Love is
a willingness to sacrifice.
—Michael Novak

"I HATE WINTER," Tony stated, as he stared out the large pane of glass in Jim's office.

"Have you always hated winter?"

Tony glared. It didn't seem to matter how many times he said that he hated the questions, that was all Jim seemed to know how to do. "No, I didn't hate it. I never noticed it."

"Didn't you live in Iowa?"

"I do live in Iowa. This," he said, gesturing with his arm, "isn't living."

Jim grinned. "All right, so you live in Iowa and never noticed winter?"

Tony turned back toward the snow-covered terrain. The colorful flowers he'd helped plant and the green grass he'd helped mow were now covered in a thick blanket of white. He noted how the sidewalks that he'd shoveled only a few hours ago held an inch or two of new accumulation. Damn, when he got out of this hellhole, he swore he'd never lift another snow shovel. Honestly, he'd probably never mow a blade of grass either, but if Claire wanted help in the gardens, he was more than willing to do that. The sound of Jim's exaggerated throat clearing reminded Tony about their conversation. Was it a conversation? It was therapy, but for the past eighteen months it was the closest thing that he'd had to conversation, other than when he had visitors.

"Iowa has winter," Tony replied. "There's snow and shit, but I was always so busy I never paid any attention. I spent most of my time working or traveling. The weather was irrelevant."

"So you didn't spend much time outside?"

Tony shrugged, walked to the chair, and sat. "Not until Claire." It was easier talking about her than it used to be. As long as they stayed away from the shit in the damn book and concentrated on their second chance, Tony actually enjoyed the walks down memory lane. Sure, they made him sad, but life was sad and Yankton sucked. If he was going to be down anyway, it might as well be while thinking about Claire.

"Tell me what you and she would do outside."

Tony closed his eyes as his cheeks rose. The grin felt nice. "She liked to walk in the woods. We have acres and acres of land covered with trees. I'd lived there for about fifteen years before she came to the estate—"

"Anthony," Jim interrupted. "Honesty. Did Claire *come* to the estate?"

Tony sighed and began again. "I'd lived there for about fifteen years before I brought Claire to the estate." He opened his eyes to see Jim nodding. "I'd never ventured out into the woods. I didn't want to. I'd surveyed the land from a helicopter after I'd purchased it. That was my only real knowledge of what lay behind the trees. I knew she liked to be outside. One time, while I was out of town, she started going out into the woods, not for hours but for entire days."

"How did you feel about her being gone all day?"

"I didn't like it. At first, I was confused. I was overseas and when I'd check the surveillance feed from her suite, I couldn't understand why she wasn't there. I called and was told she was out walking. Later, I found where she left the yard every day. It was the same place, but I couldn't see where she went. All I could do is fast forward until she returned."

"How did that make you feel, to not know where she was?"

"Stop asking me that! I'm talking. I'm answering your damn question about being outside."

"You're an intelligent man. I believe you can multitask. Try answering both questions at the same time."

Tony shifted in his seat and let out an exasperated sigh. "When I didn't know where she was, I was upset, and I was worried..." Jim started to talk, but Tony spoke over him. "I was worried that she might try to leave. She was gone all day long. There's a highway about another mile west of the lake. What if she kept walking and made it to the highway?" He looked again at Jim and shrugged. "But she didn't. I didn't even know she was at the lake until I got home and questioned her. And I was happy that she was honest with me," he added with a feigned grin. "Later, after we were married, she took me there. The first time was during a snowstorm. We got there on cross-country skis. I felt cold." This time his grin was real. "But not really. She was so excited, talking about the way everything looked in the summertime. She talked about flowers, trees, insects, and animals. I'd never realized all of that was just outside of my door. We went back in the summer, too."

Tony stood again and walked to the window. "That's why I'm not selling the estate. She loves that lake and the grounds too much."

"What about your house."

"I told you, I'm having it demolished."

"Anthony, we discussed this. You're not in the right frame of mind to make that kind of decision."

"Are you telling *me* that I can't have my own house torn down?"

Jim stood, walked closer, and leaned against the wall. "No, I'm suggesting that you wait and think this through."

"I guarantee I've thought it through. I have nothing else here to do here but think. I've thought about it until I don't want to think anymore. Other than a few personal items... and a painting... it can all go." He emphasized, "I want it gone."

"And you get what you want."

"I used to."

"Anthony, you're grasping at anything to give you a sense of control. Demolishing your home is a way for you to rid yourself of the past. It isn't that easy. If it were, there would hardly be a home that stood for more than ten years. Hell, most wouldn't stand that long."

"I know the past won't go away. I don't want it *all* to go away— just some of it."

"You've made progress, even if you don't see it. I see it."

Tony turned toward him. "Being complacent and putting up with the shit here doesn't mean I've made progress. It means I don't have a choice. I'm not going to be this person when I get out of here. I can't."

Jim nodded. "I agree with you. When you're out of here, you

won't be the man you are in here: you also won't be the man you were before."

"I sure as hell plan on it."

"How did prison change Claire?"

Tony couldn't help the grin. "It made her bold and cheeky."

"*It* did?" Jim asked.

"Yes. She was something else. I've never had anyone talk to me the w—"

"Is prison making you bolder?"

The spark left his dark eyes. "I'd say no, but I plan on being that way again after I'm out."

"Why do you think prison made her bolder?"

Tony ran his hand through his hair. "Because it did. I told you. She was so much spunkier. Damn," he said reminiscing, "I loved her retorts."

"What was she like before you kidnapped her?"

Tony stared.

"Think about that Anthony: how many times has Claire been in prison? Which time changed her the most? Could the personality that you enjoyed so much be her true personality, not the one you experienced after you kidnapped her?'

"I don't fuck'n know. She was different the first time she came— was brought to the estate. At the time it was what I thought I wanted." Tony sighed. "I liked the control." His eyes changed from dull to bright. "But not as much as I enjoyed her later. I guess I knew that she was behaving the way I wanted her to. Hell, she even said what I wanted."

"And if she didn't."

Tony shrugged. "It's like here. You do what you're supposed to do, what you need to do, or else."

"Else?"

"There are consequences."

"Anthony, I know that reading Meredith Banks' book was difficult for you, but can you see how similar your situations are?"

"I don't like to think about it."

"Tell me one benefit of being here, at Yankton."

Tony muffled a laugh. "There isn't one benefit to being here."

Jim shrugged. "Some people might disagree. I mean there are plenty of repeat felons. There must be something that's appealing."

"What? A roof over your head and three square meals a day? I have that at home in Iowa, where I live."

"You do, but that's a good start. How has your job stress been?"

"What fuck'n job stress? Tim and Patricia keep me updated, but I can't watch the stocks like I used to, I'm not involved with day-to-day decisions. Maybe you're talking about my job here?" He tilted his head toward the window. "I'm pretty pissed off about the new snow that's fallen. I just had that fuck'n sidewalk cleared."

"So, benefit number one, food and shelter. Benefit number two, less stress."

"If you're going there, be more specific," Tony corrected. "Less job stress. This place has plenty of other stress."

"All right, give me two of those stressors in this place."

Tony didn't need to think about his answer. "The damn *counts*. I hate that, and being told what to do and when to do it. Nothing, none of your so-called benefits outweighs that."

"So what would make you come back here?"

Tony squared his shoulders. "Nothing. Not one damn thing."

"Interesting." Jim moved back to his chair and leaned back. "So what if it changed? What if you could come back, still get the benefits, but the stressors were less?"

"Not interested."

"Really? Why?"

"The counts, the shit, it would always be here. I'd still remember it."

"I think our time is about up, and you have a count in less than ten minutes. Between this time and next time, think about this conversation. Oh, and don't do anything rash regarding your house."

Tony nodded. "I'll think about it, and I've already given the orders. The house is going."

Spring 2016

TONY'S JAW CLENCHED as he waited for Brent to answer his phone. Tony only had a small window of time to use the damn phone, and the next person to use it was standing a mere few feet away. How fuck'n hard was it to get some damn privacy?

"Yes, I'll accept the charges." Tony heard Brent say. "Tony, is everything all right? Why are you calling?"

"I want Patricia fired. I want you to meet her at the airport, let her get her things at Rawlings, and escort her off the property."

The shock in Brent's voice came through the line. "W-what the hell? Tony, are you thinking straight?"

"Yes, I'm thinking straight. I can't work with her anymore and I won't."

"Do you mind filling me in on what happened?"

"I'm a man. I'm not fuck'n dead, but I don't care what Roach says, I believe Claire's going to get better."

"Tony, what does that have to do with Patricia?"

"It's been happening for a while, but I didn't really notice, or I guess I wasn't paying attention. When I did, I thought if I just ignored her, it would stop. They have rules here. Shit, she almost got me in trouble."

"I'm still lost," Brent said.

"She fuck'n made a move on me. She's been saying things about wanting to help me, help me *not be so lonely*, come visit more often. Then she started talking about Nichol and how Claire was too sick to care for her. She said that she'd never do that. She'd never leave her husband and daughter. She said that she could care for Nichol like a mother, better than Claire. I about lost it. I was fuck'n wanting to get her away from me. She knew I was mad, but she started to say how she understands... I'm just lonely and frustrated. Well, she's got that right, but not for her! Years ago, before Claire and I were married, Patricia accompanied me to a few outings. It was usually last minute. She talked about that and how she wished I'd never met Claire—if I hadn't, we'd be together. Then, when the buzzer sounded for visiting time to end, she leaned over, gave me a way too good shot at her low-cut blouse, and kissed me!"

When Tony stopped talking, it wasn't Brent who replied but Courtney. She gasped and said, "She did what?! Oh no, there's no way she's getting anywhere near Nichol. Don't you worry. Aunt Cort is on this."

"You're on speaker, Tony."

"Yes, I kind of figured. I have about thirty seconds left on this call. I'm so mad I can hardly see straight. She's flying back to Iowa on the Rawlings jet right now. I want you to meet her at the airport."

Brent replied, "Not a problem. I'm behind you one hundred percent."

"So am I," Courtney chimed in.

"I don't want this to be public knowledge, only a need-to-know basis. Her leaving will be for some other reason. Work it out. Pay her. I don't give a damn. Just be sure she signs a gag order. Claire's coming back to me. I'm coming back to her. There's no way in hell I would ever..."

"I'll take care of it," Brent said, just as the phone went dead.

Summer 2016

"DO YOU BELIEVE she'll ever see it?" Jim asked about the new house Tony had been describing.

"Of course she'll see it. She'll live in it."

"Remember what we talked about. Remember the conclusion you've drawn."

Tony nodded. "I do. I get it. Claire coming back to me, remarrying me, even though I was different—or tried to be different—will always be a prison to her. I get that. That doesn't mean I can't make her life the best it can be."

"Anthony, whose decision is it, how Claire's life should be?"

"Hers." He stood and paced to the window, smiling for just a moment at the colorful view. "I know. It's hers. I'm giving her the estate—all the land and the new house. It'll all be hers. She can fuck'n sell it if she wants. My name won't be on it at all. I understand that our relationship can never be what I thought we had. I even get that maybe what we had in the South Pacific wasn't real: it was more of her conditioned response. I hate it, but I get it. It'd be like me going somewhere else with all the same people from here. The familiarity would make the same feelings come out. Without being here at Yankton, I don't think I would have gotten it, but I do." He ran his hands through his hair. "I can hear her pain and fear in that damn book. I won't do that to her again."

"Why do you think you hear that now, but you didn't six years ago?"

"We never talked about it. It happened, but we never discussed it. Besides, I didn't want to hear it then."

"Do you want to hear it now?"

"No. I hate it. I hate that I was the cause of it. I just thought we'd made it past all of that..." Tony's words trailed away.

"Can you make it past this—here?" Jim asked, motioning around the room.

Tony's shoulders straightened as he stood taller. "I *will* make it past this."

"Will you forget your time here?"

"I can try."

Jim leaned forward. "But it will always be a part of who you are. Just like the kidnapping, imprisonment, and required subjugation will always be a part of Claire. The best that she can hope for is to try to forget and move on. Tell me if you can—well, I guess you *can* since you have the means—*would* you ever consider moving to Yankton? I mean, it's a great community."

"Hell no."

"Why?" Jim asked.

"Do you need to ask?"

"Will it be easier to put this prison camp behind you in Iowa than if you lived here?"

Red tried to infiltrate Tony's thoughts. "I get it. I get what you're saying. But not only am I talking about Claire, I'm talking about Nichol too. I can't imagine not knowing where they are. I don't know what I'd do."

"You'd do what most people do: you'd get joint custody. You'd live your life and let her live hers. You're building this grand new home with the help of your friends and yet, you're not considering that Claire, if she gets better, may never want to live there. She may finally realize that she wants as far away from Iowa as you want away from here."

"When she was released from prison, she moved to California," Tony admitted.

"How will you feel when she tells you that she wants to move back to California or back to the island or anywhere?"

"I'll feel like shit, but it's her decision."

Jim smiled. "Anthony, you've made great progress over the past two years. I'm proud of you."

As Tony walked back toward his dormitory, he contemplated the session. He didn't hate Jim the way he had in the beginning. Truthfully, it felt good to talk, better than Tony had ever imagined. That didn't mean he liked all that they discussed, but in his heart, Tony knew it was true. He'd been in control of Claire's life for longer than she knew him. That wasn't a way to live. Not for her, and not for him. She would get better. When she did, she deserved, for the first time in most of her adult life, to live her own life.

So what? He was building the house for her. If she didn't want to be there, he was truthful when he said she could sell it.

He'd made progress. Tony grinned, thinking of Jim's last comment. That was definitely something Tony planned to say to Nichol as much as possible. How hard was that? *I'm proud of you.* Four words that felt better than closing the biggest deal. Yes, those would definitely be in his father vocabulary—if Claire allowed him to be with Nichol.

Tony looked at his cheap commissary watch. He had four minutes until standing count.

Chapter 21

June 2016

John

———◆———

**What you are willing to sacrifice is the
measurement of how you love.
—Jada Pinkett Smith**

"SHE CAME UP to me at the park. At the park, John! Are you listening
to me?" Emily asked.

"I'm listening to you. It sounds like you took care of it," John
replied.

"I told her to stay away, from me, from Nichol, and from
Claire." Emily turned circles in their master bedroom suite. "I was
so upset. I mean, after that damn book, she has the audacity to
come up to me! To me! And ask to talk to Claire... to do another
story?!"

John reached for his wife's hand. "Come here." He tugged her
toward the bed. "Sit, calm down. You said your piece, and you
walked away. If she bothers you again, you can call the police. She's
a reporter. She falls under the guidelines of the restraining order."

Emily sat next to her husband and sighed. "I'm just afraid..."

"Of what?"

"I said something. I told her that Claire couldn't answer her questions. I told her that Claire wasn't talking to anyone. I shouldn't have told her that much."

John's chest inflated with a deep breath. "Did you tell her it was off the record?"

Emily grinned. "I think I may have threatened her life if she repeated anything I said."

John nodded as he pulled Emily closer. "Well, I guess that could legally be interpreted as *off the record.*"

"That's how I meant it." She lay back on the soft comforter and sighed. "This feels so good."

"Did you go to Everwood this morning?" John asked.

Emily nodded. "We went for a little walk. I keep hoping she'll realize that she's outside or something. Then I helped Claire with her lunch. I swear she isn't eating when I'm not there. Not that she eats that well when I'm there."

"Did she talk?"

"Not really."

They both turned as their bedroom door opened and a rush of little feet came running in. Within seconds Nichol and Michael were up on their bed, giggling, and hugging John and Emily. Pulling Nichol into his arms, John turned and saw Becca, their nanny, standing in the doorway.

"I'm sorry, Mr. and Mrs. Vandersol. Nichol asked for you. The next thing I know—they're both running at full speed," Becca explained.

John reached around and tickled Michael's tummy, sending the noise level of the room up a few decibels. "It's all right, Becca. We needed a little positive energy in here."

"I can take them back downstairs—"

"They're fine," Emily replied. "Besides, it's about time for supper…"

A month later—July 2016

JOHN SAT IN his home office, finishing his review of a proposal, when his phone buzzed. It was a text message from Harry.

"I'D LIKE TO SPEAK TO YOU AND EMILY, IN PERSON. I CAN BE IN IOWA TOMORROW OR THE NEXT DAY. PLEASE LET ME KNOW IF WE CAN SCHEDULE SOMETHING".

John sighed. He'd meant to contact Harry since the news about Amber broke, but he didn't know what to say. Truthfully, he'd had enough fires of his own, so he wasn't anxious to step into another. John replied to the text:

"WE'LL WORK SOMETHING OUT. LET US KNOW WHEN YOU'RE IN TOWN."

"GREAT, TOMORROW NIGHT, I'LL GET BACK WITH YOU."

"SOUNDS GOOD."

His thoughts filled with their friend as John searched room to room, looking for Emily. Poor Harry had to learn that his sister had murdered his friend. Well, John's sister-in-law had been accused of attempted murder—twice—and she wasn't guilty either time. Maybe Amber wasn't either? John had read that she'd pleaded not guilty. The trial wasn't scheduled to begin until early fall.

He turned the corner to Michael's nursery and stopped at the vision of his wife and children. Emily's attention was too centered on the book and children for her to notice his presence. It was moments like this, watching the woman he loved, rocking back and forth with both Nichol and Michael in her lap, that he could forget how this all came to be. Nichol's little head drooped forward: despite her cousin's fidgeting, she was sound asleep. Emily's animated voice continued softly as she continued to read. With each page, Michael's lids grew heavier and heavier. Their son's earlier restlessness to try to stay awake gave way to the power of the story, jammies, and methodical rocking. His little head rested against his mommy and his limbs stilled. John waited as Emily continued reading.

Finally, making his presence known, he whispered, "Hey, I think they're both asleep."

Her bright green eyes peered upward from the rocking chair. "I know, but I wanted to find out what happened to Mr. Bunny. I would've lain awake all night worrying about his lost mitten," she said with a grin.

John walked closer and lifted Nichol from her arms. "I'm so glad you have one less thing to worry about." He kissed Emily. "I'll go put her in her room. How about you and I have a glass of wine and you can tell me about Mr. Bunny's mitten. I'm assuming he found it?"

"Oh, you have no idea what an ordeal it was."

After the children were both tucked in bed, John went to the kitchen to pour their wine. The stillness of the scene outside the window caught his attention. The Iowa summer sky twinkled with a blanket of stars. Silently, Emily wrapped her arms around his waist. "What are you looking at?"

"The stars. Let's go out on the deck."

"That sounds great."

A slight breeze blew Emily's hair as they made their way outside. Though the heat of the day had only lessened a bit with the setting of the sun, the fresh air was invigorating. Their home was away from neighbors and lights. Their silver illumination came from the glow of the moon and stars. Sitting on the loveseat, John wrapped one arm around Emily. "This is beautiful, isn't it?"

"It is."

"Did you ever imagine this, us living in Iowa?"

Emily giggled. "Not in a million years."

"You know, it isn't all bad. I'm surprised how much I enjoy working for Tim. Corporate law is challenging, and I like working with Brent, Tom, and, well, everyone."

Emily nodded. "All in all, things could be worse. If only..."

"Don't do that."

She took a sip of wine and peered innocently over the rim of her glass.

"She'll get better. Don't give up on her, and don't miss out on the blessings that we have by wishing..."

"I'm not. I love every minute we have with the kids. I think it was seeing Meredith last month. I'm so afraid for Claire and Nichol. I don't want the world to know what Claire's going through. Then, there're those new tests that we've authorized. I'm not sure if we made the right decision. Claire was content. Now, I'm afraid of what they'll learn." John hugged her tighter. After a moment, she went on, "And ever since Brent mentioned that Anthony's going to petition for early release, I can't stop thinking about it."

"What did your grandma used to say about borrowing—"

Emily smiled. "There's no such thing as borrowed troubles. Once you take them, no one wants them back."

"So don't do it. Leave them out there."

Nodding, she laid her head against his shoulder. The sound of crickets and cicadas filled the night. "This is nice."

John chuckled.

"What?" Emily asked.

"I was just thinking about everything you just said. I'm so glad you got the Mr. Bunny thing worked out. I can see how that would be the straw..."

Emily giggled. "Oh, you don't know! He was searching everywhere for that mitten!"

"I love you. We just need to take it one day at a time."

"I love you too. Hey?" Emily's eyes grew wide. "I've been rambling on. What about you?"

"What about me?"

"How's work... without Patricia, I mean?"

John drank another sip of his wine and wished he could tell Emily why Patricia was fired. There was no doubt that he missed having her around the office. Her boundless knowledge regarding the company helped him considerably in the beginning. Nevertheless, John respected Anthony's decision. He wasn't sure how many other men would have reacted the same way. Despite the fact that Anthony had only served two years of his four-year sentence and his wife was living in a world that no one could understand or even tap into, when push came to shove, Anthony stood up for his marriage. He'd chosen Claire over the smart, pretty, and available woman who'd worked beside him for years. John hated to admit it, but the longer he worked at Rawlings, the more respect he had for his brother-in-law.

"We're doing fine," he said. "I'll admit I miss being able to just ask her questions, but I'm an attorney. I love research and paperwork. Now, I've got more things to research."

"I think it's strange that she just decided to leave?" Though the inflection of her tone turned her statement into a question, John chose to let it go.

"Oh," John said, "Before I forget, we're getting together with Harry Baldwin tomorrow night. He's going be in town and wants to talk to us."

"Harry's going to be in Iowa? Why?"

"He didn't say."

"I don't know what to say to him... about Amber. I'm shocked."

John agreed, as the two fell silent and listened to the peaceful sounds of the Iowa night. For a few minutes they could forget about Claire's troubles, the fear over Nichol's future, Anthony's impending release, and even Mr. Bunny's mitten. For a few moments, they could be husband and wife and enjoy each other's company.

━━━━◆━━━━

HOPING THAT IT would make Harry more comfortable, Emily offered to have their get-together at their home. "I can make dinner. It'll be like old times," she suggested.

"Yes, old times—with two children running here and there," John replied.

She shrugged. "All right, new times, but it'll be more private."

John gave her a kiss, as he readied for work. "I'll let him know."

That evening after John came home, Harry arrived to their house. They hadn't seen him for almost two years, yet he'd aged beyond that. His carefree appearance was hidden behind a new mask of worry and concern. His blue eyes appeared clouded with angst. John knew the burdened feeling, too well. It hadn't been that long ago that he carried the same look. Seeing Harry reminded John that despite it all, their lives had improved.

"Harry, we're so sorry about Amber," Emily offered, as she led him to the screened porch. The shaded room with the softly rotating ceiling fan offered them the beauty of the outdoors with a refreshing breeze. "We're very familiar with false accusations. Hopefully, during the trial—"

Harry shook his head, and replied, "Thank you, time will tell; however, it doesn't look promising."

Emily offered a reassuring hug. "I'm sorry. I'm sure it was a shock."

"It was. It's actually made me rethink a lot of my choices, kind of a life inventory."

Just then, the shrill ring of children's laughter resonated from beyond the porch. "The kids are playing with their nanny in the side yard," John explained with a grin.

Light returned to Harry's blue eyes. "I bet they're getting big. I've never met your son. Michael? Is that right?"

"It is. He's almost two. It's hard to believe," John said.

"And Nichol?" Harry asked.

"She'll be three in December, and she's beautiful," Emily offered with pride.

"I bet she is. She has a beautiful mother." Harry's words carried a wave of sadness. "How is Claire doing?"

John looked at Emily, deferring to her. Even with the closest of friends she was apprehensive about sharing information.

"She hasn't changed much since you saw her last," Emily began. "I don't share it with many people, but since you two were close, I will. As much as I want to be positive, most research suggests that if recovery doesn't happen within the first twelve months, it's unlikely."

Harry nodded. "I've looked into traumatic brain injury, too."

Taking Emily's lead, John went on. "However, Claire's doctor heard this professor from Princeton speak at some medical conference. He has research showing recovery as late as four years post psychotic break. The NFL and its problems with CTE (chronic traumatic encephalopathy) has really spawned a surge in research into TBI recovery."

"Yes, I honestly think of Claire every time I see something about it on the news," Harry said.

"Emily's agreed to allow this doctor to review Claire's information and run some more tests. Once he's done with that, we're supposed to meet with him and hear what he has to say."

Harry's forehead wrinkled. "So this is good information?"

Emily feigned a grin. "We hope so, but I don't like to get my hopes up."

"It's the most encouraging news we've heard in a while. And now it's great to see you."

"Yes," Emily said, "We need to catch up, and dinner is almost ready."

After lighthearted dinner conversation, where Nichol and Michael entertained and the adults reminisced, the three friends enjoyed a glass of wine back on the porch. "Your home is beautiful. How do you like living in Iowa?"

"Better than we expected," Emily said. "It's not as exciting as living in California, and I'm okay with that. It actually reminds me a lot of Indiana."

Harry nodded. "I remember Claire saying the same thing."

"I get the feeling you wanted to tell us something, Harry? I mean, who just comes to Iowa?" John asked.

Harry leaned forward in his chair. "I actually have a lot I want to say, but I'm thinking I should just leave instead."

Emily's questioning expression met John's, before she asked, "Is it something about Amber?"

Harry inhaled. "Please, listen to everything before you comment. Let me explain it all."

John reached for Emily's hand. "We're listening," he said.

"I'm moving to North Carolina. I'll go back to California for Amber's trial, but like I said, I've been doing some re-evaluation of things. I-I, damn, this is harder than I thought."

Emily's voice softened. "Harry, I have no idea what you're going to say, but it's all right. We're your friends. You've been great to us and to Claire. You can tell us anything."

"See, that's the thing. I haven't been. Not really. Not to Claire and not to you. I haven't been honest. It wasn't that I wanted to be dishonest. It's that it was my job. And I say *was* because I've quit my job. They call it retiring, but I'm not exactly of retirement age."

"You quit your job with the CBI?" John asked.

"No," Harry went on, "with the FBI. I've been an agent with the Federal Bureau of Investigation for almost ten years."

"My grandfather was with the FBI," Emily said. Her brows knit together. "He did undercover work. Is that what you've been doing? Oh, my God, is your name really Harry? Is Amber really your sister?"

"My name is Harrison Baldwin and Amber is my half-sister; we share a mother. This was a very unusual case."

John's voice deepened. "*What* was an unusual case? Amber?"

Harry shook his head, "Amber was a byproduct. My assignment was Claire."

Emily gasped.

"Please, let me continue. I'm telling you all of this because we have become friends. I value your friendship and I wanted to apologize."

"For lying?" Emily asked.

"I was doing my job. I wasn't lying, but I feel responsible for Chester's attack on Claire. I was the one who took her to him. It was a lead I wanted to follow, and I thought if she were with me... I shouldn't have done it. I had no idea I was putting her in danger."

"He attacked her because of *him*, not you," Emily refuted.

"Chester would never have known about Claire if it weren't for me. There's more. I saw Claire in Europe before she and Rawlings went into hiding. I talked with her. She knows that I'm an agent, and she told me in no uncertain terms to leave." He grinned. "I wish she'd tell me off like that again." He refocused. "She was right, and she was determined about her decision to reunite with *him*. I know you have reasons to hate him, but I wanted you to know that her decision to remarry him was not coerced."

Before either of the Vandersols could respond, Harry went on. "I'm not supposed to tell anyone any of this, but since Claire can't, I thought you needed to know. They were both in contact with the bureau while they were away. It was a strange kind of limbo—more like a self-induced/bureau-accepted witness-protection situation. The bureau was investigating the deaths of many people, including one of our own—your grandfather—associated with the unusual poison actaea pachypoda. The connection that the bureau found was Anthony Rawlings. I was assigned to learn Claire's secrets in an effort to confirm Rawlings' connection. As you know, it wasn't him, but Ms. London. While the case was being investigated, Rawlings negotiated a one-year reprieve with Claire and Nichol in the South Pacific."

"A year? They weren't gone a year," John said.

"No," Harry agreed. "They came back early, against the wishes of the bureau."

"But why? Why did they do that? If they had clearance to stay safe—"

"Rawlings had some contact—he would never say who, although we have our suspicions. Anyway, his contact informed him of your visit to the estate."

Emily inhaled as her eyes widened. "They left that island because of *us*?"

"According to Rawlings' statement, they were concerned about your safety. When it'd been confirmed that you were traveling here to Iowa, they traveled home. Rawlings hoped to get to Ms. London before you arrived."

John looked at his wife. "Remember, we got an earlier flight."

"Oh, I can't believe how this really fits," Emily said.

"This is all classified, or most of it. Even leaving the bureau doesn't allow me to share this information, but I keep thinking about Claire. I really did care for her. I can't say we were madly in love, but we did become good friends." His eyes twinkled with memories. "The research I saw about TBI was what you said earlier, if recovery doesn't happen in the first year... Well, if she can never tell you the truth, I still thought you deserved to know."

John nodded as his mind swirled with new and old information. He and Emily weren't supposed to arrive to the Rawlings estate until later. If only...

He tried to refocus on Harry. As much as he wanted to be upset, the emotion that seemed paramount was gratitude.

"Thank you, thanks for telling us the truth. We won't share it, if that's what you want," John said.

"As long as you don't do a press release," Harry said with a grin, "I see no harm in letting you know."

John smiled. "We're not much into sharing with the media." Changing the subject, he asked, "Why North Carolina? What are you going to do there?"

"I'm thinking about starting my own investigative firm. Law enforcement has always been my dream. Entering the FBI was the ultimate fulfillment, but lately I've realized that the adrenaline rush I used to get from the dangers has been replaced. You see, I was married a long time ago. She's remarried, but I've been talking with her. We have a daughter who's almost seven. I've missed so much of my child's life." His eyes brimmed with moisture. "I don't want to miss any more. That rush now comes when I think about moving closer and getting to know my daughter. Thankfully, my ex-wife is willing to re-introduce us. Hopefully, Jillian will allow me to be part of her life."

"That's a beautiful name," Emily said.

The tips of Harry's lips turned upward. "It's silly, but my name begins with an *H*, my ex-wife's with an *I*, we used to joke about continuing the alphabet. Ilona and I were already separated when she gave birth, but I was thrilled when I heard her name."

"What about Liz?" Emily asked.

"We're taking it slowly. She's pretty devastated about Amber, but she's willing to move to North Carolina with me. They've asked her to stay at SiJo and help the new CEO: she's joining me after I get settled, maybe after the trial. I'm not sure what happened with the company. I was afraid that it would be gobbled up in some frenzy after everything went public. Liz said there was some talk of that, but then everything quieted. The board of directors have asked Simon's mother to take a role, at least temporarily. I think it's more as a figurehead, but it was a nice gesture. The new CEO is someone with a lot of experience. For Simon's sake, I hope they can keep it going."

John did know background on that, and though he appreciated Harry's candor, he couldn't reciprocate. It was Rawlings Industries, more specifically Roger Cunningham from Shedis-tics, who got the ball rolling on securing SiJo's future. It was done as discreetly as possible. Apparently, Anthony didn't want it to appear that Shedis-tics was priming the pump for a takeover. The instructions were painfully clear: it was strictly a rescue mission. SiJo would remain an independent company.

"We'll see what the future holds. Liz isn't sure how she feels about a seven-year-old daughter, and I get it. I'm hoping that once she gets to know Ilona and her husband, she'll feel more secure. I think she's worried about my being around my ex, but there's nothing to fear. We were kids when we married. I want a relationship with Jillian, and even though I'll be in North Carolina and Liz will be in California for right now, we hope to make it work. Our plan is to be together in North Carolina eventually. I'm thankful that Liz is supporting me."

John listened as Emily asked more questions and Harry willingly answered. It was so much to process, too many pieces of the puzzle that seemed to forever remain unfinished. Despite the deception, there was something pure and sad in the man before them. He'd followed his dream career and figured out that nothing compared to his family. Harry talked about the sense of loss with Amber. Even his mother was upset that he didn't use his role with the FBI to help his sister. He felt completely disconnected, until

Ilona reached out to him. Through their conversations, Harry realized that Jillian was his family—his anchor. He wasn't alone. He had roots, if only he was willing to step up and accept them. He'd chosen the FBI over his family once. He wouldn't do that again.

There was more than that in Harry's visit. There was the information about Rawlings. John couldn't comprehend that Anthony and Claire had given up their security for him and Emily. Then again, he and Emily had given up their life in California for Claire and Nichol. Harry was giving up his dream career for Jillian.

Maybe it wasn't what you give up—maybe it was what you receive.

Chapter 22

September 2016

John

———◆———

Miracles come in moments. Be ready and willing.
—Wayne Dyer

"WHAT DID THEY SAY?" Emily asked for the tenth time.

"I've told you. They just said that there'd been a development with Claire and we needed to get to Everwood as soon as possible."

John watched the passing landmarks as he drove toward Cedar Rapids. To his right, Emily fidgeted with her fingernails as she rested her elbow against the lower edge of the window. No doubt, the early morning traffic was heavier than what she usually experienced on her later drives.

"Did they say *what* development?"

"Em, I've told you the entire conversation, verbatim."

"Why didn't you ask? What if something bad happened? We're supposed to have that meeting this morning, at 8:30 AM, with that aide who's been working so well with Claire. Do you think Claire took a turn for the worse? I mean, why wouldn't they just wait and tell us when we got there? It has to be bad. Otherwise, they would've just waited."

John reached over and touched Emily's arm. "Stop. Stop trying to second-guess. I'm nervous too, but it doesn't do any good to overanalyze. We don't have enough information—yet."

"I bet it has something to do with Dr. Fairfield's treatment. So help me... if it did something. Oh, John, you didn't see how distraught she's been. She paces. She's uncooperative. That's not my sister. I mean, she's made bad decisions and done things that I don't agree with, but she's always been cooperative. Even in that damn book, she talked about how cooperative she was. I never should have allowed him to change her medications and treatment regimen. If something bad happened, it's my fault."

"Dr. Fairfield explained that those were good signs, that it showed she was becoming more aware of the world around her, instead of living in some make-believe fantasy."

Emily huffed. "I don't care what he said. What if she got upset and they had to do something to her... Oh, I hated getting those reports when she needed to be restrained. If they'd just talk to her... that calms her down. She's what... a hundred and ten pounds. It's not like she's dangerous. I don't understand. So help me... if they had to restrain her again after how well she *was* doing, I promise I'll have some heads on a platter, and the first one will be Dr. Fairfield's."

John pulled into the gate and down the long tree-lined drive. Truly, the grounds of Everwood were beautiful. He remembered how, even as a child, Claire enjoyed the outdoors. When she was young, her dad used to take her camping. John believed it was good that part of Claire's daily routine was going outside.

The change in plans both worried and disappointed John. He'd been looking forward to speaking with Claire's aide, Ms. Russel. Her reports were the most encouraging news they'd received on Claire since her ordeal began. At first, they seemed too good to be true, but her supervisor, Mrs. Bali, confirmed them. The Vandersols had tried to meet with Ms. Russel on other occasions, but each time something caused her to cancel. When Emily's phone rang this morning, while she was in the shower, John half expected it to be Everwood, canceling yet again. He should have asked more questions, but the call was brief and his initial reaction was relief that the meeting wasn't cancelled. At least, he didn't think it was cancelled. Hopefully, after they worked out this *development*, the meeting could occur.

Dr. Fairfield's assistant was waiting for them within the doors of the main facility. John couldn't decide if her bright smile was sincere or if she was trying to hide something. It looked, different.

"Good morning Valerie. What's happening with my sister?" Emily asked, impatiently.

"Good morning Mr. and Mrs. Vandersol. Your sister is fine. Please, come with me."

When Valerie led them to the elevator and pushed the button for the office floor, Emily questioned, "Why are we going to the offices? After your call this morning, I want to see Claire. I need to be sure that she's all right." John wrapped his arm reassuringly around Emily's waist.

"Mrs. Vandersol, we're going to your sister."

"Why isn't she in her room?" Emily looked at her watch. "It's still early. She should be in her room, and someone should be there helping her—"

The elevator doors opened and Valerie stepped into the hallway. Emily glared up at John. With her lips pressed together,

John knew she was refraining from commenting about Valerie's departure during Emily's speech. Inhaling deeply, she followed, as did John.

"Let me show you, before you go in," Valerie said, as she opened a door with a plate beside the frame that read *Observation*.

"Show us?" Emily asked.

"There's no sound, but you can see." She flipped a switch and a large mirrored surface became a window. In the next room, they could see Claire sitting in a chair with Dr. Brown facing her and Dr. Fairfield standing near. Dr. Brown's lips moved and then so would Claire's!

Emily covered her mouth as large tears flowed down her cheeks. "Oh, my God! Is she talking?"

"Yes, Mrs. Vandersol, she is."

Had it not been for John's steady footing, Emily would have knocked them both to floor as she fell into his chest. Valerie flipped another switch that must have signaled Dr. Fairfield. He looked up and said something to Dr. Brown, who nodded. Within seconds, Dr. Fairfield was opening the door to their room. His normally stoic expression was replaced by the largest smile John had ever seen on the good doctor's face.

"Mr. and Mrs. Vandersol, we must continue to have a guarded prognosis, but this is good. This is very good."

Emily shook her head. "I can't believe it. I want to talk to her."

"And you will. I wanted to explain a few things first."

John watched through the window as Dr. Fairfield explained the happenings of the day. The staff had entered Claire's room to wake her: when they did, she was already showered and dressed. Then, she proceeded to tell them that she didn't want eggs for breakfast; she wanted fruit. The staff was so shocked that they called Dr. Brown, who called Dr. Fairfield. The entire facility was abuzz with the news.

"Is it permanent?" John asked.

"I can't answer that with one-hundred-percent accuracy. The human brain is an amazing organ. It makes a path when medically we don't see a possibility. Something was stopping your sister-in-law from facing reality. Her DTI images told us that she was living and experiencing sensations during her episodes. The change in medication and intensive therapy has worked to essentially bring her two worlds back to one. We all dream; we all have memories. The trick is to only visit those fantasies, not to live there. Ms. Nichols was stuck in that other world. I was hopeful during her recent bouts with agitation that we were on the right track. You see, no one wants to leave that other world, assuming it's a pleasant place to be. From Ms. Nichols' tests and behaviors, I believe that where she was, she enjoyed being. As the therapy began to work, her episodes decreased. The agitation was her frustration at losing what she enjoyed. My goal was for that frustration to build to the point of action. I believe that's where we are. Ms. Nichols took action. She knows where she is. She knows her name and her daughter's name. We'll have to wait and see if her brain can handle the onslaught of information that she'll encounter with this new awakening. I recommend that her therapy be increased."

Emily's chest heaved with deep sobs. "Please, I need to see her."

Valerie handed her a tissue, as Dr. Fairfield warned, "She knows that you're on your way. She's expressed concern about you being upset with her."

"Oh God, no," Emily exclaimed. "I'm not upset. I want my sister."

"Please, calm yourself. Understand that this is very overwhelming for her."

Emily nodded. "I understand."

As John worked unsuccessfully to hold back the tears, he gratefully took a tissue offered by Dr. Fairfield's assistant. This development was more than they'd dared to hope. Taking a few deep breaths, John and Emily followed Dr. Fairfield out the door, down the hall, and into the next room. When the door opened, Claire kept her head bowed, and peered up at them through veiled lashes.

"Claire!" Emily cried, as she ran to her sister and wrapped her in her arms. The rest of the room stood by helplessly as both women hugged and cried. Eventually, John joined his family, wrapping them both in his arms.

Emily took Dr. Brown's chair and leaned forward, with her knees touching Claire's and their foreheads mere inches away, Emily held tightly to her sister's hands. "Tell us how you're doing."

"I'm... tired," Claire replied.

"Oh, Claire, thank God."

Claire's eyes widened. "You're... not mad?"

"No, no, I'm not mad. I'm thrilled. John's thrilled. We've missed you."

"I had to go," she said, her words running together.

Emily questioned, "You had to go? Where did you go?"

"Away... for N-Nichol."

"Honey, we know all about that. It's all right, you're back."

Claire sighed. "Yes."

Her sentences were short, but it was obvious that she was fully comprehending every question that anyone asked. Eventually, John knelt beside them and touched Claire's knee. When her piercing green eyes met his, John grinned. "Hey, lady, I've missed you."

Claire leaned forward and wrapped her arms around John's neck. "Thank you... thank you... for not being... upset."

"At you? Never."

Claire sniffled. "You were... I'm sorry."

"Hey, don't be sorry. Just stay with us, okay? No more going away."

She nodded. "I don't know... where... I'd go."

Everyone giggled. "That's good," Emily said, "you just stay right here with us."

"And... Nichol?" Claire asked.

Emily nodded as her gaze went to John and back to Claire. "Yes, eventually, of course, she needs you, but not yet. We need to get you better first."

A tear escaped Claire's lower lid and descended her cheek. "I understand... but... I've missed... too much."

Emily looked up to Dr. Brown. "Where's Ms. Russel? She should be here. Dr. Fairfield, I know it's been your regimen, but Ms. Russel has helped to get my sister to this point. I want to thank her."

"She should be at the meeting downstairs. I'll ask Valerie to bring her up," Dr. Fairfield offered.

John had never experienced a more emotional morning. He didn't know for sure how long they stayed in that room, but by the time they helped Claire back to her room and joined her for lunch, he knew he'd be no good to anyone at Rawlings for the rest of the day. He was spent. It was all too much: hearing his sister-in-law responding, seeing the comprehension in her eyes, and watching her feed herself, was truly a dream come true.

They never were able to thank Ms. Russel. Valerie said that she brought her up to the floor, and they'd watched through the window. She said that Ms. Russel didn't want to interrupt this important family reunion, and said that she was too emotional. She was afraid she'd upset Claire.

"Oh, I wanted so much to speak with her," Emily replied, though she and John completely understood. It'd been more emotional than either one of them had expected.

"Please... don't... stop... her from... coming," Claire said.

Emily grinned and patted Claire's knee. "Don't worry about that. Of course, we wouldn't stop her. Do you like her?"

Claire nodded. Between her posture and drooping eyelids, it was obvious she was getting tired.

"Why don't we let you rest?" John offered.

"I'll be back tomorrow," Emily said, "to see how you're doing. Will you be all right?"

"Yes... Tomorrow... will... you bring, Nichol?"

Emily pressed her lips tight and shook her head. "Honey, let's wait on that until we're sure you're all right. I showed you her picture. I'll bring some tomorrow for you to keep here in your room."

"She's so... big."

John replied, "She is, but she's still little. You'll have plenty of time with her. Right now, you concentrate on getting better. Listen to the doctors. I know you'll be feeling like your old self in no time at all."

Walking from Everwood into the autumn air, Emily squeezed John's hand. Although he felt as though he'd been through an emotional roller coaster, he couldn't help but smile. His wife looked beautiful. With her makeup gone and her eyes red, Emily's smile was the brightest he'd seen in years. "You're lovely," he whispered.

"Ha. I'm sure I look stunning. My head is throbbing and I've never been happier. Honestly, I could use a nap. Then," she added, "let's get the kids and celebrate. This was a miracle."

"I think that sounds like a great plan," John replied.

Chapter 23

Late September 2016

Brent

———◆———

If love is without sacrifice, it is selfish.
-Sadhu Vaswani

BRENT STARED AT his wife. Finally he asked, "Are you seriously going to meet Meredith Banks, the woman who wrote that vile book, at this hour of the night? Tell me again why."

Courtney reached for her purse. "Brent, I'll be fine. I'm meeting her at Short's Burgers in Iowa City."

"You're going to a bar—at 9:00 PM?"

"She said it was about Claire. She knew that Claire was getting better. I need to find out how she's gotten her information. I know I should call Emily. I do, and maybe I will. But Meredith also knew that I hadn't been allowed to see Claire. I mean, it was one thing when all Emily would say is that Claire's *not well*. Now it's different. Even though I can't tell Emily, I know she's getting better. Phil's reports have tons of great information from her medical records. However, every time I ask Emily to put me on the visitation list, she has some reason why the time isn't right."

"I don't like this," Brent said. "I don't like Meredith. Sometimes, I'm not thrilled with Emily, but I know that Emily thinks she's doing what's best for her sister."

Courtney pressed her lips together before speaking. Finally, she said, "I think Emily won't let me visit Claire because she knows that we still go see Tony every three weeks. She's mentioned more than once that if I ever am allowed to visit Claire I'm forbidden—oh, yes, she used that word, *forbidden*—from mentioning Tony's name in any form: Anthony, Tony, Rawlings, anything."

Brent shook his head. "Okay, Emily is a bit excessive. That still doesn't answer my—"

"Meredith said that if I came alone, she might be able to help me see Claire. I don't even know how she has that ability, but for Claire, I'm going to find out."

"Let me come with you."

"She said *alone*. I'm afraid if I bring you, it may scare her off. Brent, I'll be fine. I'll text you from Short's and before I head home," Courtney replied.

Brent pulled her close. "I just don't like my beautiful wife going off to a bar at night."

Courtney giggled. "You know me. You'll probably need to send a cab."

With that comment, and a quick kiss, Brent watched his wife disappear down the hall toward their garages. There was something about this whole thing that didn't seem right. He considered calling John. He'd never call Emily; she would most definitely freak out, but if he called John, and John told Emily. No. Brent sighed and recalled Tony's request last year at Yankton.

It was settled. Brent would trust Courtney's intuition. She hadn't steered him wrong in over thirty years. In the meantime, he'd work on Tony's latest request and wait by his phone. Brent didn't plan to file the papers to revoke Emily's power of attorney or request full custody of Nichol until Tony's release was assured. With that in mind, it could be in the next few weeks or it could be another year. Hell, if it were another year, Brent would undoubtedly do something else. The more he thought about Emily *forbidding* the mention of Tony's name and restricting Courtney's topics of conversation, the more it angered him. Claire was an adult. She'd been through hell, more than once, but he'd read Roach's most recent reports; she'd made her way out of purgatory—again. As much as Claire was their friend, if Brent were to analyze his feelings, he thought of her more like a daughter. After all, she wasn't much older than Caleb and Maryn. No matter what happened, he would do all he could to help her. Well, he had.

His phone buzzed.

"I JUST ARRIVED TO SHORT'S BURGER. MEREDITH ISN'T HERE YET. I THINK I COULD USE THAT DRINK! (Smiley face)"

He texted back:

"I DON'T BLAME YOU. LET ME KNOW IF YOU NEED THAT CAB."

"THE NIGHT IS YOUNG."

He smiled and lost himself once again to the motions at hand. It wasn't until nearly midnight that his phone buzzed again.

"OMG! IF YOU'RE AWAKE, YOU'LL WANT TO HEAR ALL I HAVE TO TELL YOU!"

"I'M AWAKE."

Courtney didn't wait until she was home, as soon as she was in her car, she called Brent. Instead of saying hello, he said, "Are you using your hands free?"

"No, I have two hands on the phone, and I'm driving with my knees. I was afraid I might drop it."

Brent snickered. "You're a smart-ass, but I love you."

"You're impossible, but I love you, too. Wait until you hear what Meredith has been doing..." Brent listened with bated breath as Courtney retold the story she'd just heard. It was unbelievable how Meredith had infiltrated Everwood. Truly, she and Roach should work out some kind of partnership. Between the two of them, there'd be no secrets left.

Courtney said that not only is Claire finally talking, she's asking for visitors, and Emily still won't let anyone in. It just wasn't right. Meredith believed that if Claire didn't get some positive reinforcement soon for her hard work, she'd decide that living in the real world wasn't worth the effort. It wasn't that Meredith was worried about Claire harming herself: she was worried about her mental stability. As it was, when Meredith left Claire's room tonight, Claire was crying.

"It makes me so mad. I want to drive over to the Vandersols' house and pound on their door until someone comes outside."

Brent laughed at his wife's vigor. That was one thing that could be said for Courtney: when she was in your corner, she was there forever, and most importantly, she was like a mother bear. "I don't recommend that you do that. We're still friends with Emily and John. I have to see John in the morning. I'd rather not start out the morning discussing news of how my wife was arrested on their front lawn."

"I'm going," Courtney announced.

Brent's eyes widened. "To the Vandersols 'house? Please don't."

"No, to Everwood. I'm sneaking onto the grounds. Meredith has a place where I can park. I have to walk a bit, but that's all right.

Meredith's responsible for taking Claire for her evening walk. She's going to bring Claire to me." Courtney's words came in such a rush: it was almost difficult to decipher each one.

"When?"

"Is it supposed to rain tomorrow?" Courtney asked.

Brent hit the mouse on his desk. "Let me look. I've been working and didn't hear the news." After a few clicks he had the forecast. "No, it looks clear for the next few nights."

"Then I'm going tomorrow night!"

"You know we're going to Yankton on Saturday?"

"I know!" Courtney exclaimed. "I can't wait to tell Tony."

Brent's smile widened. "I think it's just the kind of news he needs."

TONY'S DARK EYES widened. "You saw her?"

"I did!" Courtney exclaimed. "She's talking and... oh, Tony, she's better!"

Brent reached for Courtney's hand.

"W-what did they do? What happened?" Tony asked.

Courtney shook her head. "I really don't know. All I know is that they started some new treatment regimen with new medications. Meredith explained that she thinks—"

"Meredith?" Tony questioned.

"Yes!" Courtney's blue eyes shone. "As in Meredith Banks."

Tony leaned forward, his baritone voice sounding more like a growl. "If she's writing another—"

Courtney reached out and briefly touched Tony's hand. "She's not. I know. I didn't want to trust her at first either, but she swears she isn't. She said that originally that was her plan, but it changed. Tony, I think we should be happy that Meredith got to Claire. I know that I am."

He leaned back and crossed his arms over his chest. "I'm not sure I can ever be happy about Meredith Banks. How the hell do Emily and John not know that she's there?"

"She's not using her real name. Believe me, if I thought it was all for another of her sensationalized books, I'd report her." Courtney leaned forward and lowered her voice. "I may have even threatened her a little."

Tony's laugh resonated throughout the visitor's room. "You? Well, good!"

Brent interjected, "Don't laugh. She's pretty damn threatening when she wants to be."

"It was so good to see her. I know Emily thinks that she's doing what's best by Claire, but not allowing her to see anyone isn't what's best. She can't even go outside by herself. That's what Meredith does: she takes her outside after her dinner."

"You know my thoughts on Emily. I hate that she's doing that to Claire. How can she think it's for the best?"

Courtney shook her head. "I don't know. I'm not giving up."

Tony exhaled. "I've read Roach's reports. Her prognosis sounds good. What do you think?"

"I've only seen her once, but I'm so encouraged. Oh, Tony, she's back! And now if you..." Her words trailed away. "I'm sorry. I just want you to come home."

Tony grinned. "I promise, I'm ready to come home." His eyes widened. "Speaking of which, I'm pleased with the pictures of the new house. What do you think?"

Both Brent and Courtney nodded approvingly. "It's very nice," Brent said.

"It's better than *nice*," Courtney said. "It's beautiful and so homey. I'm sure you're both going to love it. Oh, and Nichol's room is perfect. I want you all there so badly."

Tony nodded, but his eyes were sad. Brent knew why, although he didn't have the heart to tell Courtney, or Tony's approval to do so. He'd known for a while. He'd prepared the preliminary petition for Tony and Claire's divorce. It had all begun months ago when Tony asked him to visit alone. As Tony's lawyer, he could see his client any day of the week, with approval. Truthfully, when Brent arrived, he was caught off-guard.

Prisoners are allowed more privacy when speaking with their attorneys. Therefore, when Brent arrived on a non-visitation day, he was led to a small individual room. Within no time, Tony was brought to him.

"Thanks for coming," Tony offered.

"Not a problem, it's your plane."

Tony grinned, but Brent could see the sadness. It'd been building for some time. It seemed like with each visit, it was more and more difficult to elicit the smiles or even smirks that Tony had once had. "I need you to start working on something for me."

"Sure, what do you need?"

"I want you to begin the petition needed to dissolve my marriage."

For more than a minute, Brent didn't respond. He stared. He looked around the room. Was this some kind of joke? After everything these two had been through. Finally, Brent leaned forward, and said, "Tony, I know they have you in some kind of counseling here, but I don't think you're thinking clearly. I saw the two of you before all this shit went down. I listened to you on the phone with the whole Patricia thing. You love your wife. I'm not sure why you think this is an answer. Is it because of her medical condition?"

"No. Don't question me—do it."

It was a tone Brent recognized. One he submitted to over the years, but times had changed. "I am questioning you. I did this once before and you regretted it. I'm not doing it again without some kind of explanation."

Running his hand through his hair, Tony looked down at the metal table. Brent's heart ached for the man before him. "I'm not good for her," Tony said.

"And?"

"And nothing. You've read the damn book. Hell, you saw her testimony. You know the things I did."

Brent couldn't hide his surprise. "That isn't an answer."

Tony lowered his voice. "It's all you're going to get. Forget for a fuck'n minute that we're friends and remember that you work for me. Remember that I'm the one who started the damn company, and I'm the one who ultimately decides who stays employed."

"You're threatening to fire me if I won't start divorce proceedings?"

"I don't make threats. Don't start the proceedings. Don't file it with the court yet. Just get everything ready."

Brent stood. "Fine, fire me. I'm not doing it without more information. Did you decide to take Patricia up on her offer and now you're feeling guilty?"

Tony's fist pounded the metal table sending shockwaves

throughout the small room. "Don't even fuck'n suggest such a thing."

Brent leaned closer and slowed his words. "Then tell me what's going on. I'm not spending my time preparing a petition if you won't tell me why."

"Claire deserves better."

Brent grinned. "All right, I'm agreeing with you."

"That's my answer. I'm no good for her, and she deserves better. I see that now. I see how much damage I did. I thought I could do what I did and then make up for it. I thought we could get past our..." he hesitated, "...start. Do you know the statistics for relationships when someone... when there's a history of..." Tony looked down. "It can never work."

"Well, excuse me if I'm wrong, but wasn't it working? Those people who came to my house with their new baby? Those people were madly in love. Hell, I'm not some kind of romantic, but I felt it. I know what I saw. You tell me that you don't love Claire. Tell me that you've fallen out of love. If you can do that, I'll do as you ask."

"You'll do as I ask, because that's your job. You want to hear my reason, fine. No, I haven't fallen out of love. I love her more than I can possibly say. I've loved her forever, since before she knew me. The months before she left the second time, and those on the island were the best months of my entire life. I'm fifty-one fuck'n years old and I have—what?—one year that I can say was fantastic. That leaves fifty that were shit, and who do I have to blame for that? Me. I screwed it all up. Claire will get better medically. I will get out of here. I want her, Nichol, and I to be a family. I want that more than I want the fuck'n air I breathe, but I won't do it to her. Claire deserves a hell of a lot better than me."

Brent listened. Finally, he said, "Why don't you let her decide?"

"Because don't you understand? I fucked up her mind. She thinks she's in love with me, because I made her think that. I did that. I took away her world. I didn't just make her the center of mine: I made me the center of hers. She's got this warped sense of who I am—who we are. It's not real." Tony leaned back. "Think about you and Courtney. You've been married for what, thirty years?"

Brent nodded, "About."

"All right, if you knew it was better for her to be without you, what would you do?"

"It's not better for Claire to be without you."

"That's not what I asked. I asked, what would you do?"

"I'd do what was best for her," Brent admitted.

"I've been a selfish bastard most of my life. I'm not saying I want to leave Claire with nothing, like I did before. I want her to have everything she'll ever need or want. She can have the estate and enough money to keep everything going. Hell, I'll pay child support and alimony. I want her to have the new house and a place to raise Nichol. I won't fight her for custody or visitation. Remember what the judge said? He said I was a danger to them. I've done some awful things. They deserve better."

Brent shook his head. "I don't agree with you. I think she'll need you. She'll need your support. Tony, I hope to hell she gets better. But if she doesn't, you'd be a selfish son-of-a-bitch to divorce her while she's in Everwood."

Tony closed his eyes. "You're right. I want her out of there. I can't get her out as long as I'm in here or if I'm not her husband. Work it out that I can make her world as right as possible. If my application for early release goes well, and I get out, I want to get her out of that place. I'll pay for whatever care she needs at home. We'll get Nichol back to Claire, then..."

"I'll get the preliminary petition filled out, but I don't want to file for your divorce, again," Brent said.

"One in a million," Tony said.

"Fine, those odds suck," Brent admitted. "Tell me the odds of one man taking an idea he started with a friend and turning it into a successful company that employs people all over the world."

Tony shrugged.

"Tell me the odds of someone finding a woman who loves him enough to not only forgive him for the crazy shit he's done, but love him, and give him one of the most beautiful, intelligent, and funny little girls I've ever seen." Brent stared. "Unless you're fuck'n planning to go to Vegas, I don't give a damn about the odds. I care that Claire gets well. I care that you get out of here. And I care that the little girl with her daddy's brown eyes, can have her mom and her dad in the next room so that when she wakes up crying from a bad dream, you both go running in to comfort her." Tony looked away, but Brent kept going. "Yeah, I'd do what was best for Courtney, but it wouldn't be a unilateral decision. We'd talk about it. I'll start your damn paperwork. Just don't ask me to actually file it."

By the time Brent stepped from the room, he was sure that his blood pressure was though the roof and that his best friend was making a terrible mistake. Well, it wasn't the first mistake his friend had made. It wasn't even the first time he'd made this particular mistake. Maybe, just maybe, Brent could convince him to never file.

The memory faded as Brent rejoined the conversation and

listened as Courtney continued to describe the house. "Wait until you see Nichol's room! It is fit for a princess."

"I can't wait. I can't wait to get out of here and see anything," Tony said.

Brent nodded. "I'm hopeful that it will happen sooner rather than later. The only step is the final review. Your acceptance of the terms of the community service was the last hurdle. Now, we just need to wait. I got the impression they were encouraged, by your record here and your history of philanthropic support. You pled guilty. In prison you've had a job, taken classes, and gone to counseling. You've even agreed to further counseling once you're released. You're established in your community. It's very promising."

"Yes, look at me. I'm the model prisoner," Tony said sarcastically. "I'm not sure I want to put my hopes in the final unit review. I've been screwed before."

"Faith," Courtney said, "have faith. Think about Claire. Three weeks ago, she wasn't talking. Now, she's doing so well. I just know everything will work out."

"I hope you're right," Tony said.

"Have you ever known me to be wrong?" Courtney asked with a smirk.

Ten days later—October 2016

WHILE AT WORK, Brent received the call. Tony's early release had been approved. In fifteen days, Tony would be able to walk out of Yankton, a free man. After calling Courtney, he began filing his petitions. The first was to revoke Emily's power of attorney. With doctors' statements regarding Claire's recent improvement, he didn't anticipate that being a problem. The next was Family Court. Whether Tony thought his family needed to be together or not, Brent surely did. He wouldn't stop until he got Mr. and Mrs. Rawlings full custody of their minor daughter.

Chapter 24

Late October 2016

Tony

————⋙•◆•⋘————

**To forgive is to set a prisoner free and
discover that the prisoner was you.
—Lewis B. Smedes**

AS THE PLANE ascended, Tony sighed at the overwhelming sense of freedom. From his Armani suit and Italian loafers to the glass of Johnnie Walker in his hand, Anthony Rawlings felt his true self re-emerging. No longer was he subjugated to the people around him. He had power: power to move mountains. He also knew that he would never again step foot inside of a federal prison. He wasn't even sure he'd ever step foot in South Dakota again. It wasn't that he intended to forget his experience—Tony didn't know if that was even possible. He did intend to move beyond it.

It was this exhilarating sense of freedom that he wanted for Claire, too. "When can we get Claire?"

"We could go tonight, but it'll be late. I recommend we go tomorrow morning. From what Meredith told Courtney—"

Tony shook his head. "That's still the strangest turn of events

I've ever heard. Who'd have thought that I'd ever feel indebted to Meredith Banks?"

"I know, right? Courtney was skeptical, until Meredith got her to Claire. Cort said that she could tell that Claire and Meredith had a mutual admiration. Meredith has risked a lot to continue this charade. Claire told Courtney that her first memories of coming out of her fog were hearing Meredith's voice, hearing her talk about *you*."

Tony took another drink of bourbon. "I can't believe she thought she killed me. I can see how traumatic that would be. No wonder she tried to block that out. Hell, I don't know what I'd do if I thought I'd killed her." Memories of a dark night in her suite came rushing back. "Actually, I do know. It's something I never want to experience again."

Changing the subject, Brent handed Tony a folder. "Here's the report from the child psychologist I hired in Iowa City. She's very reputable and having her involved helped the court's decision regarding custody of Nichol."

Tony took the file and scanned the first page. He saw the recommendation for weekly family-therapy sessions. Damn, he also had agreed to weekly anger-management sessions in order to facilitate his early release. "I thought I was going to get away from all this psychobabble bullshit."

Brent smirked. "I don't think that'll happen for a very long time. Besides, I still don't believe you're thinking straight."

Tony's eyes darkened. "Don't go there. I'm not reconsidering. Do you have the copy of the petition for divorce?"

Brent handed him an envelope. "I have the petition, but I'm not filing it."

"I don't want you to file it—not yet. Not until we get Claire home. I'm anxious to see her, but I think tomorrow is best. That'll give me some time to get everything ready."

"I agree tomorrow is better. I was going to say earlier that Meredith told Courtney that Emily visits in the morning. That's why Meredith works the later shift, to avoid her."

"I don't want to avoid her," Tony proclaimed.

Brent nodded as a smile filled his face. "That's why I think tomorrow will be better. You won't be sneaking in. You'll be going in and setting the record straight. In my opinion, if she's present, it'll help with the aftershocks."

"You're damn right. I'm not *sneaking* in. Claire's my wife, and I'm exercising my rights as a free man."

Brent's brows peaked in question.

"She is currently my wife." He tapped the breast pocket of his jacket. "This will come in the future, but for now, she's my wife." Tony didn't care for the look Brent was sending his way, but it wouldn't change his plans. Claire deserved to be free. She'd been through too much in her life, and all of it could be traced back to him.

"The house is perfect," Brent said. "Courtney's spent more time over there recently than she has at home. Between the decorators and her touch, I think you'll both love it."

"Is Eric meeting us at the airport?"

Brent grinned. "Yes, just like old times, but the rest of the staff that Courtney hired for the estate are new. She interviewed every one of them."

"Roach?"

"He'll be at the estate. I thought you'd like to see him in person."

Tony nodded and sipped more of the amber liquid. It'd been

over two years since he'd had a drop of alcohol: the aroma alone was enough to tingle his skin. The burning sensation as he swallowed rekindled the glorious feeling of weightlessness. Damn, he was glad to be back.

Eric was exactly as he'd always been. The only difference was his unusually large smile as Tony and Brent descended the plane's steps. Well, that and the vigorous handshake. Truly, Tony didn't mind. He'd retained Eric and Roach for the same reason. They weren't just part of his past: he wanted them in his future and in Claire's. They'd proven their loyalty over and over. Tony had proven his, too. No matter what the DA or US Attorney offered, Tony refused to name either of them as having knowledge of his activities. Of course, the prosecution had their suspicions, but without confirmation, that was all they had.

Tony didn't care if he were riding in a sedan or a limousine—it just felt great to be moving, going from place to place. When Eric drove the limousine through the iron gates of his estate, a feeling of anticipation, as well as one of dread, rushed over Tony. It had been a long time since he'd been on his property. After the repairs had been made on the house, Tony realized how much he hated it. That was why he'd spent so many nights sleeping on the couch in his office. Now, he wanted to like the new house. He wanted to give Claire a fresh start with new, happy memories, but until he saw the house with his own two eyes, he didn't know if that was possible.

The colorful fall trees parted and the dread disappeared. The house was so different, so new. His gaze transfixed on the grand white-brick home. That was what he saw: a home. Not a house. Not a monument. Tony didn't wait for Eric: he opened his door and stood before the home. Though in the last two and a half years, he'd only seen his daughter in pictures, he imagined her running the length of the porch and dancing around the large columns. He saw an enclosed porch and pictured Claire sitting there, reading and enjoying the fresh breeze. It was perfect.

Tony's main request during the construction was to make it open and airy. Never again would anyone keep Claire from the sun or the moon. Never again would she feel trapped. Jim had been right. Her future was her choice. She could sell this place if she wanted, but Tony had done everything in his power to make her not want to sell.

"Mr. Rawlings, would you like to enter your new home?" Eric asked, as he opened the front door. Tony had expected for it to be empty, not of furniture, but of people. Instead, he was greeted by his new staff. One by one, they introduced themselves. Courtney had thought of everything, from the estate manager, to a cook, and the cleaning staff. Even the head groundskeeper was present. When he introduced himself, Tony almost asked him about some flowers he'd seen in the front of the house, next to the mums. He'd never seen them before and worried that they wouldn't be hardy enough for the cooler nights. Then he stopped himself. Anthony Rawlings, Number 01657-3452, was a gardener, not Anthony Rawlings, CEO of Rawlings Industries. He had other, more pressing matters.

It was when they were in the kitchen that Tony heard Courtney's voice. Within seconds she was in the kitchen with her arms flung around Tony's neck. The sadness that had been threatening his tour disappeared in an instant. Her elation was contagious. From that moment on, she was his tour guide. It wasn't until she walked them into the master suite's dressing room that the sadness returned.

"Where are all of your things?" she asked, obviously perplexed.

"They were here the other day. I had the closet stocked for both you and Claire."

Tony avoided Brent's darkening expression.

"I had them moved," Tony answered.

"To where? Another room? Why would you do that?" she questioned.

Tony swallowed. "No, not to another room."

"Shit, I told you I wouldn't rent you an apartment," Brent said.

Courtney's eyes clouded in confusion. "I don't understand. I've done everything I thought you'd like. Don't you like the house?"

"I love the house. It'll be the most perfect place for Claire to raise Nichol. It's everything I asked for and more."

Her jaw clenched as sparks of understanding came to her eyes. *"For Claire to raise Nichol.* What are you saying?"

He reached for Courtney's shoulders. "Please, don't worry about it. It'll work out."

"Yes, yes, Tony, it will. As long as you and Claire have Nichol and are a family, it will work. Why did you want Brent to rent you an apartment?"

Tony glared at Brent. "When Brent wouldn't do it, I contacted Eric. I now have an apartment not far from the office."

Tears spilled over Courtney's lids. "Why, Tony? Why would you do this to Claire?"

"I'm not doing it *to* Claire: I'm doing it *for* Claire. Surely, you can understand. She's been trapped at Everwood by Emily—"

"And you're freeing her! Tomorrow, you're bringing her home," Courtney exclaimed.

"I am," Tony replied. "Before Emily, it was me. She has truly been restrained since she was a child. I won't allow that anymore. She deserves to be free."

THOUGH COURTNEY'S WORDS were still clipped, she offered her support as she and Brent followed Tony's car toward Everwood. In Brent's possession were all the documents signed, sealed, and ready. He even had the doctors' statements and the custody papers. All they needed was Claire.

The administrator of Everwood, Mr. Leason, met them at the door to the front lobby. After he and Tony shook hands, he led them to his office where Brent began explaining the documentation. As they spoke, Tony glanced around. From what little he'd seen, it was a very nice facility. He had to give that to Emily: she'd found a wonderful place. It wasn't until Tony heard his name that he focused on Brent's conversation.

"...Mr. Rawlings. Here's the document signed by Judge Wein, as Mrs. Rawlings' husband, until she's medically cleared to make her own decisions, he has medical power of attorney. With that authority, and with the support of your medical staff—I have Dr. Brown's statement—we are removing Claire Nichols Rawlings from Everwood today."

"Does Mrs. Vandersol know? Is she aware?"

"Mr. Vandersol has been informed," Brent said. Tony was shocked. John knew that he was coming and didn't have guards stationed at every door?

"Mr. Simmons, Mr. Vandersol is not Ms. Nichol's next of kin. It is *Mrs.* Vandersol."

"I can assure you that I have been as thorough as possible. We're removing *Mrs. Rawlings,*" Brent emphasized her name, "today."

"If you'll excuse me for a moment," Mr. Leason said, "I'd like to place a call to Judge Wein."

Brent handed him another paper. "Here is her direct number. We'll be outside."

Once the three of them were outside of the administrator's office, Tony asked, "John knows, and he didn't tell Emily?"

"I don't know if he told Emily or not. I sent Emily a formal request from you for permission to visit Claire. I wanted documentation of her denial. They knew you were being released. They'd been with me to Family Court regarding your rights. John's not dumb. He came to me with Emily's formal denial. He hinted that if he were I, he'd remove Emily as a roadblock. I didn't let on that I'd already started the process, but I believe he'd already figured it out. He said that if that situation ever occurred, he wouldn't fight you. I know you two have a history, but he's a good man. I even think Emily believes she's done what was right. John and I didn't talk about his future employment, but Tim and I have. We both want him to stay. Hopefully he can."

Courtney had been uncharacteristically quiet, but when Brent finished, she said, "I agree. Nichol adores them and they do her. I believe in the innocence of children. They can create a bridge capable of spanning an otherwise insurmountable gap. I can't wait for you to see Nichol."

Tony tried to process: John wasn't going to fight him. "Tim's told me how good it's been to have John at Rawlings. I can't deny they've taken good care of Nichol. I have to wonder if—"

Before he could finish his thought, Mr. Leason opened the door. "Excuse me, it seems as though you're cleared. We can bring Ms. Nic—Mrs. Rawlings to the common room—"

"No, I want to go to her immediately," Tony said.

"It's against our policy to allow men into the residential—" Was it the look Tony was giving him or the tone of his original rebuttal? No matter the reason, Mr. Leason stopped and restated his response. "I believe we can make an exception. Let me show you the way."

When they reached the door to her room, Tony said, "I know Emily's in there. I'd rather go in alone."

Courtney, Brent, and Mr. Leason nodded.

Inhaling deeply, Tony turned the knob. Two and a half years of separation ended in a split second. He saw Emily's shocked expression, but that wasn't what held his attention. It was the back of *her* head. She was right there: his wife, his life, and his envelope filled with hopes and dreams. Before he could speak, Claire stood and turned. No longer was Tony's world bland—khaki and gray. The infusion of color was almost blinding. Green—emerald green—had been returned to the spectrum.

Unbridled desire surged through him. He momentarily forgot his talk of divorce. In that second, nothing mattered but Claire. Tony needed to touch his wife, to reassure himself that she was real. Not the woman in his dreams, but the living, breathing person who consumed his thoughts. The distance between them evaporated as the rest of the room disappeared. With an invisible bond, his Claire was once again in his arms. With her cheek against his chest he wrapped her in his arms. Though her body molded perfectly to his, he needed more. Like a man in the desert needs water, like a person needs air, Tony needed her eyes. Reaching for her chin he sought the green. Instantaneously, their gazes—their connection that surpassed all else—fused.

"I've dreamt of those eyes," he whispered. Her smile washed

over him with a warmth that even sunshine couldn't provide.

"As have I."

Her voice was the melody of his soul. Then it was gone. She had turned away. "Look at me," he commanded. "I've missed you so much. Why are you looking away?"

Once again, peering upward, she asked, "Do you know? Do you know what they say about me?"

"I know. I love you."

Her pained expression broke his heart.

"They think I'm crazy."

Caressing her back, he tried to reassure her, "I think we're all crazy. That doesn't mean that I'm leaving here today without you. My love, you're coming home."

"I'm leaving here? How?" she asked.

Brent stepped forward, penetrating their bubble. Before he could speak, Claire reached out and took his hand. "I'm so thankful you're all right!"

"Me too," Brent said. "If I weren't alive, I couldn't be the one to tell you..." He grinned. "...I wouldn't be the one to help you. As long as Tony was incarcerated, Emily was your listed next of kin and held your power of attorney. I'm holding the judgment by Judge Wein: your husband is, once again, legally your next of kin. Until you're completely cleared medically, he has the power to make your medical decisions, including your release..."

Tony stared at the woman with her hand in his. She was the vision of everything and anything he'd ever wanted. As she questioned Brent about her release, and as she walked to her sister and spoke, all Tony could think about was her. She obviously wasn't crazy. There'd never been anyone to hold him captive as she could. Yes, he may have been the one who locked the door, but she was the one who held the key to his heart. As long as she was near, she'd forever have that power. He didn't mind. It could never belong to anyone else.

As they exited Mr. Leason's office for the last time, Tony saw John and Emily waiting. They stood as he and Claire approached. To Tony's surprise, John held out his hand.

"Anthony."

With his hand extended, Tony replied, "*Tony*. Please, call me Tony. Thank you, John, for all you've done while I was away. Brent tells me you've been quite helpful at Rawlings."

"It was for Nichol and Claire."

Tony nodded. "And for that, for *our* family, I thank you."

John went on, "I've been privy to many of your decisions. I want you to know that I respect them."

Tony hadn't known how this would go, but in this moment, he was relieved. "Then I hope my return won't cause you to search for another job. Rawlings Industries *and I* can always use someone like you on our side."

"Emily and I need to talk, but I think I'd like that."

Tony looked at his wife as she released his hand and wrapped her arms around John's neck. He heard tears in her voice as she said, "I had no idea you were working at Rawlings." Next, she hugged her sister. "Thank you, Emily. Thank you for not fighting this."

John explained, "Anth—I mean, *Tony's* right and you're right. We *are* a family. For our children, we need to behave like adults."

Claire stammered, "Ch-children... I can't wait to see Nichol and meet Michael."

It was Emily's turn to cry. "She's so little. She won't understand—"

John spoke the voice of reason. "Your daughter is beautiful and intelligent. She's also young. As long as we do this together, she'll make the transition just fine."

Claire peered upward. Placing her hand back into Tony's, she said, "We've missed so much. I can't wait to hold her again."

Could they make this work? Could the four of them, no, the six of them truly be a family? Tony spoke to his brother- and sister-in-law. "Thank you again, not just for Rawlings, but for taking care of Nichol. We're anxious to come and see her, but first I'd like to take Claire somewhere. It won't take long, and then we'll be over to your house. The child psychologist I consulted recommended a gradual transition before we bring her home to stay."

"I thought—" Claire started.

Emily interrupted, "Yes, gradual. I think Tony's right." Her pained smile turned toward Tony. "Thank you. This'll give us time to talk with her, to try to explain things. Let's make this as easy for Nichol as possible."

With Claire's hand once again secured, they walked through the doors. She looked up at the sky and said, "It feels so good to be free."

He knew the feeling, but she was wrong. She wasn't truly free, not yet. Despite the warmth of her hand, he knew what he needed to do. Never again would she be captive. When her beautiful green eyes met his, he said, "I want to show you something."

Chapter 25

October 2016

(Convicted — Chapter 48)

Tony

———⊷••◆••⊶———

*We should regret our mistakes and learn from them, but
never carry them forward into the future with us.*
—Lucy Maud Montgomery

UNBEKNOWNST TO CLAIRE, during their drive to the estate, Tony
waged an internal war of wills. On one side was his desire. With
Claire's hand in his, her head on his shoulder, and her trusting
gazes, that side was gaining strength by the second. He wanted her
more than life. With her beside him, he was complete. Never had
another person accepted him the way his Claire had done. Though
she knew his sins and shortcomings, she never judged. She forgave.
She forgave unforgivable acts. She forgave a man who had never
before been forgiven. It was more than that: she'd given him a child
and a life. Claire was the light to his dark and the right to his wrong.
With her beside him, he wanted to forget everything he'd learned in
prison, to forget why he was bad for her. He wanted his wife.

On the other side was his will. Throughout his life, Anthony

Rawlings could boast few attributes; however, the one that had remained strong was his word. As storms raged, he remained steadfast, knowing that above all, he was a man of his word. He'd made the decision to set Claire free. He'd spoken that edict to Jim and to his friends. Despite the desire and want, Tony knew that he had to do what was right. For the first time in their lives, Tony had to put Claire first.

Her voice pulled him from his internal struggle as she looked out the windows. "We're near the estate. What about the fire? Was there a lot of damage?"

"That's what I want to show you," he replied, anxious to see her reaction.

The iron gates opened and the trees parted. With her new home in view, Claire gasped. "What happened?"

It wasn't the reaction he'd expected. "You don't like it?"

"I-I don't know. Did the whole house burn?"

"No. There was a lot of smoke and water damage, but the fire was pretty much contained to the first level, southwest corridor."

Tony stopped the car. Before he could get to her side, she was out and standing before the large white-brick home. He watched her eyes as she took in the long porches, black shutters, and stately columns. When she didn't speak, Tony asked, "Do you want to see inside?"

"What happened to our house?"

"I had it demolished," he explained. "I built it for the wrong reasons. It was our house, but it was never a *home*. It contained too many memories."

"So you got rid of it? Tony, there were good memories there, too."

"I built that house for Nathaniel." His gaze begged for

understanding. "Claire, I had this home built for you." Tugging her hand, he led her inside, watching her response as they progressed from room to room. With each step he prayed the allure of the home would fill her with the peace and security he'd intended. Her eyes widened as they entered the polished oak foyer. Her expression warmed as her eyes scanned each room and took in the windows covering the entire back of the house. In the living room, the glass extended two stories. In the kitchen he saw the spark of approval he'd longed to see.

"Oh, this looks like a kitchen where I'd love to cook," she said.

Tony smiled. "You have a cook, but it's your kitchen. You can do whatever you'd like."

He took her down to the lower level through a theater room, fun family area, and an exercise room. It was as he opened the doors to the inside lap pool that he squeezed Claire's shoulders and said, "I couldn't build you a house without your favorite room."

Standing in awe, she finally whispered, "It's beautiful, thank you."

Still holding her hand, he led her upstairs to the bedrooms: Nichol's first and then hers. When they entered the master suite, Tony walked to the far wall and opened the draperies. As they parted, the room filled with natural light and two large French doors were exposed. Opening the doors, he beckoned her to the balcony. Stepping outside, he watched his wife as she shook her head and said "Tony, everything is so open and bright."

Lifting her hands, he kissed the soft skin and stared into her emerald eyes. "This is your glass house, one that won't shatter. I don't want you to ever feel trapped again. I want you to be able to see the sky and sun or the moon and stars whenever you desire."

She stepped closer, melting against him. "Thank you, I love it!

But how—how did you do this? You were in prison."

"I had a lot of help."

Stepping to the rail, Claire scanned the grounds below. From their view they could see a pool, a basketball court, a large play set, and the edge of the gardens. Tony couldn't be happier with the finished home. He owed his gratitude to Courtney. Everything was there, and beyond it all were Claire's woods and her lake. That was why he couldn't sell. It was why he prayed she wouldn't sell. Claire was right: despite the bad, Tony knew the estate contained good memories. He hoped those would prevail. Tony and Claire sat on a gliding seat, and he said, "Of course, you still have your island. If you'd prefer, you can move back there. Although this view is beautiful, it's difficult to compete with the view from your lanai. I just thought it might be easier on Nichol if you lived closer to John and Emily for a while."

She lifted her head from his shoulder and asked, "Why do you keep saying *you*? You mean *we*."

He couldn't put it off any longer. If he did, Tony feared he wouldn't be able to go through with his plans. Reaching into his breast pocket, he removed the envelope which Brent had given him less than twenty-four hours ago. "You and Nichol. Claire, this house, the entire estate, it's yours."

Her contented expression morphed. Tony watched as confusion became panic. With tears suddenly threatening, Claire replied, "I don't know what's in that envelope, but whatever it is, I don't want it."

Looking out over the trees, he tried to reassure her and to help her understand. Exhaling, he explained, "I tried to contact you. I wanted to be with you, to be there for you. The scene at the estate was crazy. When you pulled the trigger..."

He continued to talk, to fill in the gaps of what she knew and remembered. There was so much that had happened in the two years since that incident. How could he possibly sum it all up? How could he explain what he'd been through, what he'd done? Tony knew it hadn't just been him. She'd been through hell, too. They both had. If only they could have walked through the flames together, but they didn't. They'd both taken their own personal journey, ones that brought them back to here, back to the beginning.

He tried to express how badly he wanted to get to her, how hard he tried. He also wanted her to know that he'd taken responsibility for the things that he'd done. He confessed and accepted his fate. Tony would never burden her with how difficult it was at Yankton. After all, she'd never told him about her time in prison. They'd both suffered. The difference was that Tony was the only one responsible. He wouldn't continue to hurt her. He couldn't.

Claire shook her head and pleaded her case. She didn't say anything that he hadn't already thought. As he listened, he realized that she was doing what he'd taught her to do, what at one time he'd required of her. She was pushing her memories and fears away to attend to him. He couldn't allow that, not anymore. Claire needed to face their past and recognize that they couldn't have a future—not together. It would never be healthy. He'd caused too much damage.

"I remember it all," she refuted. "You're the one who always said the past is the past, and to think about the present or the future."

"I was wrong. You need to face it, and so do I. In all those discussions on the island, we never spoke about the things in Meredith's book—"

Tears coated her cheeks, as Claire interrupted, "Because we

were both there. During our discussions in paradise, you told me things I had no way of knowing. I know what happened between us. I also know it was a long time ago and it's over. I don't want to rehash it. I want the future."

He feigned a smile. He wanted a future too—for her. "That's what I want for you, too. I want *you* to have a future, free from all of our past. That's why I built you a new, memory-free house, and Claire, that's why Brent is ready to file for our divorce."

She didn't respond as her expression lost all understanding. He waited, wondering what she was thinking. Her eyes weren't telling him what he needed to know. He longed for the fire behind the green. Finally, Tony asked, "Did you hear me? I won't be the one to hurt you anymore, nor will Emily. You deserve fresh air and freedom. No one will ever be able to control you. Besides the money you still have invested overseas, I'm giving you the estate, a handsome settlement, and child support. With your wealth you can do anything you've ever dreamt of doing. You'll be in control of your and Nichol's future. I won't fight you on anything." Sheepishly, he added, "I do hope you'll allow me to see our daughter, but I understand if you don't." The judge had said he was an endangerment to Nichol. Did Claire feel the same? Tony tried to move on, "I think we've thought of everything regarding this house, but if there's something else you want or need, it's yours. You can have anything you want."

Her voice cracked. "You don't want *m-me*?"

Nothing could be further from the truth. He wanted her. This made so much more sense when he was back at Yankton, in Jim's office. Tony needed Claire to recognize that it wasn't her—it was him. He lifted her hand and kissed the top. "Don't ever think that. I've never wanted anyone the way I want you."

"I don't understand what you're saying."

"The reason the judge wouldn't lift the restraining order and allow me to see you was because when the judge asked me if the accounts in Meredith's book were correct, I told him yes. I admitted to everything. He ruled that I was a danger to you and Nichol."

"That's ridiculous. You never would have, nor will you ever, hurt Nichol. Obviously, we're together now, so all that legal drama is over." Her voice cracked as she asked, "Why are you throwing me away now?"

Tony stood and faced the trees as he fought the impending red. Claire wasn't thinking straight, it was his conditioning speaking, not her true emotions. Inhaling deeply, he remembered Jim's words. It would take time, but eventually, she'd understand. Tony reiterated, "I'm not throwing you away! I'm setting you free."

The pain in her voice broke his heart. With each word, another piece crumbled. She was crying and telling him she was sorry. Sorry for being crazy. Sorry for not following his rules. Sorry for disappointing him. He couldn't let her feel that way. It was like that word she used in the book. She was never the one at fault, it was all him. He was the one who was sorry.

Tony knelt before the love of his life and gently reached for her chin. "No, Claire. *I'm* the one who's disappointed *you,* over and over." With the pad of his thumb, he tenderly wiped away her tears. "While I was in prison, I learned you were finally getting better. I tried, but Emily still wouldn't allow me to contact you. She wouldn't allow hardly anyone to contact you. Courtney told me she only saw you through Meredith. She also said Emily wouldn't even let you see Nichol." The intensity of his eyes grew with each word, "I hated your sister! I was powerless to help you, and she was keeping you prisoner. I couldn't even talk to you. Hell, I heard that even your time outside was monitored."

Tony stood and once again paced the length of the balcony trying to rein in the red. Why did it need to surface around her? Tony knew why; he'd learned why. The red wasn't just anger. It was emotion: emotion that threatened his better judgment and consumed his soul. Sometimes that emotion was anger, other times desire. Claire was the spark to his dry existence. In her presence the fire grew. There had been times he'd been unable to control the blaze, but now he'd learned to dampen the flames. Once he'd calmed, Tony continued, "While in prison, I agreed to counseling. I didn't want to do it, but if doing it could help get me out of there early, I figured *what the hell*." He sat back down. "I spoke to this shrink three times a week. It started with my answering his questions. Over time, it became easier to talk. When I told him how upset I was with Emily and what she was doing to you, he asked me why I was upset. I said it was because of what she was doing. He told me to think about it more and figure out *why* I was so upset. I had two days before I saw him again. Throughout those days, I couldn't stop thinking about his question. It seemed obvious, until I realized..." His voice trailed away. Why was it so difficult to admit what Claire already knew, what she should know better than anyone else?

"What?" Claire asked, "What did you realize?"

"I was so angry with Emily, because she was doing the same thing to you that I'd done. I didn't just hate Emily. I hated myself!" He knelt before her and bowed his forehead to her knees. "I will *not* allow anyone to hurt you again. That includes me."

Claire's fingers weaved through his hair. "Tony, you were at Everwood. You heard me. I forgave Emily. And many years ago, I forgave you, too. I don't want to be free from you. I lived almost two years believing I'd killed you. I thought that was why no one mentioned your name. During that time, I fantasized about you and cried for you. Now you're here. I can touch you! I want my family back together. Besides, I'm still an outpatient. If you divorce me, they'll never allow me to have custody of Nichol. If you do this, you're not freeing me; you're abandoning me." Her tears were freely flowing once again.

Tony stood and squared his shoulders. "You're right. I don't want you to lose Nichol. We'll start with a separation..." He explained how it would work. She and Nichol could live at the estate, and he'd stay at his apartment. He didn't want to stop her from getting custody of their daughter, and with the help of a nanny, there shouldn't be any legal concerns.

It took every ounce of restraint, but he did it. Tony dampened the flame and worked to set Claire free. Eventually, Claire stood, straightened her shoulders, and silently walked past him, back into the bedroom. He didn't know what to do. His heart told him to follow her, fall at her feet, and beg for forgiveness. The pain in her eyes had been almost too much to bear. But he'd made his decision, and given his word. This was what was best for her.

Hearing his name, he turned toward the suite. Claire was speaking, "I can't see Nichol looking like this," she said, her tone emotionless. "I'm going to take a shower and clean up. I presume my closets are full, like Nichol's?"

"They are," he replied.

"Where's the staff? I'd like something to eat."

There was no emotion in her voice or her eyes. Perhaps, she too could dampen her flames. No, he knew she could. He'd taught her to do it, *required* it of her, a long time ago. He replied, "I gave them the night off. I'll go into town and get something. By the time I get back, you should be ready."

Claire nodded, turned, and walked away.

As he walked toward the car, he reassured himself that this was for the best. It was for her, and for his Claire, he'd do anything, even give her up.

Driving toward the Vandersols', Tony maintained his eyes on the road before him. He couldn't look to his right. It wasn't that he didn't believe that Claire was the most beautiful woman in the world—he did. It was that when he returned to the estate with their food, she was stunning and took his breath away. Instead of speaking, he stood mute, watching her from the doorway and trying to remember that she deserved better. It took some time, but he did what he was supposed to do. He reined in the red hunger of desire and dampened the flames. Nevertheless, with the intoxicating scent of her perfume, he didn't dare look her way. That hunger may have been subdued, but Tony knew too well that it was still present, white-hot coals merely covered with ash. The slightest infusion of fuel would set a raging fire ablaze. Maintaining his feigned indifference, he listened as she spoke.

"I don't want to tell Emily and John, not yet. I don't think they'll understand."

Tony nodded. "It might be better if we ease Nichol into the idea that her parents live in two separate homes."

Claire agreed.

When they pulled onto the Vandersols' drive, Tony noticed Claire's hands trembling. Without thinking, he reached over and covered them with his. "It'll be all right," he encouraged.

"I'm scared. What if she doesn't want us?"

"She will," he encouraged, maintaining his forward gaze.

"I haven't even asked: have you seen her?"

"No, pictures are all that I've seen." He thought of all the pictures Courtney had sent. "I was just released yesterday, and she was never brought to me. It was probably better. A little girl shouldn't be visiting her father at a federal prison camp."

"Yesterday?" Claire's eyes widened in wonder. "And you've accomplished all of this?"

"Like I said, I had help. I've been planning for my release for some time."

With his hand still on hers, he felt her stiffen as she asked, "And our *divorce?* How long have you been planning that?"

Tony pulled his hand away and glared in her direction. Damn, he thought this was done. "Claire, not now. Let's not go back there."

"Is there someone else?"

"What?" He could scarcely believe that she'd even ask such a thing. He'd told her that there had never been anyone but her. That was true. It didn't mean that there weren't women with whom he'd had physical relationships. There were, but all before her. Never had anyone else owned his heart. No one but his Claire.

"Is—there—someone—else?!" She repeated louder than the first time.

This was ridiculous. "I told you that I've never wanted anyone the way I want you."

"Well, you obviously don't want me! And you're *Anthony Rawlings.* You were in prison and your wife was crazy..."

Her argument was beyond comprehension. Sure, he'd received mail. The world was full of desperate women seeking what they comprehend to be available. He'd never responded. Hell, he'd stopped opening them. He didn't want to continue this conversation. Calming his tone, in hopes of subduing hers, he said,

"Claire, our daughter is waiting."

"I've already asked this once, don't make me ask again. Is there someone else?"

He slowed his words. "Claire, calm down."

Without warning, her petite hand slapped his cheek. The pain was minimal compared to the shock. Flashbacks of the reverse bombarded his mind. Seizing her fingers, he asked, "What the hell was that?"

"You never answer my questions. Tell me, were there letters? Did women write to you promising anything you wanted, all for the chance to take my place?"

Without releasing her fingers he said, "You're getting yourself all worked up. Calm down; Nichol is waiting."

"I deserve to know."

"Yes. Are you happy? There were letters. I didn't respond. I don't give a damn about anyone, anyone but you." Thinking not of the letters, but of Patricia, he added, "Hell, I even—"

No. He wasn't going to get into it. He wasn't going to tell her how he'd fired one of the best assistants he'd ever had because she offered him more than he'd ever want from anyone but the woman before him.

She prodded, "You even what?"

"We'll finish this discussion another time." Or not. He released her fingers. "Now, do you plan to join me, or do you plan to sit in the car all evening?"

"I plan to join you," she stoically replied.

Tony didn't notice the niceness of the Vandersols' home as they made their way up the sidewalk. His mind was too busy reining the red from their confrontation and contemplating the little girl behind the door. They last saw her two and a half years ago. To him and

Claire that was a long time, but that was nothing compared to Nichol: for her it was a lifetime. She was only a baby and now...

Emily greeted them at the door and led them to the living room. "We told Nichol she had some special guests coming to see her."

As soon as Nichol came into view, Claire reached for Tony's hand. Sitting on the floor by a dollhouse was their daughter. Time stood still as Tony took in the beautiful little girl, once again in three-dimension. The pictures he'd received paled in comparison to the vibrant child before them. She was a vision—their creation. She was the place where Claire's light met his darkness. She was everything that was good in Claire and maybe in him. Her big brown eyes were light with wonder. She was Claire—before him, before he'd hurt her and destroyed her life. Nichol was the promise of innocence. In that instant, as in the moment Madeline laid her in his arms, Tony knew that he'd willingly sacrifice his life before he allowed anyone to take that away from her.

Claire let go of Tony's hand and knelt on the floor. "Hello, Nichol," she said, feigning strength where Tony knew there was insecurity.

Their daughter stood and stared. Finally, John stepped forward, and Nichol reached for his hand. "Nichol," John said. "Can you say *hi* to the friends we told you about?"

"Hi."

Tony knelt beside Claire who reached out her hand. Nichol's small fingers shook Claire's hand as she asked, "Who are you?"

Tony laughed. "Direct, isn't she?"

With a snicker, Emily replied, "Very. I can't imagine where she gets it."

"Nichol, my name is Claire, but you can call me Mom."

Nichol's eyes grew wide as she peered from Claire to Tony. Finally, she asked, "Are you my daddy?"

His heart swelled. Never had Tony been prouder to answer, "I am."

Dropping John's grasp, she stepped forward and touched a small hand to each of their cheeks. Tony waited for her to speak. Finally, Claire said, "We're really here, honey, and we're so sorry we've been gone."

Nichol smiled, her eyes lightening to a milk chocolate. "I knew one day you'd come. Aunt Em said you were sick, and when you got better, you'd be here. Are you better?"

Claire answered, "Yes, I'm much better. Nichol, can we hug you?"

Lowering her little hands to their shoulders, she nodded. For a few seconds, Tony's envelope filled to overflowing. It was everything they had in paradise and more. He remembered their bubble during the night when Nichol would wake. Now that she was older, he saw his directness and her mother's tenderness. For an instant it was only the three of them and then without warning, Nichol released her hug and rushed to her cousin. "Mikey, know what? I have a mommy and daddy, too!" Looking up to Emily, Nichol asked, "Does that mean they're Mikey's aunt and uncle, like you and Uncle John?"

Emily looked their way and replied, "Yes, honey, it does." Reaching for her son, she said, "Michael, this is Mommy's sister, your Aunt Claire." She hesitated as Tony and Claire stood. "And— your Uncle Tony."

Claire once again put out her hand. "Hello, Michael, I'm so glad to meet you."

Michael took her hand and smiled bashfully. John's voice filled the otherwise quiet room. "Kids, if it wasn't for Uncle Tony, we wouldn't be here."

Tony's eyes went to John. So much time, so many mistakes: was he going to lay it out here? Preparing to accept what he deserved, Tony waited. However, when John spoke, it was not what Tony had expected. "Before you were born, Michael, Uncle Tony saved your mom and me from a fire. If he hadn't done that, then you wouldn't be here, either."

Was that it? Could that be John's unspoken acceptance? He'd told Brent he wouldn't fight the reuniting of Tony's family. And what had he said at Everwood? He'd said that he respected some of Tony's decisions. Could they truly put the past behind them? Tony's attention went to his daughter. Her eyes were wide with wonder as she said, "Really? You did that, Daddy?"

"Wow!" Michael gasped.

Choking back the emotion, Tony said, "I did. I'm so glad I did."

"Thank you," Emily said. "We've learned that the fire wasn't our only danger. We know what you two gave up—for us. This isn't easy for me, but thank you."

Claire hugged her sister, as they both cried.

"Why are you sad, Aunt Em?" Nichol asked.

Wiping her eyes, Emily hugged Nichol and said, "I'm not sad, sweetie. I'm happy. I'm so happy that you have your mommy and daddy again. They love you very much."

Nichol looked in their direction and smiled. "I'm happy, too."

Tony didn't intend to glance at Claire, but he did. His chest ached with pride and love, sadness and regret. It was the promise of a future swirling in a whirlwind of remorse.

Chapter 26

October 2016

(Convicted —Chapter 51 and beyond)

Tony

—◆—

I have found the paradox, that if you love until it hurts,
there can be no more hurt, only more love.
—Mother Teresa

EVERYONE WAS ADAPTING to his or her new role. Claire had stepped into the role of lady of the house: not only was she managing the staff that had already been hired, but she'd also hired a few more. Specifically, Tony wanted her to choose the head of her security, and Nichol's nanny. At first, Claire balked at the need for security, but Tony convinced her that it had always been present. It didn't matter if there was no immediate threat: the Rawlingses were people of means and as such, were potential targets. When Tony talked about Nichol, Claire agreed. She interviewed a few of the names Tony recommended, but one night she told Tony she wanted Phillip Roach. Claire argued that she was familiar with Phil, and with all the new members of the staff, she wanted the familiarity. It wasn't that Tony didn't want to grant her request. It was that Phil had been providing her security all along, just unbeknownst to her.

Tony hadn't done that because he wanted to monitor Claire's movements or distrusted her choices: it was solely about her safety. He was sure that Jim wouldn't approve. Perhaps, if he brought it up to his new therapist, he too would disapprove. That didn't matter. When it came to the safety of his family, Tony wouldn't compromise. Truth be told, Roach had been watching over Nichol and Claire for the past two years. At first, Tony wasn't sure about Phil fulfilling the position as head of security; however, Tony had told his wife that she could have whatever she wanted. She wanted Phil. Now Phil had the position. There was no doubt in Tony's mind that no one else was as devoted to his family as Philip Roach, except perhaps Eric. When it came to devotion, Eric's too was undeniable. Tony believed that with the two of them, his family was safe.

The child psychologist recommended that Claire have a nanny in place by the time Nichol moved to the estate. She said it would help with the transition if Nichol got to know her before she moved. After many interviews, Claire found a young woman with whom she felt comfortable. Her name was Shannon, and she and Nichol hit it off immediately. The child psychologist also recommended that the transition to the estate last a minimum of two weeks. During that time, Tony and Claire began the family-counseling sessions, as well as spent every evening with Nichol. After a week, the Vandersols brought Nichol to the estate. Everyone was trying to make the move as easy as possible. The two-week window was closing and everything seemed to be falling into place.

The last night before Nichol's move, Claire and Tony were encouraged when they left the Vandersols' home. As they kissed their daughter goodnight, she said, "I can't wait to go to my room tomorrow night! I can't wait to be with both of you." Her little arms hugged their faces as she added, "My momma and daddy."

On the way home, Claire did little to hide her excitement. "It's all happening so fast," she said. "I can't believe how much things have changed in just two weeks."

As he listened to Claire's chatter, Tony worked to remain stoic, to keep the red—the emotion—away. It was much more difficult than he'd anticipated. Emotion wasn't black and white or even gray as it had been in prison. In the real world, it was a rainbow of color. There was the red of desire and anger, but there was also the yellow of happiness, and dark hues of disappointment. While with Nichol, Tony allowed the color to shine. How could he not? However, when he and Claire were alone, he fought to keep it at bay. The entire process was exhausting. His plan was fine when he was at Yankton. There it had made sense, but now it was different. Instead of speaking of his wife in the abstract, she was real and so close. He longed for what they had while with Nichol—a family. Above all, he yearned for Claire.

Because it was so difficult, Tony did his best to avoid being alone with his wife. However, the night before Nichol's move, Claire asked Tony to come into the house. She said there was something she wanted to show him. Perhaps it was her excitement at Nichol's parting remark. Whatever the reason, Tony didn't want to deny her request. He liked seeing her happy. He'd caused her too much sadness.

When they entered the house, Tony questioned Claire's recently praised management skills. The staff was gone. She said she'd released them for the night. He had no idea that she'd been coming home to an empty house. As he waited for her to return from upstairs, with whatever she wanted to show him, Tony wandered from room to room. Though he planned to discuss the situation with Roach in the morning, he found it to be totally unacceptable. Slowly, unknowingly, color returned. If her managing the staff was to work, she needed to know better.

With each step up the stairs, Tony thought about his stance. It was simple. Until she retired for the evening, someone should be with her. What if she needed something? What if something happened? This wasn't debatable. As he turned the corner to enter the master suite, Tony stopped. His Claire was there, on the floor rummaging through boxes. What was packed? Was she leaving? Anything she needed was here when she moved in. As the room seeped with crimson, Tony learned that red was also the color of worry. Why would she have boxes?

Then he remembered: her things from Everwood. He'd told the staff to send everything to the estate. That had to be what it was. She wasn't leaving—was she?

From the disappointment at the lack of staff, to the worry over the boxes, the emotion he had worked for two weeks to subdue, consumed his being. As he watched his wife, Tony knew he should turn around and go back downstairs. The floodgate had opened. Emotions didn't surge singularly. Disappointment and worry were only the front-runners. Desire and need were quickly approaching. He no longer had the energy to hold it back. Though he should have stayed downstairs, he didn't turn around. Hunger colored his vision as his desire for his wife intensified.

Without turning in his direction, Claire said, "I'm sorry it took so long. I thought I knew where they were."

When she stood and their eyes met, he knew without a doubt that she could sense the change. He saw it too in her eyes. The spark he'd doused now burnt his soul. Damn, she could probably hear his heart. It was beating out of his chest as he tried to appear aloof. In a few steps, she was before him, handing him what she'd found. Tony reached for the notebooks and asked, "What are these?"

"They're my compartments," she replied.

Confused, Tony opened the top notebook, and asked, "Your compartments? What do you...?" His words trailed as he began to read:

I suppose I should start in the beginning—March 2010. No, that wasn't when I was born. It was when I began to live. Most people think I'm crazy—maybe I am. You see I began to live the day my life was taken away. Funny, I don't remember how it happened. I do know now, it never could've been stopped.

Anthony Rawlings wanted me. If I've learned one lesson in my life—and believe me, I've learned many—Anthony Rawlings always got what he wanted.

Tony didn't know if he could do this. He'd read the damn book. Why did she want him to see this? He continued:

I can't explain how it happened. I can't explain how I fell deeply and madly in love with a man who did the things that Anthony did—but I did! These feelings have been discounted by multiple people: family members, doctors, and counselors to name a few. They've told me my love wasn't and isn't real. They say I'm a victim of abuse, and as such, I don't understand the difference between love and applied behavior. How can that be true? If I don't know my own feelings, how can anyone else?

It was different than her testimony. It was different than Meredith's book. This was real and in Claire's handwriting. It was raw and vulnerable. Her therapists and doctors had told her the same thing that Jim had said—that they were wrong together. Yet, despite it all, she claimed to still love him, to never have stopped loving him, even when she thought he was dead, that she'd killed him. He continued to read:

So here I go. I've lived this story, and I've told this story. Now, I'm going to try to do both, because without reliving it, even in my mind, I can't possibly explain that I'm not crazy...

I met Anthony Rawlings on March 15, 2010. That night I worked the 4:00PM to close shift at the Red Wing in Atlanta. He came up to the bar and sat down. I remember thinking...

Tony closed his eyes. He'd lived it and he'd read it. While with Jim, he'd relived parts: parts he wanted to forget and parts he'd remember forever. Fluttering the pages of all four notebooks, he noticed every page of every book was filled with writing. Glancing up, he saw Claire leaning against the wall, her arms folded over her chest watching him. Her blank expression failed to reveal her thoughts; however, in her eyes—her damn emerald green eyes—he saw the fire he'd missed. The one he'd doused too many times, most recently with his talk of divorce.

Staring, Tony fought the urge to touch her, comfort her, and apologize for ever thinking they should be apart. Gone was his control: his desires overwhelmed him. He wanted her more than he wanted life. *How did he ever think he could let her go?*

The temperature of the suite warmed exponentially as he laid the notebooks on the dresser yet maintained their gaze, their connection. Surrendering to his need, he moved forward.

Instantaneously, mere inches separated them. Then, Claire looked away, breaking their connection.

He lifted her chin and searched for the fire. Though she didn't fight his grip, she obstinately shut her eyes. It was too late to stop. Tony knew what he wanted. "Open your eyes. Look at me," he commanded.

Instead of obeying, Claire tipped her forehead against his chest, and said, "I can't."

She could probably hear the racing of his heart as he demanded her compliance. "Look at me. I want to see your damn eyes—now!"

"Please, please, Tony," she pleaded. "Don't. I can't take another rejection, not from you."

Rejection? He could never reject her. That was the furthest thing from his mind. He lifted her chin, and this time, brushed her lips with his. With a softer tone, he asked, "Why did you show me that?"

Her lids fluttered open. "So that you'd know... I *have* faced our past—multiple times. Even knowing that past, I wanted a future."

Analyzing each word, the erratic beat of his heart stopped, perhaps all together because if what she said were true, there would no longer be a reason for his heart to continue to beat. "*Wanted? Past tense?*" he asked.

Though he still held her chin, the beautiful woman in his grasp morphed into the bold woman he'd grown to love. Her volume rose with each phrase. "*You* don't want me! You left me in the Iowa jail! You told me two weeks ago you wanted a divorce! I can't live in a fantasy! You don't want me... or a future with me! Let go of my chin and stop pretending!"

He obeyed her demand and released her chin; however, relinquishing his hold wasn't even feasible. Tony's actions weren't planned: they were visceral and carnal. He slid his hand to the back of her neck and intertwined his fingers through her hair, forcing her to keep her face tilted toward his. With his other hand, he pulled her petite body against him as his lips seized hers.

For two weeks, Tony had tried to let Claire go. He'd wanted to give her the freedom she deserved, the freedom he'd taken away. However, each day, each hour, each minute, and each second had been agony. With his lips against hers, he no longer wanted to fight his desire. He couldn't. Step by step, he pushed her backward until they were flush with the wall. Her initial resistance faded as his need intensified. Unapologetically, he tasted her sweetness as his tongue parted her lips. As he pulled her hips against his, everything came at him, more emotion than he'd allowed in years. Colorful fireworks exploded in his mind as his fist pounded the wall above her head. With his voice resonating throughout the suite sounding more like a growl, he said, "I told you before. I've *never* pretended to love you! I do love you! That's *present* tense!"

She didn't respond verbally, yet their kiss deepened, and their ragged breaths filled the large room. With each caress, her body responded to his touch. His want became more apparent and difficult to deny. When her sensual moans echoed in his ears, he could no longer resist. Tony led his wife to the bed and without hesitation, followed her onto the mattress. Her fanned hair behind her flushed face and slightly swollen lips was the most beautiful and erotic sight Tony had seen in years. Pushing her blouse upward, he searched to touch the softness of her skin.

The pulsating of the blood rushing through his veins deafened him to the outside world. He barely heard her voice the first time she told him to stop. The command didn't even compute. Then he heard her speak louder.

"I said, stop!"

His mind was a blur. What had happened? She was willing just seconds ago. The pain of his need ached as he lifted his body from hers, and she rolled out from under him.

Claire's voice was strong and determined. "You need to go. I can't do this. I won't let you hurt me again."

Damn, she was right. He was no good for her. "Claire," Tony pleaded as he stood and began to pace. "Don't you understand? That's why I wanted a divorce. I don't want to hurt you and—and I can't take it again, either. You talk about my leaving you at the jail, and this divorce." He stammered, "W-what about you?"

Claire stood and stared incredulously. "Me? What about me?"

Running his hand through his hair, he explained the obvious. "You left *me*. *You* drove away from *me*—twice! You think I don't remember that every damn time you drive away from this estate? The other day when you were gone for over three hours and driving around Bettendorf, of all places, I was scared to death that you're considering doing it again."

Claire's eyes widened as she asked, "What do you mean... the other day? How did you know that I was in Bettendorf?"

He didn't want to tell her that he'd had her followed; just like Jim, she wouldn't understand. "Claire, *they* say we're no good for one another, but in your notebooks you said you still loved me after everything. Is that still true?"

She moved closer. "Answer me. What do you know about my comings and goings?"

Tony closed his eyes and exhaled. "The reason I didn't want Roach working for you was..." Damn, he owed her honesty, even if it would upset her. "...he'd been working for me. He's been watching you since the day you came home."

Claire's eyes filled with tears, yet her voice wasn't angry. In barely a whisper, she asked, "Why? Tell me why you've had Phil following me."

He gripped her shoulders. "You have every right to be angry. That's fine, but I'm not sorry. I worry. I'll always worry. I don't want anything to happen to you ever again." His words came fast. "I don't really care *that* you go. I just need to know that you're safe."

She sank back to the bed, and he knelt before her.

"Please," he begged. "Please, tell me what you're thinking."

Her words were painful and beautiful. "I don't know. There are so many things." She shook her head. "I-I've been asked over and over, why I didn't try to escape from you in 2010 when I had opportunities. When I tell the story about us, and talk about shopping or the symphony they tell me I *should have* run or told someone."

God, he hated that she had those memories—that they both did.

Inhaling, she continued, "I didn't, because I was afraid. I was afraid that if I did, and failed, you'd punish me, hurt me."

She'd been right: he needed to leave. They'd never get beyond this. Just as he was about to stand, Claire's hands framed his cheeks and pulled his gaze back to hers. With a softer tone, she explained, "That physical pain I feared was nothing—nothing—compared to the pain of thinking you no longer cared. These last two weeks have been hell. They taught me that pain can be present, despite every physical need being met."

Unable to stop the moisture that threatened his eyes, Tony reiterated, "The divorce wasn't meant to *hurt* you."

Unexpectedly, she wrapped her arms around his neck and brushed his lips with a kiss. "Tony, maybe I should be upset that you've had me followed, but I'm not." Was it happiness he heard?

"Honestly, I'm relieved. I didn't think you cared anymore."

The tears faded as the tips of his lips moved upward. When she returned his grin, he pushed her back onto the bed and covered her body with his. "Mrs. Rawlings, I will *always* care and *always* love you. I promised you that almost six years ago."

He had. The realization hit him. He had promised that. If he didn't follow through on the divorce, it wasn't because he wasn't a man of his word—it was because he was. Tony had vowed to love her and care for her forever—twice. Claire didn't protest as his weight held her to the soft satin comforter. Removing his shirt, he added, "I've told you that I am, and despite it all, I continue to be, a man of my word."

Instead of replying, her soft hands caressed his chest as his lips trailed across her exposed collarbone and he unbuttoned her blouse. With each button he trailed a kiss lower and lower until her blouse was open and he reached the top of her slacks. Easing them down her legs he continued to worship the woman beneath him. When his lips weren't caressing her skin, they were speaking, telling her how much he'd missed her, how much he wanted her, and how much he loved her.

She reached for his face and lifted his eyes to hers, as she asked, "If we do this, if we reunite—can I trust you not to leave me, again?"

There was no way he could leave her. "I wanted to protect you. The divorce was only to keep you from getting hurt—by me."

"Don't you see? Not being with you hurt me. Every day hurt more than the one before."

Tony agreed. "It was agony. When I was in prison and we were separated by distance, it sounded good in principle, but seeing you." He lifted his head and looked down at her now nearly naked body. "And touching you." The tips of his fingers softly trailed the warm flesh from her neck to the band of her lace panties. "And not being allowed to taste you." His lips seized a now exposed nipple and gently tugged while his tongue swirled the hardening nub, eliciting moans that he loved to hear. "Was agony."

Before he could continue his seduction, Claire said, "First—first, I have a request."

A memory of a request in paradise, one made more than once, entered his mind and he grinned. Raising his brow he mused, "Yes? I think I might like this. Does it involve black satin?"

Claire snickered. "No. I want you to promise that you won't leave me, no more talk of divorce—ever. I want my *happily ever after*. Despite everything, I trust you *and* your word. If you tell me you'll never divorce me or discuss it, I'll believe you."

His heart soared. The woman beneath him was everything he wanted and more than he deserved. He wanted what she wanted, though he'd never imagined it had been within his reach. Between kisses he said, "You, my dear, are my drug. I'm so damn addicted that I can't quit you. I know, because I've tried—not for me, but for you. I failed miserably. The more I have of you, the more I need. I can never get enough. If you'll have me back—*after all, this is your estate*—if you'll allow me to move back, I'll try every day to give you exactly what you deserve. And I promise I will *never* mention divorce again."

They kissed with a passion like no one had ever experienced. It was the culmination of years of separation. It was the release of their past pain. They'd both caused it and both suffered. It was the promise of a future: one filled with endless possibilities. It was filled with a hunger that only the other could calm. She was his, and he was hers. While her nails bit into his shoulders, his fingers teased and taunted.

Breaking the spell, Tony looked into her gorgeous eyes. "I want you so badly, but I need to be honest. I can't promise you the *happy ever after*. Not because you don't deserve one, but because I know myself, and I'll probably screw it up; however, I can promise that I'll spend the rest of my life trying. Is that enough for you?"

Tony awaited her response as tears cascaded from the corners of her emerald eyes. He could stare into her gaze forever: only her answer would tell him if that were possible.

"Tony, it's more than enough. I promise that I'll never drive away to leave you again, and I'll never listen to anyone else without learning the truth from you, but..." She paused to deliver a wonderful assault of kisses to his neck, one of the places that drove him crazy and elicited growls he couldn't control. "I *will* drive away, to multiple places."

He wouldn't argue. Bold and cheeky was still his favorite.

Claire continued with a smile, "And I'll travel easier knowing Phil is there when you can't be."

His smile broadened—everything and more. "I think we have a deal."

With a playful smile, Claire teased, "Now, if you don't make love to me right this minute, I'll have you thrown off my property."

That was exactly what Tony wanted to do—to *make love*. Jim had been right about some things. He didn't just want to have sex: Tony wanted to show his wife exactly how much he loved her. "My, Mrs. Rawlings, will my lodging payments continue to be so extreme?"

She shrugged. "I don't know. I have the rest of our lives to come up with new ideas. You know, I'm very creative and let me warn you, the payments will be daunting. I hope you're up for it."

His *up-ness* was extremely evident as the red of passion colored his world. For the first time in years, Tony welcomed it. The flames of desire weren't meant to be dampened. They were meant to be fueled, and nothing fed his desire more than the sparks in the emerald eyes of the bold and cheeky woman in his arms. "I believe that you know that I am, and Mrs. Rawlings, I look forward to your challenges. Apparently, only you can decide whether I make the cut."

"Don't disappoint me. There *will* be consequences."

"Mighty fine," he whispered.

Epilogue

December 2016

(Epilogue—Convicted and beyond)

Tony

———

I am confident that, in the end, common sense and justice
will prevail. I'm an optimist, brought up on the belief that
if you wait to the end of the story, you get to see the good
people live happily ever after.
—Cat Stevens

ERIC'S SENTENCE STALLED with the sound of the opening door. All at once Tony and Claire's home office was filled with the sound of running feet and giggles. Nichol ran around Eric and Phil to the other side of the desk and launched herself into Tony's lap.

"Daddy, guess what? We're going over to Aunt Em's!"

Tony laughed and smiled up to Eric and Phil, before looking back to his beautiful daughter. "We are?"

"No! Silly. Just Mommy, Shannon, and I are going." Nichol turned her attention to the other side of the desk and asked, "Are you going too, Mr. Phil?"

Just then, Claire walked in, smiling and shaking her head.

338

"Nichol, your daddy has work to do with Mr. Eric and Mr. Phil. You shouldn't interrupt him."

Her little pig tails swung from side to side as she peered up at Tony. He marveled at the vision of his own eyes coming from Claire's questioning expression. Bashfully, she asked, "I'm not *inter-upping* you, am I?"

He hugged her tight. "You could never interrupt me, princess. You can come tell me your exciting news any time you want."

"You may regret that statement," Claire teased.

"Claire," Phil suggested, "perhaps I could drive you. The roads are very snowy."

"No, thank you. I'll take the SUV. We're just going to Emily's, and then we'll be home." She walked over to Tony and gave him a kiss on the cheek: Nichol followed her mommy's lead. "We'll be back before dinner."

"Yep!" Nichol concurred.

"Well, all right," Tony said as he lifted Nichol from his lap to the floor. "Nichol, where's Shannon?"

"She's waiting for Mommy and me."

"Can you go tell her that your mommy will be right there?"

"I can," she said with bright eyes, as she took off running toward the hallway.

Claire's questioning gaze turned back to her husband and then to Eric and Phil, as Eric closed the office door and resumed his spot beside Phil. "What's happening?" Claire asked. "By the look on your faces, I'd say we received another message."

Tony reached for her hand. They'd promised one another to be honest, in everything. It wasn't always easy, and Tony worried sometimes about how much Claire could handle. But each day she reminded him why he'd fallen in love with her. Her actions and responses reminded him that she was the strongest and bravest person he'd ever known. Even when he told her about Patricia, she handled it with grace. Perhaps if his actions had been different, she would have responded differently, but instead she was pleased. Honesty helped to make their world brighter. It cleared away the biggest threat they faced—the threat of the unknown.

"I would have told you later tonight, but since you're here, I thought you could hear it directly from Eric and Phil. Phil was just telling me about the DNA test results on the last package," he explained as he looked to Phil, imploring him to continue.

"It was definitely sealed with female saliva. Apparently, the woman's not in the federal database of known offenders, which automatically rules out Ms. London."

Claire's brow furrowed. "A woman? Who do you think would do this? Who besides Catherine would know about the Rawls-Nichols link?"

"My family connection to Nathaniel was exposed to the media during Catherine's trial," Tony said. "Still, the vendetta was kept under wraps. I suppose anyone in the courtroom could be considered a possibility."

"I'll check into the list of names," Phil offered.

"And Ma'am," Eric added, "another note arrived today. It was addressed to you: Claire Nichols-Rawls."

"Did you open it?" she asked.

"Not yet," Phil answered. "The police recommend that we bag any suspicious mailings and take them in for analysis. After the whole anthrax scare, not even letters are to be considered safe until we know for sure. Ricin is another poison that's been used in known cases. We're not taking any chances."

Claire looked from Phil to Tony. "None of the packages or

letters that we've received have tested positive, have they?"

"No," Tony reassured, as he squeezed her hand. "Eric and Phil are just being overly cautious." Turning back to Phil, Tony said, "Why don't you go ahead and drive Claire and Nichol. I need to go into the office, and Eric can take me. I like the idea of being *overly cautious* until we know more."

Claire rolled her eyes and straightened her lips. Finally, she said, "All right. Phil, I'm sure you'll be enthralled while Emily and I discuss attire to take to the island next week."

He grinned. "I'll take my iPad. You won't even know I'm there."

"Oh, no. If you're coming, you have to give us your opinion. It's a requirement."

Tony shook his head and grinned at Phil. "Hey man, better you than me."

Nudging Eric, Phil asked, "Do you want to trade?"

Eric shook his head. "Not in a million years."

Claire was almost to the door, when she looked back and said, "Excuse me, I heard that."

Just then, the door flew open and they all heard Nichol's excited voice as she said, "Momma, hurry up! Come on, Momma." She tugged on Claire's hand.

Tony watched the green of his wife's eyes shimmer as they made contact with his own. He knew what she was thinking and did his best to appear innocent.

"So demanding," Claire muttered under her breath. "Just like someone else I know."

This time it was Tony's turn. After a feigned cough, he murmured, "Umm, I heard that."

Phil waited until Claire was gone before he said, "I've been searching for Patricia."

Tony's stomach knotted. "Is there evidence or is this intuition?"

Phil shrugged. "I just want to rule her out. Eric and I were brainstorming about women in-the-know with a grudge." With a smirk, he added, "The list isn't as long as you'd expect."

Eric said, "We talked about past house staff, but everyone's been cleared. It's just Patricia who's MIA."

"I won't be satisfied until I've found her," Phil confirmed.

"Keep us posted," Tony said.

"Yes, sir."

October 2017

Harry

IT WAS HIS first parent-teacher conference. Jillian had just recently begun third grade, and Harry was thrilled with his new more involved role. Ron and Ilona had been wonderful. Jillian was even spending the night at Harry's house every other weekend.

He'd learned so much in the past year. It wasn't only about his new investigative agency and his new surroundings, but Harry also learned the names of all the Disney princesses, to only months later be informed by his daughter that she was too old for princesses. The new craze included dolls that looked like Zombie Barbies. Harry truly hoped that craze would pass soon. To avoid the DVD's she brought over and watched, Harry had introduced her to Nancy Drew. He didn't think she was too young to get some tough-girl detective work. After all, someday she could take over his new company. Regardless what they did, Harry enjoyed spending time with his favorite girl.

When Harry had gone back to California for Amber's trial, he told Liz the truth. He let her know, in confidence, that he'd been the one to first suspect Amber in connection with Simon's death. He told her that it was the picture that she'd mentioned. There was no other way that his sister would have gotten that picture than from the perpetrators of his kidnapping and ambush.

Liz didn't take the news well. Not only was she upset at Harry for telling the FBI, she was upset that she'd added fuel to his firestorm of suspicions. She claimed that she couldn't move to North Carolina due to SiJo. Liz said that they needed her experience and knowledge, but Harry suspected that wasn't the full truth. Somehow, after months of trying to make their long-distance relationship work, Harry didn't care. He'd told himself that Jillian would be his number-one concern, and he'd meant that. All in all, he was content.

Harry pulled up to Jillian's school at 6:45 PM. Their conference was scheduled for 7:00 PM. As soon as he opened the door to the school, Harry saw Ron, Ilona, and Jillian. When his daughter saw him, she ran and grabbed his hand and pulled him toward her parents.

Ron extended his hand. "Hi, Harry, are you ready for this?"

He grinned. "Yeah, I am. I'm kind of excited about it."

Ilona, who was straightening Jillian's blonde ponytail, looked up. "Well, Jillian is quite the little genius, just like her mother, so I don't expect any surprises." She looked into their daughter's eyes. "Should I?"

"No, Mom," Jillian replied, as they all laughed.

Harry had no idea what to expect. To him it was all a surprise.

At exactly 6:58 PM, the school bell buzzed and they heard the announcement:

The 6:40 PM session of parent-teacher conferences is now complete. Please exit the classrooms for the 7:00 PM session. Thank you.

With the anticipation building, Harry accepted Jillian's hand as she led him to her class. The walls were covered in posters, colorful letters, and math equations. Harry's gaze scanned the room, taking in the colorful posters and tiny desks. His light blue eyes stopped on the large desk at the front of the room. Behind the desk, smiling and extending her hand to Ilona, was one of the most beautiful brunettes he'd ever seen. When her green eyes met his, he momentarily forgot his own name. It was Jillian who came to his rescue.

"Miss Oliver, this is my other dad, Harry."

Harry extended his hand. "Hello, *Miss* Oliver..."

February 2018

Phil

PHIL PUSHED HIS way through the lobby of the hospital. He couldn't believe he was going through this again. Well, it wasn't him; it was her. After the first time, he'd never wanted to experience this kind of anxiety again. It was more than anxiety: it was the helplessness. Phil told himself he never could have stopped it. But why would Claire willingly put herself in this danger again.

The first time, she'd almost died.

Over the years, he'd unapologetically done what he needed to do to keep Claire and Nichol safe. It had been a long time since they'd received a threatening package or letter. Rawlings and Claire hypothesized that the mysterious sender became bored and moved on. Eric knew the truth. Patricia was the one to take herself off the radar. Having her disappear permanently went unnoticed. Phil maintained his position. No one would threaten or harm his family. That was until now—the overwhelming sense of helplessness grew.

Perspiration moistened his brow as his shoes pounded the tile floor of the nearly empty corridor. Determined, Phil made his way toward her room. It was nearly midnight and visiting hours were over: he didn't care. As he rounded the corner, he was surprised by the number of people he saw. Scanning the sea of familiar faces, Phil's eyes met Courtney Simmons. Immediately, she stood and walked toward him. Her reassuring smile did little to quiet his frantic nerves.

Taking his hands in hers, she said, "Phil, don't look so worried. Women give birth all the time. Claire will be fine. She has the best doctors that money can buy."

Peering over her head, he saw Brent Simmons as well as John and Emily Vandersol. Turning back to Courtney he asked, "I thought you and Emily were going to be with her, well until..."

Courtney giggled. "Well, it's *that* time. We were in there, but things started moving fast," she squeezed his hand, "not *too* fast, just moving. We left Claire and Tony alone with the doctors to experience this together. From what I hear, this will be Claire's first conscious delivery."

Phil nodded. The memories of that day and night, four years ago, were what haunted him as he drove frantically to get back to the hospital. He would've been here sooner if he hadn't been taking Nichol and Shannon back to the estate after their visit. Phil didn't think things would progress so fast: last time she'd been in labor for almost twenty-four hours. "I hope this time isn't anything like that time," he said.

"There's no reason to suspect it will be. She was doing great when Emily and I left the room..." Courtney looked at her watch. "...about twenty-five minutes ago." She tugged at his hand. "Come, sit down with all of us."

Phil accepted her invitation and tried to get lost in their conversations. He didn't want to think about what Claire could be going through.

"...I was worried, but she reassured me that once all the medication was out of her system, she had her doctor's okay to become pregnant," Emily said.

John squeezed his wife's knee. "I think after we found out that Beth was on her way, Claire had baby fever."

"Oh, Nichol is so excited about Beth," Courtney said. "Every time I see her, she tells me about her little cousin. I think she's holding out hope she's going to have a little sister."

Emily sighed. "I know. I'm afraid she's going to be disappointed. We've all told her that the doctors said she's getting a brother."

"At least Michael's happy," John said. "He didn't want to be the only boy."

"Has anyone gotten them to spill the name?" Brent asked. "I've tried and tried, and Tony wouldn't tell."

All of them shook their heads.

Phil continued to listen as the minutes ticked to hours. He was teetering between sleep and mental breakdown when Rawlings came into the room wearing a paper gown and the biggest smile Phil had ever seen. "Claire and baby Rawlings are both doing great," he said. "The nurse said that you can come in, one at a time."

Emily and Courtney jumped up, as Courtney offered, "After you, but hurry."

When his turn finally arrived, Phil opened the door. Despite the late—or rather early—hour, Claire's emerald eyes shone and her smile beamed.

"I'm not holding him until he gets bigger, so don't ask," Phil offered jokingly.

"He'll be bigger tomorrow," Claire replied.

"I think he already is," Tony said, sitting on the edge of Claire's bed, gazing at his green-eyed son in her arms.

"I think you'll need a pay increase if we keep adding charges to your watch," Claire joked.

"No one will tell his name?"

Claire smiled at Tony and said, "We kind of want to explain it, so everyone understands."

Tony offered, "We put a lot of time and thought into his name. We knew we wanted to find the right one, one we both wanted and felt good about—"

"Like Nichol," Claire interrupted. "Phil, may we introduce you to our son, Nathaniel Sherman Rawlings."

Phil's eyes widened.

"It may seem strange," Claire continued, "but the way we look at it, the truth is that even though people make mistakes, it doesn't stop the reason you loved them in the first place. Tony and I both loved and respected our grandfathers. More importantly, had it not been for them, we wouldn't be here today." She looked at the sleeping bundle in her arms. "And neither would Nate."

Tony smiled, kissed Claire's cheek, and turned his shining brown gaze to Phil. "Put on your running shoes, my man. Between Nichol and Nate, I'm pretty sure there will be consequences."

THE END

Note From Aleatha

Dear Readers,

Thank you, from the bottom of my heart for this amazing journey!

All my love,

~Aleatha

Glossary of CONSEQUENCE SERIES Characters

-Primary Characters-

Anthony (Tony) Rawlings: *billionaire, entrepreneur, founder of Rawlings Industries*

Anton Rawls *(birth name): son of Samuel, grandson of Nathaniel (birth name)*

Claire Nichols Rawlings: *meteorologist, bartender, woman whose life changed forever, wife and ex-wife of Anthony Rawlings*

Aliases: *Lauren Michaels, Isabelle Alexander, C. Marie Rawls*

Nathaniel (Nate) Sherman Rawlings: son of Claire and Anthony Rawlings

Nichol Courtney Rawlings: daughter of Claire and Anthony Rawlings

Brent Simmons: *Rawlings attorney, Tony's best friend*

Catherine Marie London (Rawls): *housekeeper, friend of Anthony Rawlings, 2nd wife of Nathaniel Rawls, Anton Rawls' step-grandmother*

Courtney Simmons: *Brent Simmons' wife*

Emily (Nichols) Vandersol: *Claire's older sister*

Harrison Baldwin: *half-brother of Amber McCoy, president of security at SiJo Gaming*

John Vandersol: *Emily's husband, Claire's brother-in-law, attorney*

Liz Matherly: *personal assistant to Amber McCoy, love interest of Harrison Baldwin*

Meredith Banks Russel: *reporter, sorority sister of Claire Nichols*

Phillip Roach: *private investigator hired by Anthony Rawlings*

-Secondary Characters-

Amber McCoy: *Simon Johnson's fiancée, CEO of SiJo Gaming*

Derek Burke: *husband of Sophia Rossi, great-grandnephew of Jonathon Burke*

Eric Hensley: *Tony's driver and assistant*

Nathaniel Rawls: *grandfather of Anton Rawls, father of Samuel Rawls, owner-founder of Rawls Corporation*

Patricia: *personal assistant to Anthony Rawlings, corporate Rawlings Industries*

Sophia Rossi Burke: *adopted daughter of Carlo and Silvia Rossi, wife of Derek Burke, biological daughter of Marie London, and owner of an art studio in Provincetown, MA*

-Tertiary Characters-

Abbey: *nurse*

Allison Burke: *daughter of Jonathon Burke*

Amanda Rawls: *Samuel Rawls' wife, Anton's mother*

Andrew McCain: *pilot for Rawlings Industries*

Anne Robinson: *Vanity Fair reporter*

Becca: *Vandersols' nanny*

Bev Miller: *designer, wife of Tom Miller*

Bonnie: *wife of Chance*

Brad Clark: *wedding consultant*

Caleb Simmons: *son of Brent and Courtney Simmons*

Cameron Andrews: *private investigator hired by Anthony Rawlings*

Carlo Rossi: *married to Silvia Rossi, adoptive father of Sophia Rossi Burke*

Carlos: *house staff at the Rawlings' estate*

Dr. Carly Brown: *Claire's primary doctor at Everwood*

Cassie: *Sophia's assistant at her art studio on the Cape*

Chance: *associate of Elijah Summer*

Charles: *housekeeper, Anthony's Chicago apartment*

Cindy: *maid at the Rawlings estate, adopted daughter of Allison Burke and her husband*

Clay Winters: *bodyguard hired by Anthony Rawlings*

Connie: *Nathaniel Rawls' secretary*

Danielle (Danni): *personal assistant to Derek Burke*

David Field: *Rawlings negotiator*

Elijah (Eli) Summer: *entertainment entrepreneur, friend of Tony's*

Elizabeth Nichols: *wife of Sherman Nichols, Claire and Emily's grandmother*

Elizabeth (Beth) Vandersol: *daughter of John and Emily Vandersol*

Dr. Fairfield: *research doctor at Everwood*

Agent Ferguson: *FBI agent*

Francis: *groundskeeper in paradise, married to Madeline*

Mr. George: *curator of an art studio in Palo Alto, California*

Agent Hart: *FBI agent*

Officer Hastings: *police officer in Iowa City*

Hillary Cunningham: *wife of Roger Cunningham*

Ilona (Baldwin) George: *ex-wife of Harrison Baldwin, mother of Jillian*

Agent Jackson: *FBI agent, Boston field office*

Jan: *housekeeper, Anthony's New York apartment*

Jane Allyson: *court-appointed counsel*

Jared Clawson: *CFO Rawls Corporation*

Jerry Russel: *husband of Meredith Banks Russel*

Jillian (Baldwin) George: *daughter of Harrison Baldwin and Ilona (Baldwin) George*

Judge Jefferies: *court judge, Iowa City*

Jim: *therapist at Yankton Federal Prison Camp*

Mr. and Mrs. Johnson: *Simon Johnson's parents*

Jonas Smithers: *Anthony Rawlings' first business partner in Company Smithers Rawlings (CSR)*

Jonathon Burke: *securities officer whose testimony helped to incriminate Nathanial Rawls*

Jordon Nichols: *father of Claire and Emily Nichols, married to Shirley, son of Sherman*

Julia: *Caleb Simmons' wife*

Kayla: *nurse*

Keaton: *love interest of Amber McCoy*

Kelli: *secretary, Rawlings Industries, New York office*

Kirstin: *Marcus Evergreen's secretary*

Mr. Leason: *administrator of Everwood*

Dr. Leonard: *physician*

Dr. Logan: *physician*

Madeline: *housekeeper in paradise, married to Francis*

Marcus: *driver for SiJo Gaming*

Marcus Evergreen: *Iowa City prosecutor*

Mary Ann Combs: *longtime companion of Elijah Summer, Tony's friend*

Maryn Simmons: *daughter of Courtney and Brent Simmons*

Michael Vandersol: *son of Emily and John Vandersol*

Sergeant Miles: *police officer, St. Louis*

Monica Thompson: *wedding planner*

Naiade: *housekeeper in Fiji*

Chief Newburgh: *chief of police, Iowa City Police Department*

Officer O'Brien: *police officer, Iowa City Police Department*

Miss Oliver: *Jillian (Baldwin) George's teacher*

Patrick Chester: *neighbor of Samuel and Amanda Rawls*

Paul Task: *court-appointed counsel*

Quinn: *personal assistant of Jane Allyson, Esquire*

Judge Reynolds: *court judge, Iowa City*

Richard Bosley: *governor of Iowa*

Richard Bosley II: *son of Richard Bosley, banker in Michigan*

Roger Cunningham: *president of Shedis-tics*

Ronald George: *second husband of Ilona (Baldwin) George*

Ryan Bosley: *son of Richard II and Sarah Bosley*

Samuel Rawls: *son of Nathaniel and Sharron Rawls, husband of Amanda Rawls, father of Anton Rawls*

Sarah Bosley: *wife of Richard Bosley II*

Shannon: *Nichol Rawlings' nanny*

Sharon Michaels: *attorney for Rawlings Industries*

Sharron Rawls: *wife of Nathaniel Rawls*

Shaun Stivert: *photographer for Vanity Fair*

Sheldon Preston: *governor of Iowa*

Shelly: *Anthony Rawlings' publicist*

Sherman Nichols: *grandfather of Claire Nichols, FBI agent who helped to incriminate Nathaniel Rawls. FBI alias: Cole Mathews*

Sherry: *assistant to Dr. Carly Brown*

Shirley Nichols: *wife of Jordon Nichols, mother of Claire and Emily*

Silvia Rossi: *married to Carlo Rossi, adopted mother of Sophia Rossi Burke*

Simon Johnson: *first love and classmate of Claire Nichols, gaming entrepreneur*

Dr. Sizemore: *obstetrician and gynecologist*

Sue Bronson: *Tim Bronson's wife*

Judge Temple: *court judge, Iowa City*

Terri: *nurse*

Tim Bronson: *vice president, corporate Rawlings Industries*

Tom Miller: *Rawlings attorney, friend of Tony's*

Tory Garrett: *pilot for Rawlings Industries*

Valerie: *assistant to Dr. Fairfield*

Dr. Warner: *psychologist at female federal penitentiary*

Judge Wein: *court judge, Iowa City*

SAC Williams: *Special Agent in Charge of the San Francisco FBI field office*

THE CONSEQUENCES SERIES
Timeline

-1921-
Nathaniel Rawls—born

-1943-
Nathaniel Rawls—home from WWII

Nathaniel Rawls marries Sharron Parkinson

Nathaniel begins working for BNG Textiles

-1944-
Samuel Rawls—born to Nathaniel and Sharron

-1953-
BNG Textiles becomes Rawls Textiles

-1956-
Rawls Textiles becomes Rawls Corporation

-1962-
Catherine Marie London—born

-1963-
Samuel Rawls marries Amanda

-1965-

FEBRUARY 12

Anton Rawls—born to Samuel and Amanda

-1975-

Rawls Corporation goes public

-1980-

JULY 19

Sophia Rossi (London)—born/adopted by Carlo and Silvia Rossi

AUGUST 31

Emily Nichols—born to Jordon and Shirley Nichols

-1983-

Sharron Rawls exhibits symptoms of Alzheimer's disease

Marie London starts to work for Sharron Rawls

Anton Rawls graduates from Blair Academy High School

OCTOBER 17

Claire Nichols—born to Jordon and Shirley Nichols

-1985-

Nathaniel Rawls begins affair with Marie London

Marie London loses baby

Sharron Rawls dies

-1986-

Rawls Corporation falls

-1987-

Anton Rawls graduates from NYU

Nathaniel Rawls found guilty of multiple counts of insider trading, misappropriation of funds, price fixing, and securities fraud

-1988-

Nathaniel Rawls marries Catherine Marie London

Anton Rawls graduates with Master's degree

-1989-

Nathaniel Rawls—dies

Samuel and Amanda Rawls—die

-1990-

Anton Rawls changes his name to Anthony Rawlings

Anthony Rawlings begins CSR-Company Smithers Rawlings with Jonas Smithers

-1994-

Anthony Rawlings buys out Jonas Smithers and CSR becomes Rawlings Industries

-1996-

Rawlings Industries begins to diversify

-1997-

Sherman Nichols—dies

-2002-

Claire Nichols—graduates high school

Claire Nichols—attends Valparaiso University

-2003-

Simon Johnson begins internship at Shedis-tics in California

-2004-

Jordon and Shirley Nichols—die

-2005-

Emily Nichols—marries John Vandersol

-2007-

Claire Nichols—graduates from Valparaiso, degree in meteorology

Claire Nichols—moves from Indiana to New York for internship

-2008-

Claire Nichols—moves to Atlanta, Georgia, for job at WKPZ

Simon Johnson begins SiJo Gaming Corporation

-2009-

WKPZ—purchased by large corporation resulting in lay-offs

Jillian Baldwin is born

-2010-

MARCH

Anthony Rawlings—enters the Red Wing in Atlanta, Georgia

Anthony Rawlings—takes Claire Nichols on a date

Claire Nichols—wakes at Anthony's estate

MAY

Claire Nichols—liberties begin to increase

Anthony Rawlings—takes Claire Nichols to symphony and introduces "Tony"

SEPTEMBER

Meredith Banks' article appears—Claire Nichols' accident

DECEMBER 18

Anthony Rawlings—marries Claire Nichols

-2011-

APRIL

Vanity Fair article appears

SEPTEMBER

Anthony and Claire Rawlings attend a symposium in Chicago where Claire sees Simon Johnson, her college boyfriend

NOVEMBER

Simon Johnson—dies in airplane accident

-2012-

JANUARY

Claire Rawlings drives away from the Rawlings estate

Anthony Rawlings—poisoned

Claire Rawlings—arrested for attempted murder

MARCH

Anthony Rawlings divorces Claire Nichols

APRIL

Claire Nichols pleads no contest to attempted murder charges

OCTOBER

Claire Nichols receives box of information while in prison

-2013-

MARCH

Petition for pardon is filed with Governor Bosley on behalf of Claire Nichols

Petition for pardon is granted; Claire Nichols is released from prison and moves to Palo Alto, California

Tony learns of Claire's release, hires Phillip Roach, and contacts Claire

APRIL

Claire and Courtney vacation in Texas

Tony travels to California. He and Claire have dinner and reconnect

MAY

Claire meets with Meredith Banks in San Diego

Claire and Harry connect

Claire and Harry visit Patrick Chester

Claire attends the National Center for Learning Disabilities annual gala where Tony is the keynote speaker

Claire takes a home pregnancy test

JUNE

Caleb Simmons weds his fiancée, Julia. Tony asks Claire to accompany him to the wedding

Claire is attacked by Patrick Chester

Claire moves back to Iowa

JULY

First mailing arrives to Iowa addressed to *Claire Nichols-Rawls*

SEPTEMBER

Tony leaves for a ten-day business trip to Europe

Claire leaves Iowa

OCTOBER

Claire moves to paradise

Phil Roach takes Tony to paradise

OCTOBER 27

Anthony Rawlings and Claire Nichols remarry

DECEMBER

DECEMBER 19

Nichol Courtney Rawlings born

-2014-

MARCH

Tony and Claire Rawlings return to the United States

Incident at Rawlings estate

Claire Rawlings suffers a psychotic break

Tony and Claire are arrested

Anthony Rawlings is booked for crimes against the state of Iowa and the United States

Claire Rawlings is booked for attempted murder

Catherine Marie London is booked for crimes against the state of Iowa and the United States

A protective order is filed against Anthony Rawlings

JUNE

Anthony Rawlings pleads guilty to kidnapping and is sentenced to four years at Yankton, Federal Prison Camp, Yankton, South Dakota

JULY

Michael Vandersol is born to Emily and John Vandersol

NOVEMBER

Catherine Marie London's case goes before a grand jury

-2015-

JULY

Catherine Marie London is convicted of crimes against the state of

Iowa and the United States

AUGUST

Amber McCoy is arrested for crimes against the state of California and the United States

-2016-

SPRING

Anthony Rawlings fires his assistant, Patricia

Tony begins construction on new home

JUNE

Meredith Banks approaches Emily Vandersol in park

Meredith Banks goes undercover at Everwood to learn about Claire Rawlings

JULY

Harrison Baldwin retires from FBI and moves to North Carolina

SEPTEMBER

Claire Rawlings begins to speak

Tony starts petition to terminate the marriage of Anthony and Claire Rawlings

Courtney Simmons meets with Meredith Banks and sees Claire

OCTOBER

Anthony Rawlings' early release from Yankton Federal Prison Camp is approved

FIFTEEN DAYS LATER

Anthony Rawlings is released from Yankton Federal Prison Camp

Tony signs Claire out of Everwood

Tony gives Claire the Rawlings estate and asks her for a divorce

Tony and Claire go to see Nichol for the first time in 2 ½ years

Tony and Claire reunite

DECEMBER
Nichol Rawlings' third birthday is celebrated in paradise with family and friends

-2017-
APRIL
Elizabeth (Beth) Vandersol is born to John and Emily Vandersol
OCTOBER
Harrison Baldwin meets Miss Oliver

-2018-
FEBRUARY 7
Nathaniel (Nate) Sherman Rawlings is born to Tony and Claire Rawlings

Books by
NEW YORK TIMES BESTSELLING AUTHOR
Aleatha Romig

CONSEQUENCES
(Book #1)
Released August 2011

TRUTH
(Book #2)
Released October 2012

CONVICTED
(Book #3)
Released October 2013

REVEALED: THE MISSING YEARS
(Book #4)
Previously titled: Behind His Eyes Convicted: The Missing Years
Re-released June 2014

BEHIND HIS EYES—CONSEQUENCES
(Book #1.5)
Released January 2014

BEHIND HIS EYES—TRUTH
(Book #2.5)
Released March 2014

Aleatha Romig

Aleatha Romig is a New York Times and USA Today bestselling author, who has been voted #1 "New Author to Read" on Goodreads, July 2012 through 2014!

Aleatha has lived most of her life in Indiana, growing up in Mishawaka, graduating from Indiana University, and currently living south of Indianapolis. Together with her high-school sweetheart and husband of twenty-eight years, they've raised three children. Before she became a full-time author, she worked days as a dental hygienist and spent her nights writing. Now, when she's not imagining mind-blowing twists and turns, she likes to spend her time with her family and friends. Her pastimes include exercising, reading, and creating heroes/anti-heroes who haunt your dreams!

Aleatha enjoys traveling, especially when there is a beach involved. In 2011, she had the opportunity to visit Sydney, Australia, to visit her daughter studying at the University of Wollongong. Her dream is to travel to places in her novels and around the world.

CONSEQUENCES, her first novel, was released in August, 2011, by Xlibris Publishing. Then in October of 2012, Ms. Romig re-released CONSEQUENCES as an indie author. TRUTH, the sequel, was released October 30, 2012, CONVICTED, was released October 8, 2013 and the final installment of the Consequences Series REVEALED: THE MISSING YEARS was re-released in June of

2014! She has also released the CONSEQUENCES READING COMPANIONS: BEHIND HIS EYES- Consequences and BEHIND HIS EYES- Truth.

Aleatha is a "Published Author's Network" member of the Romance Writers of America and represented by Danielle Egan-Miller of Brown and Miller Literary Associates.

Share Your Thoughts

Please share your thoughts about
REVEALED: THE MISSING YEARS on:
Goodreads.com/Aleatha Romig
Tell your friends!!

Stay Connected with Aleatha

"Like" Aleatha Romig @ http://www.Facebook.com/AleathaRomig to learn the latest information regarding Consequences, Truth, Convicted, REVEALED: THE MISSING YEARS and the Behind His Eyes Companions as well as other writing endeavors.

And, "Follow" @aleatharomig on Twitter!

Email Aleatha: aleatharomig@gmail.com / Check out her blog: http://aleatharomig.blogspot.com

What to read after the CONSEQUENCES SERIES

Absolutely amazing! I have not been this captivated by a book, by a series, in years! Thank you to everyone who told me to read these.
—Aleatha Romig

CAPTIVE IN THE *dark*

CJ Roberts

USA Today bestselling author

CHAPTER 3

EXCERPT

I AWOKE, GASPING and disoriented, the edges of the dream dissipating, but not the dread lingering inside me. The darkness was so complete, for a second, I thought I hadn't woken from my nightmare. Then slowly, frame by frame, it all came back to me. And as each frame was cataloged and stored away in my mental library, a faint but growing concept took hold, that this nightmare was reality, *my* reality. I suddenly found myself longing for the dream. Any nightmare would be better than this. My heart sank to new depths, eyes burning in the darkness. I looked around dispassionately, noticing familiar objects, but none of them mine. As the haze cleared, ever more steadily into cold hard reality, I thought, *I really have been kidnapped.* It hit, hard, those words in neon, in my head. I looked around again, surrounded by strangeness. Unfamiliar space. *I really am in some strange place.*

I wanted to cry.

I wanted to cry for not seeing this coming. I wanted to cry for the uncertainty of my future. I wanted to cry for wanting to cry. I wanted to cry because I was most likely going to die before I got to experience life. But mostly, I wanted to cry for being so horribly, tragically, stupidly female.

I'd had so many fantasies about that day he'd helped me on the sidewalk. I'd felt like a princess who'd stumbled across a knight in shining armor. Jesus Christ, I'd even asked him for a ride! I had been so disappointed when he said no, and when he mentioned meeting another woman, my heart had sunken into my stomach. I cursed myself for not wearing something cuter. Shamefully, I had fantasized about his perfect hair, his enigmatic smile, and the exact shade of his eyes almost every day since.

I closed my eyes.

What an idiot I'd been, a damned foolish little girl.

Had I learned nothing from my mother's mistakes? Apparently not. Somehow I'd still managed to go all retarded at the sight of some handsome asshole with a nice smile. And just like her, I'd gotten good and fucked by him, too. I'd let a man ruin my life. For some reason beyond my understanding, I hated my mother in that moment. It broke my heart even more.

I wiped angrily at the tears that threatened to escape my eyes. I had to focus on a way to get out of here, not on a way to feel sorry for myself.

The only light came from the dim glow coming off a nearby nightlight. The pain had subsided into an overall soreness, but my headache still raged. I was unbound, lying under the same thick comforter, covered from head to toe in a thin layer of sweat. I pushed the comforter away.

I expected to find my naked body under the comforter. Instead I found satin: a camisole and panties. I clutched frantically at the fabric. Who had dressed me? Dressing meant touching and touching could mean too many things. Caleb? Had he dressed me? The thought filled me with dread. And underneath that, something else entirely more horrible: unwelcome curiosity.

Fending off my conflicting emotions, I set about inspecting my body. I was sore all over, even my hair hurt, but between my legs I didn't feel noticeably different. No soreness on the inside to suggest what I couldn't bring myself to think might happen to me at some point. I was momentarily relieved, but one more look around my new prison and my relief evaporated. I had to get out of here. I slid out of bed.

The room appeared rundown, with yellowing wallpaper and thin, stained carpet. The bed, a huge wrought iron four-poster, was the only piece of furniture that appeared new. It hardly seemed like the kind of thing that belonged in a place like this. Not that I knew much about places like this. The linen on the bed smelled of fabric softener. It was the same kind I washed my family's clothes in at home. My stomach clenched. I didn't hate my mother, I loved her. I should have told her more often, even if she didn't always tell me. Tears stung my eyes, but I couldn't fall apart right now. I had to think of a way to escape.

My first instinct was to try the door, but I dismissed that idea as stupid. For one, I remembered it being locked. For another, if it wasn't, the chances were good I'd run right into my captors. The look in that guy Jair's eyes flashed through my mind, and a violent shiver of fear ran down my spine.

Instead, I crept to a set of curtains and pulled them back. The window was boarded shut. I barely contained an exasperated scream. I slipped my fingers around the edges of the wood trying to pull it up, but it proved impossible. *Damn.*

The door opened behind me without warning. I spun around,

slamming my back against the wall as if I could somehow manage to blend into the curtains. The door hadn't been locked. Had he been waiting for me?

Light, soft and low, filtered through, casting shadows across the floor. Caleb. My legs shook with fear as he shut the door and walked toward me. He looked like the Devil himself, dressed in black slacks and a black button up shirt, stepping slowly, deliberately. Still handsome enough to make my insides clench and my heart stutter. It was pure perversion.

In the fall of light from the door, his shadow loomed, long and dark. Unbidden, words once made ominous by Poe manifested as flesh in the man before me: *"Suddenly I heard a tapping, as of someone gently rapping, rapping at my chamber door."*

Crap, crap, crap. Okay, that last part was me.

Caleb raised his hand as if to hit me, and I threw my arms up to protect my face. His hand slammed against the wall. While I cringed, the bastard laughed. Slowly, I moved to bring my arms down and cover my breasts. Caleb grabbed both my wrists in his left hand and pressed them to the wall over my head. Pinned between him and the wall, I reacted like a frightened hamster. I froze, as if my stillness would discourage his predatory nature. Like a snake that only eats live mice.

"Are you hungry?" he asked.

I heard the question, but the words had no meaning. My brain ceased to function as it should. The only thing my mind could focus on was his closeness. The intense warmth of his firm fingers pressed into my wrists. The clean, wet smell of his skin in the air around me. The invisible pressure of his gaze upon me. What was this?

When I failed to respond, the fingers of his right hand trailed across the underside of my right breast, the fabric of my camisole made his fingers balmy satin against my flesh. Our earlier exchange forced its way into my consciousness. *"Go fuck yourself."*

"...I'd much rather fuck you."

My knees slightly buckled and my nipples hardened. I took a sharp breath and leaned away from his touch, forcing my tightly shut eyes into the skin of my upraised arm.

His lips caressed the shell of my ear, "Are you going to answer? Or must I force you again?"

Food? My stomach suddenly twisted sharply. A primal pain. Yes, there was my hunger, when he reminded me of it. I was absolutely starving. I mustered up my courage by taking a deep breath. "Yes."

I felt his smile against my ear, and then his fingers held my chin. In my peripheral vision, I watched him lean into me. His breath was cool against my heated flesh.

"Yes," he repeated my response, "you're hungry? Yes, you're going to answer? Or yes, I have to force you again?"

My heart raced. I felt his breath on my cheek. There was suddenly not enough air, as if his proximity sucked it out of my lungs.

"Or is it just yes?"

My lips parted and my lungs pulled in deep, bringing in as much air as they could. It didn't seem like much. I forced myself to answer through my panic.

"Yes," I stammered, "I'm hungry."

I knew he smiled, though I couldn't see it. A shiver, so strong my body nearly jerked toward his, ran down my spine.

He kissed me softly on the cheek. I think I whimpered. Then he walked out of the room, leaving me paralyzed even after I heard the door shut.

Caleb returned shortly with a wheeled cart laden with food. My stomach gnawed as I smelled the meat and bread. It was difficult to control the urge to run toward the food. Then Jair followed him into the room carrying a chair.

Seeing Jair made me wish the floor would open up and swallow me. Earlier, when Jair had sought to rape me, I had—once again—tried to find protection in Caleb's arms. I suppose that, somewhere in my head, I'd clung to the hope that this man, this Caleb, would protect me. All I could see was that horrible, feral look in Jair's eyes. He wanted to *hurt* me.

The door shut and I looked up to find Caleb sitting next to the food. We were alone again. Fear and hunger tore at my insides.

"Come here," he said. His voice startled me, but I moved to walk toward him. "Stop. I want you to crawl over here."

My legs shook. *Crawl? Are you kidding me? Just run. Run right now.* He stood, looking straight at me. *Run where? See how quickly he slams you to the ground and drugs you again!* My knees hit the floor. What choice did I have? I put my head down but I could still feel his eyes on me like a weight that promised his hand. My knees and my palms moved across the ground until I reached the tops of his shoes.

I was trapped. I was nearly naked. Weak. Scared. I was his.

He bent and gathered my hair in both his hands. Slowly, he lifted my head until our eyes met. He looked at me intently; his brows were knit together, his mouth set in a hard line. "I wish he hadn't done this to you," he said while stroking the corner of my left eye. "You really are a very pretty girl; it's a shame."

My heart twisted. A memory, *the* memory ripped through my defenses and surfaced at the forefront of my mind. My stepfather had thought I was pretty, too. I was a pretty *thing*, and pretty things did not fare well in this world, not in the hands of men like him. Instinctively, my hands grabbed his wrists in an effort to guide his hands from my hair, but he held me firmly. Not roughly, just firmly. Without words, he made himself clear; he wasn't done looking at me yet. Incapable of holding his gaze, I averted my eyes to some point just beyond him.

The very air around me seemed to shift to accommodate him. His breath skated across my cheek, and beneath my trembling, sweaty hands, his forearms hinted at his immense strength. I shut my eyes and took a deep breath in the hopes of calming down. The smell of him mingled with the food and rushed into my lungs. The combination did strange primal things to me. I suddenly felt carnivorous. I wanted to tear the flesh from his bones with my teeth and drink his blood.

Unable to help myself, I whispered, "It's your fault he did it. All of this is your fault. You're no better than he is." It felt good to say the words. I felt I should have said them sooner.

A bead of sweat trickled down the side of my neck, its slow crawl over my collarbone, across my chest, and into the well of my breasts served to remind me of my body. My soft, breakable body.

He sighed deeply and let out a slow breath. I shivered, unable to discern whether the sigh meant he had calmed or he was about to slap me senseless.

His voice, thinly coated with civility, filled my head, "I'd watch what you say to me, Pet. There is a world of difference between me and *him*. One that I think you'll learn to appreciate, despite yourself. But make no mistake; I am still capable of things you can't imagine. Provoke me again and I'll prove it." He let me go.

I sank without thinking, back down to all fours, once again staring at his shoes. I was sure I'd completely break down if I tried to imagine all the things I wasn't capable of imagining, because I could imagine some pretty horrible things. In fact, I was imagining some of those horrible things when his voice interrupted my thoughts.

"You're entire life is going to change. You should try to accept that, because there's no possible way to avoid it. Like it or not, fight it or don't, your old life is over. It was over long before you woke up here."

There were no words, no me, no here. This was crazy. I had awoken with sweat and fear to this, this darkness. Fear, pain, hunger, this man—eating at me. I wanted to put my head to the tops of his shoes. To stop. The words hung in the air like a speech bubble, still clinging to his lips. How long before? Before that day on the street?

I thought about my mom again. She was far from perfect, but I loved her more than I loved anyone. He was telling me I'd never see her again, that I'd never see anyone I loved again. I should have expected those types of words. Every villain had a similar speech, "Don't try to get away, it's impossible," but until then, I hadn't realized how truly terrifying those words were.

And he stood above me, as if he were a god who had torn the sun away, not caring for my devastation. "Address me as *Master*. Every time you forget, I will be forced to remind you. So you can choose to obey or choose punishment. It's entirely up to you."

My head snapped up and my shocked, horrified, pissed off eyes met his. I wasn't going to call him *Master*. No. Fucking. Way. I was sure he could see the determination in my eyes. The unspoken challenge behind them that screamed, *Just try and make me asshole. Just try.*

He lifted a brow, and his eyes responded, *With pleasure, Pet.*

Just give me a reason.

Rather than risk a fight I couldn't possibly win, I returned my eyes to the ground. I was going to get out of here. I just had to be smart.

"Do you understand?" he said smugly.

Yes, Master. The words remained unspoken, their absence duly noted.

"Do. You," he leaned forward, "Under. Stand?" He drew out each word, as if speaking to a child or someone who doesn't understand English.

My tongue pushed against my teeth. I stared at his legs, unable to answer him, unable to fight him. A lump began to form in my throat, and I swallowed hard to keep it down, but the tears eventually came. These were not the tears of pain or fear but of frustration.

"Very well then, I guess you're not hungry. But I am."

At the mention of food my mouth surged again with saliva. The smell of the food twisted my stomach into tight knots. While he tore off pieces of bread, my nails dug into the thin carpet where my tears now dripped onto the floor. What did he want from me that he couldn't just take? I sniffled, trying not to sob. He touched me again, stroking the back of my head.

"Look at me."

I wiped the tears from my face and looked up at him. He sat back in his chair, head cocked to one side. He appeared to be considering something. I hoped whatever *it* was wouldn't cause me more humiliation, but I doubted it. He picked up a piece of cut meat from his plate and slowly stuck it in his mouth, all the while looking at my face. Every tear that sprang from my eye I quickly wiped away with the back of my hand. Next, he picked up a piece of cubed beef. I swallowed hard. He leaned forward and held the delicious smelling morsel to my lips. With an almost unabashed relief I opened my mouth, but he snatched it away.

He offered again. And again. Each time I crawled closer and closer, until I was pressed between his legs, my hands on either side of his body. Suddenly I threw my arms up around his hand and wrapped my mouth around his fingers to get the food away from him. *Oh my god, so good.*

His fingers were thick and salty against my tongue, but I managed to wrest the meat from between them. He moved quickly, his fingers found my tongue and pinched viciously while his other hand dug into the sides of my neck. He squeezed, making me open my mouth in shock as pain cascaded down my throat. The food fell from between my lips to the floor and I howled around his fingers at the loss. He let go of my tongue, and his hands found control along the sides of my head as he tilted it up toward his. "I've been entirely too kind and you're going to learn just how civil I've been. You're very proud and very spoiled, and I'm going to beat it out of you twice."

Then he stood up with enough force to push me backward onto the floor. He walked out of the room and shut the door. This time I heard the lock.

Beside me the food beckoned.

Books by C.J. Roberts

CAPTIVE IN THE DARK
Seduced IN THE DARK
EPILOGUE

CPSIA information can be obtained at www.ICGtesting.com
Printed in the USA
BVOW04s0220101114

74411BV00002B/49/P